SURVIVAL INSTINCTS

A DYSTOPIAN NOVEL

MAY DAWNEY

Dedicated to whoever has both the good sense and governmental power to prevent this work of fiction from becoming reality in the future.

CHAPTER 1

THE FIRST SIGN THAT NEW York City would be special was the zebra. It pushed through the shrubbery and onto the sun-flooded interstate no more than thirty feet from Lynn. Its hooves clicked on the cracked asphalt as it weaved its way leisurely through the thick throng of rusted car skeletons.

Lynn stopped.

Skeever, at her heels, did too.

At least for now, the zebra didn't notice them. It plucked at a tuft of grass with nimble lips.

Lynn blinked consciously, wondering if the animal would go away if she did. It didn't. If this animal was what she thought it was, she was staring at an Old-World relic. The striped horses had been kept in carefully constructed habitats in the hearts of cities. Lynn realized she should probably have felt awed by the experience, but her only thought was *dinner*. She quietly reached down to her belt and undid the leather strap that held her tomahawk in place.

Skeever growled. His ears had turned back, and he bared his teeth.

Shit. Lynn hurried to reach down and muzzle him, but it was too late.

The zebra's ears twitched. Its head shot up and swung toward the source of the sound. A shudder ran through its compact body as it spotted her.

Lynn met its eyes.

The zebra shied to the side. A single blade of grass dangled forgotten from between its lips. Keen animal intelligence underlay its gaze, sizing her up.

Don't you go anywhere, now. She reached for her weapon as quickly as she dared. Thirty feet away, wind from the side. She would have to get closer for a clean throw or risk only injuring it and tracking it until it succumbed to blood loss. She tensed and sped forward.

Instantly, the zebra's eyes widened, and it threw its head back. It rushed off, bleating in panic.

At the very last moment, Lynn stopped her axe from leaving her hand. "Dammit." She let her momentum fall away.

Skeever excitedly caught up with her.

Just as she reached down to pet him, a group of the striped animals broke through the vegetation onto the road and streamed around the car wrecks. Their hooves hitting asphalt and their bleating cries caused such a cacophony that she froze from the sheer unfamiliarity of it. Lynn spent her life being quiet, among people who spent their lives being quiet. This was glorious and frightening, and Lynn could only watch the procession pass.

Skeever barked and ran after the unexpected newcomers. But when the last of them disappeared into the shrubbery, he retreated, tail between his hind legs. He pressed his bulk against her.

"Wow." Lynn took a deep, steadying breath. For a moment, she had forgotten that was dinner, running off. She regrettably tracked the herd's departure by ear and considered her options. She *could* try to hunt them down, but the odds of catching up before nightfall were nil. Besides, they were going the wrong way.

"Look behind you only to make sure there is nothing there that might kill you," her father used to say. Lynn had adopted that creed, and it had kept her alive so far. Today was not the day to go against it.

She glanced one more time at the wall of green into which the zebras had disappeared and shook her head. *It's a damn weird day.* "Come on, Skeever. We'll find something to eat in there." With only a small pang of regret, Lynn walked away from the herd.

Ahead, past the remnants of cars and a precarious-looking bridge, lay New York City. Lynn had puzzled its name together from the rusty signs overhead. It sounded vaguely familiar. Perhaps she'd heard about it from the odd traveler she'd met on her meandering journey, or perhaps her parents had told her stories before they had died. If someone *had* told her about the city, she'd forgotten the details. All she'd learned about it during the approach was that it was big. Really big.

New York City was most likely the biggest Old-World city she had ever encountered. It stretched out for miles, bordered by water, and boasted a host of towering concrete giants. The massive towers gleamed in patches—glass and metal reflecting in the midafternoon sun—and Lynn could almost picture them in their full glory, standing proud as pinnacles of human ability. Now they were shadows of their former selves, crumbling and weighed down by history, just like the human race.

It was a depressing thought for a beautiful late-summer afternoon, inspired by the failed hunt. They were running out of food, and Lynn worried. If she hadn't been worried, she would never have taken on a city like New York straight on.

Skeever trotted ahead with wagging tail, sniffing at the bones of drivers and passengers in the mess of cars. Some sat propped up against the faded interior like gristly puppets; others lay piled on seats and nearly rusted-through floors as heaps of bones and rags.

She had asked her father once why they buried the bones of recently deceased strangers but not the bones of the pre-war people littering the world.

"Lynn," he had told her six-year-old self. "Everything that lives has a spark in them. It's what makes us alive instead of dead. It's in that sparrow over there and even in the grass we sit on. That's why we always thank our kills for giving up their life so we can eat and stay strong. Do you understand?"

She *had* understood. Things that moved, things that grew bigger, they were different from things that were dead. She had seen enough dead things—trees, hunted game, people—to understand the difference. "But why do we bury *people* and not bones?"

"We bury people because that way, we give back what we took to stay alive. When we bury people, their bodies feed the grass and the bushes and the trees so they can grow bigger. The animals eat the grass and fruit and vegetables. We eat the animals and the fruit and vegetables as well. This way, nothing is lost, and everyone gets to eat. We don't bury the bones, because they don't have anything to give back anymore."

She had carefully pondered the difference between a person who had just died and a person who had died during the war. It had sparked another question. "Why don't we bury the bad people?"

He had paused then. Her father never spoke without thinking about it carefully first. It had made her impatient as a child, but as an adult she admired it. As much as Lynn would have liked to be as thoughtful as her father, she was too impulsive to do his spirit justice.

"Some people do things that we don't want others to ever do again. We don't want their spark to live on, so we leave them for the predators we'll never eat ourselves. That way their evil disappears, and the world becomes a little better."

This discussion was one of her most vivid memories of her father. He'd put it so black-and-white that the distinction between honorable and dishonorable had made sense to her young mind. She had discovered that nothing in this world—except for zebras—was ever black-and-white, especially not when it came to honor.

Lynn frowned. Her mind had wandered. She stopped to check her surroundings for danger.

Skeever looked up at her questioningly. He whined and took a step forward, urging her on. He obviously didn't think there was anything to worry about.

His behavior settled Lynn, but it had still been stupid to let her mind wander in the Wilds. She smiled wryly when she pictured how her father would have reacted to her lapse in attention. "Distracted, then dead," he used to say. It was hard to argue with that.

"Sorry, boy." She started to walk again. An exit came up just after the surprisingly sturdy bridge, and she went down it, crawling over cars to do so.

Skeever planned his own route. Once down, he darted ahead, although he checked on her every few seconds.

They were quickly swallowed by New York City's maze of buildings. They surrounded her, intact, crumbled, and everywhere in between. A brick building towered over her to the left. Tree branches emerged from its shattered windows. The row of houses to her right was in ruins and completely overgrown by an assortment of tall grasses, low bushes, and large oak trees.

A group of small monkeys with big brown eyes regarded her from the canopy of the oaks and yipped. They tilted their little heads to the side as she passed and shook a branch here and there, but monkeys this size weren't dangerous. They were also hard to turn into food. Monkeys were another remnant of the ancient zoos, but unlike zebras, Lynn had seen them before. She had discovered they were too quick to kill with a throwing axe, so she let them be.

A glance at the sky told her she wasn't going to be making any more miles today. Already, the sun lowered toward New York City's crumbled skyline. Braving the night without shelter would be suicide-by-predator. "I think it's time we find a place to hole up for the night, whatcha say, boy?" It would be a hungry night, but at least there would be another day to search for food afterward.

Skeever's head lifted at the sound of her voice. He wagged his tail.

She smiled. *I can't believe I almost left you behind.* How could it be that only three days had passed since she'd found him? It felt as if he'd been with her forever. She scratched the underside of his jaw with her free hand. The nametag on his collar jiggled. "What did you do before you met me, hm? Who was the man you were with? Who named you Skeever?"

Skeever tilted his head to the side and gave her better access to the underside of his muzzle.

"Too bad you can't talk. Maybe then you'd have some answers for me." She considered that. "Well, maybe it's for the best. You already make enough noise as it is." She patted his flank, then straightened up again. Yeah, it was good not to be alone. She'd been alone for so long, she had forgotten how good it felt to have someone to talk to, to rely on—even if it was a dog.

Looking about, she wondered what the wisest course of action was. There were undoubtedly familiar and unfamiliar animals in the city that used the buildings around her for shelter. At least a portion of those would happily make a meal out of her. She needed a place she could secure—someplace with a heavy door and not too many holes in the walls. There was no place like that around here; the area had been too heavily bombed during the war. She would have to keep moving.

The second she stepped forward, a loud noise echoed through the streets. Instinctively, she dropped into a battle stance. For a split second, she thought her foot had activated some kind of trap, but then the sound rose again. *What the hell is that?* Adrenaline-induced sweat made her fumble as she grabbed for her tomahawk.

Skeever yelped and turned to the source of the sound—somewhere ahead, to the right. Ears flat, he growled and tensed to the point where he seemed to vibrate.

It sounded again.

The hairs on the back of her neck stood on end. *Animal. It has to be an animal.* Dread settled coldly in her gut. "Shit, I'm going to have to check." If she didn't, she would never be able to sleep tonight. She reached down with her free hand to stroke Skeever's rough-haired back. "You be quiet, understood?"

Skeever looked up.

Lynn took a deep, steadying breath. "Yeah, I know. This sucks." Staying low, she moved toward the sound. "I don't like it either."

He caught up after a few steps, then passed her and sniffed the ground ahead.

"We just have to know." She gripped her tomahawk tighter. Time to discover what monsters the streets of New York City housed.

Lynn ducked low and parted the grass in front of her. Another deafening cry came from the bottom of the hill. An enormous gray animal lashed its elongated snout at a group of eight or nine hunters.

An elephant! Surely it couldn't be anything else.

It threw its trunk up and trumpeted its despair as another spear pierced its weathered gray skin. The weapon stuck to it until the monstrous animal threw itself against a building that promptly lost its façade. The spear snapped like a twig, and the man who had thrown it sprang away just in time to avoid both the elephant's stomping feet and falling debris.

"Cody!" a red-haired woman screamed. She tried to get to him, but the age-worn tusks blocked her way, so she jumped back.

Another woman waved a machete in the air the front of the animal to draw its ire. "Look over here, you! Dammit, Dani! Kill this thing!"

The elephant turned away from the redhead and focused its lashing tusks and trunk on the machete-wielder.

"Keep it busy!" Another hunter rushed up to the animal's now-exposed side, her long hair trailing behind her as she fearlessly hurled her spear. The weapon hit its target.

The elephant threw back its head and lifted its trunk. It trumpeted the sound that had drawn Lynn here.

Skeever barked and tried to pull free from the hold Lynn had on his collar.

She yanked on the thick leather. "Shut up!"

A shot rang out.

Lynn gasped. This was only the second time in her life she'd heard a gunshot.

Skeever struggled and whined.

She lifted her head higher to locate the gun that had been fired—and its wielder.

A black man knelt down just outside the flurry of activity to fiddle with a pistol, either to repair or reload it; Lynn couldn't tell.

The elephant whined and drew Lynn's attention. Another streak ran down its hide, adding to the look of morbid camouflage in an increasingly reddening area of battle.

Lynn could taste the blood in the air.

Cody had gotten up and shouted for the animal's attention. He waved his empty hands and feigned forward with another loud cry.

The frenzied animal stepped back and threw up its trunk skittishly. Its small brain seemed too overloaded with sensations and emotions to choose a course of action.

Something gleaming caught the light before it lodged deeply into the animal's neck.

The elephant trumpeted again, then stumbled.

Seemingly out of nowhere, the machete-wielder emerged at its rear and slashed across the back of a leg.

Blood gushed.

The elephant let out a chilling cry of pain and sagged through the leg. Its flanks heaved with each breath.

Skeever squirmed in his position half under her body, fighting the hand around his collar.

The swarm of people descended on the elephant like a chaotic but hell-bent swarm of lethal locusts. More spears pierced its sides; blades slashed.

Death by a thousand cuts. The words bubbled up from the depth of her mind without a solid memory attached to it.

Skeever contorted.

She flattened him to the ground more, wrestling him down.

The elephant fell with a dull thud that was not celebrated.

Was it dead? Eager to confirm the group's victory, Lynn pushed up to see over the tall grass.

The second her attention drifted away from him, Skeever yanked away and raced across the street, barking like mad before fastening his teeth to the elephant's waving trunk.

The group was thrown into chaos, caught between surprise and the last vestiges of the hunt.

"Skeever!" She forgot about the danger and gripped her tomahawk as she jumped up and sprinted forward, toward the circle of people and the animal in the last throes of its death struggle.

One of the hunters either did not see or did not pay attention to Skeever as she jumped atop the fallen animal and sank a spear deep into its neck. The machete-wielder, however, stopped dead in her tracks. The man named Cody managed to yank her back just in time to avoid a lashing of the animal's trunk as it flew past, lifting Skeever off his legs.

The dog growled and bit down harder on the trunk, refusing to be dislodged.

Lynn shouldered past a slender man and struck at the elephant's head once as she dodged past its wicked-looking tusks. The blow connected and scraped across strong bone before cutting deep into the cheek.

The elephant thrashed and threw off the hunter, who then disappeared behind its back, out of Lynn's view.

Lynn wrapped her arm around Skeever's writhing bulk and pulled. "Let go!"

To her great surprise, he did.

Lynn fell, but her backpack cushioned most of the impact. Something crunched to bits inside. She scrambled, arm still locked around Skeever, and got out of the way just before a tusk landed heavily on the spot she'd occupied a second earlier. She rolled out of the way and curled into a ball around the twisting dog, gaze on the elephant and its attackers.

The hunter the machete-wielder had called Dani clambered up the animal's back. She was young, covered in blood. Her face was stilled in concentration, and she didn't look Lynn's way even once. She gripped and leveraged one of the spears stuck in the elephant's back, and the animal shuddered once; then a crack loud enough to reach Lynn's ears indicated that either the spear or the animal's vertebrae had given way.

The elephant went slack.

Dani slipped and tumbled off the animal, spear and all.

The other hunters backed off. They watched. They waited.

Lynn swallowed heavily. She still struggled with Skeever, who fought against her grip.

Silence fell.

The elephant's breathing slowed and then, anti-climactically, ceased.

Lynn exhaled along with it, then inhaled deeply. She was very aware the elephant's chest didn't rise with hers.

When she released Skeever, he jumped away like a bucking bull, released from the barn come spring. For a second, Lynn forgot she was probably in trouble and smiled.

Then chaos returned.

"You!" A young man, barely more than a boy, reacted before anyone else could. Mere seconds after the elephant had gone down, he lunged at her with a bloodied knife, his face contorted in anger so deep that it almost froze Lynn in place. Almost. If it had, she would have died then and there. Adrenaline pushed its way through her system, and she rolled out of the way of the first attack, crushing more items in her backpack.

Metal hit asphalt.

The boy's momentum caused him to fall, but he lashed out again even as he sprawled.

Lynn pulled up her legs to get clear of the knife, then kicked. She hit him in the face hard enough to make him drop the knife—it was a lucky shot, and she knew it. She wouldn't get another.

The boy groaned, but his bloodied—probably broken—nose didn't deter him even a little. He scrambled over her, pulling at her leg and clothes for leverage, then grabbed for her hair. He yanked—hard.

She cried out and instinctively covered his hand with her own. His weight prevented her from filling her lungs. Panic surged. Her heart galloped to the point of bursting. *Air!* She remembered her training and blindly clawed at her attacker's face, going for the eyes in animalistic instinct.

He turned his head to the side to avoid her nails and punched her in the face. Then he closed his hands around her windpipe and squeezed.

She pounded at his arms. She tried to fight. She tried to defend herself, but her strength wore down fast. Her heartbeat pounded inside her skull, drowning out any other sound. Her vision became blurry. Her world distilled to gray eyes filled with tears. His mouth moved, but Lynn couldn't focus long enough to understand what he was saying.

In the distance she could hear more yelling and barking, but neither fully registered. His weight pushed her down onto something sharp in her pack.

His grip lessened just enough for her to gasp for breath as he punched her again.

Pain exploded across her cheek. She wheezed, and the oxygen tasted like copper.

He lifted his fist again.

She tilted her head to the side as much as she could to protect it, but the blow never came.

The pressure lifted, first from her neck, then from her chest. Instinctively, she gasped for air, which tore up her throat on its way down. She breathed blood and nearly choked on it. Coughing, she rolled onto her side and tried to get up. Like a newborn lamb, she struck out with her legs and found them incapable of carrying weight. She sank to the ground again and sucked in sand with her oxygen. Damn, that hurt. But she couldn't rest. She tried to slither away.

People were fighting around her. The noise of their brawling just barely topped the pounding of her heart. She scooted forward, away. The other foot, another few inches. *Repeat.* She reached out to plant her fingers in the dirt and placed her hand upon the sticky handle of a knife by accident. Her shaking hand closed around it almost without conscious thought. She took strength from it: now she could defend herself, at least.

Skeever barked, and someone was shouting, but it was all far away.

Her heartbeat pounded in her ears. Every breath burned her lungs and throat. She opened her eyes to see, but her left eye had swollen shut and the other was watery with tears. They did her no good.

Someone grabbed her and pulled her over with a heave, causing her to flounder like a turtle on its back because of the backpack.

In a blind panic, Lynn tried to fight them off. She swung the knife up, but it was knocked from her hand instantly. When she kicked and twisted around to bite, her attacker locked their arms under Lynn's armpits and pressed her into their body to control her movements. Her back arched awkwardly, and she couldn't use her legs anymore or risk tipping them both over and relinquishing even more control. "Le—" Her voice broke as agony seared up her throat. She coughed again, which caused even more pain.

"Stop struggling!" The command was a breathless one.

At least she was giving her attacker something of a fight. Lynn squirmed even harder, invigorated by this tiny perceived victory.

"Dammit!" The grip fell away.

Lynn scrambled again but didn't get far. The struggle had sapped the last of her energy, and she fell face forward as she tried to clamber up.

They let her; the hands didn't return.

The next one to touch her was Skeever as he nuzzled the back of her head. He sniffed at her hair and whimpered. The familiarity of it almost had her break down in tears. "Sk—" Her voice came out in a rasp, and it hurt, so she stopped herself. She reached out and limply wrapped her arm around him. Using his sturdy bulk as a leverage point, she sat up shakily.

A few feet away, the woman named Dani sat on her haunches, inspecting her.

Lynn jumped.

Dani raised her hands, showing her palms. "I'm not here to hurt you."

Yeah, right. She was hotly aware they were all looking at her and that most brandished weapons.

They had dragged the boy who had attacked her away. While he struggled against the grip of Cody and another male, he seemed calmer. He clutched his forearm and glared at her, angry but not like someone who had only just been thwarted in a second attempt on her life.

Lynn frowned. Had it been Dani who'd grabbed her the second time? Now she had a moment to think, she remembered the voice *had* sounded female. She looked back at Dani. If she had been the one to grab her, she hadn't hurt Lynn.

Dani lowered her hands and stayed squatted, watching her.

They looked like a pack of wolves to her, ready to pounce.

Slowly, she slid off her pack. This time she wouldn't be encumbered by it if they attacked her again.

Skeever circled her.

The black man with the pistol stood a few steps apart, arms folded across his chest as he glanced around the square that had served as a hunting ground. He didn't seem interested in current affairs. The pistol gleamed in his holster, definitely on display. There were others, but the machete-wielder whistled sharply, and Lynn's attention jerked back to her before she could take them in.

Skeever whined. He glanced at her with his trusting eyes and then to the machete-wielder. Slowly, he pulled away from her and trotted over to the stranger, tail between his legs. He pressed against her submissively.

As Lynn adjusted her balance, something stung in her back. Great. Another injury. She ignored it; she needed what little reason was left in her adrenaline-sodden brain to figure out Skeever's odd behavior. It hit her like the boy's punch: Skeever *knew* these people.

The machete-wielder didn't reach down to pet him; her one hand still held the bloody blade, and the sleeve on the other side of her body was bunched up near the shoulder, made redundant by the lack of a right arm. "Can you talk?" Her voice was cold and hard.

To spare her throat, Lynn should have shook her head, but she nodded instead. With the strength of the bold and proud, she stood.

When she wobbled, Dani shot up and took her arm.

Lynn shook her off and gave her a death glare.

She backed off with a shrug. "Suit yourself."

"Did you kill him?" the machete-wielder cut in.

"W-Who?" Pain flared again, but she clenched her fist and refused to back off. Gauntlets were obviously being thrown, and she'd just had to fight for her life. She'd be damned if she showed weakness now. Besides, she was finally getting answers to questions she hadn't even had time to formulate, such as why the boy had attacked her. Surely it had nothing to do with the elephant.

"The man who owned the dog. Did you kill him?"

Realization hit like a bucket of ice water. "N-No." She cleared her throat in the hopes of getting out more than a rasp and winced. *Ouch*. "I found him dead."

The severe woman searched her features through narrowed eyes. Seconds passed. She was, perhaps, in her forties. Her short hair was graying at the temples, but most of it was a dirty blonde that was now splattered red. Her angular jaw was set, and, along with cold gray eyes and a hooked nose, it made her look avian. "What did he look like?"

Lynn steeled herself for a full sentence. The more she spoke, the worse her throat felt. "Mid-forties, maybe? Brown hair." *That could be anyone. Shit.* She racked her brain for something that had stood out, but she hadn't exactly lingered. Then she remembered something she'd puzzled on at the time. "He had a cord on his belt with a bird skull and a small metal tag with the letter R on it."

That was enough. The bird-skull memento obviously registered. Machete-wielder's eyes watered, and her lips set into a thin line. She did not cry. Instead, she holstered her machete and held out her one hand to her son. He *had* to be her son, Lynn thought. The resemblance was too striking even though his hair was darker. And he would have cause to attack her if he thought she'd killed his father.

Which I didn't.

The boy broke free angrily now that the men restraining him lessened their hold. He stepped forward and flung his arms around the machete-wielder's torso in a way only a teenage boy could: too proud for a gentle hug, too young to go without comfort altogether.

The machete-wielder whispered something to him and wrapped her arm across his shoulders.

Lynn glanced away out of a vague sense of intruding and found Dani looking at her. Lynn stared right back. The brunette was about her age, Lynn guessed, maybe twenty-seven or twenty-eight. She was covered nearly head to toe in blood, but it didn't all belong to the elephant. Near her left temple ran a small but angry-looking gash, and a trickle of blood soaked her cured leather top.

"Take her to the Homestead."

Lynn looked up sharply.

"—and take those weapons off her."

Dani nodded at the machete-wielder. "I will."

Lynn was fairly certain she would not get a say in the matter. A glance at the faces around her confirmed her suspicion. Still, not all of them were looking at her with murder in their eyes; that was just the boy. The rest of the expressions ran the gamut between disinterest and curiosity. Only two refused to meet her gaze when she looked at them.

"Skeever, come!" The machete-wielder turned on her heel and strode off.

Skeever glanced at Lynn but then jogged away.

Lynn's heart sank.

After a few seconds, Dani turned to her and sighed. "His name was Richard, and he was Kate's partner. Dean, the guy who attacked you, was his son."

"I figured." Her voice sounded oddly flat in her own ears, a combination of a lower tone to spare her voice and her conflicting emotions. She felt sympathy for the group in losing one of their own, but she was also angry. No, not angry—indignant. She hadn't done a damn thing wrong, and yet this guy, Dean, had gone off on her so ferociously that she could have ended up dead. She brought her hand to her throat and rubbed carefully. It felt swollen and hot.

Dani ignored her tone and extended her hand. "I'm Dani."

Lynn regarded the dirty appendage for a few moments, then took it. "Yeah, I got that." They shook. How long had it been since she had last touched a human being? In a friendly matter, that was. Well, friendly-ish. "Lynn." She tried not to sound too pissed off. It wasn't Dani's fault Dean had lost it.

Dani scanned her with a slight squint.

Lynn didn't like to be examined. "It's not going to get prettier." How bad was the damage to her face anyway? Her left eye was still swollen shut, but her right had cleared up considerably. She resisted the urge to feel at her face even when Dani released her and stuffed both hands into her coat pockets instead.

"I di—"

"Dani! Kate didn't say to babysit her. C'mere and pull your weight, will you?" Cody stood bare-chested and bloody atop the carcass. He glowered at Dani and completely ignored Lynn.

While they'd talked, the rest of the group had begun to dismantle the elephant. Initial cuts to the skin had been made already.

"Coming." Dani's voice did not show the annoyance Lynn's would have. Or maybe it did, in its metered neutrality. She glanced at Lynn. "Are you going to run off the moment I turn around?"

Lynn considered it. "Probably not." She wanted to, but that Kate woman had taken Skeever away, and she wanted him back.

Dani inspected her again. "Then why not make yourself useful while you're with us, hm?"

"Let's not pretend it's a voluntary stay." The painful rasp made the statement sound reproachful, to say the least, and she didn't try to bend it into anything else.

Dani just shrugged. "Do what you want, but we like people who pull their weight much better than people who watch others work. We might be more inclined to believe hard workers too."

Lynn searched Dani's eyes. The implications were clear: they didn't trust her, nor her story. Lynn probably wouldn't have trusted her story either, but it still pissed her off. She nodded. "Fine. I'll help."

"Good choice, Wilder." Dani extended her hand, palm up. "Your weapons?"

"What exactly did you want me to cut with if I gave you those?" She pointedly arched her brow. No way was she handing her weapons over without a fight while everyone else was armed to the teeth.

Dani seemed to ponder that. "Right. Afterward, then."

Lynn didn't grace that with a reply. When she shrugged off her jacket and set aside her boots, everyone watched her, some more obvious than others. The redhead stared openly as she exchanged words with a muscular but lanky man. He was carving out one of the animal's destructive tusks but managed to glance at Lynn every few seconds. Whether it was in distrust or curiosity, Lynn couldn't tell.

Cody definitely eyed her in distrust. When she stepped up, confidently brandishing a knife, he watched her every step of the way, as if she were going to throw the knife into his back if he didn't.

She ignored him. Getting used to the feeling of stepping barefooted through a mixture of sand and coagulating blood took all of her brain power. It was like stepping on a field of gritty snails. She shivered. *Time to get to work.*

The setting sun cast a red glow on the grass Lynn sank down onto. They had worked hard, and her limbs were sore. Her back was killing her. At least the throbbing in her throat had lessened some.

The ragged remains of the carcass drew flies downwind. Three loaded-up stretchers made from straight poles and braided vines lay in front of Lynn's stretched-out legs to be taken to the Homestead.

Lynn had been assigned to watch the stretchers while Cody and a small man everyone called Eduardo hauled the animal's tusks and sacks of bones up to the second story of a nearby building to be collected another day. Dani knelt at a puddle, busily washing the worst of the gore off her hands, arms, and face. Lynn had tried to do the same yet still felt disgusting. Every time she moved, her blood-crusted clothes tore away from her skin. It was everywhere. She shuddered.

The redhead woman, Ren, lowered herself down next to her with a groan. She seemed to be in her thirties and, like all of them, was covered in gore from head to toe. "Stick a fork in me, I am done." She leaned back on her hands, then let herself fall into the grass all the way. Her impressive chest heaved. "I think we did well, though."

Ren's proximity made her nervous, but she didn't radiate enough of a threat for Lynn to move her aching body. She nodded and gave the area a once-over. They'd been making enough ruckus to keep the scavengers away, but now that the work was winding down, the clearing would soon become the site of a feeding frenzy.

"Now Cody and Eduardo just need to hurry up and get here, and I'll be happy. Don't you have the feeling we're being watched by all sorts?"

Lynn glanced at her sidelong. *Why are you suddenly talking to me? You've all been silently side-eying me for hours.* She gave a noncommittal hum. Her knife and tomahawk pressed against the underside of her legs. It was a reminder she wasn't defenseless—yet. The hard work seemed to have made the group forgetful, and she refused to tempt fate by keeping her weapons in plain sight. "How far away is the Homestead anyway?"

"Not far. Half of an hour at most." She glanced at the stretchers. "With all of *that* anyway."

Having grown up in settlements, Lynn was familiar with the division of a day into twenty-four segments called *hours*. She'd spent most of her life without access to a sundial, however, and she couldn't envision the length of time Ren indicated in relation to distance.

Dani plopped down next to Lynn, stretched out her legs, and shook out her hair. Most of it remained stuck to her skull because of the blood and water, but a small braid on the side of her head with a little dark bead on it was heavy enough to overcome the stickiness. It swung wildly and drew Lynn's attention.

Lynn scooted backward a little so she wouldn't be flanked by the two women anymore. Her weapons dug into her flesh as she dragged them along.

"I'm ready to go." Dani glanced back at her, then focused on Ren. "Where are the boys?"

Ren shrugged. "They'll be here."

"If they don't hurry up, we'll be lion food soon." Dani's gaze darted around. Her hand lay on the spear by her side, then she drew the shaft onto her lap.

Lynn assumed lions here were like wolves on the open road: the top dog of the predator hierarchy. She had no desire to run into one; she'd come face-to-face with enough entirely foreign animals today. *Speaking of which...* "Where's the guy with the gun?"

Ren sat up and looked around as if she only now realized they were a man short. "Yeah, where *is* Flint?"

Flint? Lynn frowned at the odd-sounding name.

"Over there." Dani pointed with the tip of her spear. The shaft was made of some sort of metal, Lynn noticed now, not wood.

Flint sat on his haunches by the carcass, his back to them.

Ren hummed and settled onto the grass again.

"That's not his name, by the way," Dani said. She must have spotted Lynn's confused look. "But we call him that because—" She paused to look at Ren. "Do you know his birth name?"

Ren shook her head and got even more debris in her hair as it brushed along the ground. "No. He's always just been Flint. I bet Kate knows, though."

"How many more are there?"

"That's it," Ren said. "Oh, and Tobias, Kate's younger son."

Damn, another kid growing up without a dad. That caused a pang of misery in Lynn. She kept it out of her voice, though. "Another kid, huh."

Ren nodded with a grim expression. "Yeah."

"Such a mess." Dani sighed.

Lynn didn't respond to that, but she knew very well what it was like to grow up without a father, and she didn't wish it on anyone—not even Dean and most certainly not his kid brother. "How old is he?"

"He's what? Six now?" Ren checked the statement with Dani.

Dani nodded. "Should be."

"And you left him alone?" The words slipped out before she could press her lips together.

"He's six, not two." Dani shrugged. "You haven't seen the Homestead."

Lynn hummed, unconvinced of the wisdom of leaving a child alone anywhere in the Wilds, even if it was in a building. She didn't get time to ponder it.

"They're back." Dani pointed the spear and got up.

Lynn looked up.

Cody and Eduardo talked animatedly as they stepped out of the building, although both looked around for danger as soon as they were clear of the doorframe.

Lynn stood and brushed sand and grass off her clothing—or tried to. A lot of it stuck to the drying blood. She plucked at the husks until the men came closer, then straightened. She didn't want to appear anything but strong and confident around Cody. He looked down on her enough as it was.

"Hey, babe." Cody helped Ren up and kissed her before she could reply.

Lynn looked away from the intimate moment.

"We should go."

The dark, low voice made her jump and whirl around.

Flint stood behind her. His slightly yellowish eyes studied her. She tried to divine what he thought of her, but his face was completely unreadable.

Lynn realized they hadn't been properly introduced yet. The chance to do so passed when Dani nudged her.

"You're about my height, right?"

Lynn nodded, attention diverted.

"Good, then you're with me. Cody and Flint will take the second stretcher, and Ren and Eduardo take the last."

Lynn gathered her pack and stuffed her clean jacket into it as everyone else answered in the affirmative. After a glance over her shoulder, she slipped her tomahawk into the depths of her backpack and closed it. She hated to stick her dirty feet into her boots, but she did so anyway so she could slip her knife into it.

After a minute, Dani was back and loomed over her.

Lynn swallowed and slowly tilted her head up. Had Dani seen her? Did she remember she was supposed to take Lynn's weapons?

"Front or back?"

"Huh?" Lynn groaned internally. *Very eloquent, Tanner.*

"The stretcher. Front or back?"

"Back."

"Fine with me." Dani twirled her spear, then pressed something on the shaft. Instantly, the compartments of the metal tube folded in on themselves, and the spear shortened to half its original size.

Lynn raised an eyebrow.

Dani either didn't notice or ignored it. From her pocket she produced a piece of rope with a loop on one end and a little pouch on the other. She slid the loop over the tip of the spear and pulled it tight, then settled the bud of the weapon into the pouch as if she had done it so often it'd become routine. It probably had. She hung the spear across her torso like a shoulder bag, then nodded at her backpack. "If you're so adamant about keeping your weapons, keep one of 'em at the ready. If we get attacked, you're not my priority."

Lynn's heart skipped a beat as she realized she'd been found out, but she set her jaw and looked up with defiance. "I can take care of myself, *Settler.*" She stood and hoisted her heavy backpack onto her protesting shoulders.

"Whatever you say." Dani turned and walked over to the stretchers. The bloody tip of her spear bobbed over her shoulder.

"Bitch," Lynn muttered under her breath. She followed and took her place opposite Dani between the two poles.

Dani bent down with her, and they lifted together.

Every single one of her muscles protested as she bore the stretcher's considerable weight. "Damn."

Dani's shoulders squared. "Don't you dare drop it."

"Not going to." Lynn adjusted her grip so the weight was more evenly distributed.

The muscles in Dani's arms stood out under the skin. "Are you sure?"

"Very sure." She wasn't, but she would be damned if she was going to admit weakness.

Next to them, the others got ready as well.

"Everyone set?" Cody checked on the group, but his gaze slid over Lynn as if she didn't exist.

Asshole.

"Set," Dani and Ren said in unison.

"Let's go home."

CHAPTER 2

The Homestead rose up above Lynn like the last behemoth of the Old World. In an otherwise leveled city block, it stood as the sole reminder of civilization-that-was. Nature had left her trace; the marble façade had lost its shine, and of the letters above the entrance only two remained, one a C and one an R. They were specked with imperfection now, but Lynn could picture how they would have gleamed proudly in the sunlight when people had still come here to work. Would they have noticed, she wondered? Would the letters have given them a sense of pride? Of belonging? Did they now? She took in the small group of people around her. It must be nice to have a home.

To her, the Homestead felt like a lion's den she was about to walk into. Lynn understood now why the group had felt comfortable leaving Kate's youngest alone: the place was a fortress. The windows on the first and second story of the building had been fortified with wooden planks and metal plates. They had even hoisted some stripped car doors in front of them, nailed to the boards with strips of metal and leather or held in place with chains extended from the windows above. Each chain was secured to the ground by rocks. The building's doors had been fortified with wood and metal as well, but Lynn was more impressed by the barbed-wire-wrapped piece of metal fence installed in front of the doors like a swing gate. It was a menacing deterrent for anyone and anything foolish enough to come close.

"Is this all yours?" she asked.

Dani shook her head. "No, just the fifth floor and the roof. We don't use the rest. Well, we use *that* as a lookout point." She inclined her head toward a rig that hung in front of a shattered or removed window on the third floor.

Not even knowing most of the building was deserted could lessen Lynn's anxiety over entering it. *Is Skeever really worth this?* A sharp pain in her chest reminded her he was.

"Flint, put it down for a second." Cody and the black man lowered their stretcher. He undid the wiring that held the panel in place and swung it out, then pushed one of the fortified doors open. The doorway revealed nothing but darkness. "Go first."

Ren and Eduardo carried their load up the three steps to the door and disappeared inside.

Lynn looked up at the building again. Once inside, she would be completely at their mercy. She dared a glance to the side. How far would she get if she ran now? She still had her backpack and her weapons. They knew this area much better than she did, but maybe if she ran fast enough, she could find a place to hide.

I'm so tired. Just the thought of running made her limbs ache. She looked up again. *And Skeever is in there.* It was ridiculous to risk her life on something like that, but there wasn't much more to her life than that dog.

Dani stepped forward.

Lynn tensed. Dani's momentum pulled her toward the entrance. She leaned into the pull so she wouldn't have to move her feet and could delay the inevitable, but the stretcher was too heavy. She took a step to avoid falling over. Then she took another. Her throat tightened as she passed Cody and stepped into the building.

The swing gate crashed against the stone of the building with a thunderous rattle. Lynn jumped. The noise echoed horribly in the building's cavernous lobby until it died and left behind an oppressive silence.

She craned her neck to look behind her and watched Cody push the door shut.

Her fate had been sealed—at least for now.

She couldn't linger on her fear long. The red light of the setting sun, projected from cracks between the boards covering the windows, didn't illuminate much of the dirt-caked marble flooring, and she stumbled when Dani's momentum caught up with her. Tufts of grass struggled for foothold in various larger and smaller cracks. Stepping on them upset her balance as

Dani forced her along; just staying upright required all of her balance and brainpower. Their motions threw up dust and pollen, making it even harder to see. She blinked to help her eyes adjust. If she wanted to plan her escape, she needed to soak in every detail of her surroundings.

Once she could see again, she realized sunlight wasn't the only illumination after all. Jars with crude, lit wicks in them had been placed on the floor, interspersed along the walls. They gave off just enough light so the group could make their way to the end of the hall. The thick smoke that curled up from them carried the heavy scent of animal fat into the air and made her eyes water. She tried and failed to wipe them on her shoulder and jumped when Cody and Flint pushed past her. They disappeared into a hallway off the entry hall.

Dani guided them deftly past a chunky receptionist station and several interlinked seats.

After a glance back at Ren, who fell in line behind her, Lynn underwent the torture of walking up five flights of stairs with limbs and a brain that had gone numb with the strain of the day, not knowing what would await her once she made it upstairs.

"Kate? It's us!" Cody and Flint lowered their stretcher.

Eduardo and Ren followed their example, then sagged to the floor.

Dani guided Lynn past them and set down the stretcher.

Lynn gratefully complied. Her shoulders stung; her lower back felt compressed, and her feet were sore. Her arms were too numb to ache. Sweat ran down her neck and spine. Forcing her to carry the heavy stretcher with its unstable load had been the most diabolical and effective way to trap her: she had rarely been this physically exhausted, and her fighting spirit had been dampened considerably. She took off her heavy backpack and leaned against the wall for support.

"Kate?" Cody took a step down the hallway and listened.

Still no answer.

Lynn took in what she could see of the Homestead. The hallway was like any other she had raided in her life: dusty carpets and doors leading into boardrooms. She supposed they were no longer boardrooms now, if the group lived here. They would be bedrooms now, living rooms, storerooms, and whatever else they needed.

"Do you think they…?" Ren didn't finish her sentence.

Lynn glanced from her to Cody.

"I dunno." Cody stared down the hallway intently. "I'll go check. Take care of this stuff, will you?"

Lynn bit back a groan, but Ren got to her feet instantly.

"All right, final effort." Ren actually smiled.

Only Eduardo echoed it. Dani was too busy scrambling to her feet to smile, and Flint, it seemed, didn't smile at all. He stood stoically by and nodded at her when she glanced up at him.

Lynn looked away, then forced herself upright. "Where does it go?"

"The kitchen." Ren took charge.

"I'll go blow out the candles downstairs." Eduardo got up with an agility and ease that made Lynn jealous. He disappeared through the door again.

Lifting the stretcher for a second time was murder on her arms and back, but she managed. Step by grueling step, she followed Dani down the hallway and into a fairly spacious room. The term *kitchen* was deceiving. Kitchens had a stove or a fireplace, something to cook on. The Homestead's kitchen was more of a breakroom—she'd seen them before in office buildings, complete with machines to make drinks and others that used to hold packaged food. There were none of those machines in the Homestead's kitchen. Instead, barrels and boxes were stacked along the walls. Thick wooden planks and Old-World desks served as spaces for meal preparation. Tables dominated much of the room, creating space for indoor meals and now, Lynn supposed, for sorting meat from fat and bones.

"On the tables, please."

Lynn grunted in accordance. With the last of her strength, she lifted her load onto the table, set it down, and then stumbled to the side, out of the way of the others. Completely wiped, she slid down the wall. "Damn."

"Double damn." Dani lowered herself down next to her, then leaned her head back against the wall and closed her eyes. Her chest rose and fell rapidly. Beads of sweat slid down her neck and forehead.

Lynn pulled her legs in to avoid getting stepped on. Next to her hand lay a carved wooden animal, probably a horse. She picked it up and turned the crudely carved animal around in her hands. There were a variety of toys strewn about, Lynn now realized. Drawings—drawn straight on—littered the walls. *Kids' stuff. How rare was that these days?*

When she looked up again, she found that Flint was the only one who had remained standing. He leaned against the window, looking out into the falling darkness. The others had taken seats around the tables.

"What a day." Ren sighed. She dragged the sleeve of her loose woolen sweater over her forehead. Her face was red, and although she was still smiling, she looked just about done.

Lynn could relate.

"I should get the smokehouse ready." Ren's voice was filled with an intense unwillingness to move.

"I'll help you, Ren." Eduardo didn't get up either. "Do you think they are okay?"

"Kate and Dean? Sure." She didn't sound very sure, though. "Well, I'm sure they made it home safe. I'm sure they're not, you know, *okay*."

Eduardo reached over to rub Ren's arm.

Flint sighed deeply enough for Lynn to notice.

"Come on." Dani stood and held out her hand for Lynn to take.

Lynn hesitated. She stared suspiciously at the extremity. "Where are we going?"

"To the roof. To work." Dani wiggled her fingers. "Come on."

Lynn considered getting up without help, but antagonizing Dani wouldn't do her any good. She took Dani's hand, which was calloused and warm, and stood. The second she had her balance, she let go.

"We'll be right there," Ren said.

"Take your time." Dani picked up a slab of meat and strode out.

Lynn dug her fingers into the yielding, bloody flesh as well and lifted a large slab that instantly made her arms tremble. She hoisted it onto her shoulder for relief and strode out without looking at any of the others.

Dani had waited for her just a few paces around the corner.

Lynn almost bumped into her.

"I didn't think you had it in you." Dani smirked ever so slightly. The blood from the meat soaked through her leather jacket, but because it was already a dark crimson, it didn't matter anymore. All of them were covered in blood.

Lynn watched it trickle down. "I'm tougher than I look."

"Good to know."

It seemed as if she had gained some of Dani's respect. Not that she needed it. Lynn arched a brow. "Can we go now?"

"Sure." Dani watched her a few seconds longer, then turned away and strode down the narrow hallway.

Lynn followed along and took in every little detail. At equal intervals, both sides revealed a door and a tall, narrow window next to it. Almost all of them had been covered by curtains; the others were dark.

Living quarters? Storerooms? She peered into the darkness of an uncovered window but saw nothing. *Is Dean hiding in one of these?* The thought made her tense. "Is one of these yours?" If Lynn got Dani talking, maybe she'd tell her more about the layout of the floor and where its residents resided.

"No." Dani didn't even turn her head.

She tried again. "It's a nice setup you have here."

Now Dani looked about. "Thanks. You know, I've gotten so used to it, I hardly notice anymore."

The words reminded her of the camps she'd lived in as a child. "I remember." When it became apparent Dani wasn't going to say anything else, Lynn fed her another question to keep her talking. "Have you been with these people long?"

"Almost two years. Back then Cody, Eduardo, and Ren weren't there yet. Some other guy died from an infected wound a few days after I arrived."

"Sucks."

Dani shrugged.

What more could you say? An infected wound was a death sentence unless you managed to make it through on bed rest, herbal remedies, and first aid alone. Lynn had seen plenty of good people die over nothing but a cold or diarrhea. There was no medication, and the big machines Lynn had once seen in a hospital she had raided had all been fried in the war. Besides, there was no one who could have operated the equipment even if it had survived, nor power to run it.

"Through here." Dani directed her through a door and then up a smaller staircase. When she put her weight against a heavy door, it gave way with a high-pitched creak. She held it open for Lynn with her ass, hands occupied with the heavy slab of meat.

Lynn slipped past and forgot all about planning her escape. She didn't even feel her sore limbs and still slightly hot features anymore. When she uttered an appreciative "wow," she barely noticed her sore throat. Before her was paradise. Half of the rooftop was taken up by a garden, partly domed by a greenhouse made of sheets of glass set in a wooden frame. Lynn recognized beans, squashes, lettuce, carrots, tomatoes, and a variety of herbs in low beds. Potato plants grew in barrels.

The other half of the rooftop was covered with an assortment of sheds and roofed areas, including a seating area, several small workshops—metal and wood by the looks of it—and a shed for what Lynn assumed would be gardening tools. A water tank towered over the concrete structure that housed the staircase. The center feature of the roof was a wide circle of stones on a bed of sand and tiles in which a fire had burned to coals. The dim glow cast shadows across four benches set around it in a square.

The same fat-burning candles as well as several torches illuminated the terrace and workstations.

"Pretty good, right?" Dani asked.

Lynn slowly dragged her gaze over to her dark-haired companion and nodded, awestruck. "Brilliant," she said. "Absolutely brilliant."

It was. It was secure from predators and the very few people who would ever wander into the area, provided an excellent lookout, and, above all, made the group largely self-sufficient.

As if Dani could read her mind, she pointed to the garden. "What we can't eat or store, we trade for wool or food we don't produce ourselves. To the south is another small settlement with sheep and goats, for example." Dani stepped out onto the roof and the door fell shut.

The sound brought Lynn back to reality. This was still enemy territory. She took it all in. "What do you make yourselves?"

"Cody is a metalworker; Flint works mostly with bone and ivory, and Eduardo and Dean are our resident woodworkers. Ren and Eduardo tend the garden." Dani pushed forward, straight across the roof.

Lynn followed and listened, soaking up the information like a sponge. Information was power: the more she knew about the group, the better she could protect herself against them. "How about Kate?"

"Kate is in charge, pretty much; she's our spokesperson and is in charge of inventory and trade. Richard was our scout."

"And you?"

Dani stood a little straighter. "I hunt, help where I can, and do the leatherworking. Ren tried to teach me to knit once, but I almost stabbed her with a needle out of frustration, so we gave up on that." She grinned.

Lynn smiled despite her tumbling thoughts. It was all so...well organized. Everyone had defined roles and skills to contribute, and they seemed to get along. The group was large enough to cover all bases but small enough to depend on each other for survival, which must help keep the peace between them. Lynn had been in groups too small to function properly, which led to famine and infighting, and groups too large, which made people complacent and greedy. Both had splintered. This group actually had a shot of making it—if they managed to survive the loss of one of their own. She decided not to put focus on that. "You guys have one of the best setups of any group I've encountered so far."

"Thanks." Dani took in the rooftop again. "Kate and Richard started it all, including the garden. Kate's decent at gardening too, but with the one arm, she tends to get frustrated with it."

"What's up with that, anyway?"

"Huh? Oh, the arm? Born that way. No story." Dani turned to her, walking backward a few paces. "Trust me, in a few days, you won't even notice it anymore."

"I guess." She wasn't planning on being around long enough to get used to anything.

Without another word, Dani guided her to a workbench in the shed she had previously pointed to when she had spoken of her own activities. She dumped the slab of meat on a heavily stained workbench. Wood cuttings and dried grass covered the floor, probably to absorb the blood that came off her kills. It was a small workstation that they barely fitted into together, but it was well stocked with knives of various sizes and other tools of the trade.

Lynn disposed of her share of the meat and straightened with a groan. Her wet shirt stuck to her skin. Lynn hoped she would soon be able to wash properly. After the work was done.

"We'll smoke most of the meat so we can store it longer and trade it with other settlements. Ren and the others will poke up the fire and set up the smokehouse. Do you know how to butcher?"

"Not formally or anything, but I can cut meat into strips. Just tell me what size, and I'll be good."

"Where's your axe?" Dani's tone was casual, but it was a clear reminder that she knew Lynn was still armed.

"It's a tomahawk. And it's in my pack." Lynn met her eyes defiantly.

Dani examined her a few moments longer and then pulled a knife off a rack: a long blade with a wicked edge. She turned over the jagged slab in front of her, cut off a thin but long strip, and held it up for Lynn to see.

"No problem."

Dani hesitated, then tossed the blade in the air in a display of showmanship and caught it by the sharp end by pinching it between her fingers before the cutting edge could cut into the palm. It was a well-practiced and impressive trick, a way to show she knew how to handle a blade without coming right out and saying it.

Lynn caught the warning that underlay the gesture loud and clear.

Dani offered the handle to Lynn, leveling the tip of the blade with her own belly in the process. "Then I guess you get to borrow a knife of mine."

Their gazes met and held.

A test? Lynn inhaled slowly, then took the knife. She tried to emote that she wouldn't run Dani through the second she let go. She might have if it would have given her an advantage, but without knowing where Skeever was, she couldn't make her escape.

After a few moments, Dani released her grip and did not look down at the blade.

Lynn lowered it.

Dani swallowed heavily, and Lynn's attention was drawn to her throat. She pulled her gaze away instantly as she realized staring at the neck of someone who was worried you'd kill them with their own blade was a bad idea. As casually as she could, she took Dani's place. She silently pulled the slab of meat over, cut along the sinew, pulled it out, and set it aside.

Dani watched her—not just her hands but her face. "You seem to have it handled, Wilder. I need to go help Ren, but I'll get you a few new chunks soon, okay?" Dani's tone was casual, but there was a touch of tension underneath. Maybe she was reconsidering leaving a stranger alone with a wall of knives.

"See you soon." Lynn forced a little smile, which she hoped would steady Dani's nerves.

After a few moments of inspection, Dani turned and walked away without another word.

Lynn watched her go, and the knots in her stomach loosened more with every step Dani took. Being left alone gave her a chance to take stock of her situation and make a plan. It was fairly simple: she needed to find Skeever and then make a break for it. For now, she would cooperate and learn all she could. If they wanted her to do chores, then that was what she would do—right until she made her move.

The chunk of meat fell heavily on the cutting block. Lynn had seen Dani coming so she wasn't caught by surprise, but she still had to keep herself from jumping at the suddenness of it all. That first day when she'd had Skeever, she had jumped skittishly at everything he had done as well. In her world, sudden movement usually meant sudden death.

"More to cut up. I'm going to help Ren and Eduardo set up the smokehouse." Dani left without waiting for an answer.

Lynn watched her go again, then let her gaze veer out over the rooftop for Dean, but he wasn't there. She'd spent most of her time at the cutting block assessing the group and its dynamic. Lynn observed them the way she would a herd of animals or stalking predators: with the razor-sharp focus of one trying to stay alive. If she understood the mechanics of their hierarchy, she would be able to use it against them—at least that's what she hoped.

Of those whose physical strength and power over the group she respected the most, only Cody was within sight. He worked the main fire into a frenzy before allowing it to dim down to blazing coals that warped the sky above them with their heat. He and Kate seemed to be the group's alphas.

As her gaze landed on him, he looked up.

She glanced away and watched Ren, Eduardo, and Dani drag wooden panels to the fireplace instead.

Lynn didn't fear Eduardo's strength, but she was quite sure both he and Ren would go along with the wishes of the pack when push came to shove, and that made them dangerous to her in their own right. She wasn't sure what Dani would do, which made her a liability.

Ren and Dani set up the outer panels around the fire and laid more paneling over the tops of them to create a roof. Eduardo and Cody installed support beams and racks into the created chamber. Both came out sweaty and coughing even though they'd tied strips of fabric around their heads to cover their mouths and noses.

Cody and Ren were obviously involved, as the kiss had made clear before, and they definitely behaved like a couple: he helped her lift the heavy things; she berated him for doing it, and once it was done, she kissed him as a way of saying thanks.

Lynn was also starting to suspect that Eduardo was romantically involved with Cody. The two men shared intimate moments such as wiping soot off each other's cheeks or exchanging a kiss here and there—while Ren and Eduardo seemed to be friends or at least not overtly romantic.

Whatever their relationship was, Ren, Cody, and Eduardo seemed to form a unit of which Eduardo was at the bottom. Not far behind the others, but either his subdued personality or Cody's and Ren's outspoken ones had pushed him somewhat to the periphery. He dipped his head more often and was sent off for retrieval of materials and tools by the others. Lynn wondered if the three even realized they were doing it.

Her gaze slid to Dani, who most definitely was not part of that unit. They all reacted differently to her, less intimate. Lynn could easily establish where Dani fit into the general hierarchy of the four: on par with Cody or just a fraction below him, but well above Ren and Eduardo. Dani allowed Ren's hand on her shoulder a moment, for example, but she avoided Cody's touch if she could.

It struck her how closely groups of people resembled groups of monkeys.

Lynn almost cut into her thumb as she twisted her head about to track Flint's progress across the roof. Flint was a bit of a mystery to her. His movements and facial expressions were completely controlled. No one reached out to Flint, which could mean they were either afraid of him or he was above all of them in standing. Maybe he had just found a way to avoid the hierarchy altogether. Not being able to slot him into the equation she was building in her head frustrated Lynn, but there was nothing she could do about it but keep observing. That was made harder by the fact that Flint seemed to have eyes in the back of his head; whenever she looked at him, he stared her down. It was unnerving.

Her thoughts were interrupted by Dani, who joined her with more meat. "Let me help."

Lynn stepped aside, making room. "Is the, uh, hut ready?"

"The smokehouse? Yeah. We'll hang these to dry soon." Dani took another knife from the rack, tested its sharpness on the meat, and began to cut when the blade proved sharp enough.

Lynn watched her hands, then her profile, and reminded herself to get back to work.

Dani didn't talk. They stood close together in the cramped space, and although Lynn tried to keep herself away enough not to, their shoulders and arms brushed on occasion.

Tensely, Lynn allowed her to invade her personal space.

"Dean and Kate are in their rooms." Dani kept working with her head down.

"Hm?" Lynn looked up from the meat.

"Kate. The boys." Dani shrugged. "They won't open the door for Cody or talk to him. He's worried."

Lynn frowned. "Why are you telling me this?"

"Dunno."

Then Lynn caught on to the stiffness in her shoulders and her set jaw. *Cody is not the only one worried.* Lynn needed to find out how close everyone was to each other and who might be willing to go against Kate and Dean. Dani would be strong enough to, but now that Lynn recognized the worry in her tone, she wondered how willing she would be to defy them. Of course she couldn't come right out and ask. She had to go the long way 'round. "Are they close, Cody and Kate?"

Dani regarded her. "You know, just because he has two partners doesn't mean he sleeps with everything that moves." Her voice was sharp all of a sudden.

Lynn's face heated. "That is...not even close to what I meant," she managed. *Shit.* "Why should I care that he has two partners? I've seen weirder things, trust me." She groaned inwardly. "That's also not what I meant." She took a deep breath.

Dani scowled at her. "What *did* you mean?"

"I meant—" She inhaled to steady her frayed emotions and collect her tumbling thoughts. "That I have no idea what I'm talking about and I should just keep my trap shut."

Dani remained focused on her a few seconds longer, face unreadable as she examined Lynn's features. Then the tension in her shoulders and face ebbed away. "Damn right you do." A smile tugged at the corners of her mouth as she got back to work.

Lynn exhaled as silently as she could. Crisis averted. She watched her a few moments, but when Dani didn't acknowledge her further, she shook her head and got back to work. Keeping her mouth shut for now would most likely gain her the most in the long run, but she wasn't happy with it. She felt the pressure of time ticking away as the pile of slabs got smaller and the baskets of strips became fuller.

"Cody cares about Kate and the other way around too." Dani broke the silence after several minutes. "Richard was hardly here when he was still alive. Cody helps out with Dean. Toby is all but glued to Eduardo, but Cody is the only one who can handle Dean when he's in a mood. Cody cares about Dean, and caring about Kate came easy, I guess. There is nothing between them, though. Not as far as I'm aware."

"Wouldn't be any of my business, anyway," Lynn interjected.

"True. Same for me."

Lynn hesitated, then said carefully, "I really didn't mean anything by it."

Dani shrugged and kept her head down. "You never know. People are assholes."

Lynn chuckled despite herself and nodded. "Yeah, that they are. Most of them, anyway." Now that the tension had lessened some, she resumed her questioning. "What about Flint?" She looked past Dani and found him near a torch, scraping tissue from what seemed to be one of the elephant's molars. He seemed unaware of anything around him, but Lynn very much doubted that was the case.

Ren crossed her field of vision before disappearing through the door to the staircase.

"Flint is…Flint." Dani shrugged as she rubbed her cheek on her shoulder. The motion left behind a streak of red that made her look like one of those tribal warrior types who had succumbed to the craziness of life in the Wilds and now worshipped a log in the shape of a duck or something.

"Tired?"

The question shook Lynn from her musings. It took her a moment to realize Dani had caught her staring. *Damn it.* "No, I was just—" She let the words hang in the minimal space between them, unsure of how to end the sentence without running the risk of upsetting Dani again, just when she was finally getting some answers out of her. She shrugged as she cast a sideways glance at Dani. "Nothing. Forget it. I probably am tired."

Dani cracked her neck and arched her back. "Yeah, same. I'm so done for today."

"How much longer?" Lynn turned another slab over in her hands and cut into it.

"Finish these cuts, hang 'em up, get clean, make dinner… I dunno, half the night?" Dani glanced at her with a shrug that seemed almost apologetic.

Lynn stifled a groan. "Great." She licked her lips and tasted blood. *Yuck.* "Um, and what happens after dinner? To me?"

Dani's hands faltered before she resumed working. "I don't know, Wilder. Wrong person to ask. I'm just here to keep an eye on you. Kate or Cody will figure out what to do with you for the night." Her tone had turned gruff again. "Just cut and you'll get dinner."

A mixture of annoyance and fear pumped through Lynn's veins. She gritted her teeth and forced the blade through the meat. "Yes, ma'am." *At least now I know where your place is in the group.*

CHAPTER 3

REN STOOD BY THE TABLE, cutting bits of flesh away from large globs of fatty tissue.

Lynn halted just short of the threshold. "Ren?"

The redhead looked up from her work and gave her the once-over. "What can I do for you, Lynn?" She looked tired, but she tried to hide it behind a smile.

Lynn took a small step forward, into the kitchen. "Dani told me to come see you for a checkup now we're done with the meat."

Ren sighed, but nodded. "Sure." She wiped her hands thoroughly clean on a rag. "Take a seat."

She did.

Ren placed a bowl of water in front of Lynn and handed her a few large handfuls of soft wool. "Wash up."

Lynn began the careful and painful scrubbing. She watched the water turn redder and redder as coagulated blood softened and was absorbed into the wool, then squeezed out into the bowl with the water. How much of the blood was hers, and how much of it belonged to the elephant?

Ren inspected her out of the corner of her eye as she cleared, then cleaned the table. She tossed a bloody rag into a barrel in the corner, then pulled a clean one from a cupboard. She wetted it and returned to scrubbing. Again, the rag ended up in the barrel.

Lynn dropped the wool into the water and watched the wad disappear into the swirling red.

"Are you done?" Ren pulled up a chair and sat.

Lynn nodded.

"Okay, let's see what we have here." Ren took a soft hold of her jaw and tipped her face toward her as she ran her gaze appraisingly over Lynn's skin.

Ren had the greenest eyes Lynn had ever seen—including her own. She looked away from them, to a charcoal drawing of a flower on the wall. She didn't like to be touched—really didn't like to be touched—but when Ren's cool and calloused fingers touched her stinging skin, she forced herself not to flinch away.

"How did you end up here today?" Ren's voice was soft.

"You guys made me come."

Ren didn't take it as a joke, which was good, because Lynn hadn't intended it as one. "I meant in New York City. Are you local?"

Lynn considered the harm in telling Ren and found none but her own discomfort. "No, I spent last winter up north, in a camp near what used to be Ottawa. Nearly froze my ass off. When everyone dispersed in the spring, I decided that I was going to be somewhere warm next winter. So that's why I'm heading south."

"All alone?"

Lynn tensed. Then she realized Ren's tone wasn't interrogatory but concerned. "Yeah." She had to force herself to share more. "I'm usually on my own." It was a vague response, but even that small addition dredged up a lot of memories. She instinctively pulled the layers of armor a little tighter around herself.

"That's hard on a person." Ren's voice was void of judgment. Her fingers slid lower, to Lynn's throat.

Lynn shrugged, then tilted her head at Ren's gentle guidance. "Practical, I would say."

"Practical?"

When Ren's fingers probed especially sensitive skin, Lynn hissed.

"Sorry."

"It's fine." Lynn licked her lips.

"You said it was practical to stay alone?"

The touch hurt, and she felt very vulnerable letting Ren inspect her neck, so she allowed herself to talk, hoping to distract them both. "When you're alone, at least you have nothing to lose."

Ren's gaze drifted to Lynn's eyes before she continued the inspection. "Perhaps. But you miss out on a lot that way—people to rely on, to love."

Here was an opening she wasn't going to pass up. "Like you and Cody and Eduardo?" She kept her voice carefully neutral.

"Like us." She tugged at Lynn's chin until her head turned to the side.

Lynn's view of the flower was replaced with the dark of the outside world. When Ren didn't volunteer more, Lynn asked, "How long have you been together?"

Ren's gaze lifted to hers and held it.

A shiver of warning slid up her spine. *Damn, did I push it too far?* Ren spoke before she could backtrack.

"Cody and I have been together for years, almost seventeen now. Eduardo joined us eleven years ago." Ren's voice was pitched to a chipper lilt that didn't resonate with the guardedness in her eyes.

Lynn inspected her. *You don't like sharing either, do you?*

Ren looked away so she could pick up a clean bit of wool, wet it, and apply it to Lynn's temple.

It stung, and Lynn hissed. There was definitely something there. *A cut or a bruise?*

Ren leaned back, then wiped her hands on her pants and stood. "You have a shallow cut on your temple, a split lip, and your eye is swollen and bruised. I don't think anything is broken, but even if it was, there is nothing we can do." Ren strode to one of the mounted cupboards and opened a door.

Lynn touched her right eye and winced. Definitely swollen. Definitely bruised. The taut skin felt alien under her fingers.

"Your throat is bruised as well, but I don't think there will be permanent damage."

Lynn huffed. "That's something, at least."

Ren took something from the cupboard and closed the door. "I know you're angry—"

"Yeah, I am." Lynn set her jaw, then unclenched it as pain shot up the right side of her face. "He could have strangled me."

"He didn't."

"Maybe not, but he tenderized the side of my face pretty well."

Ren sighed as she sat down next to her again and unscrewed the cap of the Old-World tin container. Once, it had probably been blue with strong, white lettering, but the colors had mostly faded now. "We were all in shock, I guess."

Lynn dragged her gaze back up from the tin. "Is that supposed to be an apology?"

Ren reached up and tilted Lynn's head to the side. "That depends."

Whatever was in the tin stung when Ren applied it to her cut. She flinched. "On what?"

"On if you really didn't kill Richard."

Lynn jerked her face free so she could glare at her. "I didn't. I told you."

A few seconds passed as Ren examined her eyes. "People say a lot of things."

Lynn set her jaw and broke the staring contest.

"Why don't you tell me what happened, hm? Maybe more details will convince me." Ren renewed her hold on her chin and continued to rub the stinging concoction onto the worst of the cuts and bruises.

"Not much to tell. I needed a place to sleep, so I went into this Old-World shop for cars. One of the doors inside was locked. As soon as I tried to open it, I heard barking. I wanted to head out then, but if there was a guard dog, maybe there was something to guard, you know?"

"You were looking to steal someone else's things?" Ren's voice was neutral.

Lynn tensed. "Only if there was something useful."

"Right."

Lynn tried to turn her head to gauge Ren's mood, but her grip was too strong. She decided to just push on. *I'll be out of here soon anyway. Who cares what she thinks.* "Anyway, I was going to let the dog grab my arm, then kill him, but he didn't attack me. He stood over—" A second passed as she fumbled for the dead man's name. "Richard's body and threatened to attack, but he didn't come closer. He just growled at me. He was definitely not rabid, so I figured it might be worth it to see if he could be handled."

Ren hummed. Her fingers didn't stop dabbing.

The ointment no longer stung.

"When he finally let me in and I could examine Richard, he was long gone. He'd been bitten by a snake. Skeever mauled it, but I guess the damage was done." She paused again.

"Then what happened?"

Lynn tried to look at her, but again Ren's hold on her jaw tightened.

"Almost done."

Lynn settled with difficulty. She didn't like to sit for extended periods of time. "I buried him and took Skeever. Couldn't let him die there as well, could I?"

Ren finally let her chin go. "If that's the truth, then thank you for taking care of Richard."

Lynn checked her expression. It didn't look as if Ren believed her. *Whatever.* "I just did what any decent human being would do." Truthfully, she had only buried Richard because of the conversation her six-year-old self had had with her father; no one dug a grave for the fun of it.

"Right." Ren sighed and sat up. "About Dean..."

"If you are going to tell me to forgive him, I can spare you the lecture." She stubbornly met Ren's marvelously green eyes.

"I was going to ask you if I have to worry about you getting revenge for that cut." Ren's voice wasn't accusatory. She was simply asking, probably so she could deal with things accordingly—including locking Lynn away until Kate had gotten from her what she needed, Lynn suspected.

Lynn had to admit she had considered taking some kind of revenge. But Dean hadn't seriously injured her, and he *had* just lost his father. "If you keep him off my back while I'm here, he has nothing to fear. I won't be here long anyway, just a bed for the night." A reminder—a warning. At least that was how it was intended. She hoped it didn't come across as a plea. To enforce her words, she stood and briskly pushed past Ren's legs.

Ren had to twist to get her legs out of the way or risk injury.

As Lynn walked to the window and looked out into the darkness, she felt Ren's gaze prickling on her back. The sensation reminded her that something in her pack had broken during the struggle with Dean, and with the memory, the experience of being choked returned as well. She shuddered and willed her anger to wash away her fear. "If he comes at me again, though, I'll be ready for him."

Ren hesitated. "That's fair. Thank you." She stood with a groan and put the ointment away in the overhead cupboard. "I should go help the boys. Could you take that?" She pointed to a pot, which contained the fatty tissue she'd been working on when Lynn had come in. The underlying message that Lynn was expected to come up with her was crystal clear, and Lynn resigned herself to the inevitable.

"A good hunter is someone who doesn't just see their prey but also knows at every moment that they will not become prey themselves." Her father had taught her that, just like he had taught her how to cast a sweeping glance over an area and analyze it in an instant. She noted the location of every fire, torch, and fat-burning lamp on the rooftop as she came up to make sure no one was hiding in their shadows.

The air was saturated with the scent of smoke and drying meat, which meant everyone was working and not busy plotting her death. Ren walked ahead of her to a makeshift table by one of the fires. Flint sat nearby, busily carving something. Eduardo disappeared into the smoke shed. Dani processed meat in her workstation. Cody, Kate, and the kids were nowhere to be seen.

Is that everyone?

She racked her brain to make sure she had them all accounted for: Kate, Dean, Tobias, Cody, Ren, Eduardo, Flint, Dani. She checked their positions again—of those in view, anyway—and relaxed a bit. Balancing the pot on her knee, she closed the door behind her before she caught up to Ren. As long as she kept them all in sight, she'd be okay.

The birds had fallen silent, but monkeys and other nighttime critters had filled the silence left after their songs had ended. Bats danced overhead. She marked the shape of their shadows so she wouldn't jump any time one swept by. Time to free her hands.

As she crossed the roof to join Ren at the table, she felt exposed. All eyes seemed to be on her, but when she looked up, no one was looking—not even Dani.

Ren gestured at the table. "Right there will be fine."

Lynn put the pot down. She lingered.

"Why don't you cut up the carrots, hm?" Ren suggested.

Stoically, Lynn took up one of the knives on the table and went to work. She ignored the way Ren stared at her now weapon-filled hand before returning to peeling potatoes without comment.

After a few minutes, Ren cleared her throat. "Were you born in Canada?"

Lynn blinked. Canada? She tried to remember what she'd told Ren before, why she would bring up Canada, but her frayed mind refused to recall.

"You mentioned a camp in Ottawa."

"Oh. No. I uh… I was born near what used to be Detroit. But my parents traveled a lot."

Ren glanced at her. "I suppose they are…?"

"Dead? Yeah. Long ago." Lynn didn't like to talk about it. She didn't like talking about herself at all.

"I'm sorry." Ren seemed genuinely sympathetic.

Lynn shrugged. "It happens." She kept her gaze down. She was so tired that her emotions lay close to the surface, and she refused to cry over her dead parents in front of Ren. It had been twenty years since her father had passed away and even longer since she'd lost her mother. She'd managed without them. She needed to steer the conversation away from her own life because talking about her sorry past wasn't doing anyone any good.

"Ren, can I talk to you?"

At the sound of Cody's voice so close by, Lynn whirled around and instinctively leveled the little knife in her hand with Cody's chest. Her heart skipped, then sped to a gallop.

Ren froze next to her.

Cody's eyes widened. His hands went up. Then he smirked. "Careful now, girlie. I came to talk to my wife."

Lynn realized her mistake—Cody wasn't going to hurt her—and lowered the knife. Her hand trembled, and she pressed it and the blade against her thigh. She turned away. "S-Sorry."

"That's what happens when you bring in Wilders," Cody said. "Ren? Can we talk? Privately?"

Her attention still on Lynn, Ren followed him a small distance out onto the roof. She only turned her head away once Cody started talking.

They were looking at her. Lynn could feel their gazes like pinpricks on her skin. It wasn't just Cody and Ren; the others were watching her too: Eduardo from the opening of the smoke house, Dani from her work shed, and Flint from across the rooftop as he carved. Were they mocking her? Were they afraid of the crazy girl? The Wilder, as this group seemed to call outsiders? Maybe they should be. Years on the road had made her jumpy.

Being here, unsure of what was going to happen to her, playing games and desperately scheming to secure any advantage wore on her.

She was so hungry and so tired—now that the adrenaline had worn off again, she could feel just how hungry and tired she was—that she wasn't thinking straight. Still, life was pretty messed up if your first reaction to being spooked was to plant a knife into someone's chest. She shook her head as she straightened and tightened her grip on the blade. It felt foreign in her hand now, as if it had betrayed her. Her hand shook slightly.

Once she started chopping again, head down, the gazes lifted one by one until the pinpricks disappeared altogether. Lynn tried to listen in on Cody and Ren's conversation, but their words were drowned out by the noises of the night. The merry sputtering of the fires around her, the sounds of people working, and loud animal howls, yips, and cries all covered the softly spoken words.

She focused on chopping vegetables.

Several minutes later, Ren approached cautiously and with enough noise to warn Lynn of her approach.

She glanced up, then back to her carrots.

"Feeling better?"

Lynn shrugged. "I guess. Was that about me?"

Ren stepped up to the table and glanced at the knife. She picked up her own again and resumed peeling. "Not exactly. Kate came out of her room. They're just dealing with the loss right now. I—"

"Hey, you!"

Lynn almost dropped the knife but rushed to grip it instead as she whirled. She had been sure her adrenaline had been exhausted, but her body found a hidden reserve. Her heart rate spiked again, and cold sweat promptly ran down her spine. Any other time she would have scolded herself for jumping at ghosts *again*, but this time the reaction was justified. She would recognize that voice anywhere.

Dean stood a few feet away, backpack around his shoulders. A wicked-looking knife—about twice the size of hers—gleamed in his clenched fist. The anger was still in his eyes.

Lynn swallowed. She relaxed her muscles so she wouldn't lock up when he came at her. This time it would be a fair fight—as fair as could be with the size difference in the blades at their disposal. She mentally rehearsed the moves: *sidestep, upswing for the throat, feint left, get behind him, gut stab.* Lethal force. She knew that look: if she didn't end it, he would.

Ren turned slowly.

"You know where he is, right? My dad? Take me to him." Dean pushed forward.

The cocking of a gun echoed through the darkness to her right, and to her left Ren took a step forward. She spotted Dani as she came out of her workstation, spear extended and leveled. Apparently, no one trusted this to go well, although Lynn wondered who they were protecting: her or Dean. *Time to make a last stand, Tanner, but don't you dare lash out first. They'll kill you deader than dead in an instant.*

"Take me to him!"

She took a deep breath. "No."

He stepped forward again. "Take me to him!" he emphasized every word this time.

"Dean…" Ren's soothing voice barely made it over the echo of his bellow.

Lynn held Dean's gaze. Sweat prickled icily on her back. Her mind struggled to catch up to this turn of events. "You tried to kill me."

"But I didn't. Take me to him!"

"It's dark." The thought of being out there, with Dean, in the dark nearly paralyzed her with fear.

He squinted but didn't advance. "We'll take torches."

"Dean, I need you to dro—"

"And walk around like targets for predators? No way!" Lynn twisted the knife to get a better grip. "And even if it wasn't dark, there is no way I am going anywhere with you."

Dean's eyes narrowed dangerously, and he stepped forward.

Ren took up position in front of Lynn. "Dee, think ab—"

Dean slid to the side to restore his line of vision.

Ren's body obscured Lynn's view of the knife, so she sidestepped too, to make sure he couldn't trap her against the table should he lunge around Ren.

"I'm not leaving my dad out there another night, and *you* know where he is! So you are going to shut u—"

Lynn bristled and pushed forward, urged on by her anger. "Hey, asshat, read my lips: no! It's a two-day journey at least, three if I can't find my way back right away. Besides, he was buried with proper honors! I know you're hurting, but—"

He uttered a broken warrior's cry—the cry of a man knowing he was committing suicide but doing it anyway—and lunged.

Ren jumped aside with a small yelp of fear.

The storm that had been raging inside Lynn's skull settled in an instant. Calmly, she brought up the knife and sidestepped as planned. There was something about the possibility of imminent death that was very soothing.

Before Dean could reach her, someone burst into her field of vision from the left and smashed into him. The force knocked both over into a tangled heap of legs, arms, and grunts. They fought for control of the knife.

Cody. Lynn sucked in a breath. It was Cody who had come to her rescue—or maybe Dean's, depending on how he judged their odds.

Ren rushed forward to help but ended up on the periphery, bouncing from one foot to the other, yelling.

Taken by surprise by the sudden turn of events, Lynn watched the ensuing struggle as if she were miles away.

Ren yelled, but the meaning of the words didn't sink in.

She spotted Flint now, his face grim and his gun raised in one hand as he watched. Dani gripped her spear, waiting. Eduardo had held up a hand uselessly near the smokehouse, in a quiet and completely ignored stop sign.

"Dean! Pipe down!"

Cody's voice snapped her attention back to the struggle. He had Dean pinned down, but the boy bucked and contorted, still struggling. Cody was out of breath, but he was a strong man with a level head. He spent only the energy he had to while Dean was wasting his with his thrashing. This fight was over, even if Dean hadn't realized it yet.

She straightened and relaxed her tense and sore muscles. The adrenaline drained from her and left her dizzy and unbalanced. She gripped the table for support and felt the handle of the knife dig into her palm.

The movement seemed to catch Ren's attention, and her gaze settled on Lynn.

Why does she look so afraid? Then Lynn remembered the promise she had made, that if Dean came after her again, she would kill him.

Dean began to cry in ragged sobs.

She glanced down at him. Snot and spit left streaks on the boy's face. Despite what she'd said—and thought—earlier, she didn't need petty revenge. To show they needn't worry about her, Lynn placed the knife on the table and pushed it away. She stepped back on unsteady legs.

Dean caught his second wind and pushed hard enough to almost tip Cody over.

Cody scrambled to solidify his hold.

"No! Dad is out there! Who knows if he's being eaten right now or—or—" His voice broke.

Lynn shuddered. She shouldn't be watching this. It was too embarrassing to see someone so utterly stripped of their walls. To busy her eyes, she looked over at Dani, who stood in the same spot but had lowered her spear. She wasn't watching the fight; she stared at Lynn with an unreadable expression.

Why was she looking at her like that? She managed to hold the gaze a few seconds but then had to look away. She couldn't deal with Dani right now—or her own emotions.

Cody embraced Dean, and Dean buried his face in Cody's sweater. He cried openly now that the fight had drained out of him.

Lynn licked her lips. "I meant what I said."

Ren tensed.

"I'm not going anywhere with him."

Ren deflated. She turned back and watched her husband console the grieving youth. "I don't blame you." Her voice only just carried over all the nighttime noises.

Lynn resumed her staring as well, as painful as it was. She finally had time to process this attack, this plea. Why did Dean want to collect his father's body? She'd buried him, all good and proper. There were big stones on his grave. Only the most determined of animals would manage to get down to him in the deep hole she'd spent an entire morning digging. He was safe, buried, gone.

When she looked up, Dani was still watching, but now her gaze alternated between her and Dean.

Dani met and held her gaze for a second before she turned and disappeared into the shadows of the workshop.

With a pang of unease, Lynn returned her gaze to the two men embracing on the floor, one stoic and supportive, the other small and broken.

There was no need to get Richard's body. None at all. But the threat of it loomed over her now. It might have been Dean's idea, but it was one of those ideas that could—would—spread until they all became convinced their loved one needed to be with them. She'd seen it before, this mob mentality. Another chill went down her spine. Her imprisonment and the subsequent punishment for the crime of being at the wrong place at the wrong time were solidifying, and there was nothing she could do about it.

Kate made her first appearance of the night once dinner was served around the fireplace. A young carbon copy of his brother clung to her hand. Dean didn't come up to the roof with them, and neither did Skeever. The quiet conversation between the members of the group—which had not involved Lynn in any way, shape, or form pretty much since the confrontation with Dean—died down as Kate and the boy came to a halt beside the benches.

Lynn tensed and surreptitiously glanced up from her food.

Kate looked like shit, pale and numb. Her eyes were bloodshot, her face void of expression. The hairdo that not even killing an elephant had managed to dishevel had largely escaped from the bun on the back of her head.

This can't be good. Lynn looked away. Perhaps avoiding eye contact could delay the inevitable. Not keeping an eye on Kate made her uncomfortable, so she glanced back as she took another bite.

"Would you like some elephant stew, Katherine?" Cody asked.

Kate shook her head.

The young boy Lynn presumed to be Toby clung to her leg. When Kate tried to pass him off to Ren, he started crying and pressed his face more tightly against her.

Kate sighed and—with the dignity of a woman too proud to collapse in front of others—laid her hand on the boy's head and kept him close.

Another candid glance told Lynn that everyone but Cody studied their food with acute attention. The atmosphere was charged.

Lynn took another spoonful of meat, potato, and vegetable pulp. She was quite content staying out of this mess. Her thoughts had turned inward the more the group had ignored her as the night went on. They had watched her, but without chores to dole out—ones they trusted her with, anyway—they had let her be as long as she stayed seated. The food had made her sleepy, and it had become impossible to remain on guard at all times. None of them had moved from their chosen seat since they'd sat and had left Lynn alone to valiantly struggle for wakefulness. Well, Kate's appearance had woken her up just fine.

"Lynn, could I talk to you a minute?"

Lynn jumped despite anticipating Kate's question. *Deep breath.* "I guess." She put the bowl down reluctantly and stepped out of the square of benches.

After barely sparing her a glance for most of the evening, everyone now stared at her.

"Ren, take him, please?" Kate tried to pry Toby off her again, but every time she'd loosened one hand, Toby's other had taken a renewed hold.

Toby whimpered and pressed his face more tightly against her leg.

"Sure." Ren got up and lifted the boy.

The second she did, Toby started crying. "Mommy, no!" He took a big gulp of air and released a cry so high and sharp it was physically uncomfortable.

Lynn turned her head to the side to angle her ear away from the source of the sound.

"It's okay, baby. I'll be right back." Kate reached out to stroke his hair but retracted her hand quickly when Toby tried to grab at it.

"I've got him." Ren lifted Toby into her arms and rocked him to calm him down.

He kicked at her, pushed, and clawed until she was forced to sit down quickly and take hold of his hands.

The anguish on Kate's face made Lynn uncomfortable, but not as much as the sheer volume of Toby's shrieks did. She fingered the strap that usually held her tomahawk in an almost subconscious effort to regain her composure. She hated noise. The warmed metal of the knife in her boot reminded her that, while vulnerable and alone, she was not defenseless.

Still, no one had taken it from her. Lynn suspected that they might have actually forgotten this time.

Kate guided her wordlessly away from the fire and into the shadows. Once she stopped, Lynn halted at a safe distance and eyed her.

"Let's make this brief." Kate had to raise her voice to be heard over her son's cries. "My husband was an honorable man. He did what he had to do for his family."

"I don't doubt that."

"We want to bring him home."

It was strangely anti-climactic to hear the actual words. "Why can't he stay buried where he is?" She didn't even try to take the edge out of her voice.

Kate regarded her. "I don't trust you. You say he was killed by a snake, but for all we know you killed him and took his stuff."

"I didn't."

"I know you didn't take anything. We went through your backpack, but that doesn't prove you didn't kill him. You did take Skeever."

Lynn's anger rose. "You did *what*?" She took a step closer.

Kate's gaze hardened. Her hand slid down to the hilt of her machete. "Careful, Lynn."

"Or what?" Her whole body tensed as she prepared to grab her knife, consequences be damned.

"Or we'll be a lot less friendly to you from here on out."

Lynn set her jaw but forced her body to relax. "I'm not doing it."

Emotions and schemes played in the cold gray of Kate's eyes. "I don't think you have a choice."

"Oh, I have plenty of choices."

Kate smirked. "Really? Like what? I know you still have that knife in your boot—and you'll be handing that over—but even with that knife, we'll kill you before you can do any real damage to us."

The telltale sounds of the group behind her rising as one and Dani's spear extending sent a shiver down Lynn's spine. Her heart thumped in her chest. "You will never know where Richard's body is if you kill me."

"True, but I think you value your life too much to risk dying right here, right now."

Dammit! Everything in Lynn screamed to turn around so she could see the Homesteaders coming, but she fought the urge. "I'll draw you a damn map, and you can get him yourself." Even agreeing to that felt like admitting defeat.

Kate shook her head instantly. "I'm not that stupid, Lynn. Who says it's accurate? Who says you'd not be leading us into a trap? No, you're coming with us."

Lynn swallowed as reality hit. There was no way around this; she could put up a good fight, but at the end of the day, Kate had the power. She could make Lynn go back under armed escort if that was what it took. Cody, Flint, and Dani together would be able to control and guard her around the clock, even out there, where she was much better equipped for survival. No, she couldn't fight this, but she could try to survive it. "I have demands."

Kate frowned. "Demands?"

The ruckus behind Lynn continued.

"Yes." She needed to make sure she would be in control at all times out there, which meant she needed to avoid an armed escort—or at least one she couldn't take in a direct fight. "I'll do it if Dani comes with me. Just Dani—and Skeever."

Kate's gaze darted to the group, lingered, then returned. "Why would I agree to something as ludicrous as that? You'll take off the first chance you get."

Damn right I will! "It's a risk you're going to have to take. See, you can force me to take all of you, but I swear I'll make it hell on you. I'll lead you through every wolf-packed, snake-infested, crater-pocked hell terrain I can find in the hopes it'll kill you all." Lynn all but hissed the words out, and in the moment, she wasn't even bluffing. She didn't know if she could stand by and watch anyone get mauled, but as she stared into Kate's squinted eyes, she knew she might be able to with Kate and Cody and the whole damn lot.

Seconds ticked away. Kate was considering the proposal, and Lynn knew she had her. She could all but see the gears in Kate's head turn. Again, Kate glanced past Lynn to the group—probably at Dani.

Finally, she set her jaw and nodded once, sharply. "You can take Daniela."

Murmurs started up all around her. Lynn caught slivers of the conversations.

"...did she want Dani?"

"...how come Kate didn't...?"

"We should have forced..."

She ignored them. *Dani's full name is Daniela.* Lynn suppressed the thought. Now was *so* not the time for that. "And Skeever." As she said it, a deep longing for her companion settled in her heart. "He's used to being out there. He'll hear danger coming long before we do. I plan to live through the insanity of walking around with a buffet for carnivores—"

Kate flinched at the description of her husband's body.

Lynn relished her discomfort. "...and I need Skeever to do it."

Again, Kate first held out but then gave in. "Okay." Her eyes had gone colder than Lynn had ever seen them. She was undoubtedly planning murder.

Dizzying relief flooded Lynn's system, but she held it at bay. If she wanted a shot at making it through this affair now that she'd antagonized the whole lot, she needed to get out of here quickly. "Good. Now, I want to wash myself, and I want enough food and water for a weeklong trip as well as any equipment I can think of." Unlike everyone else, she was still covered in blood and dressed in her blood-soaked clothes. She hated it.

"Agreed."

"Dani and I are leaving in the morning, after breakfast. Have everything ready then." Without waiting for Kate to speak again, she turned on her heel, squared her shoulders, and pushed straight through the throng.

Everyone stared at her, weapons still at the ready.

In a stroke of masochism, she searched for Dani's eyes in the crowd. She half expected her not to be there, but she was, standing next to Cody.

Their gazes locked.

Dani's emotions had been impossible to read so far, but the events of the last few minutes had shattered the mask. There was fear in Dani's eyes, mixed with shock and surprise.

Lynn set her jaw and met the gazes of the others. Her heart pounded in her throat hard enough that she feared it would be obvious how terrified she was. She used it as fuel to darken her voice. "Which of you assholes wants to show me where I can wash up, hm?"

CHAPTER 4

A STRANGER LOOKED BACK AT her in the dirty bathroom mirror, a thinner and bloodier version of herself that Lynn had not met before. She'd seen herself in a real mirror for the last time in Canada, almost a year back. And the intervening time had been—she struggled for a word. Terrifying? Stressful? What was that word Old Lady Sana had liked? Eschaton? The end of days and all the horrors that came with it?

Her hands trembled as she submerged them in the hot water Eduardo had brought her after Cody had locked her into this Old-World bathroom with nothing but a candle and a set of clean clothes from her pack. She was still reeling from her confrontation with Kate—and she hadn't wrapped her head around the fact that she would be going back for Richard's body. She ran the conversation over and over in her head and thought of a thousand things she could have said and done differently, but it didn't matter now. The damage was done. All pretense of hospitality was gone now, and truthfully, it was a relief. They had all known she was a prisoner here; it was about time it showed in more than being watched.

"Clean yourself up." The words reverberated back to her off tiles and the doors of disused toilet cubicles. Even her voice sounded unfamiliar, as if her reflection had spoken the command. She shivered. "And stop talking to yourself."

It didn't solve anything anyway. It didn't blunt her fear, and every word still caused sharp discomfort in her throat. Besides, one of them was out there, outside of the locked door, waiting for her to clean up so they could take her to her room for the night. It could be Cody or even Flint. Lynn had heard male voices talking, but she didn't know these people well enough to tell who it was. Neither was a very appealing option.

She tilted her head back and inspected the bruises underneath the film of dried blood still coating her skin. She could actually make out the shapes of Dean's fingers, wrapped around her neck like the wings of a moth. When she swallowed, the moth shivered as if trying to peel off and fly. For a second, the visceral image of not just the bruises but the skin and flesh below tearing off to fly away overwhelmed her. The blood staining her neck and chest seemed to be hers, gushing from the flayed skin. She quickly tilted her head back down to chase the vision away. One thing was clear: she needed sleep to restore her sanity from beyond these tattered remains.

The stab of longing to hold Skeever again came up so suddenly and so strongly that she doubled over and had to put her hands on the bottom of the bucket in front of her to keep from crumpling. She needed *him*. If she hadn't found him—that brilliant ray of happy hope—she may not have made it even these extra days. She could feel in her very bones that she was wearing ragged out there alone. Most of the time, she didn't allow herself to feel it, but it was true: slowly but surely, she was starving and going insane. People weren't built to be alone, and she'd been alone for so long until Skeever came along.

She'd been hard-pressed to hunt for herself lately, but Skeever brought her game he'd hunted. He'd warned her of danger and kept her warm when her deprived body had failed to do so. His desire to go anywhere as long as it was forward had urged her onward. Seeing the simple joy of life in his eyes had allowed her to experience the world that way herself again, even if just a little. Not having him near her now was physically painful. She felt it in her gut as if someone had reached in, gripped fast, and twisted.

Stop thinking about him.

She straightened and took a ball of wet wool out of the bucket. Streams slid down her arm as she began to soak the caked grime loose. As she scrubbed, blood and dirt accumulated over many days came off reluctantly. It clung to scars and burn marks. She watched them reappear and let their presence and the memory of how she had gotten them soothe her. They were mementos of times she'd cheated the Reaper. She certainly looked like one of his prey—big eyes, small breasts, protruding ribs and clavicles, and muscles built by causing death.

She pondered the issue as she worked up to her shoulder. Diluted red ran down to her breast, where the stream split to each side of it. The chilled drops traversed her belly and were soaked up by her blonde bush below, darkening the hairs to a faded pink that amused Lynn. "You must really like me, hm, Mister Reaper?" She forgave herself for talking to herself again. Where she rubbed higher up her shoulder, fading bite marks appeared.

A Wilder, Cody had called her. Every settlement had different names for the people who stayed put and those who traveled. *Wilder* was one of the more accurate ones for the travelers. She met her eyes again in the mirror. *Wild.* Yeah, that was as good a descriptor of her as any. There were certainly days where she could form no more sophisticated thoughts than kill or be killed, eat or starve, make a fire or freeze.

I need to stop thinking.

She put the wool down and leaned forward to guide her hair and as much of her head as she could into the bucket, then held her breath as she let the warmth of the water soak loose the caked blood. If only it would also soften her equally caked thoughts.

When the oxygen in her lungs ran low, memories of Dean's hands around her throat pushed at the edges of her mind. She held her breath until her heartbeat quickened. When her lungs started to hurt, she gripped the edge of the bucket more tightly but stayed submerged. It wasn't the same as being choked, but a flutter of fear sprang to life. This time she would harness it.

One, two, three... She counted to fifteen, struggling against the memories and the urge to pull her head free. Next time someone choked her, she wouldn't panic.

Eighteen, nineteen, twenty...

Her nails dug into the wood. She whimpered and bubbles escaped. Next time, she wouldn't be reduced to crawling away like a pathetic bug, out of her mind with terror, barely grasping what was happening to her.

Twenty-eight, twenty-nine, thirty.

She yanked her head out with a gasp. Water streamed down her face, and she coughed. Another gasp of air. She forced herself to look into the mirror. Her hair stuck to her skull in odd angles, and streams of water ran down her chest. Her eyes were intense again, hard and angry. *Good.* Anger was fuel. She would need it to make her escape—and she would have to escape, if not tonight, then as soon as she could ditch Dani somewhere.

The pain and hardness in her reflection's smile chilled her.

"I hope you like to run, Reaper," she told her reflection. "Because I'm going to dash."

"Took your sweet time." Of course it was Cody they'd gotten to wait for her.

Lynn made sure the candle balanced securely in her hand before she adjusted her grip on the wad of bloody clothes. "Bite me." She felt recovered enough to stare him square in the eye. It was good to be clean, to wear clothes that were relatively clean. She could run her hand through her hair again without getting stuck in the tangles. Some of her sanity had returned with a good meal, a proper wash, and a revealing conversation with her own reflection.

He laughed, but his eyes remained cold. Since her confrontation with Kate, the thin layer of civility between them had been stripped away, leaving only mistrust. "Such a delicate flower."

"Bite me." She accentuated each word. *I won't have to deal with you much longer anyway.*

He looked down at her with a mocking smirk and pushed away from the wall. "Come on, flower girl. Time for a nap."

She bit her tongue and followed him.

When he stopped at a door, she stopped. "Mine?"

"Yeah. Sorry the view isn't great."

She squared her shoulders and pushed past him with as much bravery as she could muster. The view was, indeed, rather disappointing: it was a windowless room. *Room* was also somewhat of an overstatement. In *ye olden days*, it had probably been a supply closet. A rickety shelving unit lined the back wall, and she could identify some brooms, mops, and buckets in the light of her candle.

"I'll need your knife now."

She tried not to tense. "I'll be needing it again in the morning anyway." She made sure her expression was neutral and turned around.

"Yeah, I don't really care. Either you give it up now, or I get it off your person." He stood in the doorway, blocking her.

A little shiver coursed down her spine. She was suddenly very aware the room had only one exit and he controlled it.

She had options—tossing the candle at his face and making a run for it was the best one that came to mind—but that would give her absolutely no time to find Skeever or even find the exit before they would be upon her. She wasn't sure where she was on the floor, and if she permanently burned someone, she'd better be damn sure she could get away. And she wasn't.

Slowly, she reached down, slid the blade from her boot, and turned it around so she could hand him the hilt.

He took it. "Is that it?"

She nodded.

"Traveling light?"

"The bare minimum."

He forced her to hold his gaze. He probably didn't believe her, but it was true. She used to have more and even better weapons, but shit happened.

"It doesn't matter anyway. Sleep tight, flower girl." He stepped back and pulled the door shut before Lynn could even move.

The lock clicked shut. "Get some sleep. Bright and early tomorrow." He chuckled dryly.

Dread spread like burning wildfire, but she fought it. Of course they were going to lock her in. She picked up the candle and turned to the shelves. *I don't like not having a weapon, though.* Maybe there was something on there that would help her. There were brooms and mops, a few buckets, some bottles, the contents of which had long evaporated, a few bars of now-dry and cracked soap, boxes of something powdery she didn't bother to decipher the name of, and a bunch of other little knickknacks.

An idea for an improvised weapon formed slowly in her mind's eye. A crude dagger, a dangerous one even to herself, but it was something. She picked up one of the bottles and turned it over in her hands as she waited for Cody's footsteps to disappear down the hall. After wrapping the glass vessel in her bloody shirt, she mashed it. She waited with bated breath to see if anyone came for her, but after a minute or so, she dared to take a breath and uncovered the shards.

After careful inspection, she picked one that was about half an inch thick, the shape of a curved triangle. She wrapped the rest of the evidence of her activities in her shirt and stuffed the package behind some boxes on the lowest shelf.

Lynn used the shard to cut off a few strands of the mop head. They were coarse, and she could knot them together easily, even with slightly trembling hands. She ran the resulting string through the animal fat that had melted in the candle bowl and worked it into the fibers to make them more supple, less liable to break or tear once she began to work with them. Before the excess fat could harden up, she squeezed it out of the string and wiped her glistening hands on her pants.

Now came the tricky part. While the string dried, Lynn took the glass shard to the only metal thing in the room: the frame of the shelving unit. She turned the glass in her hands until she could decide on the cutting edge, then she began the tedious and sometimes painful work of dulling the other tips by grinding them over the sharpest edge of the unit's leg. She worked low, right by the floor, to minimize the noise, but she jumped at each little sound. Every time the metal sang when she tried to go too fast or when something on the shelves rattled because of the force she put on the leg, she stopped and checked the door, waiting for Cody to barge in.

He never did.

It had to be past midnight when she was finally satisfied with her work. By the time she sat up, her back was stiff, one of her legs fast asleep, and she'd cut herself more times than she could count. At least all the cuts were shallow.

She gently stroked the glass dust off her hands and suppressed a groan as she straightened. Her fingers tingled because she'd gripped the glass so hard and so long. They refused to close around the shard. *Come on already.* Every second without some kind of weapon felt like an eternity. She sat up on her knees near the small flame and stretched and clenched her fingers to bring life back into them.

When she could feel her fingertips again, she laid the string over one of the three tips of the shard and pressed it down with her thumb. Then she wound the string over the dulled tips, crossing between one tip and the other until the string formed a handle. She knotted the end around the string that covered the hollow of the glass to secure it. The fat made everything slippery and the work harder, but the string didn't tear and stayed in place once she put tension on it.

The resulting weapon was crude, but the now string-covered straight edge fit into the crease where her fingers met her palm. She could curl her thumb and pinkie over the string on either side of the dulled tips for grip and control. The result was a weapon she could drag across the side of someone's neck or face—or even their arm or side—as if raking them with her nails, just much more effective. She stood on nearly numb legs and practiced the attack a few times: push her arm out and then yank back, cutting deep. She grinned as she turned the blade over in her hands.

It works.

With that thought, lethargy set in. She'd risen to this occasion on adrenaline alone, and her relief over finishing the weapon's construction washed most of that away. The door was locked, so she wasn't going anywhere. Even if she found a way out, Skeever was damn-knew-where in the complex, and she would probably have to fight her way out with nothing but this improvised weapon. It made much more sense to go to sleep now and make a break for it once she only had Dani to worry about. It was time to sleep and rest up for tomorrow, because it was going to be a make-or-break day.

"Lynn?"

She shot up before she was fully awake and scrambled for her shard. "Yeah?" She winced at the wobble in her voice. Years of experience in waking up to threats allowed her to instantly dredge up the details of her current predicament. The shard had dropped onto the ground, and she gripped it. She stuffed it into her boot the exact moment the door was pushed open.

Eduardo smiled at her, but he stayed in the hallway, keeping distance between them. "You slept well, yes?"

"Fine." She stared at him expectantly. The glass dug into the skin of her ankle a little, but probably not enough to draw blood.

"It is breakfast time. Are you hungry?"

She nodded.

"All right. Come."

Lynn picked up the nearly extinguished candle as well as her bundle of bloody clothes and stood. She bit back a groan—sleeping on the floor had left her stiff and sore. Hauling the heavy stretchers yesterday probably had something to do with it too.

Eduardo guided her away from her cell.

Sounds of conversation floated to her from the kitchen. The voices quieted the moment she walked in, but a flurry of gray fur, sprawling limbs, and a lolling tongue careened into her hard enough to nearly knock her over.

Skeever! Despite her discomfort around these people, she instantly dropped to a knee and wrapped him in her arms. She let him lick her entire face and grinned as she tried to restrain him. "Shhhh, shhh, Skeeve! Skeever, shhh." Lynn could have cried over feeling Skeever's robust form and hearing his soft little whining noises.

"Skeever!" Kate's tone was as cold as a bucket of ice water.

Skeever whined and looked up but didn't move from Lynn's side.

Lynn searched for Kate amidst the others gathered around the table.

Their gazes met.

Kate snapped her fingers by her chair.

Skeever trotted over, low to the ground, and settled by her chair, shivering.

Yeah, assert your authority, bitch. I'm taking him with me when we leave, and he isn't coming back. Lynn got up slowly, keeping eye contact. "Good morning to you too."

Kate's jaw set. "Sit—"

Lynn almost told her to shove it.

Dean glared at her from beside his mother. Toby, on her other side, looked up at her wide-eyed. Cody watched her with that damn smirk; Eduardo had slipped past her during her embrace with Skeever and smiled at her tentatively. Lynn wondered where Dani, Ren, and Flint were. Without a word, she sat down on the only chair around the table without a person on each side.

No one ate of the bread, fruit spread, and cheeses on the table.

Lynn's stomach growled in the silence.

Cody's smirk deepened, but he didn't comment on her hunger. "Sleep well?"

"Great. I always sleep well in captivity." She didn't return the question. She didn't really want to know, and she had absolutely no interest in conforming to social norms.

Silence fell again, and no one filled it until Ren entered, bearing two large bowls.

Cody got up and took them from her before putting them on the table.

Ren sat next to Lynn and nodded curtly.

Lynn nodded back.

"All right, let's eat." Cody pushed the bowls over to Kate, who used her fork to skewer two pieces of bacon and placed them on Toby's plate. She scooped some eggs onto it and added a piece of bread. While she leaned over to talk softly in his ear—probably to coax him into eating some of it, as he made no move toward his knife and fork—Dean took the bowls and helped himself to a full plate.

Lynn didn't react to any of it. She sat and waited. Her stomach growled again. "Where's Dani?"

"Packing." Ren cast her a reproachful glance.

Don't blame me for taking her with me; blame Kate for this whole endeavor. Lynn watched the progress of the bowls around the table.

Cody took his share, then Ren, who wordlessly passed the bowls along to Lynn.

Lynn took as much as Cody. If they thought she was actually going to get Richard, she was entitled to a generous helping—and if they disagreed, they could piss off. She reached over her plate to take three slices of bread from the basket, lathered them freely with butter, and ate one in five bites, barely chewing. She was famished. The more she ate, the more she became aware of it.

They were probably looking at her, but she couldn't be bothered to care. Everything tasted so good: warm and crispy bread, molten butter, fatty bacon, fluffy eggs. Much better than scraps of meat, scavenged roots, and maybe some traded-for cheese. She didn't even bother with a knife and fork. She ate like the Wilder they thought she was and was perfectly content doing so.

The chair next to her scraped over the floor.

Lynn jumped and dropped her bread. *Dani.* She stared at her, trying to read her.

Dani sat but didn't look at her. Ren pushed the bowls past Lynn toward Dani, who quietly took the remainder of the bacon and eggs.

Lynn couldn't read her. *What else is new?*

Silence fell again, but this time Lynn was aware how tense it was.

Ren and Eduardo were silent; Kate was busy trying to get Toby to eat, and Cody and Dean kept staring at her. It was annoying, but she didn't care half as much about that as she did about the fact that Dani didn't look in her direction so completely that it had to be deliberate.

Lynn scooped the last of the eggs into her mouth—wastefulness was a sin—and looked at Dani.

She'd shoveled most of her breakfast in quietly.

Lynn pushed her chair back and stood. "I think it's time to go."

Slowly, Dani pushed her chair out and stood. Her hand trembled, but she grabbed the chair to hide it. "Okay." She nodded without meeting Lynn's eyes, but she met Kate's.

Kate stood. "Dani has provisions packed and a blanket for a stretcher to carry…" She faltered. "…him on."

"Right." The tension was making Lynn's skin crawl, and she planned to rush through the goodbyes. "Backpack, weapons?"

"In the hallway." Kate extended her hand. "By the door."

Lynn took great joy in seeing the anger on Kate's face as she called Skeever over. Without bothering to react, she turned and walked out, both Skeever and Dani on her heels. Some of the others followed at a greater distance, but she didn't bother to check who. Kate, probably. Maybe Cody and Dean.

Her backpack and jacket were, indeed, waiting by the door. Lynn slipped on her jacket and fished her tomahawk out of her backpack. Its familiar weight against her hip settled her. She hoisted her gear onto her shoulders and took Dani in. Now that Dani had her jacket on, her backpack strapped around her shoulders, and her folded spear in her hand, she looked like the elephant slayer Lynn had first met. "Ready?"

Dani's guarded eyes finally met hers. "Yeah."

Cody pushed her aside and undid a heavy padlock on the door. He pulled her knife from his belt and handed it over. "Come back soon, flower girl. Don't get eaten."

For a split second, Lynn entertained the thought to fuck it all and plant the knife in his chest. She restrained herself. "Fuck off."

He grinned.

Kate—the only other person who'd followed her—stepped up and opened her mouth as if to say something, but then just turned and left.

Skeever took two steps in Kate's direction and whined. When Lynn clicked her tongue, he turned to her and pressed against her leg instead.

"Right, then." She slid her knife into the boot not occupied by the glass shard and straightened. "Let's go." She pushed the door open and headed out onto the staircase without looking back.

A single pair of footsteps followed her down the steps.

Just one loose end to take care of and I'll be on my way again, with Skeever.

The dog rushed down ahead of her, sniffing busily.

It was so good to have him back. She trusted his nose as he traversed the lobby and only cast casual glances through the near-dark hallway. If he didn't think there was any danger, she was inclined to believe him. She needed to focus on the uneven floor so she wouldn't trip.

When they came to the doors, Dani opened them. After staring out for a while, she wordlessly undid the wire that held the swing gate closed.

Lynn grabbed Skeever by the collar. "Heel."

He whimpered but obeyed, vibrating with excitement.

She stepped out with him. The area around the Homestead was deserted as far as she could tell. It was a bright day, and it would warm up soon. She considered stripping off her jacket but didn't want to lose the layer of protection.

Dani closed the doors and tied up the fence.

Lynn let Skeever go so he could explore the area around the Homestead.

He darted off but circled right back to sniff along the wall, tail wagging.

Dani unfolded the spear. Her gaze darted around to the ruined buildings. When nothing moved, she walked past Lynn into the small square in front of the Homestead.

Skeever brushed up against the building, lifted his hind leg, and peed lengthily.

Lynn couldn't picture a more perfect goodbye to this shithole.

CHAPTER 5

LYNN SET OFF FROM THE Homestead at a firm pace. She felt Flint's gaze on her from the lookout rig hanging off the side of the building but refused to acknowledge him. Instead, she tried to gauge the mood of her travel companion.

Dani glanced back once, then set off, away from the Homestead, with strong strides that carried her past Lynn. She seemed to have withdrawn into herself even more than before—not looking at her, not speaking, not even acknowledging Skeever. It would have worried Lynn if Dani hadn't continuously scanned her surroundings, presumably employing reflexes engrained in her by whoever had taught her to hunt. Her gaze was alert but not frantic, and she appeared to be holding her own.

Skeever bounded ahead and sniffed at the crumbled walls of the buildings in front of him—the same they'd passed through on the way in yesterday—and then beyond as they passed the barrier.

At least you're happy. She returned her attention to Dani's stiff back.

She trudged on, but to where?

"Dani...?"

No reply.

"Dani, come on. Stop." She gritted her teeth. "Please?"

Dani tensed. She took a breath, then slowed and turned. Her grip on the spear tightened. "What?"

Lynn's focus slid from Dani's unreadable face, down to the sharp tip now leveled in her direction. "Maybe we should talk about where we're going?"

Skeever circled them before he shot past Dani to sniff at a crooked oak.

"Okay." Dani wiggled her weapon. "Talk."

"Right." Lynn checked the position of the sun. "That's east. I came from the north so..." Faced with Dani's spear, she pointed north with her tomahawk and not her unencumbered hand to assert her own dominance. "That way?"

"No. That's lion territory. If we're going north, we can go that way." She pointed with her spear. "I know a route that goes west, then curls up to the northeast."

Lynn ached a brow. "Why aren't we going back to the hunting ground? I can find my way from there."

"Can't. We hunted in lion territory. They'll be all over the area now, feasting on the bones."

"Okay." Lynn lowered her tomahawk. "We'll go that way, then." She would have liked to take the direct route and make her escape sooner rather than later, but she conceded to common sense. Speed wouldn't do her any good if she was too dead to capitalize on it.

Dani stared at her as if she was going to say something but then only nodded and turned on her heel. With the same brisk pace as before, she picked her way across the overgrown street.

Lynn hurried to catch up.

When she got within a foot or two, Dani glanced back and increased her pace.

Lynn walked faster.

Dani matched her again.

Oh for fuck's sake! Apparently, Dani was staging her own little rebellion. Lynn shook her head and fell back. If she pushed, she would wear herself out before noon, and she couldn't afford that. She needed to be as fresh as possible when she made her escape.

When Lynn wasn't on her heels anymore, Dani didn't turn or even glance back. As the road's condition deteriorated, she picked her way carefully, held her pace, and kept the sun at her back. She didn't talk or acknowledge Lynn in any other way.

Now that their course was set, Lynn didn't mind the silence; getting used to being out in the Wilds again took all her attention. Even just a few hundred feet from the Homestead, plant and animal life encroached. The lush bushes and rustling trees stood as stark reminders that every reclaimed inch of the city was predator territory. The yoke of it settled on her like a lead weight. She tried to ease its burden by paying even more attention to her surroundings but with only marginal success.

Dani's route diverged from the path they'd taken yesterday, and the distinction between *street* and *building* became even less defined. The remnants of houses had spilled onto every available space between them, be they gardens, alleyways, or streets. Without Skeever, Lynn would have backed up slowly and looked for another path. Eyes seemed to stare out at her from every shadow; danger appeared to lurk around every corner and behind every pile of overgrown rubble.

They got farther and farther away from the Homestead, and her insides still writhed like maggots in her gut. She took a few short breaths to gain control of her emotions, but they refused to settle. With a scowl, she wiped her clammy hands on her pants to better her grip on her tomahawk.

Dani picked her way across the debris a few feet ahead. She paused so Skeever could pass her and watched his progress before following along, all without sparing Lynn a glance.

Lynn followed in Dani's literal footsteps while her thoughts flitted as confusedly as the flocks of birds overhead, drawing her attention inward. She eyed Dani's back. She seemed oblivious to the dread Lynn felt as hotly as the sun on her neck. Did she not realize what Lynn couldn't shake: that New York City was too massive to get a grip on? That they were infinitely small and pathetically underequipped to handle it? Lynn took a shuddering breath and released it. *Why can't I get a grip? Isn't this what I do best?*

Over the course of her life, Lynn had spent years in various incarnations of the Wilds. She'd grown up in the ashes of Old-World Chicago, had lived in the outskirts of Ottawa, and had traveled through Detroit and Toronto in between. She'd experienced the same claustrophobic sense of disconnect in those areas as she did now, but she'd also felt…not in control perhaps, but capable. Not now. Her thoughts kept flitting to Dani.

Dammit, that's it! The thought struck her that the difference between then and now was that she had a human companion. Dani's presence threw her off-balance.

Lynn's only other true traveling companion had been her father. While he'd shielded her from a lot of his fears and worries, she'd known, understood, and loved his core being. Dani was a mystery to her. She played her emotions close to the chest, and they hadn't shared more than a few words prior to and since departing. Dani could harm her, help her, or do nothing in any situation they ended up in, and the fact that Lynn didn't know which was more likely to happen forced her to divide her attention. She came to an unpleasant conclusion: if she wanted her equilibrium back, she had to connect with her at least a little. They may travel together for just a day or so, but a lot could happen in that time. She stifled a groan. *Fine, let's bond.* She inhaled deeply. "So, uh…Daniela, huh?"

"Don't even try." Dani didn't look back.

Thrown off-balance by the instant rebuke, Lynn needed a few seconds to answer. "Try what?"

"To get me to talk to you. I'm not going to."

Lynn pushed forward to bridge the gap between them. "Look, I get that you're angry. I just—"

Dani whirled around and brought her spear parallel with Lynn's gut again.

Lynn jerked to a halt and stepped back on instinct. She raised her hands to chest level and showed Dani one open palm and the handle of her tomahawk, held in place with her thumb as she lifted the other hand as well. Her heartbeat rabbited. This was not what she'd had in mind when she struck up the conversation. "Easy."

The spear's tip shuddered with the force of the grip Dani had on its shaft. Her heartbeat surged through a bulging vein on the side of her neck. "This trip wasn't my idea."

She examined Dani, trying to sort out this sudden explosive reaction. "Not mine either."

"Opinions are divided about that one." Dani forced the words out through a tightly set jaw.

Lynn checked on Skeever to make sure he wasn't tensing up or otherwise showing signs of impending danger.

He didn't.

It began to dawn on her that perhaps most of Dani's ire wasn't directed at her but at Kate. She relaxed her posture. "Kate made me do this, you know? If you didn't want to come, you could have taken it up with her. She could have called this whole thing off."

Dani threw her free arm up. "You think I didn't?" She laughed, but it was a hollow sound. "I talked to her for over an hour last night—I reasoned with her, pleaded with her, threatened her. Do you know what she said?" She jabbed the spear in Lynn's direction.

Lynn took another cautious step back. "I can guess."

Dani shook her head. "I doubt it. She said I owed it to her. *I* owed it to *her* to do this."

"Why?"

"Because she took me into the Homestead. As if I haven't proven my worth ten times over since!" Dani thrust the spear again.

"Um, could you...?" Lynn motioned at the weapon, but Dani either didn't hear her or chose to ignore the request.

"I am the one who goes out to set snares and hunt game. I help around the Homestead. I carry my weight!" Dani pounded her chest in a proud and very masculine gesture that was strangely enticing. Not that Lynn had time to focus on such things.

"I'm sure you do carry your weight."

Dani snorted. "Oh, don't even start." She jabbed at Lynn again but not with the intent to harm as the spear tip didn't get close. "You have no idea who I am, and I haven't forgotten you chose me to come with you because it might've given you an edge." She waved the tip of the spear around in a circle as if to indicate Lynn's whole person. "Anything you say or do, I'm taking as an attempt to make your life better. You don't give a shit about anyone else—least of all me."

A confusing mix of anger and embarrassment shot through Lynn's system. She opened her mouth and closed it again when she discovered she didn't have a reply to that. It was true that she'd tried to give herself an edge by taking Dani, but she didn't consider herself a selfish person, as Dani seemed to imply. She lowered her hands with the palms down, trying to placate her. "I don't have to know you to know you pulled your weight. They would have kicked you out long ago if you hadn't."

The tip of Dani's spear drooped an inch or so as she seemed to ponder that. "I guess." She brought up the weapon again. "But you dragged me into this, so don't think I'm only pissed at Kate."

Lynn shrugged in what she hoped would come across as casual but not unsympathetic. "Sorry. You're a decent person who is strong enough to lift dead weight—literally—but also someone who I think I can take in a fight should you get it into your head to, well, do this." She nodded toward the spear.

Dani dropped her gaze to the weapon and seemed to register the implied threat of it for the first time. She lifted the tip and let the shaft slide through her loosened fist until the bud settled onto the sand by her feet.

Lynn instantly relaxed a little. "Thanks for that."

Dani remained silent. The blood still throbbed through the protruding vein on her neck, but it seemed to have slowed a little. Her chin had dropped to her chest, and she clutched the spear as if it was the thing that held her upright instead of the other way around. She'd drifted even further into herself—and away from Lynn.

Lynn realized once more how inept she was at handling human emotion. She couldn't identify what underlay Dani's body language, and she wouldn't know what to say to make her feel better even if she tried. She licked her lips. "Um...maybe we should move on?"

Dani swallowed. "Yeah, I guess." Her voice cracked halfway through the sentence. She checked the position of the sun before she lifted her spear again. "This way."

Lynn let her get ahead a few paces to give her the space she had insisted on before, then patted her thigh to draw Skeever's attention.

He looked up from a pile of rubble he'd been sniffing and trotted over. After a brush against her leg, he pushed on ahead.

As he passed, Dani ran her fingers over his spine, exhaled audibly, and fell in line.

Dani's words chafed against her mind like badly sewn pants against her thighs. Lynn supposed Dani had a point: she had definitely taken every opportunity to bend the situation to her advantage since the Homesteaders had captured her, but was it selfish to do so when they'd threatened her freedom and her life? The will to live wasn't selfish, was it? *Well...* Okay, so it was selfish, but was it *bad*?

She ran her hand through her hair and shook it out as she glanced left, then right. *Jeez.* Maybe she should just leave well enough alone for now; this conversation hadn't made her feel better at all.

The longer they walked, the higher the buildings rose into the sky. Lynn craned her neck to look up at the skeletal behemoths, impressed by their size and cowed by the hidden signs of life in the brambles. Vines stretched from building to building like oversized webs. While the fantastical spiders that would have made them never appeared, other animals were everywhere. Innumerable types of birds nested in the ivy and other creepers that covered every inch of the towers. Several times, Lynn spotted deer in the distance. Monkeys yipped and hollered as they scattered along the road before rushing up the sides of the buildings. Twice she heard elephants trumpeting, but they didn't come into view.

Lynn took a deep breath. She decided she hated New York. *Too many hiding places, too much noise.* She had to fight to keep her hand steady and her pace constant. The urge to rush through this part of the city was hard to quench.

Dani led her silently.

At first the silence had felt like a continuation of the previous cold shoulder, but now Lynn began to reconsider.

Since their talk, much of the stiffness had drained from Dani's posture, and her attentiveness seemed to have suffered for it. She kept her head down and only looked up every dozen steps or so. Dani clutched her spear in both hands, against her chest. The position rendered the weapon useless, but Dani didn't seem to notice or care.

Lynn cared. Her life, at least partly, depended on Dani. She bit back a groan at the daunting task of another minefield of a conversation, but it had to be done. "Hey, Dani?"

"Hm?" Dani's head jerked up as if she had been deeply in thought.

Lynn lengthened her strides until she was level with her.

This time, Dani didn't speed up.

That's progress. She glanced to the side. "I don't know how to say this without sounding like a bitch, so—"

Dani raised a brow and smirked.

Right. Dani already thought she was a bitch. *Whatever.* "I, uh...need you to pay attention to what's happening."

Dani stopped and planted a hand on her hip. She squinted. "I am paying attention."

Lynn snorted. "Right. What's the name of this street, hm?"

Dani's expression darkened, and she pushed out her chin.

Lynn instantly realized her error. *No, not bitchy at all, Tanner. Very friendly behavior right there, not suspicious or condescending whatsoever. Dammit, you're trying to get her to cooperate!*

"I'm going to go back to watching what happens around me now." Dani whirled back around and briskly stalked forward. The stiffness had returned to her spine and shoulders.

Thoroughly dismissed, Lynn fell back a step and bit her tongue. If she opened her mouth, the resulting conversation would undoubtedly turn into another argument. She cracked her neck to drain some of the tension out of it and shook out her arms. *You're an idiot. Do what you do best and make it through alive. This talking thing is not for you.*

She returned her attention to New York City. Despite the outward beauty of its greenery specked with flowers and fruits, Lynn could only think of it as a malicious whole. It was impossible to comprehend that people had once lived in this bastion of nature. Only a few hundred years ago, mankind had dominated these streets. They'd tamed the Wilds with asphalt and cement. Human beings had denied entrance to all this life and had caged the animals who now ruled supreme.

What would it have been like to walk these streets in awe of the architecture or even with indifference to its massiveness? It was unimaginable that they hadn't tried to hear predators coming over the cacophony of the warning calls of birds or struggled to look past upturned cars for signs of movement. Maybe they'd taken a leisurely stroll through these streets with their kids or sat in these cars until they could move forward and go home. Insanity—or maybe this life was insane.

Skeever jerked to a halt.

Dani bumped against him but caught herself on the side of one of the cars before she lost her balance completely. "What—?" She frowned.

"Quiet." Lynn gripped her tomahawk as her skin crawled.

Skeever growled.

Dani fumbled her spear into position, apparently now catching on to what Lynn had guessed the moment Skeever had stopped: he'd sensed something. And whenever Skeever sensed something and growled, it was something he perceived as predator, not prey.

Lynn scanned the area. Nothing moved in the sea of wrecks ahead. Not in the doorways or windows of the buildings around them either. A troop of monkeys clambered up a tower behind them, but Skeever stared dead ahead, so that wasn't it. She pushed past Dani to grab his collar before he could attack whatever it was he'd heard or smelled. She wasn't about to let him blunder into a fight he couldn't finish.

"Do you see anything?" Dani held the spear with both hands again, but at least the tip pointed forward now.

"No." Lynn straightened as much as she could with her hand around Skeever's collar. "Could you climb up one of 'em?" She nodded toward the car beside them.

Dani nodded. "Right." She turned and clambered up the rusted metal with the ease of practice. Once she'd gotten her footing, she scanned the area slowly, from left to right.

Skeever pulled against Lynn's hold and showed his teeth.

She braced against his force and glanced up. She itched to prompt Dani but bit her tongue. Dani was a hunter; looking for predators and prey was what she specialized in.

The hairs on the back of Lynn's neck stood on end. Either the glare of the sun reflecting off innumerable cars and trucks hid whatever approached or the vehicles themselves blocked it, but whatever the reason, Lynn saw nothing. She looked up at Dani, desperate for information.

Dani seemed to have forgotten about her. She stared ahead with laser focus. After a few seconds, she lowered herself into a battle stance and gripped her spear.

A spike of alarm coursed up Lynn's spine, and she found herself fighting rising panic. *She's going to attack it—whatever* it *is*. Her adrenaline surged so violently she felt dizzy. *No, no, no, no.* Presented with the suffocating threat of the Wilds, some people went on the offensive to gain a sense of control that they were desperate for. It inevitably left them wide open to the First Law of the Wilds: the second you exposed yourself, it devoured you.

Dani took off before Lynn could raise her hand to yank her down.

Lynn's heart arrested, then lunged into a gallop.

Within moments Dani disappeared between the rows of vehicles. The top of her head appeared briefly whenever she passed a slope in the metal.

Shit! Shit, shit, shit! Lynn raised her tomahawk and looked around frantically. *What do I do?*

Skeever yanked again.

Lynn lost her grip.

He shot away, barked loudly, and disappeared between the cars.

Losing sight of him made Lynn's stomach churn. *Decide!* She sprinted after him, forcing herself to blindly charge past wrecks. Every time she did, she expected something to jump her, but nothing did. Her heart beat so loudly it sounded like a drum in her ears: *thump-thump, thump-thump, thump-thump.* She spotted Dani two rows of cars away. Relief flooded her system. She leaped the hood of a car to get to her—right into the aftermath of the hunt, kill made. Lynn tried to soak it all up with eyes unwilling to focus on anything longer than a second.

A massive gray shape lay sprawled on a narrow strip of ground between wrecks.

Dani's spear protruded from its chest, still trembling.

Dani stood motionless over the carcass.

Skeever bit down on its throat, seemingly uninterested that it was already dead. He growled and shook hard.

Then it registered what she was looking at: a wolf.

Oh no. The heat in her veins turned to ice and became solid, constricting her chest. There was always more than one wolf. Cold sweat ran down her back. She looked around wildly. "Skeever! Come here." Lynn slapped her thigh.

Skeever growled but relinquished his hold with a whine. He licked his faintly reddened nuzzle and trotted back to Lynn. After shaking himself out, he pressed against her leg. Then his head jerked up, and he sniffed the air.

A sense of impending doom rushed up like storm clouds hounded by gale strength winds. The hairs on her arms stood on end. "We need to go!"

"What's your problem? It's dead." Dani glared at her over the body of the slain wolf. She casually yanked the spear from its chest. "There was just one."

There is never just one, she wanted to shout. But if she got into a shouting match, they would be here forever.

A growl started up so low in Skeever's throat that Lynn felt it more than she heard it.

Fear threatened to overtake her. She knew it with absolute certainty now: they were coming; the First Law dictated it.

Dani still seemed oblivious to what was as clear as day to Lynn. She looked around but without urgency.

I could just leave her. She considered it, but only for a moment. She was not a murderer. Lynn gripped Dani's arm. "We need to go!" She dragged her along.

"Let me g—" Dani's gaze shifted from Lynn's face to something behind her. Her eyes widened.

Too late! Lynn let go of Dani and raised her tomahawk even as she whirled around.

Skeever twisted and shot past her. He snarled and impacted audibly with something.

"Skeever!" Dani's voice was shrill.

Finally, Lynn zeroed in on a second wolf.

Skeever's momentum must have thrown the wiry animal over mere seconds before it would have jumped on Lynn. It snapped at Skeever's shoulder as he stood over it and bit down on its throat with all his might. They both snarled and tumbled over the uneven ground.

The wolf raked the sharp claws at the ends of powerful hind legs across Skeever's side. Tufts of bloody hair flew free.

Without thought, Lynn raised the tomahawk and sprang forward. She twisted her arm to get past Skeever in the tangled mess of fur and limbs and brought the sharp edge down with force. The blade connected with the side of the wolf's head just as it spotted her coming.

Its jaws missed her arm by inches.

Bone crushed under the impact of the blow, then gave way.

A guttural yowl of pain started low in the wolf's throat.

Lynn tripped but held on to the tomahawk, jerking it sideward as she fell. Pain tore through her shoulder, but she ignored it; she didn't have time for pain. Her heart hammered in her chest to the tune of: *get away, get away, get away!* She let go of the tomahawk and scrambled back, then kicked the weapon with all her might.

The sudden jerk halted the wolf's outcry. The yellow eyes widened before they abruptly dimmed. Its hind legs twitched but didn't raise again.

Skeever still bit down. He renewed his hold and growled as he shook.

Dani stood wide-eyed, staring, spear raised.

Lynn sucked in air. Every ounce of wisdom in her body told her to get the fuck up, but she was transfixed by the fact she was still alive.

It's dead. Relief rushed over her but was replaced with ice-cold fear a frantic heartbeat later. Something sharp scratched over metal somewhere nearby. When she jumped up, her legs didn't hold her and she sank to her knees. Her heaving, shallow breaths were making her light-headed. *Breathe!* She lowered her head and inhaled deeply. Her tomahawk stuck out of the wolf's skull only a few steps away, but it felt like miles. She pulled her knife free from her boot instead and stood again.

"Behind you!"

Lynn turned just before the wolf was upon her. Its weight was crushing, and she went down in a sprawl. The knife fell from her hand and skidded over the ground, under one of the cars nearby, out of reach.

Dani's spear flew uselessly overhead.

The animal went for her throat right away. Its breath smelled like death. Saliva dripped onto her cheek.

In a flash of panic, Lynn leaned her head away as far as it would go and pushed her arm up like a pitiful shield. Pain as hot and acute as fire flared through it as the wolf bit into it. Even through her coat and sweater, the teeth sank deep into her flesh, and she cried out. Her back arched like a bow over her backpack.

Dani screamed her name, which seemed like an especially useless thing to do right now.

The wolf snarled and clambered more firmly upon her. It raked her thigh on the way up.

Another guttural cry tore from her throat. She tried not to move her arm. Maybe if she didn't move it, the wolf wouldn't shake it. If it did, she knew her limb would snap like a twig. Sweat pearled and ran down her neck, and her heartbeat rocketed. Her bladder threatened to let go. She had to close her eyes against the horror of it all so she could think.

The wolf bit down harder.

For a second, the pain became so intense Lynn thought she would black out. *Think!* She remembered the shard weapon in her boot. With great effort she managed to draw up her leg and reach down. She pulled the shard free and opened her eyes so she could aim her thrusts. The sight of the bared teeth around her own arm caused a wave of panic so strong that her stomach lunged up. She managed to choke vomit down. Panic tore at the frayed remnants of her self-control. *Focus, dammit!*

The wolf growled and bit down harder.

Lynn set her jaw and kneed it in the side as hard as she could.

The wolf yelped and turned its head to bite at her leg. The move freed her arm—and left the wolf's neck exposed.

Lynn's breath seized. Her heart thundered. *This is it!* Her throbbing arm fell to her chest. She gripped the shard more firmly and stabbed. For a heart-stopping second the thick hide resisted—then the glass cut through and sliced deep.

The wolf uttered a cry so chilling that Lynn nearly dropped the shard. She sucked in a ragged breath and yanked the shard down as hard as she could. Hot blood dripped down and squirted across her arm.

The large muzzle swung back to her face, and she lifted her bloody arm in defense even as she tore the improvised knife through flesh and muscle again.

Skeever crashed over her. The force of his impact pushed the dying wolf off her.

It snarled, but Skeever's bulk kept it from standing up.

Skeever found purchase on its throat and tore.

Lynn pressed her bloody arm against her chest and scrambled forward without thought. Her mind had blanked in the face of death. She fell over the wolf as she overbalanced from the weight of her pack but stabbed even as she did so.

Skeever tore again, and this time a large chunk of fur and flesh gave way.

The lights in the wolf's eyes went out entirely.

Lynn couldn't stop her arm from lifting and coming down to drive the shard in again and again and again. A ragged laugh clawed its way up her insides, but she couldn't let it out. If she let it out, she would fall apart.

Dani fell by her side and grabbed her arm. She shouted something.

The rush of blood in Lynn's ear washed it away. She should stop stabbing; there could be more wolves. *Why can't I stop?*

"Lynn!" Dani yanked at her arm.

She dropped the bloody shard and fell back on her ass, trembling. Lynn fought for breath, for control. *Focus!* She tore her gaze away from the wolf's ruined neck and stared up at Dani. It was only then that she fully registered Dani was there.

"Oh shit, shit, shit. Lynn? Are you okay?" Dani kept her hands in the air above Lynn's arm as if she was afraid to touch her. "I couldn't find my spear. The axe stuck. Shit, are you okay? Does it hurt?"

The barrage of high-pitched questions made Lynn's head scream in agony. "Shhhh," she rasped. "S-Shut up. Are there m-more?" Her entire body went cold all at once, and she could barely focus her thoughts.

Dani seemed reluctant to look away, but after a few seconds, she seemed to get a grip on the panic that had dominated her features. She stood, then hesitantly stepped away from Lynn and climbed onto a car, spear in hand.

The sight brought back bad memories, but Lynn couldn't worry about Dani's actions right now. With effort she drew her legs under her and stood. Pain flared in her hip and shoulder, but mostly in her arm. Blood seeped up through the bite marks in her coat. She looked down at the wolf again.

Skeever had torn away much of its throat and chewed noisily on its flesh. The dog looked a mess—blood everywhere, tufts of hair missing—and he trembled.

"It looks clear." Dani jumped down. "Can you—do you want to move?"

Lynn nodded. She felt cold and numb. *Shock.* This was shock; it must be.

"Let me get the—" Dani yanked repeatedly at Lynn's tomahawk until it came free.

Lynn watched her without really registering anything about the scene. Fatigue crept in as silently as the wolves had. She needed a place to collapse, to gather her wits and tend to her wounds. Her gaze slid down to Skeever. His left hip was covered in blood, and he drew the leg up whenever it lowered to the ground. She needed to inspect his wounds as well. A deeper sense of lethargy blanketed her. Now if only she could will her feet into motion.

"Do you...?" Dani hesitated. "Do you want me to carry your pack?"

Lynn lifted her head and stared. A bitter and somewhat manic laugh bubbled up inside of her so fiercely that Lynn thought she might explode if she didn't let it out. "Y-You nearly got me killed, and now you want to carry my pack?" She didn't recognize the high pitch to her voice.

Dani's eyes widened before she looked away. "I just thought you might be hurting." Her voice was no more than a whisper.

The laugh welled up again like a living entity, even harder to suppress this time. "Of course I'm hurting!" She felt ragged and raw inside and out. The chaotic tumble inside her skull intensified, and she struggled to keep her train of thought. As the wind picked up, the smell of death invaded her senses. Blood and piss and shit: that was what life was about out here in the Wilds. "You just don't get what it's like out here, do you?"

Dani opened her mouth to speak.

Lynn cut her off with a wave of her bloody hand. Now that the floodgates were open, Lynn couldn't stop her raging emotions from bursting out. "It's not like hunting!" She pointed to the mangled form of the nearest wolf, imposing even in death. "We're not in control; they are."

Dani followed the motion of her hand and stared at the cadaver. Her gaze lingered on the wolf when Lynn pressed on.

"It's not like...like hunting an elephant; it's not planned out. Out here, you don't get to go home and pull a gate shut!" She was being loud—too loud—but she couldn't quiet herself. A tremor started in her injured arm and spread to her entire body within seconds.

Dani folded her arms across her chest and scuffed the ground with the tip of her boot. "I saw only one, and I took it out."

"Gah!" Lynn kicked a car. "You need to get it through your skull that life out in the Wilds isn't just taking out one threat! Everything is a threat!" She crouched down and fumbled her knife out from under the car where it had slid. Her head buzzed as if it were filled with angry bees. She stood shakily and pointed the blade at Dani's chest. "The second you drop your guard in the Wilds, you die."

Dani stepped back. Her gaze slid down, eyes wide. Her spear came up with a jolt.

Lynn's barely noticed. Her head pounded in tune with the throbbing pain in her mangled arm. "So if you're going to keep charging wolves and putting me in harm's way, I'd rather fight it out now, because I'm not going to let you kill me without a fight."

Dani stared at the knife. Her eyes watered, and she blinked to clear them even as she looked away. She swallowed with difficulty, then swallowed again. "I think we should go." Her voice cracked.

After a few more seconds of pressing the point, Lynn cradled her arm again. "Damn right we should."

CHAPTER 6

DANI TURNED AWAY FROM THE road. "We're here." Relief was evident in her tone.

Lynn came to a halt and inspected the meandering cement path. It was cracked and overgrown, and led to a sprawling brick building almost entirely hidden from view by a curtain of trees and brush. The promised shelter appeared structurally sound save for the glass entrance doors, which had been shattered. Much of the copper lettering on the overhang was gone, but Lynn could piece together the word *chapel.*

When Dani had said she knew a place nearby that was usually secure, Lynn had agreed to wait before she inspected the damage to her arm. Since then, there had been no reprieve from her chilling thoughts about the damage the wolf's teeth might have caused. They had traveled in complete silence. Her fingers had gone cold and stiff. Her coat sleeve was bloody. Several times she'd been on the verge of telling Dani to stop out in the open or to find a hole in the wall to use as temporary refuge, but every time the promise of safety had won out over her barely suppressed panic. She hurried after Dani.

Skeever shot ahead.

Dani only just managed to grab the dog by his collar before he could blunder in.

He sniffed busily within the bounds she allowed.

Lynn scanned Skeever's raised tail, his scraping front paw, and his eagerly extended head. It was his hunting pose, not his attacking pose. He still favored his left leg, but it didn't hinder him as he clambered over the bramble. "Well, he smells something in there." She hoisted her arm higher up against her chest and gripped her shoulder with her numb fingers. Hopefully, she had remembered her father's words correctly, and the arm elevated like this would stop the bleeding.

"Rats, probably." Dani took a step forward to balance herself as Skeever pulled against her hold. She frowned. "But something bigger could have wandered in. The last time I was here, the doors were still intact."

"Let him go. He's good at sensing danger. If he's gearing up to hunt rats, it's probably clear." From what Lynn could see of the chapel beyond, it wasn't that big anyway; not much room for anything to hide.

Skeever sprang forward with a crisp bark.

Dani entered more slowly with her spear raised, but only a few seconds later she lifted the shaft so it rested against her shoulder. "All clear."

Lynn swallowed. Now that they had arrived, a mixture of relief and dread filled her. She couldn't help feeling as if she were walking toward her sentencing. Had the incisors ripped her skin from flesh and flesh from bone? How much blood had she lost? How much grime had gotten into the wounds? If they got infected, would she lose her arm—or her life? Her chest seemed to compress and prevented air from getting into her lungs. She attempted to distract herself by looking around.

The chapel consisted of a single carpeted room probably twenty by fifteen paces across. It was filled with rows of dust-caked and partially destroyed chairs. The high ceiling sloped up to a point at the center and was covered with slim wooden boards, many of them on the verge of falling down. A kaleidoscope of colors spread across the wall opposite the door. Their source was a stained-glass window that Lynn only glanced at in favor of further inspection of her unfamiliar surroundings.

Skeever growled and yipped.

Something small scurried past.

A faded American flag moved in the breeze as Skeever chased the rodent into the left-hand side of the room. The tattered cloth hung over half a dozen upturned coffins.

Coffins? In a church? Lynn frowned. "What is this place?"

"Cemetery." Dani jiggled a chair leg jammed behind the handles of a set of secondary entrance doors on the right. She pushed then pulled at it until she seemed satisfied the door was properly barred. "This was the place where they held the uh...services, I guess." She motioned to the coffins. "Busy day."

Lynn snorted despite herself.

Dani smiled fleetingly. "I'll stand guard so you can..." She nodded toward Lynn's arm, then busied herself by standing sentry at the main entrance.

Despite Dani's outward hardening, Lynn suspected she felt responsible for what had happened—and she should.

Lynn slid her tomahawk into the loop on her belt and pulled up a chair. *All right, let's do this.* Careful with her arm, she lowered her pack onto the seat. With every button she popped on her jacket, she drew a slow breath, but her hands weren't steady and her heartbeat continued to thunder. She shrugged her jacket down her good right arm and peeled it off her throbbing left arm. As the heavy leather slid over the wound, sharp pain forced her to suck in a shuddering breath. She soldiered on. Her coat fell to the floor and threw up dust. Less blood than she'd expected had soaked into the wool of her sweater. It was a hopeful sign, which nevertheless proved nothing. She paused.

Dani hadn't moved.

Skeever noisily chewed on something in a corner.

Lynn had as much privacy as she was going to get, but she still turned her back to Dani. She didn't want Dani to see either her arm or her expression before she'd had a chance to come to grips with how it looked. Her hand trembled, and she flexed and clenched, flexed and clenched to steady it. She gripped her wrist and fastened her gaze on the display of colors on the wall. *Deep breath.* She pushed up her sleeve. The wool tore loose where blood had already dried, and pain coursed up her arm. She puffed out her breath. The force of her pulse inside her skull was giving her a headache.

Breathe. Look down. Just...look down. She did.

Relief flooded her system as strong as a wave. *Oh thank fuck.*

The upper canines had punctured her skin and had torn into the flesh below, but the incisors had only broken the skin in a few places. She turned her arm over. Bruises had already started to form, and her skin was torn in a few more places. She was lucky that her coat and sweater had protected her against what she'd feared the most: the tearing away of the skin from the flesh that was so telling of a wolf's bite. This, if treated properly, would heal. With a little luck and a lot of care, it wouldn't get infected. She wouldn't lose her arm.

She pressed her eyes shut. *Thank fuck.* A lump constricted her throat, and she swallowed. "It's not as bad as I thought." She sounded hoarse. Her legs threatened to give out. *I need to sit down.* She lowered her pack from the chair and slumped onto it.

Dani had turned and lingered by the door. She glanced away when Lynn looked up. "Good."

"I'd say so." Lynn examined her.

A little bit of the tension had drained from Dani's posture. Something else was different too. The distance between them was the same as it had been since they'd left the Homestead, but unlike that first frustrating half morning, Dani now seemed to be repelled by Lynn's presence where before Dani's anger had repelled Lynn.

When Lynn realized she was frowning, she straightened out her face. "I need water."

"Right!" Dani cast a quick look outside, then walked back, slipping off her backpack. She lowered herself and it to the floor by Lynn's legs and pulled her water sack from its depths. "Here."

Lynn took the sack and pulled the bone stopper from the neck with her teeth. She dropped it to her lap and pondered how to proceed. The thought of jugging perfectly good water over her arm didn't sit well with her.

"Do you need help?" Dani's tone was deceptively light.

"No!" Lynn winced as the reflexive snap left her mouth. *Deep breath. No need to take her head off. Shit happened; you're alive.* "No, but I could use a bowl and something to wash with." *There, I'll become a socially capable being yet.* But why should she? She wasn't sticking around. Her nerves were too frayed for these types of thoughts, she decided, and focused on the task at hand.

Dani rummaged through her backpack and came up with a rag and a bowl. "Here." She was still down on a knee and offered Lynn the tools.

Lynn took them, happy to note her hand cooperated fully even though her arm smarted. She poured some water into the bowl and handed the sack back to Dani. "Thanks."

Dani nodded. She sat on the dirty ground and stretched out her legs before rotating her ankle joints.

Were Dani's feet sore already? Lynn resisted the urge to roll her eyes. It wasn't even noon. *It's a good thing you get to go home soon.* To her surprise she felt a little bit of guilt after the thought struck her. She covered her confusion by wetting the rag. Why was she feeling guilty? She had nothing to feel guilty about. *Right?* Of course that wasn't entirely true. When she abandoned Dani somewhere, Dani would have to find her way back to the Homestead alone. If she came face-to-face with another roving band of wolves, she would be on her own.

Dani had pulled another rag from her pack and started cleaning her spear.

Less thinking, more cleaning. She rubbed the coarse wool over her sensitive skin and winced. Despite what she'd told Dani earlier, Lynn wasn't used to getting hurt quite this often. Yes, at least once a day she came across something that could potentially kill her, but more often than not she managed to sidestep the crumbling edge of a ledge, go around the packs of wolves or roving dogs, and stave off starvation, dehydration, and hypothermia. She had skills, and they kept her safe—usually. When other people entered the equation, all bets were off, it seemed. Her ponderings caused her to brush too close to the worst cluster of wounds. Pain flared up her arm, and she hissed.

"You okay?"

Even though Lynn avoided looking at her, she could feel Dani's gaze on her. She didn't want to talk about it. "How do you know this place?"

"It's one of our hideaways when we go hunting," Dani said after several seconds of silence. She scratched a stain off the metal shaft. "One of our farthest."

"Do you guys ever stay out overnight?" She forced herself not to make a sound of discomfort as she scraped the wool along the underside of her arm.

"No, never." All emotion had drained out of Dani's voice.

Lynn paused to stare at her. "Never?"

Dani shook her head. "I haven't spent a night outside of the Homestead since I arrived."

She tried to pass it off as something unimportant, but ever since the wolves, Lynn thought she was getting better at reading Dani's expression and body language. The thought was a little unsettling; if she was getting better at reading Dani, maybe Dani was getting better at reading her too. And Dani had already been pretty good at it to start. "How long ago was that again?"

"When summer comes, it'll be two years." Dani folded and extended the spear experimentally and inspected it, seemingly to busy her eyes.

Lynn kept her gaze on her wounds as she cleaned them of her blood. Thankfully, her cleaning confirmed her earlier assessment. "So, how scared shitless are you right now?"

Dani tensed, and the grip on her spear tightened.

For a second, Lynn thought she'd pushed the tentative comradery too far, then she realized what she was seeing in Dani wasn't anger but fear. She swallowed. "Sorry, that was insensitive."

"Whatever." Dani began to pace.

Skeever, roused by the movement, trotted over from the corner and followed her back and forth across the small chapel. He bounded ahead. Within seconds he returned with the mangled remains of the rat in his jaws and brushed his head against Dani's hand to get her to take his offering and throw it.

Dani pushed him away twice before she tossed the dead rodent across the room. Disgust crinkled her features. She wiped the tips of her fingers on her pants.

If Dani was afraid now, how scared would she be when she was alone out here? Lynn sighed and focused on cleaning her injuries—injuries she'd sustained because of Dani's stupidity. Fuck Dani and her fear.

"Is it safe?" Dani scanned the site before them hesitantly.

"It's defendable." Lynn let Skeever sniff through the rubble in front of what had been a house pre-war. Its top stories had collapsed, but unlike its brethren in the area, its outer walls still stood.

Dani glared at her. *Defendable* was apparently not a satisfactory criterion for someone used to an almost absolute guarantee of safety when she slept.

"It's the best option we have." Lynn glanced around. This section of the city had been decimated by the bombers. The tallest things around were the trees that had grown on and through the grass-covered remnants of civilization.

Dani had urged them on well beyond what Lynn felt comfortable with, unwilling to agree to a sleeping place this open, but the destruction in this area had been complete. As imperfect as this shelter was, Lynn knew they could make it work. And she needed to make it work too; the dull throbbing in her arm had worsened to a steady pulsing. Swinging her arm as they walked, bumping it against her body by accident, and reluctantly using it to climb over obstructions had taken its toll. It was also getting dark quickly now.

"Come on. Let's look inside." Lynn clambered through the gap in the structure that had once held a door. It was now the start of a steep slope of debris. When she pushed aside a variety of green creepers, she upset a mass of spiders. She shook them off without a second thought, planted her fingers into the dirt between the stones, and hauled herself up. She bit back a grunt of pain.

Skeever scrambled up after her, tail low. He overtook her.

Lynn stood up. *Inside* was better described as *on top of*. The building's innards had compacted into a rubble layer as thick as its entire first story. The collapse had created a fairly level and spacious surface to camp on. As far as hideouts went, this was a decent one. Walled in on three sides, sheltered from the wind, and as long as it didn't rain, a fire would keep them warm. As Lynn stood, she could look out over the ruined walls but saw little more than sunset-red-colored treetops.

Skeever beelined for something in the far left corner and circled, nose to the ground, panting loud enough for Lynn to hear him the entire length of the space away.

Carefully, she tested the solidity of the ceiling-turned-floor as she made her way over to him.

It held.

She crouched down by a collection of bones and dry scat and pulverized some of the feces between her fingers. It was old. Either it was a single dropping of a bear or multiple droppings of something smaller. Wolverine? Dog? Lynn didn't like any of the options; they were all fiercely territorial and wouldn't take kindly to intruders. The skeleton was the size of a small doe, but it was hard to tell what it had been exactly, with many of its parts missing—including the skull. More wolves? This not knowing was going to haunt her in the long, dark night.

Skeever sniffed her fingers, then licked them. His tail trembled between his legs.

You don't like it either, do you, boy? She scratched along his jaw.

"Are we staying?"

Lynn's heart stuttered. She whirled around. "Dammit! Don't sneak up on me!"

Dani flinched, then her features hardened. She drew herself up to her full height even as the tip of the spear lowered loosely to Lynn's chest height. "Don't yell at me." Her tone was metered. Her eyes narrowed. "You knew I was coming up after you. Tell me what you've found."

Lynn's heartbeat settled to a strong thumping, ready for battle, a powerful pulse that steadied her. She straightened slowly and pushed the tip of the spear aside before stepping past it, into Dani's personal space. The motion rendered Dani's weapon ineffective, but Lynn didn't need much room to swing her tomahawk. The smooth wood of the handle settled against her skin as she tightened her grip.

Dani's eyes widened; she knew it too.

Lynn allowed only a fraction of the smirk that tugged at the corners of her mouth. *That's right, Dani. Don't forget you're in my world now.* She pushed forward.

Dani had to attack, take a step back, or fall over. She stepped back.

Lynn's blood ran hot in her veins, victorious. Her dominance established, she relented. "Something used this as a lair, but not for a while. So yes, we are going to bar whatever we can, and then we're going to stay. Agreed?"

"Y-Yes." Dani broke the eye contact. She turned and walked away, shoulders slumped. "I'll start on the door."

Lynn considered protesting. Could she trust Dani to build adequate defenses? She'd said herself that she hadn't spent a night out in the Wilds for years. But Lynn was so tired. Hauling heavy with her weakened arm would worsen the injury, and she knew it. "Don't fuck up."

Dani tensed and she slowed her step, but only a second. Then she tilted her head up and marched off without looking back.

Lynn watched her slip down the slope until she disappeared completely. She loosened the grip on her tomahawk and deflated with a slow release of her breath. Dani'd had a point, she realized; Lynn should have never let herself be caught by surprise like that. Of course Dani would follow her up. *Stupid.* She shook her head. At least Dani now remembered who held the power between them. Lynn wondered why that mattered so damn much to her, but it did. Maybe it was because she'd let Dani push her until sundown was upon them instead of setting up camp when light had still been abundant. Lynn liked to have everything set up to perfection before darkness fell. Now she would have to scramble to get that done. She cracked her neck on both sides and rotated her sore shoulder with care. Time to make the best of it. First step: clear a spot to camp down.

A short time later, she added twigs to a small fire built on dried scat and leaves. It would take more time and more wood to build the fire up to one stable and hot enough to heat up some food or water, but even this crisp, little fire offered relief from the rapidly encroaching darkness.

Sounds of grunting and dragging reached her ears again. Dani had been busy too.

Skeever barked, but it was his happy bark.

What is she doing, anyway? Lynn added a few more twigs and bits of bark to the fire. She tightened the ring of stones around it and got up. Tomahawk in hand, she walked back to the slope and stared down into the twilight. Her eyes adjusted quickly.

Dani was dragging a man-sized branch into the hole in the wall. The crown of leaves sealed it up behind her and Skeever. Other leafed branches lay nearby and she piled them on, creating a hedge of sorts to keep the predators out.

Lynn analyzed the improvised barricade. It wouldn't stop anything from coming in, but it would make a hell of a noise while their attacker struggled.

Dani stepped back and crouched. She got her fingers under a heavy-looking piece of debris—something that seemed to have been part of the roof—and pushed up with the obvious intent of tipping it up and over against the branches to create an even more solid barrier.

Lynn had to begrudgingly admit it would solidify the barrier greatly if she got the solid piece of wreckage in place.

Dani managed to hoist the sagging slab onto her thighs but then faltered.

"Coming down." Lynn slid down to her.

The well-defined muscles in Dani's arms trembled with fatigue or strain. "I've got it." She forced the words out through gritted teeth.

"You don't." Lynn knelt down, reached beneath the debris, and checked for sharp edges. She found something squishy that wiggled instead. Shuddering, she brushed it off and took a hold. "On three." *This is going to hurt.* She braced herself. "One...two...three!"

Dani pushed.

Lynn set her jaw and put tension on her arms. Pain seared through her injured forearm like lightning, and she had to lessen her grip or risk dropping the whole thing.

Even with the force of three and a half arms, they managed.

Skeever bounced around them excitedly as the slab crashed onto the thick branches and against the wall. It slid to the side; a piece broke off, and it threatened to topple. Then it settled.

A victorious thrill coursed through Lynn. She cradled her arm against her chest and flexed her fingers to ease the pins and needles. "That should do it."

Dani put her hands on her hips and sucked in air. "I've got this." She shot Lynn a glare, then began to stuff the gaping holes of the two front windows with more leafy branches.

Lynn rolled her eyes. *Whatever.* "Skeever, come." She snapped her fingers.

Skeever shot up the slope.

Lynn followed him a lot slower, trying not to use her throbbing arm. *Serves you right for trying to help. Let the stuck-up bitch figure things out herself if that's what she wants.*

Even in the few minutes she'd been away, the fire had died down to small, flickering flames looking for sustenance to fuel their young life.

Still scowling, Lynn fed them scat and twigs and poked the fire up again.

Skeever dropped down by her legs and exhaled audibly.

Eventually the grunting and mumbled swearing and the rustling of drying leaves below her stopped.

Lynn was hungry. They'd walked far today; she'd fought with wolves and Dani, and perhaps more importantly, she was back in the Wilds. All had taken their toll. They'd eaten jerky and bread with sour goat cheese while walking, but that was long gone.

As if roused by her thoughts, her stomach growled. *Soon.* The fire was scarcely hot enough to heat anything up now, but it would do with patience.

Lynn bit back a smirk. *Patience was never your strong suit, Tanner.*

Skeever lifted his head and stared out into the deepening darkness.

Lynn followed his gaze even as her hand settled on the handle of the tomahawk she'd laid next to her.

Dani came up and dropped down heavily by the fire without sparing Lynn a glance. She frowned and leaned to the side as she reached under her butt and pulled a piece of warped metal out of the rubble. Dani tossed it across the plain of their hideout.

It clanged onto the debris somewhere in the darkness.

Skeever shot after it, almost catching fire as he sailed past its flames, yapping eagerly.

Lynn let go of her weapon and straightened.

More carefully, Dani straightened as well, then stuck out her legs along the fire.

Here was an opportunity for small talk, Lynn realized. She stubbornly refused to take it. "You have the food."

Dani glared at her but got up with a groan. She pulled her pack away from the wall and into the circle of light cast by the now healthy fire.

Skeever returned and offered the bent iron bar to Dani, tail wagging.

Dani grunted. "Not now, Skeever. Go." She pushed against his flank. "Go!"

Skeever turned a circle and looked expectantly up at Lynn.

Lynn grinned. "How about food instead, hm?" She drew her aching legs under her and untied a stiffening rat from her backpack: Skeever's second catch of the day. She held it up.

Skeever promptly dropped the bar from his mouth, then trotted along.

She took him to a spot just outside the circle of light, not wanting to watch him demolish his meal while she ate. "Down."

Skeever hesitated. He whined, then turned on the spot she had indicated and sagged down.

She laid the rat between his legs and watched him as he tore into it.

His tail drummed excitedly on the rubble.

Tiny bones cracked under the force of his jaws.

Lynn shuddered, not so much at the sound but at the realization that the wolf could have done that to her arm with ease. She rubbed the appendage in question.

By the time she returned to the fire, the sight of a jar awaited her. She recognized yesterday's elephant stew, and her mouth watered.

Dani had settled her shoulders against her pack. Her eyes were closed. The firelight flickered across her features. Her wrestling contest with the branches and rubble had left her face and neck smeared with dirt.

Lynn squatted next to her pack and took out a spoon and a bowl before rummaging around for two old cans. They were dented and blackened but held water—and elephant stew—just fine.

Dani's head shot up, and her eyes blinked open sleepily. They settled on Lynn for a moment, then drooped again.

Amateur. Lynn shook her head with a smirk. She opened the jar and filled both cans to the halfway point for the first round of dinner. After securing the lid, she kneeled by the fire, pushed the sticks aside to expose some of the red glowing embers, and dug both cans in.

Weariness had claimed Dani again. Her head bobbed. She'd crossed her arms in front of her chest, but one arm was threatening to slip from the tangle.

As much as Lynn scoffed at Dani's surrender to exhaustion, there was also something enviable about it; Dani apparently lacked the terrifying experiences that even a few minutes of inattentiveness could cause out here—like the way the wolves had been upon them in seconds today—that would have her fight her exhaustion no matter what.

The same exhaustion Dani felt, Lynn felt too. Perhaps more so because she hadn't even come close to recovery during her night locked up in the Homestead's disused closet. Yet Lynn couldn't imagine napping like this around Dani and most certainly not without having her weapons within reach.

Dani's spear lay above her head. Her knife hung on her belt but was secured by a strap. If something barged in now—or if Lynn attacked her—it would take Dani precious seconds to free her knife. Seconds were all it took out here.

Lynn stirred the stew and tasted it. The potato was still stone cold. She sighed and shifted. It upset some of the leaves under her feet.

Dani shot awake again and sat up, looking around and then at Lynn. Her eyes narrowed as if Lynn was somehow the cause of her drowsiness.

With a snort, Lynn returned her attention to the cans. She stirred again and made sure to scrape the bottom. "Almost done."

Silence. Dani shifted until she sat close by the fire, cross-legged, and rubbed her eyes and cheeks with the flat of her hands, spreading even more dirt on them.

I should get away tonight, when she sleeps. They were far enough away from the Homestead, and Dani was too tired to follow her into the dark. The thought should have brought her elation, but it caused a heavy weariness instead. Lynn was exhausted too. Traveling in the dark was a terrifying prospect even when she didn't ache all over. Unable to reach an instant decision, Lynn's thoughts dissolved when Dani moved.

Dani opened her pack and pulled out her own spoon and wooden bowl.

Lynn tried the stew again. It was hot enough. She pulled the sleeve of her sweater from under her jacket and covered her fingers with it before gripping the edge of one of the cans. Heat seeped through the wool instantly so she hurried to lean over the embers and put the container down in the rubble by Dani's legs.

"Thanks." Even Dani's voice was weary with sleep.

Lynn hummed and liberated the second portion from the fire.

Dani employed the same trick Lynn had used to draw the hot can farther along the ground before she tipped its contents into the bowl and scraped out the tin.

They ate without speaking, but it wasn't quiet. Skeever hadn't quite finished his meal—he liked to play with it, Lynn had discovered—and the sound of snapping bones and scraping nails rose up from the corner. The wind rustled the leaves of the trees all around them. Owls hooted. The fire popped and crackled. In the distance something howled.

Lynn shivered. She scooted forward a bit to chase away the sudden chill that seeped into her bones. She scraped her spoon along the bottom of her bowl and finished off her first portion, then her second after it finished cooking.

Dani had finished too. She stared into the fire with half-lidded eyes. Fatigue radiated off her.

The silence between them stretched to the point where it got uncomfortable to Lynn. Despite herself, she put her bowl down loudly. The spoon rattled against the edge.

Dani's head shot up, and her now-alert gaze settled upon Lynn.

"How are your feet?"

Dani squinted. "Why do you ask?"

"I think you should take your boots off. If you have blisters, they could get infected if you don't air 'em." She nodded toward the leather-and-rubber contraptions around Dani's feet.

Dani looked down too. She hesitated, then untangled her legs and went to work untying the leather strings. Her jaw set as if to steady herself before she pulled her boots off. She put them by the fire with a slightly trembling hand.

Even from here, Lynn could see blisters along the edges of her little and big toes. She'd guessed correctly: Dani wasn't used to walking this long. The chapel had been an outpost for the Homesteaders—and it was almost within spitting distance of the Homestead. It had been a long time since Lynn had suffered from sore feet, but she could imagine the discomfort.

Dani produced Ren's medicine from her pack and spot-treated each blister in turn. She muffled a groan that mixed pain and relief as she applied the ointment.

Skeever entered the circle of light while busily licking his muzzle. He brushed against Lynn's back before he lay down with his head on her lap.

She tore her gaze away from Dani and smiled at him. "Hey, boy, good food?"

He sighed and licked his lips again.

Lynn stroked Skeever's head. *I haven't sat by a campfire with other people since that couple near Plattsburgh.* How long ago had that been? Two months? Of course she'd sat by the Homestead fire with the others yesterday, but that was different. Settlement fires weren't like campfires made on the fly, kept small so as not to attract anything or anyone. Settlement fires never went out. They became beacons of homeliness: three meals a day, heat at night, all produced on flames easily brought back to life from dulled but still lively embers. They were kept differently, smelled differently, served a different purpose. The contrast had never been as stark as now, with the ambivalent memories of the Homestead still so fresh.

"Here." Dani extended the jar. "For your arm."

"Thanks." Lynn took it. She considered packing it away, but since she would use it on her arm later, she decided to put it by her tomahawk instead.

Dani stretched her legs out and wiggled her now-glistening toes.

"Better?" It fell from Lynn's lips before she could stop it.

Dani's toes stopped moving. She nodded slowly. "Yeah." A pause. "Thanks."

"Welcome. How much longer until we can turn north?"

Dani hesitated. "Somewhere in the afternoon, I think."

"Afternoon?" She frowned. "It took me, like, two hours to get from the interstate to where you guys hunted the elephant." It was a vague estimate; connecting passing time with distance was not her strong suit.

"Yeah, but I don't know that route." Dani ran her finger along the inside of her bowl. She sucked the digit clean with an air of nonchalance that was incongruent with the tension in her shoulders and the way she avoided Lynn's gaze.

Lynn squinted at her. Was there something going on? Something she needed to worry about? She could see no possible advantage for Dani if she deliberately lengthened their journey—unless she planned to lead Lynn into a trap. Then a thought struck her. "Do you even know where we are?"

Dani tensed even more, then shrugged. "Sort of."

"Sort of?" She didn't hold back the sharpness in her tone.

Dani glared at her. "Hey, don't even start! We don't come out this far! Flint told me the routes out of New York that he knows are still intact—or at least which were intact a few years ago—and I'm just…working with that."

Lynn rolled her eyes emphatically. "So, basically you have no idea where we are or where we're going."

"Well…" Dani plucked at her pant leg. "I just need to find the bridge."

Lynn fought her impatience. "Which bridge?"

The shadows the fire cast made it hard to read Dani's expression as she looked up. "Um, a bridge with two pointy towers that leads to Bronx." She hesitated. "We should have made it across today. According to Flint, it was maybe an hour away from the cemetery, along the big 278 street."

An hour? They'd walked at least half a day since the cemetery. Anger bubbled as hotly as the stew had in the cans. "So you're basically saying we walked half a day in the wrong direction and you have no idea where we are?"

Dani's silence spoke volumes.

Lynn's mind raced. She'd counted on Dani to take her out of the city or at least toward the edge of it. Once she ditched Dani, she had planned on heading straight on, leaving New York behind, and never looking back. Now *straight on* might lead her deeper into the city. If that happened, it could take days, even weeks to get free from New York's clutches. "Shit!"

"We can backtrack tomorrow." Dani's tone had lost its bravado. "Follow the road back to the cemetery and then past it. I'm sure we're on the right road. We just…went the wrong way."

Lynn sighed. *Shake it off. It happened. Move on. Nothing can be done about it now.* "Yeah, I guess we don't have a choice."

Dani swallowed. "I'm sorry."

Lynn snorted. "I bet. Next time you don't know what the fuck you're doing, tell me, okay?"

Instead of rising to the bait as Lynn had expected, Dani met her gaze and nodded. She appeared to be on the verge of tears. "I will."

CHAPTER 7

Lynn cursed herself for not paying better attention yesterday; they'd gone almost straight south instead of west. The position of the sun as it rose to the left was a glaringly obvious sign that Dani hadn't had a clue where they were going. She should have noticed, but the pain in her arm had increased to the point of distraction—which had caused her to focus more on her immediate surroundings instead of something as far away as the sun. That was her excuse, anyway. Now she trudged back along the remnants of the same broad street they had taken yesterday.

Dani walked parallel to her whenever the rugged terrain allowed, keeping a steady five feet between them. The night hadn't done her a kindness. In the pale light of morning her expression was truly blank, not just shielded like before.

Lynn suspected that the reality of her situation had sunk in. Unlike Lynn, who had settled into her well-practiced habit of dozing without ever falling fully asleep, Dani had drifted into sleep only to awake with a start whenever something scurried, howled, or otherwise made noise nearby. In the darkest hours before daybreak, she'd curled up into a ball and sobbed noiselessly until she'd drifted off into fitful sleep once more.

The blankness of Dani's mood worried Lynn a little, but her thoughts were occupied with a much more pressing issue: she couldn't tell if her arm hurt worse or less today. It felt different: tight and stinging. She'd cleaned the bite marks yesterday evening and again this morning. At least a few of the wounds needed stitches; they'd begun to bleed again at the lightest of touches, and the wool she'd tied over it with leather strips had greedily sucked up its share.

Too bad she didn't have anything on her to stitch them with.

Her wounds would heal, Lynn knew from experience, but as long as they remained open, the risk of infection was severe. It would also take a long, messy time without stitches. For now, she'd slathered the whole area with the thyme ointment Ren had given her, and she'd bandaged it all up as tightly as she could stand. She'd have to figure out something to stitch it with. Eventually.

Lynn took in the overgrown rubble, the slightly swaying trees, the scurrying hares and rabbits.

Skeever saw them too. He zigzagged ahead of them and sniffed constantly. His tail was raised and flitted from side to side.

Speaking of other missing items and future plans... "We should try to find a map." She molded her voice to a tone of airy neutrality.

Dani regarded her suspiciously. "A map?"

Lynn glanced at her but then quickly diverted her gaze. "Yeah." She cleared her throat. "So this doesn't happen again." She motioned in a wide arc to encompass not only the perceived path, but also the entire experience of having to make their way over the crater-pocked, partially buried, car-strewn mess of a road again. *And not at all so I can better plan my escape.*

"I...guess."

"Easier said than done, though." Lynn chuckled and hoped it didn't come across forced. "A gas station, maybe? If it's intact, paper might have survived."

Dani was silent for a few seconds. "Okay, but only if we see one beside the road or something. We don't want more delays."

Lynn nodded. Triumph blazed in her chest, and she struggled to quench it so she wouldn't give herself away. "Absolutely." A map would allow her to plan her escape route—and Dani knew it too. Lynn was sure of that. Dani was anything but stupid. She glanced aside.

Dani seemed even gloomier.

What was she thinking about? Was she hatching her own plans to get Lynn to stay? Had she been surprised Lynn had still been there come dawn? What she wouldn't give for the opportunity to sift through Dani's thoughts even once. For now, she would have to take Dani's compliance at face value and fake innocence as much as possible. She had to focus on finding a very specific needle in a thoroughly destroyed haystack. Lynn sighed and let her gaze glide over the pulverized city block.

Dani passed the cemetery without looking at it once. She drew up her shoulders, gripped her spear more tightly, and quickened her pace. The effect was marred by a small limp that had developed because of her blisters, which seemed to be worse on her right foot.

Lynn inspected her as she went on ahead, then turned her head toward the cemetery out of a perverse urge to drive home the fact that she could have been a day farther along. She couldn't see the chapel from this angle—and through the growth that had overtaken the cemetery and buildings beyond—but she knew it had to be there.

Barely a hundred feet after the crumpled overhead road they'd been tracking turned west, they passed one of the many defensive barriers the Old Worlders had constructed before society's complete collapse. It was a haphazard affair of upturned cars, barbed wire, tanks, and turrets. Every rusty firing nozzle pointed at the sky in eternal vigilance for a threat that would never come again.

The wide-open swing gates revealed a strip of leveled buildings, but then houses and shops rose up as pristine as possible after centuries of exposure to Mother Nature's insatiable desire to reclaim what humanity had taken from her. Among them stood—as if planted there by grace herself—an overgrown gas station. Its telltale pumps had survived, somewhat protected by a faded canopy, which had once been multi-colored.

Lynn's heart stumbled. "Dani." She inclined her head. "Over there."

Dani frowned as she surveyed the general area Lynn's nod had indicated. Then her eyes widened. "Unbelievable."

Lynn grinned. "Come on. Let's have a look."

Skeever swerved to catch up with a few seconds' delay.

Lynn pressed her face to the glass and held her hand over her eyes to shield them as she peered inside.

Intact. All of it. The shelving units were empty except for a toppled can or two. Everything was caked with the dust of ages.

Dani reached past her to check the door handle. "Locked."

"Step back." Lynn bashed the glass in with her tomahawk. It splintered into thick cubes that tumbled over the floor on both sides of the door. Like a flock of cooped-up pigeons, stale air that smelled vaguely of rot rushed past.

Skeever whined.

The corner of Dani's mouth curled downward into a grimace. "Gross."

"Uh-huh." Lynn settled her gaze on Skeever. "You stay out here. Stay."

Skeever tilted his head. Big eyes examined her. He planted his butt.

Dani entered the gas station.

Lynn followed Dani in and zeroed in on her back. What if Dani found a map and destroyed it?

Dani leisurely strolled past the shelves in the left aisle. She didn't look like a woman hell-bent on getting rid of vital evidence.

Lynn exhaled slowly and diverted her gaze to take in the rest of the shop. Glass crunched underfoot. The scent of death seemed to have seeped into the walls and was ever-present. She went around the shop counterclockwise, and kept her eyes open for a map as well as anything else of use. There wasn't much to salvage here; whatever had been left behind had spoiled and dehydrated in their containers, leaving them caked and mangled. Magazines lay scattered and curled across the floor. When she stepped on them, they flaked like autumn leaves. Lynn scoured the newspaper stands for a map.

"Oh no." Dani stood in the doorframe to the back room.

Lynn's chest constricted. "What?" She hurried over.

Dani stepped back to let her pass. She'd gone a little pale.

They lay side by side on a blanket that had once been red. It had soaked up the waste of decomposition as best it could before the blackened slosh had spread across the tiles. *Well, that explains the smell.* Dani seemed to find the sight off-putting, but Lynn looked beyond them and zeroed in on a desk against the opposite wall, a sturdy gray metal thing with drawers. Her mouth went dry. "Come on." She hooked her fingers around Dani's upper arm and turned her around. "Let's find a map."

Dani shook herself out and focused on the shop instead. "I don't think there are any here."

Lynn scrutinized the floor plan. Had she missed an aisle? Any of the racks?

"Maybe we should just go? Flint said to cross the bridges and then take the exit east. We could figure out how to go from there from the signs." Dani walked over to the counter and lifted up a magazine, which crumpled under her touch. She wiped the flakes from her hand.

Lynn glanced into the back room again. "I'm going to have a look in there, then I'll be right out."

Dani's fingers twitched. "Do you need help?" Her voice was light. Deceptively light, perhaps.

"Nah." *Casual, casual.* "Go another round through the shop, see if you can find anything useful. I'll be right back."

Dani hesitated, then nodded. "Okay." Whatever swirled in the depth of her eyes was undefinable to Lynn.

Thankfully, the desk drawers weren't locked. She took a deep breath and started pulling them out. The top drawer was full of small items such as pens and paperclips. Her five-year-old self would have loved to stumble upon this hoard of treasures. Anything Old World had mesmerized her. Now she pulled the entire drawer out and scattered its contents over the desk for easier access. *I'm so fucking jaded.* The thought brought on a wry smile, but no feelings of guilt or sadness.

The second drawer was disappointingly empty, a single key and a plastic box with small, weird-looking lightbulbs its only contents. She closed the drawer and pulled out another.

It was filled with papers, and her heart rate spiked. She steadied the container on her thigh and slipped it from its rail. Instead of tipping it over, she balanced it on the precarious pile of office supplies from drawer number one and took the contents out one at a time. Her hands trembled a little. She shook them to get them to steady and winced at the stab of pain that coursed up her arm. "Dammit. Idiot." She rolled her eyes, then focused back on the trove.

Even paper kept in a dark drawer, in a protected space, suffered decay. It wasn't as abused as the magazines in the shop, but some of the flimsier scraps crumbled under her careful touch. The ink had faded on most of the papers. She scanned barely legible receipts, folders with pages full of numbers, and a magazine with images of naked women that she flipped through without much hope for a map. Then, almost at the bottom, she found a colorful booklet. It took some time for her to sound out the bold, white letters on a faded, blue field and to form them into words that spelled: *The Ultimate New York City Bike Guide.*

Lynn licked her lips with a tongue that had suddenly gone dry. She lifted the thin book out and cracked it open. The pages held a lot of very small text, intercut with pictures of happy people with helmets on, rushing down roads with backdrops of bridges, pristine architecture, and well-kept parks. She didn't bother with the words but found herself holding her breath as she studied the pictures for details on the verge of fading forever. Was this what it was like? This...ideal? Perfect families in a perfect world? Something seemed to settle on her chest, making it almost impossible to breathe. For the first time in her life, she felt truly jealous of the Old Worlders.

"Lynn?" Dani hadn't snuck up on her this time; she'd spoken softly from the doorway.

Lynn turned. "Hey."

"Did you find anything?"

Lynn hesitated, but the evidence was in her hands, in plain view. "Maybe."

Careful not to disturb the bones, Dani came over. Despite what she might think about the possibility of a map, she soaked up the pictures as well.

Her closeness made Lynn's skin crawl, but she resisted the urge to create distance.

Pressed against Lynn's side, Dani slid her gaze over the pages as Lynn flipped them oh-so-carefully. She didn't comment.

There were only fourteen pages, and their numbers dwindled down fast. Lynn started out only interested in locating a map, but every page sucked her in more. The pictures were mesmerizing. Clean, happy people, doing things just because they could. All the cars were shiny and new. When Lynn could make out the facial details of the drivers, they were always smiling—waving sometimes. The office fell away as she thumbed through the aged booklet.

She had almost forgotten about the quest for a map when she turned the page and it was suddenly there. It had been printed on pages ten and eleven, with whitish shapes for land, blue strokes for water. Very little of it was labeled. It was a deadly simple map. Hudson River marked the left edge, and something called *Eastchester Bay* capped the top. Six colored lines ran across a section of the white shape labeled *Manhattan*. The map would have been useless were it not for the lines marked with little red and blue shields Lynn knew from her journey over many of America's interstates: the map provided an overview of the major roads. More importantly, dead in the center was the road marked *278*, and it led over water, then curved up north—exactly as Flint had told Dani. She swallowed down her nerves. "There." She pointed. "We're somewhere there."

Dani frowned. "You might be right."

"I am. Look." She traced the road down south, making sure not to touch the fragile paper. "That's the fork. I must have come into New York over this bridge." She pointed at a stretch of white over the field of blue marked *Whitestone Bridge*. "And we went through this part called Queens to get here."

Dani nodded. "So where do we go, exactly?"

Lynn gestured vaguely above the map. "Somewhere there. It's not on the map, I think. It took two days to get to the bridge, and we walked from here..." She pointed out their starting point east of Queens. "...to here..." She circled an area to indicate their former camp. "In a day."

"Okay, makes sense. So, which road did you come down on?"

Lynn glanced at Dani and hesitated. Could it harm her to tell Dani? She couldn't think of a reason—she wasn't going that way again; telling Dani might even show some sort of trust, and yet... "The 95." It stung like an alcohol-soaked wound.

Dani leaned forward a bit more and found the road. "It's in Bronx. That seems to match with what Flint told me."

"Yeah." It snaked up past the Eastchester Bay before disappearing off the map. "If we go up to the 278, it'll take us to the 95." She followed the line that said 278 with her finger, drifting to the west for a couple of miles before swinging northeast. Even as she did that, she was already searching the map for something else entirely: her escape route. Her best way out was the 95 in the opposite direction to where Dani thought they were going. The road came down from the north and then curved west to a crossing over Hudson River called *George Washington Bridge* before eventually turning south.

If she took the 87 exit west, right after an unmarked bridge, instead of following the 278 as Dani thought they would, it would take her to the 95. Even if she missed that exit for some reason or couldn't manage to shake Dani, there would be three others along their route that would take her to the same point.

"We really went the long way 'round." Dani straightened and sighed.

"Yep." Lynn still studied the map. She needed to imprint it, just in case Dani took it away or it fell apart completely. "So let's get going, hm? We should be able to get here tonight." The hairs on her arms stood on end as she tempted fate by pointing at a spot just before the split toward the 89, the exit she was going to take.

"Yeah, let's." Dani swallowed and searched her face.

Lynn casually closed the booklet, knelt down, and very carefully stored it in her bag. A tingle of excitement buzzed through her as she closed her backpack and hoisted it onto her shoulders. She felt as if she was getting away with something. For a horrible moment, she thought she would giggle, but of course she didn't. "Okay, ready." As she stepped outside, reality settled heavily upon her again. Yes, she had a plan now, but she would still have to execute it.

New York's defenses had achieved what they'd set out to do before they'd fallen: the road up to the bridge had survived. It curved northward and gained elevation until it was level with the crossing. Two gleaming towers peeked over the water, which was a hopeful sign the bridge itself had survived too.

The increasing elevation pushed them above the treetops. A firm wind whipped Lynn's hair about. It carried scents of an ocean she couldn't see and the ever-present smell of soil and decomposition. She brushed her hair aside so she could soak in the view. On the right was an almost unbroken field of leaves, but on the left a clump of buildings pierced the uniformity—vestiges of concrete and glass, which almost all bore the burden of ever-climbing ivy.

"Why do you think they built the roads like this? Like...high up?"

Lynn swung her gaze away from the wide-open view with regret. Seeing so much clear sky above her made her feel as if she could breathe again. "I don't know. Maybe it was easier, or they needed the room below. I guess you could walk and drive there, too. I'm sure it'll go down eventually."

Dani kept looking at the left-hand side view. She hesitated. "It's weird, isn't it? A few hundred years ago, there were hundreds of people living right here—maybe thousands."

Lynn shrugged. "More than that, I think. If every house had at least one person living in it, that's…what? A million or something?" It was a word that had very little meaning, especially in terms of people. *Are there even a million people left on the planet? There must be, right?*

Dani stepped up to the railing and gripped the wire mesh with one hand.

It groaned and creaked under the sudden force.

Instinctively, Lynn checked her surroundings for anything drawn to the sound even as the wind dispersed it.

"I can't even imagine a million people." Dani's voice barely carried to her ears. "Were they in these cars when the bombs fell?" She didn't turn her head to look at the metal constructs that lay strewn about like the husks of giant beetles. "Trying to get out of the city?"

It was an obviously rhetoric question; Lynn didn't know what had happened here any more than Dani did. Maybe they had left their cars and had walked home to be with their families. Maybe they'd thrown themselves over the edge of the bridge. She shuddered at the thought and turned so abruptly she startled Skeever.

He jumped back, whimpered, and stepped in place nervously until she reached out to pet him.

"We should go, Dani."

Dani frowned at her.

Lynn could see the questions swimming in her eyes, but what was the use of talking about the Old World? "We don't have much daylight left." Lynn didn't have to look back to know Dani's gaze was on her as she walked off. After years of hyperawareness in the Wilds, she knew when she was being watched.

The bridge was massive and far more of a death trap than the ramp leading up to it had suggested. It hadn't survived either the war or the ravages of time entirely intact; large chunks had fallen into the swiftly churning water below. Lynn had to lead them around the gaps and over piles of rubble. Her aching arm had taken a hit, and Dani's complexion had gone paler and paler. Lynn took her time for safety's sake.

By the time they reached the other side, the sun had noticeably changed position.

Lynn looked up at it and made an educated guess about the speed of its descent. "We still have some daylight left." She glanced at Dani. "Wanna try to make a push to get off this island thingy we're on?" It was going to be tight; the road seemed to stretch out like a snake through grass and the head was nowhere to be seen. If they made it, though—or at least came close—they would be in spitting distance of the 89 exit Lynn had her eye on. If she dared to make a run for it during the night, she would be home free.

"I don't know."

A few paces ahead, Skeever came to a halt and looked back. He panted, and his tongue hung out of his mouth. The crawl across the bridge seemed to have tempered his boundless enthusiasm.

Lynn turned her head to Dani. "Why not?"

Dani shrugged. "I just don't want to risk camping out on the side of the road if we can't find somewhere secure." She didn't meet Lynn's eyes.

"That's quite a different tune than yesterday's." An icy hand wrapped around Lynn's spine where it met her skull. Was Dani on to her plan? "What's going on?"

Dani set her jaw and looked away.

"Earth to Dani. Tick-tock." Lynn's insides knotted.

"My feet hurt, okay?" A little smile tugged at her lips. "I just don't want to walk anymore."

The hold on her neck lifted. Lynn laughed, as much out of amusement as relief. The tension in her gut lessened. "Well, we could rest for a few minutes, but I think your feet will only hurt worse when you start walking again."

"I know." Dani sighed. "I'm going to sit down long enough to get some food out, and then we'll go on, all right?"

A few minutes can't hurt. Besides, they were relatively safe here: they had a somewhat clear view over the treetops, and nothing bigger than rabbits moved along the road that wound away from the bridge. "Sure. I could eat."

Dani sighed when she sank down to the asphalt. "Ohhh, that's good."

Skeever beelined back and went straight for Dani's face, lapping over her cheek before she could open her eyes.

"Skeever, no!" Dani groaned, but her voice held a little laugh. She pushed at the dog. "I was having a moment here!"

Skeever panted even harder and went around her to get close on the other side.

Dani fought him off with a chuckle.

Lynn tested the sturdiness of the railing before she leaned against it. She watched the two and found herself smiling. "Tell you what: if we make it off the island before nightfall, we'll find a way down to the water so you can soak your feet."

"Are you dangling a carrot?" Dani squinted up at her, eyes lit. She managed to get Skeever to settle across her lap.

Lynn grinned. "Maybe."

Dani laughed, then twisted to drag her backpack up to Skeever's hind legs. "Well, it's working." She pulled out a bag and handed Lynn a chunk of bread from it before unwrapping the two-thirds of a small cheese wheel that had remained after yesterday's lunch. She cut off another third, divided it, and gave Lynn her half. All the while she had to twist and turn to keep the food away from Skeever's muzzle and wagging tail.

Lynn pulled the bread apart and smushed the cheese between the halves. She hummed at the sour taste as it hit her taste buds.

"It's actually a nice day." Dani looked up at the clear blue sky. The muscles of her jaw flexed as she chewed.

Lynn took another bite and contemplated her surroundings. She supposed it was true; everything man-made was decaying, but nature blossomed. The area was green and lush, with flecks of color breaking up the singular palette. The relentless barrage of sun, wind, and rain had reduced most of the cars here to a state of collapse, making them less present somehow. Birds and monkeys sang and yowled in chorus. Lynn could see how—if the world had been a little less deadly—it might be enjoyable. That was a dangerous thought. Letting down your guard was a surefire way to get killed. "We should go before your feet give out entirely."

Dani sighed. "Yeah, you're right." She held her bread with her teeth and pushed Skeever off her.

He got up reluctantly and went straight for her lunch.

Lynn took pity. She pushed away from the railing and grabbed the dog's collar. "Come here, you."

He struggled against the hold but stayed in place after another firm yank.

Dani sent her a look of gratitude and hurried to stand up. A flash of agony scrunched up her face, and she groaned around her lunch. After she closed her backpack, she shook out her feet one at a time. She took a bite, chewed, and swallowed. "This," she said, "is torture."

Lynn couldn't help grinning. "I thought you were supposed to be the big, bad hunter? You must be used to walking."

"Not for days on end!" Dani hoisted her backpack onto her shoulders. "Besides, most of what I do is either short tracks from trap to trap or lots and lots of lying in wait with a short dash at the end. I can stand for hours, sit on my haunches for ages, but walking? Not my thing."

Lynn let Skeever go and watched him bounce around a few times before circling them and racing off. She gave Dani's shoulder a teasing pat. "Well, you'll either get used to it really fast or be in agony for the rest of the trip, won't you?"

Dani slumped a little. "Don't remind me."

For the first time, Lynn found herself sympathizing with Dani's plight a little.

"I think we should have taken the other lane after all." Dani leaned against the fence over the divider to peer at the other side of the road.

Lynn climbed one of the abandoned cars and looked out over the mess ahead. Why was this road system so bloody massive? Had the Old Worlders navigated this tangle of supersized roads with ease, or had they been as confused as Lynn was by all the overhead signs, exits, and rows upon rows of lanes? "I don't know. I think our exit is still up ahead. The last sign said Manhattan to the right, didn't it? And that's not the one we want. I think that if we head on, we should be directed off this interstate and onto the right one eventually."

Dani looked back at her with a frown. "Maybe."

Lynn put her hands on her hips and sighed. She scanned the horizon. It was a mess of green and roads, a convergence point for a number of lanes as they swirled from the streets below onto the height of the overpass. "The map said we were on an island, so we have to go over another bridge to get off. I don't think we have yet. If we go straight on, we'll cross the water and we'll come to another split. There we make sure we go on along the 278." *Well, that's your plan anyway.*

Dani climbed the stone divider and gripped the fence with her fingers. She brought her hand up to shield her eyes from the rapidly fading sunlight and peered out over the road as if searching for a divine sign.

Skeever crawled into a car, out of sight.

Lynn kept her balance on the car's roof while she turned to look back at the weird little houses with the boom barriers that they had just passed. Signs above had read *cash* and *E-ZPass*. Neither had meant anything to her.

"Okay, I guess you're right." Dani jumped down and hissed. She shook out her feet again.

Lynn climbed down carefully to spare her arm. *Fine pair we make.* She bit back a snort. "So onward?"

"Onward." Dani squinted. "Skeever?"

"He's in there." Lynn nodded at the skeletal vehicle that was distinguishable from the rest only by the fact that its roof hadn't rusted away completely.

"What's he doing in there?"

Lynn heard the high-pitched squealing long before she glimpsed inside. "Lunch."

"Lunch of—oh!" Dani swiveled away. She swallowed, presumably to keep her own down.

Skeever pulled a wormy little creature, a baby rat, from the tattered remains of the backseat cushioning. He threw his head back, crushed the small meal, and swallowed. His tail pounded the back of the passenger seat.

Lynn grinned at Dani. "How can you be a hunter and yet be so damn squeamish?"

"There is a big—" She paused and swallowed. The hand not around her spear lay on her abdomen. "Big difference between butchering an animal and then roasting it over a nice fire or eating live mice."

"Rats."

"What?"

"Those are rats. The tail." She held her thumb and index finger a few inches apart. "Rat."

Dani squinted. "Is that really what matters here?"

"Probably not." Lynn grinned. "But I can't help being just a little bit amused."

"Whatever." Dani scrunched up her features when a high-pitched cry sounded, then cut off abruptly.

Lynn leaned against the car's frame as she waited for Skeever to finish his meal. "Be happy he catches most of his own food." She was; if he didn't, she wouldn't be able to keep him.

Dani didn't reply. She walked over to the railing and looked down.

Lynn listened to the birds, enjoyed the sun, and made sure they were still alone. Respite, but she was also getting anxious. She really wanted to make it over the bridge today. "Skeeve, come on." She pushed away from the car and snapped her fingers at knee-height. "You're done."

Skeever tilted his head up. His reddened tongue lolled. His enthusiasm seemed to have returned as his stomach had filled.

"Coming?" Lynn had already walked off.

Dani fell in line with a glare at Skeever.

Skeever licked his lips and trotted off, head in the wind.

Lynn stared out ahead. They must be getting close to the bridge leading off this island now. When they did, how was she going to find her route out of New York? Would it be listed on any signs? The sun sank lower as she studied every sign, either on the side of the road or overhead. The anxiety returned in the form of sweaty hands and a swelling heartbeat that worsened the painful pulsing in her arm. What if it wasn't listed?

The next overhead sign said something about bridges that meant nothing to Lynn, but the one after that said to take the next right for the 278 East. Far more important was the red and blue shield above the sign next to it, which read: *87 North.* Her exit.

Lynn expressly focused on the road that led east. "That's the one, right?"

Dani glanced up at the signs. "278 to *Bruckner expwy* and *New England?"*

"The 278 part is correct, according to the map. I have no idea what the other things are. They aren't on the map, I think. Want me to check?" Lynn moved to slide her backpack off.

Dani shook her head. "No, we don't have a choice anyway. East is where we want to go. The 278 is the road we were looking for, not the 87. So let's take the exit and find somewhere to sleep tonight." She peered up at the rapidly sinking sun. "I don't think I'll get to soak my feet."

Lynn nodded. "'Fraid not." She stole a glance at the *87* sign one more time before she followed Dani over the bridge and toward the first exit.

The lock clicked under Lynn's gentle prodding. A flash of pride surged in her chest. *If only I'd had these when they locked me up in that damn closet.* She would have been out of New York by now. "There we go." Almost every building on this street had been secured with a roll-up garage door and a small roll-up next to it with, presumably, a regular door behind it. This door was the only one without a security grate and had thus become the target of her lock-picking skills. She stowed her tools and picked up her tomahawk. While crouched to the side of the door, she pushed the metal door open.

It creaked horribly.

Dani jumped. She clutched her spear and whipped her head about to look down both sides of the street.

Lynn stood and peered inside. She inhaled deeply. *Dust. Mold.* It didn't smell of animals or death.

Skeever almost knocked her over in his hurry to explore the inside of the garage.

The only bit of light from a source other than the door opening came from small holes in the metal grate right next to it. The garage was small and still held a big, red car that filled up almost the entire space.

Skeever didn't growl nor bark. She could hear him sniffing in the echoing brick box.

"Let's go in." A quick inspection revealed Skeever's nose had been right: the space was deserted. Lynn slid off her pack and groaned when her shoulders came to life with an explosion of pinpricks.

Dani closed the door behind her quickly, minimizing the duration of the noise, then pushed the room's sole chair under the handle to bar it.

Lynn tried to open the driver's side door. It gave. When she pulled the handle, the rubber seals around the edges of the door panel extended for the last time, then crumbled into dust. She threw her hair back and bent down to peer inside. The upholstering was fairly intact. No signs of snakes, poisonous spiders, deadly traps, or anything else that might cause harm. Nothing scurried away, and if there were ratholes, they weren't apparent.

She slid in gingerly and laid her tomahawk on her lap so she had her hands free to run along the leather-covered steering wheel. Dust came away in flakes and tickled her nose unpleasantly. She grinned in spite of it.

When Dani pulled the passenger side door open, the sound of the rubber seals coming unstuck echoed through the garage.

Skeever scratched at the concrete floor in a corner.

The pedals under Lynn's feet moved to various degrees, which heightened both the experience and her sense of glee. She'd never seen a car this intact and could almost imagine how it would be to drive it.

Dani slid in and stilled.

"Have you e—?" The words died on Lynn's lips as the last of the daylight caught on something metallic in Dani's lap.

Dani's fingers tightened around the handle of her long butchers' knife.

Amusement turned acidic in Lynn's gut. Her hand twitched as a prelude to lifting from the wheel.

"Don't." Dani's tone was short. She turned her head to look at her and tilted the tip of the knife in Lynn's direction with a minute motion of her wrist. The rest of her body was tense. "Don't take your hands away."

Lynn swallowed and tightened her hold on the steering wheel instead. Dani was a hunter and had a hunter's reflexes. There was no way Lynn could grab, angle, lift, and bring down her tomahawk before Dani ran her through. *Options!* She could throw herself out of the car and hope Dani didn't get her first—hope the tomahawk wouldn't skitter away into the solidifying darkness and leave her defenseless while she grabbed her knife. She could try a bare-handed attack and pray she could get the knife out of Dani's hand. *Risks, risks, risks.* "What are you doing?"

"We need to talk." Dani's voice strained like something bound and prodded.

"Since when do we talk with weapons?" Lynn tried to put amusement into her voice, but the tightness in her throat mangled it to something shrill and adversarial. She set her jaw and forced herself to look away from the knife and up to Dani's face.

"Since we're at a...uh...well, a fork in the road. Literally." Dani managed a little snort.

When their gazes met, Lynn's insides churned. *She knows.* Instinct took over. *Deny it!* "Fork? What are you talking about?"

"Don't *do* that!"

Lynn startled. Her hand flitted away from the steering wheel.

"Last warning! Keep 'em on the wheel, or I'll have to—to—"

"Do what, Dani? Are you going to kill me?" Lynn halted her hand but didn't move it back. These inches closer to a weapon were too hard earned. She took her fear and turned it to anger. "Hm? Is that the plan? Spit it out!"

"I don't know!" The shout seemed to drain some of Dani's hostility. She slumped into the seat, but the knife didn't budge. That wasn't anger in her eyes now; that was desperation. "I don't know, Lynn. What do you want me to say? To do?"

Lynn stared her down. She took advantage of Dani's inner turmoil by lowering her hand a few inches more. "What's going on?" Back to neutral, maybe a bit of care. She needed to figure out what chord to strike to get out of this situation—and fast.

"Could you not lie to me?" The unspoken *for once* was as loud as Dani's voice in the claustrophobically small space.

Lynn didn't react. She wondered if Dani could hear her heart pounding.

Dani took a deep breath. "When you run away tonight, were you going to kill me first?"

"What?" Lynn frowned and shook her head. "No, I wasn't."

Dani inspected her. "That's stupid."

Lynn felt dizzy, a physical reaction to the continually shifting tone of the conversation. "Wha—why?"

"I could hunt you down."

Lynn shorted. "No offense, but I sincerely doubt that." She nodded at Dani's feet. "You can barely walk, and you're exhausted. Yeah, you have the food, but I've been without food before. And I'll have Skeever. You'd limp back to the Homestead instead of coming after me."

Dani's hand around the knife twitched.

Lynn's gaze flitted down. "Tell me I'm wrong."

"You're wrong."

Too quick, too shaky. "I'm not."

Dani's eyes narrowed, and she sat up straighter. "You are."

Lynn's certainty faltered. She was silent for several seconds. "Even if you did, Dani..." She felt the strong urge to drive this point home, just in case Dani was really stupid enough to come after her. "You won't be able to catch up. You're a good hunter—you must be—but you're not used to the Wilds. You can't track me on the roads; you can't move as fast as me, and you'd be in danger the whole time." She reached out toward Dani but withdrew before she touched her.

Dani squinted at the hand, but her posture had slumped as if the dose of reality Lynn had unloaded onto her shoulders was weighing her down.

Lynn seized the moment. "Really, Dani. You're so much better off just letting me go. Tell them I died or something or that I knocked you out and ran away. That you tried to find me but couldn't. They'd take you back. They wouldn't be angry."

Dani seemed to consider the proposal. The knife remained trained firmly on Lynn.

"I could tell you where to go, and you can have the map. I'll tell you all the markers I remember. You can go back to the Homestead; the whole group can go out to get him, and it'll be much safer than just you and me. All you have to do is agree to let me go, okay? Think about it. You didn't want to come out here either, did you?"

The almost imperceptible headshake felt like a major victory.

"Good." Lynn smiled softly, and risked a now-deliberate move of her hand toward Dani as a sign of comradery.

Dani tensed. Her features were becoming harder and harder to decipher now that the light had drained away almost entirely.

"Sorry." Lynn shifted and forced her body to relax even though every fiber in her being pushed at her to grab her tomahawk. "Didn't mean to startle you." She smiled. "Do you have a candle or something?"

Dani nodded.

"Okay, how about we get that lit, eat something, and we'll talk, okay? We'll have a rest, and I'll tell you all I know. Then I just...get my things and leave. You can sleep here tonight, safe and sound. You know the way home, and if you leave really early tomorrow, maybe you can even make it to the Homestead by nightfall. Sounds good, right?"

Dani dipped her head down. She lowered the knife onto her lap. "I can't."

Even in the confined space, Lynn struggled to hear her. She frowned. "Why not?"

Dani's head came up again. Her expressions were now entirely obscured by darkness. "Because you're wrong."

Lynn waited for an explanation.

It didn't come.

"What am I wrong about?"

"I can't go back. Kate won't let me in."

If Lynn could have one wish granted right now, it would be to be able to look Dani in the eye and tell if she was lying. "She won't leave you to die at the gate, Dani."

Dani was silent for so long that Lynn got ready to prod her again. "That's what she said."

Could anyone manufacture the intricate layering of pain, anger, and fear in Dani's voice? Lynn couldn't, but she wasn't a very good liar. The question was: how good a liar was Dani? "She literally told you that unless you came back with Richard's body, she wouldn't let you back in?"

Dani shifted. Another pause—shorter this time. "Yes."

Lynn turned fully toward her now. "And you believe her?"

"Kate's a woman of her word." A little tremble to her voice betrayed she wasn't exactly sure of Kate's actions if Dani went back.

"Even if she is, she must have said it as a heat-of-the-moment kind of thing, Dani. You know that." She scrambled to find the right words to convince Dani. "I don't know Kate very well, and I can't say I like her, but you said it yourself: you've been useful. And you like each other, right?"

Dani's clothes rustled as she seemed to shrug. "Would you risk it if you were me?"

Lynn opted not to answer that. "And what about the others, hm? Ren? Eduardo?"

"You must have realized Kate and Cody are in charge. Dean would side with his mom. Ren and Eduardo might vote for me, but that's still three against two."

"Flint?"

Dani sighed. "I don't know. But even if he voted in favor of me, not every vote is equal. Trust me, I have been thinking about this since the moment I realized you were not really going to get Richard's body with me."

Lynn chose strategic silence.

"I always suspected you had other plans—you agreed too easily—but I hoped that maybe I was wrong."

Dani's nearly disembodied voice in the darkness tore into Lynn's gut as if it'd been the knife still on Dani's lap. "Damn it, Dani." Her resolve wobbled. Time to change tactics. "Okay, say they would kick you out like that." She snapped her fingers. "Then why would you even want to go back?"

Silence. "I don't have anyone else."

Lynn squeezed her eyes shut and pinched the bridge of her nose. *Now what?* She couldn't go through with this stupid suicide mission for Richard's body. Neither did she want to kill Dani to get away from her. She could still escape, of course, but what if Dani did follow her? Did she want her death on her conscience? Obviously, she couldn't convince Dani to go home, so it was time to adapt. "Okay, you know me. Come with me. We'll take the 87, go west, forget about this whole insane idea of getting Richard's body." In the stillness—Skeever seemed to have fallen asleep somewhere—Lynn could hear Dani swallow.

"I don't trust you. You were going to leave me here without another thought. What guarantee do I have you won't leave me somewhere else? You said it yourself: I'm a hunter—a good one—but I'm not a Wilder like you." Her voice broke on the last syllable, and she sniffed as if she was fighting tears.

Shit. She couldn't really blame Dani. Put in Dani's shoes, Lynn wouldn't trust herself either. "Getting Richard's body is lunacy."

"I know." Dani sniffed again. "I don't have a choice."

Lynn pondered that. Dani had plenty of choices, didn't she? Testing the theory that Kate wouldn't let her back in and running away with Lynn were two of the most obvious ones, but there were probably more.

"If you tell me where he is, I'll get him myself." Dani's voice shook. "I'll figure out how to get him to the Homestead."

Lynn groaned. "You can't be serious."

Dani shifted. The leather of her seat squeaked.

Lynn tore her forgotten left hand from the steering wheel and gripped her tomahawk. Her hand felt numb. She couldn't see a damn thing.

"Here's the candle. Light it." Dani sniffed.

The pool of dread in Lynn's stomach sloshed uneasily. When something bumped her arm, she jumped, but she took the candle from Dani instead of braining her with the tomahawk. *Progress.*

"We can look at the map, and you can tell me all the markers you remember. I can find it."

"Right." Lynn sighed. She peered into the darkness, at the form beside her, but didn't have the emotional tools to reenter this conversation and come to a different result—one that wouldn't leave her with an acidy rock in her gut. "Sounds like a great plan."

CHAPTER 8

THE FLAME'S FLICKERING LIGHT CAST deep shadows across Dani's face as she studied the map.

Lynn studied Dani instead. Dani had taken her shoes off again and had stretched her legs out on the concrete floor. Her feet were a mess of blisters—both popped and unpopped—but Dani paid them no heed. Her entire focus was on the map.

"So I just follow the 95 north, then take the second exit once it curves east?" Dani looked up at her.

Lynn nodded. It would have been easier to pinpoint the location of the body if the map had extended that far north, but it didn't. "I think it was the second one, yes. I found him in a white building, right off the exit. It used to be a place where they sold cars. It took me two days to get from Richard's body to where you were hunting elephant." She traced the 95 down the map. "Two full days, one night."

"Any other landmarks?" Dani squinted at the map as if the missing part would mysteriously appear if she only focused hard enough.

"Um…not really." She racked her brain. "The road to the car shop was one of those overhead ones, so the exit sloped up. There's a railway parallel to the 95. It was on my left when I took off, so it should be on your right. I think the station was right at the exit. Go up, then right so you're crossing the tracks, and then it's on the right again. Big white building, huge parking lot. Across the road from the building is a driveway into a yard. The house is white with an orange slate roof, I think. Once you reach the house, go left into the yard. It's overgrown, but there is a little stone path about ten feet in. Take it. Somewhere there, on the right, you'll find the grave covered with stones."

"Okay." Dani inhaled as if to sigh but seemed to restrain herself. She sat up and nodded. "Okay."

Lynn could almost feel the worry radiate off her. "Confident?"

Dani tensed a moment, then shrugged. "Sure. It's just one road, one exit, and there it is, right?"

"Right." There was a little bit more to it than that, but why bring that up now? She had told Dani all she remembered; that was all she could do.

"When, um...are you leaving?" Dani looked up at her through her lashes.

Lynn shrugged. "Soon, I guess."

"Okay." Dani inspected her. "I think I owe you some food for the road."

"Owe me? Why?"

"For telling me where Richard is, I guess. And half of it was meant for you. Maybe it helps." She shrugged.

Lynn watched her. Was Dani trying to get her to reconsider? Even if she was, Lynn wasn't prideful enough to say no to free food. "Okay, thanks."

"Hand me my backpack?"

Lynn got up from the floor and retrieved it from its spot by the passenger side door. It weighed even more than her own. Dani's shoulders must be as sore as her feet.

Skeever lifted his head from his paws and watched her from the corner he'd settled into.

"Here you go." She sat back down on the cold concrete.

Skeever rested his head again, sighed, and went back to sleep.

Dani pulled out and divided a packet of beef jerky strips, a bunch of carrots, another small wheel of cheese, four apples, four large potatoes, a small sack of flour, some oatmeal, green beans, and a turnip. "There."

Lynn stared at the collection by her leg. She hadn't seen this much food in months. Without foraging and hunting, it wouldn't last her long, but it was a potential life-saving emergency supply and many of these foodstuffs she hadn't eaten in months—some even years. Oatmeal? She barely remembered it. Beef in any form and potatoes she hadn't eaten since Ottawa. She'd traded a fishhook for flour about a month back and had enjoyed flatbread for two weeks before the supply ran out. Her mouth watered. "T-Thanks."

Dani cocked her head a little. "Welcome." She paused a moment, then added, "There's a lot more at the Homestead, you know?"

Maybe it was the sparkle in Dani's eyes or the softness in her tone, but something about the way she said it caused a tingle of warning to course down Lynn's spine. "Good thing you're going back soon, then." To drive the point home, she packed the food away in bags and satchels.

Dani's smile wavered a little, then strengthened as she sat up a little straighter. "Yeah, exactly." Her gaze veered away, and she cleared her throat. "Maybe you should stay until morning." She glanced at her from under her eyelashes. "It's safer to travel by day."

There was certainly logic to that. Dani seemed agreeable to the whole divide-and-conquer thing, so why not get a good night's sleep? This place was as much of a fortress as she was ever going to find. "Yeah. I guess. First or second watch?"

"Do we need to keep watch? We're pretty secure...right?" Dani's expression was hard to read in the candle's flickering light, but there was a note of defiance in her voice.

Lynn glanced at Skeever in his corner and figured Dani had a point. Damn, she was just too tired to focus on things like this right now.

"Yeah, okay. I'm gonna get some sleep. Take the back. You'll be able to stretch out better. Your back must be killing you." She got up without waiting for a reply, hoisted her pack onto the driver's seat, and walked around the car to get into the passenger side. Lynn stubbornly closed her eyes and leaned her head back to shut the world out—both the outer world in the form of Dani and her internal turmoil. Dani's sudden cooperation left Lynn feeling unbalanced—and wondering when the other shoe would drop.

Dani opened the back door and slipped in quietly, bumping Lynn's seat. Then she moved more solidly and stretched out through the gap between the front seats.

Lynn tensed. She blinked her eyes open.

Dani put the candle on the dashboard. She balanced it carefully, checked to make sure the window didn't get too hot, and withdrew, all without acknowledging Lynn just a few inches from her.

When Dani left her space, Lynn exhaled slowly, making sure it was inaudible. She shifted to get the stiffness out of her shoulders and neck. She really hated having people so close by; it reminded her of how easily they could hurt her, but Dani in particular provoked a nervousness low in her gut. She was a Homesteader, one of her captors and her guard…but by allowing Lynn to get away, she was risking that bond. If Dani was telling the truth, she might end up homeless just because she'd tried to help Lynn. *That's the crux, isn't it? Is she telling the truth?*

"If the mechanism still works, you can tip the seat back." Dani's soft voice sounded almost as if she were right next to her ear in the confined space.

Despite herself, Lynn jumped and tried to make out Dani in the mirror that hung from the car's front window. Her thoughts shattered. "Huh?"

In the light of the candle, Dani smiled at her. "The seat. The back tips back in cars—or they used to. You can get more comfortable. There's probably a handle or a knob somewhere. On the edge of the seat."

"Oh. Right." Lynn didn't know about things like that, but she searched along the sides until she did find a handle. She pulled it and pushed until the back tipped and she was lying down much more comfortably. *Huh. Well then.*

"Better, right?"

Lynn shrugged. "Yeah, this is good. I guess."

Dani's smile widened in a see-I-know-what-I'm-doing sort of way.

Lynn rolled her eyes. "'Night." She laid her tomahawk across her lap and wished the familiarity of its weight would settle her more than it did. With a sigh, she shrugged off her coat, wrapped it around her like a blanket, and turned onto her side. She pressed her back against the door in an effort to get comfortable.

Dani stretched out on the back seat. It took her a long time to settle, but then her soft breathing evened out rapidly. She stilled. A minute passed in tranquility, then another.

Lynn sighed. Sadly, not even knowing Dani was asleep coaxed sleep out to come to Lynn as well. Time ticked away. The world outside was dead quiet. Lynn could usually doze anywhere and at any time, but not tonight. She was hyperfocused on Dani, and her brain was driving her up the wall. She felt very, very confined in the tiny car, locked in the garage.

How anyone could actually sleep—deep sleep—while out in the Wilds was beyond Lynn. It confirmed her conclusion that Dani wasn't a wanderer; she was used to protective walls and a soft bed. She wasn't trained to sleep with one eye open and planting a knife into anything that moved purely on reflex. There was something soothing about that; humanity needed people who weren't jaded to the point of numbness. *Just not out here. Not with me.*

By midnight, Lynn became restless and weary. She had never been very good at staying still. If she had been alone, she would have scavenged or moved on. Then again, if she had been alone, she would probably be asleep by now.

Dani whimpered. It was a tiny sound, but in the quiet of the night it seemed deafening.

Lynn turned around to check what was wrong. Numbness and pain flared up simultaneously from her stiff back and cramped legs.

Dani was still asleep, but her face had scrunched up into a frown. She was having a nightmare—a pretty bad one by the looks of it. Her blanket slid off as she knocked her knee against the back of Lynn's seat.

A glint caught Lynn's eye.

Dani's prized knife poked out from under her torso. It looked as if she had pressed the flat of the blade to her chest the way Lynn usually did but had dropped it as she'd rolled onto her front. Now the blade stuck out from under her belly, tip to Lynn. It was a miracle she hadn't cut herself yet.

Dani jerked, and her arm narrowly missed the sharp edge.

"Shit." She checked Dani's face to find her out cold. Carefully, Lynn set down the tomahawk on the driver's seat and turned until she could reach the knife tip through the gap between the seats. Her jacket slid off her shoulders. When she pulled gently, the blade didn't budge an inch; the weight of Dani's body pushed it down into the leather.

Dani whimpered and rolled farther onto her belly and buried the knife even more.

Lynn paused to reassess her strategy. *I could just wake her.* But then she would have to explain why she even cared in the first place. Human decency was only a good excuse when you hadn't just told the other party to march off alone on a suicide mission. Lynn sat up on her knees to get a better view.

Okay, just get in there and see if you can wiggle it loose or something. The new technique worked a little. The blade shimmied forward as she wiggled and pulled with slow, deliberate movements. Triumph bubbled up as the hilt oh so slowly came into view.

Then Dani groaned, hooked her arm around Lynn's forearm, and hugged it close.

Lynn tensed.

Dani sighed contentedly.

The blade fell to the mat on the floor with a dull thud.

I'm trapped. The realization dawned on Lynn very slowly. She shifted.

Dani's hold intensified. Her face scrunched up.

Baffled, Lynn sat with her front pressed against the backrest, knees planted firmly on the seat and her arm caught in a sleeping vice. *What the hell?* The thought was followed by a more practical one. *Now what?*

Again, she could just pull her hand free and be done with the whole thing. Dani would wake up for sure, but she could blow her off. It might be slightly awkward; she would have to explain the what and why, but the problem would be fixed. It was the sensible thing to do...but Dani was quiet again. Her features had mellowed. Her deep breathing blew a lock of hair up from her cheek on every exhale. The nightmare had passed.

Well, shit. Lynn sat and stared. *She'll let go soon. She'll shift, I'll pull away, and the moment will be over. No one has to explain anything, and we'll go on our merry way.*

But Dani didn't. If anything, the hold intensified as she sank deeper into obliviousness. After two days of walking and a night almost entirely without sleep, Dani slept the sleep of the dead.

Lynn sat and did the only thing she could do as her legs went prickly, then numb and her shoulder joint started to ache, then whine, then scream: watch.

She watched the slow rise and fall of Dani's chest, the slivers of expression that traversed her features—hints of a smile, the barest glimpse of a frown—and the way a tiny droplet of drool made its way down from the corner of Dani's mouth to the ancient leather below.

It should be boring, excruciating even, but it wasn't. Dani's features changed every few seconds, and the wavering light filled the in between with motion. Lynn studied the strong jawline and pronounced cheekbones that had captured her attention when they'd first met. She located the small braid in Dani's loosened hair and traced it to its source on the side of her head, just behind her ear. She counted little scars and marks—twelve that she could see—left there by claws, teeth, fires, and random accidents.

When the small holes in the garage door started to reveal light, Dani stirred.

Lynn jumped; even in the awkward position, she'd nodded off. It took her a few seconds to realize that Dani was waking up and—more importantly—that her arm was free. It could have been free for seconds or hours, Lynn didn't know, but it was free. *What time is it?*

But that wasn't the priority. She had to turn around and pretend none of this had happened. A groan escaped her as she sat up. Every muscle in her body protested the movement.

Dani yawned. "Is it time?"

For a second, the meaning of the words eluded Lynn. Then she remembered: parting ways, Dani's quest. "Y-Yeah, the sun is coming up."

Dani sat. She cracked her neck. "I think I actually slept."

Lynn chuckled somewhat nervously. "Yeah, I think you did." She smiled despite herself.

Dani smiled back.

Something fluttered in Lynn's gut.

After a few seconds, Dani tilted her head. "Are you okay?"

Shit! "Yeah, totally. Just some stiffness, you know?"

Before Dani could ask more questions, Lynn opened the door and all but fell out on legs that hadn't quite gotten circulation back. She wobbled, caught herself on the door, then was bowled over by something big and hairy.

Skeever landed on top of her. The force of the impact expelled the air from her lungs. He barked, and his tail hit the inside paneling of the door in rapid taps as he assaulted her face with his wet nose and wetter tongue.

"Skeever, no! Stop! Dammit!" But she only halfheartedly pushed at his head, laughing as every lick and nudge allowed her to get a little more distance from the abnormality of the night.

"You're good with him." Dani stood over them, apple in hand. She took a bite and smiled. Rest had done her good; she looked strong and confident.

Lynn pushed Skeever's muzzle under her armpit and looked up from the floor with as much dignity as she could manage. "We get along." She smiled.

"Are you—" The smile became tense. "Taking him?"

Shit. They hadn't talked about that yet. She cleared her face of emotions and kept a struggling Skeever down. "Yeah."

Dani paused a few seconds. "They'll be pissed."

"They can kick rocks."

The silence was awkward. Very awkward. They hadn't spoken much yesterday either, but Lynn realized now that Dani had definitely been the one to keep the conversation going throughout the day, even if it had been in short bursts. She'd given up on that today, and the result was a trek that felt hollow and tense. It was also headed in the wrong direction—for Lynn, at least. She'd walked Dani to the interstate, and when Dani had turned right, she'd found herself following along.

Dani hadn't questioned her about it, but a few minutes in, she was casting more and more confused glances her way.

Maybe it was time for an explanation. "I thought I would walk you to the next intersection and turn west there."

Dani scanned the tree line. She nodded after a moment. "Yeah, that's fine."

Silence.

"I guess I wanna make sure you're on your way."

"Okay."

With nothing more to say, Lynn pressed her lips together and walked.

The road was solid the first part of the way. From their elevated position, they had a good view over an almost obscured strip of water, and Lynn wondered if Dani was thinking about that soak of her feet Lynn had promised her last night. She didn't ask; she wasn't sure how to.

Before long, she didn't have to worry about it anymore. The road worsened, and large chunks of it had come off on the edges. They were soon forced onto a single lane that was riddled with cracks. To make matters worse, the canopy had encroached on the deck, and they had to pick their way carefully over and under cars and tree limbs.

Dani hacked at the overhanging branches when they became too tangled to traverse. "Fucking *nature*." Her grumbled complaint was the first words out of her since their short conversation at the start of the hike.

Lynn stayed behind her and kept an eye out for any dangers. The noise Dani made seemed to scare off even the ever-present monkeys, though. They howled in the distance and rattled the tree branches, but the sound didn't come closer.

Skeever had one of Dani's hacked-off branches in his mouth and lagged behind because he kept getting it stuck on debris.

His tenacity made Lynn smile for what felt like the first time today.

"How long have we been walking?"

Dani's voice jerked Lynn back to reality. She instinctively looked up for the position of the sun but saw only leaves. "I have no idea. A few hours?"

"Based on the map and how far we came yesterday, I think we should have been at the exit you wanted already. We may have passed it." Dani stopped and massaged her chopping arm.

"Maybe." Lynn had thought about that. "We've been pretty much crawling along. I think it's still ahead."

Dani pondered that and nodded. "Maybe. Take over for a while?" She stepped back to let Lynn pass in the narrow opening.

Lynn ducked under a massive branch and then took a shortcut through the branches.

Dani followed her every move.

Skeever took the long way around. He whined when he had to abandon his stick. When Lynn had to chop a path, he soon claimed a new one. Then Lynn spotted a sign, half-hidden by branches and nearly knocked over by the twisted metal of what had once been an overhead crossbeam. She ducked under a thigh-sized branch and tried to get a better look. "Can you read that?"

Dani shook her head. "No. Do you think it's the sign that says it's your exit coming up?"

Lynn shrugged. "Maybe. I guess we should check. There's a branch there that looks strong enough to climb up on."

Dani nodded and handed Lynn her spear before shrugging off her bag. "I'll go. I'm a good climber."

Lynn hesitated. Could she trust Dani to tell her the truth about what the sign said? She'd been very cooperative since their confrontation. What if she was just luring Lynn farther along? *There will be more signs. If she lies to you now, you'll find out soon enough.*

Dani was agile, Lynn had to admit. She disappeared into the overhanging branches, and soon the entire canopy shook. Dani poked her head out a few moments later, from a branch Lynn hadn't expected her to reach yet. "The road splits ahead. According to the map, you're taking the left lane."

Lynn nodded. A vague sense of dread gripped her.

Dani disappeared, then dropped down from an overhead branch. She rubbed her green-stained hands on her pants and picked up her bag. "Last few hundred feet or so." She smiled, but her eyes remained dim and troubled. Before Lynn could inspect her further, she turned away.

Skeever hurried after her, leaving Lynn to catch up through the foliage.

It was slow going. The road worsened. Lynn had to carry Skeever through the trees several times—to his great dismay. The parts of the road that were intact were littered with debris and car husks. It seemed as if there had been an accident here, or maybe the impact from the bombs had thrown the cars around. Those last few hundred feet took probably an hour, but then they reached a split that could only be their point of divergence.

Dani stopped.

Lynn did too.

"Right, try not to die." Dani gripped her spear, turned on her heel, and walked off.

Lynn's heart dropped to her stomach. She stared, dumbfounded. She had expected a struggle or at least a last-ditch effort to convince her to come with her, but Dani's mind seemed made up.

Skeever sauntered past her to catch up with Dani.

Belatedly, she grabbed him.

He pulled against her grip.

"You too!" Lynn called after her.

Dani folded her spear as she walked and slung it across her back. Her shoulders were up high, tense, and she didn't acknowledge Lynn again before she disappeared into the foliage. Branches snapped, and leaves rustled. Then silence fell.

She was gone.

It took Lynn a minute to put herself in motion again. She guided an unwilling Skeever along the other road of the fork.

He kept doing what she refused to do herself: look in the direction Dani had disappeared in.

Lynn was free; she had Skeever, and she had food. Everything she had planned had come to fruition. It was even better than they'd planned, actually, because she hadn't had to hurt Dani or abandon her without her knowledge. It was, for all intents and purposes, a perfect getaway.

So why did she feel so shitty?

Well, the answer to that wasn't hard to find: Dani was going to get herself killed. Maybe not on the way to Richard, but as soon as she dug him up, the scent of his rotting flesh was going to draw any scavenger in the area. Wolves, wild dogs, probably even lions—all would flock to her and rip her to shreds if she got between them and their prey. And Dani would. She wouldn't let Richard get eaten.

Her stomach twisted, but she chopped at another branch and pushed her way through the narrow opening she created. Another step away. Another. Another. She managed to push forward by focusing on her cutting. Then the road restored itself—one moment it was in crumbles; the next it was made up of four lanes and void of trees. The forest expelled her into bright sunshine, and she had to shield her eyes until the stinging stopped.

Skeever shot ahead.

Lynn shivered despite the heat radiating from the sun. Within seconds, sweat streaked down her back and between her breasts under layers of leather and wool, but she didn't dare take off either. The sudden openness of the landscape made her feel unsafe in a whole different way than the claustrophobic tunnel she'd just exited. She had gotten used to having someone watching her back while in the open—not consciously, but as soon as she stepped farther into the glare, she became aware of how exposed her back was. She scanned her environment for anything moving that wasn't vegetation.

Birds chirped leisurely in the branches of trees that swayed in the funneled breeze.

Rabbits were abundant here, making homes in the mulch of leaves accumulated over years. Small shrubs had grown in the mulch, spilling onto the road and providing the rabbits cover from predators like hawks and hungry dogs. They scattered when Skeever charged at them in hot pursuit.

Lynn watched him scramble over half-buried cars and under the last branches extending over the deck for as long as it took her to adjust to seeing the sky again.

Long enough for Skeever to drop a rabbit by her feet.

She smiled. With Skeever by her side, she would be fine.

Well before sunset, Lynn pulled the gate shut on a small loading dock wedged in between three brick buildings. Four steps led up to a cement platform in front of another roll-up door that wouldn't budge. "Guess we're roughing it outside tonight."

Skeever sniffed through his new domain and didn't pay her any heed.

Lynn didn't mind. She had a fire to start, water to boil, and dinner to roast. Beside the rabbit, Skeever had also chased down a hare, so dinner would be abundant tonight.

The sun went down long before she'd gotten the fire going. The wood she'd scavenged the last part of today's hike wasn't as dry as she'd hoped, but with enough patience and fire starters, she managed. She made quick work of skinning both the rabbit and the hare. She thought about tanning the hides but decided against it once she considered the effort of cleaning and stretching the hides, coupled with the disgusting chore of cooking the brains to make a preserving paste. Besides, that would mean a delay in dinner; with only two hands, she couldn't both rotate the meat and work the hides. She shook her head and tossed the furs down to the rubble below the platform.

Dani would kill me.

She paused. Where had that come from? Who cared what Dani thought? Dani was gone, history. She didn't owe Dani anything—least of all some tiny furs she couldn't properly preserve right now anyway.

"Get out of my head, will you?" For all Lynn knew, Dani was dead. *Or dying in a ditch.* "Shut up." She drove a skewer through the rabbit and secured it above the fire.

Beside the risk of death, that was definitely the worst thing about being out in the Wilds alone: far too much time to think.

By the time the rabbit was cooked, the hounds had come out.

Skeever kept rushing the chain link to chase them off, and for now he succeeded.

Lynn watched their vague outlines passing along the gate like shadows, just out of the firelight's reach. Their eyes caught the light every once in a while. She was worried, but not more than usual. She'd bound the gate with plenty of rope; it wasn't going anywhere. Since it was also almost twice her height, she didn't expect the dogs to be able to jump it. Maybe some feline predator could climb it, or a human, but not the dogs. Because of that, the roaming pack served as involuntary guards. Their presence would keep anything else at bay.

"Let 'em be, Skeeve." She sucked the flesh from between the rabbit's ribs. "Come here!"

Reluctantly, he did. He walked up the steps with his tail between his legs.

She tossed him the rabbit carcass.

Instantly, he crunched it down into digestible chunks. He didn't even take the time to lay down as he usually did when she passed him something to chew.

Lynn smiled. It was so good to have him here. The threat of losing him had gotten her in trouble, but here they were, together.

Skeever audibly crushed the rabbit's skull.

Lynn shivered at the sound, imagining another skull being crushed.

"Dani chose her own fate." Saying it out loud did not make her believe it, but it did make her feel less alone. She pulled the hare from the spit and tested the meat. "Eat and sleep, Tanner. Eat and sleep. Look behind you only to make sure there is nothing there that might kill you."

Even with that reminder, the delicious, fatty hare went down like gravel and turned sour in her gut. When she lay down to sleep, she pressed the flat of her knife against her chest and remembered how badly that had almost gone for Dani. Lynn had slept like this for years, though, and didn't move around as Dani did.

When Skeever joined her, she closed her eyes and exhaled slowly to settle herself. She nodded off quickly, but not before wondering if Dani had found a good place to sleep.

CHAPTER 9

Lynn awoke with a start. *What was that?* She peered into the darkness. When she didn't instantly see danger approaching, she cast a quick glance at the fire. Its steady flames told her she couldn't have been asleep for more than a minute or two.

Skeever's head was up and tilted to one side. He had heard something too. A growl started low in his throat.

Lynn laid her hand on the nape of his neck.

He quieted.

She exchanged her knife for her tomahawk and stood.

Nothing moved in the circle of light, nor in the shadows just beyond. She could see the fence; it was intact and closed. The edges of the roof were clear as well. "Go check."

Skeever made his way down the steps. He sniffed the rubble with his tail between his legs.

Lynn followed him down. Once she put the fire at her back, her eyes adjusted to the darkness and the blackness beyond the gate became a little less absolute.

Wind caressed the trees and set the shrubbery atremble. Something scurried along the debris-strewn road—a rat? A raccoon? One of the seemingly thousands of cats in the area?—and disappeared. The dogs were nowhere in sight.

She pressed herself against the gate and peered out into the shadow world beyond. *What's out there?*

Skeever leaned against her leg. He kept his head low as he stared out.

Seconds ticked by. An owl hooted. Bats danced overhead in an intricate choreographed piece that nearly cost them their lives as they zipped past brick and wood. Whatever presence had woken her up had dissolved back into the night.

As she expelled her breath in a huff, Lynn tried to release the tension in her body with it. She had only marginal success; tension was inevitable at night. She reached down and stroked Skeever's back, smoothing down fur. "Come on, Skeeve. Back to bed."

It was a well-practiced, age-old tradition to wake up several times during the night. The routine of investigation and fruitless search was grating, but inevitable. Sleep deprivation was the price of staying alive in the Wilds.

She sat back down on the blankets. The small fire had dimmed considerably in the minutes she'd left it unattended, so she was forced to build it back up before she could lie down again.

Skeever sank down by her side. He stretched his paws out and laid his head on them.

Lynn scratched behind his ear. She stared out at the fence again. It was a night filled with activity just beyond what her senses could perceive. Leaves rustled, monkeys howled in the distance, and unseen creatures ambling through the undergrowth made much more noise than could reasonably be expected from something so small. Even the swooshing dives of the bats, the greedily burning fire, and Skeever's whimpered exhales fractured whatever odds of silence there could possibly be. For all its birds, zebras, and elephants, the world during daytime often felt hollow and lifeless. Never the night.

Lynn added another branch to the fire. She envisioned the map she'd given Dani and wondered how far toward the 95 Dani could have gotten yesterday. It depended on the vegetation, of course. If the road had restored itself for her like it had done for Lynn, she would have covered a lot more ground than if it hadn't. But Dani wasn't used to long hikes. Her blisters would have affected her speed and duration of travel. Would she have risked not finding a place to rest before nightfall? Lynn didn't think so.

Lynn had put in...what? Half a day's travel after their split around noon? Dani would more than likely have put in less. She would have left herself plenty of time to make fortifications, a fire, and some food. They were probably a day's hike apart.

Not that it matters.

She tossed her stick into the fire and watched it burn. Then she lay down against Skeever's flank. As part of the routine, she placed her tomahawk within easy reach, took her knife, and flattened it to her chest again.

Time for another few minutes of nodding off.

The pattern held until daybreak. Lynn went through rapid cycles of wakefulness and rest until the sky had gone from black to gray. She'd let the fire go out as soon as natural light returned to the world. Not having to tend a fire meant she could roll over and go back to sleep much quicker. Every extra minute of sleep was welcome, after all.

That was the theory.

In reality, Lynn lay awake until dawn. She stared up at the lightening sky while she massaged her belly. An apple-sized ball was stuck in her gut, but she couldn't feel it with her hand. She blamed it on her food, but she knew it wasn't.

It was Dani. The ball consisted of conglomerated worry and guilt, and it refused to shift. She sat up in the idle hope of dislodging it.

Skeever lifted his head, sighed, and laid it back down. He hadn't gotten much sleep either last night, thanks to critters and probably Lynn's restlessness.

"Sorry, Skeever." She scratched him behind one ear until he smacked his lips. *Now what?* It was a bit too early to leave, but she could get herself ready to go as soon as the world lightened a bit more. She pulled her pack to her and retrieved salty goat cheese and the second of the—now badly bruised—apples Dani had given her.

Dani again.

Lynn felt the urge to toss the apple away as hard as she could. They were a day's travel away from each other, and here Lynn was, thinking only of Dani. She bit into the apple instead. No way would she let Dani cost her food as well as sleep.

Skeever rolled over onto his side and stretched lazily, giving her clear access to his belly.

She rubbed it absentmindedly. All of this thinking wasn't doing her any favors. She had to get moving. Usually, she would let the sun come up a little more, but she couldn't sit here any longer. "Come on, boy. Early day today."

Something in her words or her tone seemed to convey the message. He stood and stretched.

Lynn packed her backpack and stomped out the remains of the fire. With the apple and cheese in one hand and her tomahawk in the other, she left her shelter behind in a controlled rush.

Skeever seemed surprised by her hurry; he lagged behind for a few seconds, then shot ahead, keeping her in view as he began the hunt for breakfast in the near dark.

Walking was usually meditative. The repetitive motion as well as the constant vigilance left little room for stray thoughts—which was exactly what Lynn had been hoping for. Yet the meditative mood wouldn't come. She'd gotten close to it after she'd reached the highway, but the feeling abandoned her before she could fully settle into it.

She glanced at Skeever. If anyone had told her a fortnight ago that she'd let a group capture her just because she would otherwise lose possession of a dog, she'd have laughed in their faces. Yet she had done exactly that. Had adopting him been the catalyst to start caring about people again?

Skeever was loyal, quietly supportive, and a good hunter. He'd made himself indispensable very quickly, but beyond that fact, it was also really nice to have someone to spend time with.

And she had to admit—stupidity and inexperience aside—Dani had made a good travel companion. She was talkative without being a blabbermouth, smart, and willing to learn. If she stopped attacking wolves and grew some calluses on her feet, Dani could make a good Wilder one day.

Lynn glanced behind her and found nothing but cracked asphalt, wrecked cars, and vegetation wherever it could find a foothold. The world was, as always, desolate. Even with the birds singing in the trees, a group of monkeys upsetting branches in the distance, and small critters scurrying between the piles of rubble, it felt empty. Some days, that thought calmed Lynn. After all, empty was good; it meant there weren't any predators.

Today, the world around her felt hollow, and Lynn realized the sentiment extended to her internal world as well.

I'm lonely. The realization struck with absolute certainty. *Even with Skeever, even after months of being alone and never minding it at all, today I feel lonely.* She swallowed. "Skeever, come here."

Skeever trotted back leisurely and bumped her leg.

Lynn crouched down in the middle of the road and wrapped her arms around him. She buried her face into his fur. He smelled of earth, smoke, and dew-dampened dog. It was familiar and soothing, but it didn't take away the hollow feeling inside of her.

Skeever squirmed and tried to bite her ponytail.

Lynn held on. "Did I make a mistake?" Skeever's fur absorbed the whispered words. *Not just for Dani, but for myself?* A lump had formed in her throat, and she swallowed it down. She didn't show emotion—didn't feel things.

But she did.

Right now, she was feeling regret, loneliness, and a throbbing headache. The latter wasn't technically an emotion, but it bloomed so suddenly that it rapidly overtook everything else. She stroked Skeever's flank and inhaled once more before pulling back.

Instantly, Skeever assaulted her face with his tongue and dead-rat breath.

Grinning, she ducked and gripped both sides of his head. "Shhhh... shhhh...what are you so happy about, huh?" She rubbed his cheeks. "Huh?"

Skeever barked, either out of excitement or to free himself...or maybe both.

Lynn glanced around reflexively, but the road was still abandoned. "Come on, Skeeve. Gotta go. I need to think." She stood again.

Skeever jumped and then rushed forward.

Lynn watched him go as she walked. *At least you got over a bad night's sleep fast.* She shook herself. Now more than ever, she needed to find her meditative mood because she had to think about things—important things. The most important of all being which way she was going to go at the intersection with the 95: away from Dani or toward her. It was her last chance to catch up, but if she went after Dani, she'd also be agreeing to get Richard's body.

With an early start and a fairly intact road, Lynn made it to the 95 well before midday. Despite her resolution to make a decision, she'd spent most of her time doing the exact opposite. The meditative mood had hit her, and she'd allowed herself to drift pleasantly. She'd marched away the morning by meticulously scouring her surroundings, playing fetch with Skeever, and eating while on the go.

Now that she got closer to the intersection, large signs started to appear overhead—or under feet when the signs had come crashing down. They were, as always, a confusing mess. The 95, according to the signs, ran north to south, but Lynn had the map fresh in mind and knew it to run east to west instead. Looking at the larger picture, the 95 did come down from the north and might eventually turn south again once it looped around New York City. So, north for Dani, south for a clean escape.

The road split, and north became left, and south became right. She had a choice to make, and she wasn't ready. Not by a long shot.

Skeever dallied around her legs.

Lynn had come to one decision in between putting off making any: if she was going after Dani, she would convince her to forget about the Homesteaders that had sent her out to die and come with her. Now that she'd reached the split, Lynn had to do some math to see if it was even possible to catch up before Dani reached Richard's body. Once that happened, it was too late.

Midday. Lynn looked up at the sun. Dani had to be one day of walking dawn-to-dusk away, at a minimum, depending on how accurate Lynn's memory of the map and her prediction of Dani's speed were. If she was wrong about the map or Dani was a lot slower, Lynn might end up ahead of her, but even if that happened, she would wait at the car dealership and make a final plea. The thought filled the hollow in her belly with a flutter of excitement.

She had to do it. Even if she couldn't quite explain to herself why, she trusted her gut—and her gut told her that she didn't want to be alone anymore. That she wanted another person to keep watch part of the night so she wouldn't be continually exhausted anymore. That she wanted the protection of another pair of eyes to scout the area while she hunted or gathered a meal. She wanted more out of life than survival—and she'd only felt that when she'd been young enough to let people in.

Lynn renewed the hold on her tomahawk and looked into the gloom of an overcast but warm day. The first step onto the left fork of the road was hard, but then her steps became lighter and easier. The road pulled at her. It seemed to urge her on and whisper *find Dani, find Dani, find Dani.*

She increased her pace.

Skeever darted ahead, down the slope, and onto the 95 heading north.

Easier said than done, road. But Lynn was certain it could be done. She could find Dani, talk her out of this plan now that Dani had experienced life in the Wilds alone, and get her to come with Lynn. It would all work out.

The convergence of roads spread out before her like a petrified spider web, unbending and unyielding in the stiff afternoon breeze. It was late—later than Lynn would have liked. The sun had started to set already, but she'd had her mind set on reaching this point before the day was done. She searched the lanes and ramps leading up to them for a lone figure but didn't spot Dani. *That would have been too easy.* Dani must have come past here already. A badly bombed road had slowed Lynn down, and even if the 278 had befallen the same fate, Dani must have reached this point before her.

The question was: how long before her?

Skeever followed her closely as she began to maneuver the web to get to the 95 leading north. He looked as exhausted as Lynn felt; his tongue lolled, and he hadn't shot out ahead of her in a long time. His limp—courtesy of the wolf attack—had returned.

Lynn felt like limping too. Even with her hardened feet and well-trained leg muscles, she was trembling with exhaustion. She wasn't used to walking from sunup to sundown with only a few minutes of rest for some food. The straps of her backpack dug into her shoulders, and her own wolf-induced injuries were throbbing. She hoisted her arm up against her chest again in an effort to alleviate the pain and licked her dry lips. Her water had run out long ago. "Just a little farther, Skeeve."

She followed the sign that read *95 to New Haven.* Once she smelled water, she dared a quick trip to the edge of the deck and stared down into a broad, rushing river. She groaned. It was going to take to sundown at least to get down to ground level and then backtrack under the mass of overhead roads. There was no other choice, though. She couldn't live without water.

It took her even longer than she'd expected. By the time she'd drunk her fill and topped off her bottles, darkness already encroached. And this was a bad place to be stuck at during the night; the many underpasses offered plenty of shadows for animals and humans to make their homes in. She hurried back up the slope, but her calves strained against every step and her already-tight lower back seized up entirely by the time she made it back onto to the right road.

Skeever whined as he caught up, stopped, then caught up again.

"Almost," she assured him. "Almost."

Once she was certain she'd left the spiderweb behind and was now securely on the road Dani was on, she broke into a big building, which had been painted blue at some point. It could have been a school; the walls inside still held many of their bright colors, and the tables and chairs she found inside the large rooms were tiny.

Lynn shied away from these spaces; they all had windows to the outside, and she didn't want to be seen. She examined every room, walked every hallway, to see if the building was as empty as it had appeared. Once she was satisfied it was, she returned to a small office at the heart of the building and barricaded herself and Skeever in by upturning the desk.

As soon as she unrolled her bedding, Skeever sank down on it and went to sleep.

Lynn tried to feed him an apple.

He didn't even look at it.

She ate it herself while she took off her boots, then lay down. A moan escaped her when every single muscle in her body seemed to relax at the same time. Walking sunup to sundown wasn't good for the body.

Skeever sighed and tilted his head up to connect with her arm.

"Sleep well, Skeever. Up early tomorrow. I'm hoping your nose will help me find Dani."

He licked his lips and exhaled in a huff.

Lynn remembered to get her knife, groped for it blindly, and pressed it against her torso. *That'll have to do for tonight.* She was too exhausted for more. Within minutes, she sank into a deep, exhausted sleep that not even her survival instincts woke her from.

So hungry! Lynn groaned and blinked her eyes open. Her limbs felt leaden, but above all, her stomach gnarled hungrily, and her head pounded. She knew that feeling, and it frightened her. After the headache would come the dizziness and then the general weakness. She had to eat.

Lynn messily gathered her things and forced herself to slow down as she made her way out. Anything could have wandered in last night.

Skeever didn't seem worried. He sniffed the hallways with his natural optimism and hurried outside once Lynn held the door open for him.

She cast a look at the outside world. It was later than she'd thought. The sun was already visible on the horizon. She should have gotten up earlier or made up for lost time by leaving now, but her stomach growled for attention.

Tiny chairs provided wood for a small fire, where she cooked oatmeal with apple, two flatbreads, and beef jerky and carrot soup.

Skeever caught a blackbird and ate it noisily.

She scooped every bit of oatmeal out of the tin, ate half the soup, and left one of the flatbreads. She could have eaten the rest as well—easily so—but decided to leave it as a snack for the road. At least her headache was going down now that her stomach was full. Lynn ran her hands through her hair.

The memory of her naked body in the mirror haunted her. *Bone and muscle, that's all you are.* She needed more food, more rest, and a life where she wasn't a forced march and a missed meal away from death. Without the supplies Dani had offered her, she would be forced to hunt or take Skeever's bird from him in order to get some energy back.

She swallowed. Yeah. She needed to get to Dani, and she needed to convince her to stay.

Yesterday's cloud coverage hadn't gotten any lighter. Lynn couldn't tell accurately how gray the sky would remain because the sun wasn't yet up high enough, but she was worried. Even the hint she got of how the sky would light up later promised her one thing: rain. Lots and lots of rain.

Lynn bit into her flatbread and chewed slowly. If it started to rain, she would have to find shelter or risk getting sick in soaked clothes.

Thinking about that possibility wouldn't do any good. She had to make more progress than Dani today or she could never hope to overtake her. Lynn packed and got up. Her legs protested with sharp stabs. "Come on, boy. Dani's out there. Gotta find her." She patted her thigh.

He got up with great reluctance and trotted over.

She stroked his head and pulled some downy feathers from under his lip and from between his teeth. "Time to go."

Skeever seemed to grasp that there was no escaping the inevitable and took up his usual spot ahead of her, sniffing the ground. She helped him onto the 95 by hoisting him over a divider and turned north.

Judging by the angle of the slowly rising sun—as best as she could guess its location in the sky through the dense clouds—she hadn't made it to the road she'd come down on yet. She was still traveling east. The vegetation around the road decreased in density. The bombings must have been less intense here, a fact reinforced by the buildings lining the road. All were overgrown with ivy and other creepers; all were in dangerous stages of neglect, but time and nature's reclaiming touch were the primary causes, not complete destruction. The roads and walkways had survived the war and had stunted the growth of trees.

Bushes, grass, and weeds still grew abundant, but the claustrophobia that Lynn had felt while encased in forest was gone. She was no longer on a raised track either; as soon as she'd left the massive conglomeration of roads, the 95 had become a regular street that ran straight down an urban area.

Lynn's guard was up. It was good to have sky overhead again, but every hedgerow, house entrance, fence, or corner promised dangers that were invisible—until it was too late. Whenever they approached a danger point, she slowed and held her tomahawk ready to strike.

A pack of at least fifteen dogs crossed an intersection maybe two hundred feet from her, and Lynn hurried to muzzle Skeever before he could bark. She pulled him into an alley after casting a quick glance down its length to see if it was occupied, and waited. A pack of dogs usually didn't attack on sight, but risking it would be foolish.

Skeever growled low in his throat.

Lynn tapped him on the nose to shush him. She counted seconds, up to a hundred. Then she peered around the corner.

The pack was gone.

She waited until Skeever's fur had settled, then let go of his muzzle.

He didn't bark, nor did he pull against the hold she still had on his collar.

As soon as she let him go, he shook himself out and then looked up with big, brown, trusting eyes.

She smiled at him and stroked his head. "Good boy."

Once they crossed the intersection, the dogs were nowhere in sight.

By noon, Lynn was getting very tired of playing hide-and-seek with deadly critters. It slowed her down when she could least afford it. She chewed on a pear she'd pulled from a tree in one of the yards as she tried to strategize.

If Dani had even made it this far, she might have left the 95. So no matter how long and fast Lynn walked, they would miss each other in this crumbling maze. Dani could be on a parallel road right now, and Lynn would never know it. The car dealership was a good back-up plan, but Lynn was pretty hell-bent on meeting up far earlier—preferably before the rain came.

As the sun had climbed the sky, light patches had started to form cracks in the gray blanketing the sky, but rain was definitely on the horizon. Based on the increasing strength of the wind and years of experience, Lynn estimated it would start coming down in buckets before she would usually make camp, near the end of the afternoon. Darker clouds were moving in from the northwest, and they promised not just rain but thunderstorms. She shouldn't be surprised, given the heat of the last few days.

Skeever perked his ears and stopped dead in his tracks. His tail shuddered.

Lynn looked around but saw nothing. She was about to urge him on when her far less accurate human ears picked up on what he'd heard: geese. Her stomach rumbled at the thought of meat. She cocked her head. Their telltale gurgling squawks came from somewhere to their left. "Go."

Skeever went off, sniffing the ground as he pulled into a light run.

She followed him cautiously, keeping her eyes peeled for geese and dangers alike. Geese were horrid creatures—vicious monsters that attacked without provocation. Their beaks came equipped with razor-sharp edges that did terrible damage to any exposed skin. They also tasted delicious, and they were slow enough for a dog or a well-thrown tomahawk to kill.

Skeever tracked their squawking to a fenced-in yard. It was so overgrown that even climbing the chain-link fence wouldn't give Lynn a vantage point, so she circled it, and the house, for a way in.

The calls of the birds seemed to egg Skeever on. He rushed ahead of her. Then he disappeared.

Before Lynn could fully grasp that he'd found an opening in the fence large enough to squeeze through, chaos ensued in the yard. Lynn didn't have to see what was happening to place the noises. That was the sound of a startled gaggle of geese fleeing for their lives now that an excited dog had gotten into their sanctuary. Most of the settlements Lynn had lived in as a child had a hen house. One night, a fox had snuck into one of them, and Lynn had been awoken by the hens' frantic flapping and clucking. This sounded almost exactly the same, the only difference being that the geese fought back and hissed angrily. The garden wasn't big enough for the geese to spread their wings and take off, so they were going on the offensive.

Lynn hurried to find the opening but didn't dare crawl through when she found it. She'd meet frantic geese who'd chew her face off. So she lifted her tomahawk instead and waited for any escaping geese to come her way.

The panicked flapping sounds decreased, and the hisses grew louder and more frequent.

Skeever yelped.

The bushes rustled.

Lynn steadied her tomahawk and braced to swing.

What emerged was definitely a goose, but its neck was lodged firmly between Skeever's jaws.

Skeever wiggled his way through the narrow opening with the dead bird forming a stumbling block between his front legs. He didn't let it hinder him too much, though: as soon as he was out, he ran.

Lynn didn't hesitate to bolt after him, because the remaining geese were hot on his tail.

The gaggle pursued them much longer than Lynn had expected them to, but eventually they raised themselves up as tall as they could, flapped their wings, and hissed as they held their ground.

Lynn laughed, checked behind her, and slowed. "Skeever! Skeeve! Stop!" She was slightly out of breath, but her blood was pumping. Her mind felt light and unencumbered. Lynn hadn't felt this alive in a long time. She checked her surroundings quickly, then looked back at the geese.

They still stood at attention, but the sting had gone out of their warning.

Skeever trotted back. When she reached out, he released the goose with only the slightest of possessive growls.

She stroked his head, then checked his back and flanks for injuries. He had a few tufts of hair missing, but her fingers came away with only a few specks of blood. The geese had taken a nip out of his left ear, but nothing too serious. She made a mental note to keep an eye on the little injury. "Silly dog." She smiled and hugged him. "Good job."

He trembled against her slightly but let himself be hugged.

"Good boy." She looked up again to find the geese retreating. *Good riddance!*

They'd ended up somewhere farther along the 95, just past a tunnel. Stone walls rose up on either side. "Come on, let's get a better view and then gut this thing." Lynn took the goose by the snapped neck and walked up the slope on legs that protested every step after her sprint.

Once she'd gotten a bit of an overview again—or at least wasn't in a hole anymore—she made quick work of the goose. She plucked the majority of its feathers from its belly and neck, then cut it open from the neck to the poop hole. The guts came out easily, and she tossed them to Skeever as his reward—all but the intestines to spare him a mouthful of feces. Then she cut its esophagus and gently extracted the crop and gizzard. She carefully cut out the little sack that held the goose's stomach juice and tossed the remainder to Skeever, who hurried to snatch up his treat.

Grass was never hard to find, and she stuffed the carcass with it to the point of bursting. Then she wrapped it up with ivy vine to keep it closed. It was a rush job, and she still had a lot of plucking to do before she would be able to cook it, but for now, this would do. She wiped her hands on her pants and tied the goose to her backpack by its neck so it could air and keep until dinner.

Skeever had long finished his share of the kill, but he didn't show any interest in the rest of the goose. He sniffed around the area and whimpered softly.

Lynn looked up from the knot she'd been tying. "Everything okay?" She reached for the tomahawk by her knee and stood. Nothing jumped out at her, but that didn't mean anything. She reached down blindly and hoisted her backpack onto her shoulders.

Skeever trotted forward, then waited for her to catch up.

As soon as he did, he hurried on. He kept his head low to the ground and sniffed.

A sliver of hope began to glow in Lynn's chest, and she picked up the pace. Did he smell Dani? Was she close?

The deck climbed again, with the overhead signs still announcing she was on the 95 to New Haven. It curved north and went down again to meet another road, the part of the 95 Lynn had traveled down on. And there, in the distance, was a little, person-shaped figure.

Lynn's breath hitched. *I did it!*

Skeever hurried down the ramp.

Lynn waved frantically. "Dani!"

CHAPTER 10

The figure raised a hand above their eyes and looked back at her.

Lynn rushed forward. She'd done it! She'd somehow managed to do the impossible: find a single woman in the Wilds!

The figure still didn't move.

Surely, she can figure out who it is? Relief turned acidic in her gut. *Why isn't she moving?* She gripped the shaft of her tomahawk to assure herself that she'd be ready to fight, just in case she'd been wrong about the identity of the figure.

Skeever didn't seem to share her concern. He sniffed along and picked his way around cars and other obstacles.

The figure stood motionless at the bottom of the ramp and watched.

As Lynn got closer, more details became distinguishable. The shaft in the person's hand was definitely a gleaming spear. Their hair was brown and either really short or pulled back into Dani's usual ponytail. They weren't very tall, and more than likely, they were female. Once Lynn got close enough to make out the details that mattered, like facial features and clothing, her confidence returned. It was Dani.

What am I going to say? She'd spent a day and a half pushing herself to the top of her abilities to catch up, but she hadn't thought about what she would do or say when she did. She'd assumed it would work itself out. Dani would be surprised, maybe angry, but most likely also relieved. In the few rare instances Lynn had thought this far ahead, Dani had always reacted to her call.

Skeever reached Dani first. He ran up to her, barked, and jumped.

She pushed him back down and away. Her gaze remained trained on Lynn.

Lynn groped around her mind for something to say, but when she was only a few feet away, nothing had come to her other than "hi." She came to a halt.

Dani's expression was flat. Her jaw was set, her gaze sharp. At least she looked unharmed, just a little dirtier than the last time Lynn had seen her.

Skeever jumped around Dani. He licked her spear hand to get attention.

Seconds ticked by as Dani ignored him and stared at Lynn. "Hi."

Lynn frowned. This was not how it was supposed to go. She licked her suddenly dry lips and swallowed. Her brain shut down, but not saying anything wasn't an option. She scuffed at the sand blown onto the road. "I brought dinner."

"Great." Dani's voice was as flat as her expression. "What are you doing here?"

Lynn lowered her head and shrugged. Her heart rate had spiked, and her hands were clammy. She slid her tomahawk into its loop around her belt before it could send out the wrong signal. "I dunno." *Bullshit!* The right answer was: *I got lonely and I couldn't stop thinking about you,* but she couldn't say that. Not when Dani was so antagonistic.

"You don't know?" Dani drew the words out to make them sound at least twice as long—and spiteful.

"I—"

"Lynn, I swear on my father's grave that if you give me a reason that's all about you right now, I'll gut you."

Lynn looked up to check Dani's eyes for intent and realized Dani wasn't joking or exaggerating. She considered and closed her mouth.

Dani huffed. "Thought so." She shook her head, turned, and walked off.

Skeever hurried after her. He tried to force himself between her legs and almost made her trip.

She still ignored him.

Lynn stood frozen, mind racing. *Now what?*

Dani kept walking.

When the distance between them passed twenty feet, Lynn managed to snap herself out of her thoughts of failure. She hurried forward. Her calves cramped and forced her to slow. "Dani!" She closed the distance with difficulty and fell in line next to her. "Please stop."

"Why?" Dani looked stoically ahead of her.

"I-I still think it's a bad idea to dig up his body. I still think it'll get you killed. But I don't want you to get killed. You're the first person in forever that I—I—" She faltered.

"Selfish." Dani almost snorted the word. She glanced aside. "You don't want to see me killed because...why? Because you'd miss me? Who cares, Lynn? Who cares who you'll miss once they're dead. You should have come with me just because you don't want to see me die—see anyone die, for that matter. You're here because you've realized you'd apparently miss me if I died, and that's..." She waved her free hand as if she were tossing something away. "...useless to me."

Lynn's cheeks grew hot while the rest of her went cold. "I'm s—"

"Sorry? Yeah, I don't care." Dani bit out the words with the sharpness of goose teeth. They cut just as deeply, too.

Lynn ran a shaky hand through her hair and took out her tomahawk again. They were traveling now. Even though her insides were squirming and her thoughts swam, she tried to be mindful of the world around her. The eight-lane road offered plenty of vantage to calm her worries, though. Except for some kind of ungulate in the distance, the world was void of visible life.

Skeever whined again and fell in line beside Dani, head down, either feeling the tension or missing the love.

Lynn felt bad for him. She took a deep breath. "I'm used to being alone." When no reply came, she continued. "My mom died when I was very young, my dad died when I was six, and every other person I've ever loved died before I was twelve. I promised myself I wouldn't care about anyone ever again. And I haven't. I've always kept myself away from people and never put myself in a position where I had to rely on someone. I... made sure I could make it on my own, no matter what." She glanced to the side.

Dani stared ahead, but she appeared to be listening.

Tendrils of hope wrapped around Lynn's heart. She pushed on. "I shouldn't have left. I should have realized it was a terrible thing to do. I still don't want to dig up a corpse and walk around with it—because I want to live, and I want you and Skeever to live—but I should have stayed with you and tried to convince you not to go through with it." She took a deep breath. "I know you're not used to being out here, and I—I thought maybe you'd died already, and then I thought of you dying at all, and I...I realized I'd made a mistake. And you're right, I should have felt that way because of you, not because of me, but I'm just...just not used to thinking that way. It's been a very long time since I...well, since I thought about anyone but myself."

Dani glanced at her for only a second.

Lynn's heart fluttered like a bird taking to the sky. *That's something.* She had to keep talking. If she kept talking, Dani would listen, and she wouldn't leave. "Please, don't go through with it." She hated to beg, but the situation warranted it. "Please, just turn around and come with me. I know I haven't given you a lot of reasons to trust me, but at least you'd be alive. Please?" She resisted the urge to reach out and take Dani's arm.

"I can't." Dani ran her hand over her tied-back hair. "I'm not like you, Lynn. I can't just...not care about other people. They're my family, and they want their family back—I want my family back. We've been over this." She sounded tired now. "Besides, it was you who got me into this mess in the first place. You volunteered me, remember?"

Lynn flinched. "Yeah. I didn't know you then."

"Selfish." Dani's lip curled up almost imperceptibly. "You should have let them all come, then we'd have been safe—or at least much safer. But you wanted only me to go with you because you had no intention of ever going through with it, did you?"

Lynn took a deep breath, then shook her head.

"Thought so. Kate warned me about that too. She wanted to let the group follow us at a distance, so when you ditched me or tried to hurt me, they could catch up and force you to lead them to Richard's body."

Lynn's head shot up. "What? Kate wanted to—?" She looked behind her on instinct.

"I told her not to. I didn't want to put more people at risk. I always knew you would ditch me, but I know what I can do. I am strong, and I am a good hunter. I can make it home with Richard's body—I know I can. And I told Kate that, too."

"I-I thought she'd made you go?" Lynn's head was reeling.

"Kate wants Richard's body back, yes. I realized pretty quickly that me going was the only choice to get it; you'd deadlocked all other options. I didn't want to go out here alone and risk dying, but if you had spotted the rest of the group following us, you might not have told me where Richard's body is. You stuck around long enough to tell me that, at least."

Lynn's brain had seized to function. Deep down, she'd probably known already that Kate and Dani had seen through her plan to get away, but to know that the group had strategized to get what they needed without her even realizing stumped her. They had suspected she was going to try to escape and that when she did, the location of Richard's body would be lost to them. Instead of locking her up and trying to get the information through force, they had trusted Dani to play along and manipulate Lynn into either taking her to the body or to get its location from her before she escaped. Dani had managed both while always making Lynn feel as if she was in control of the situation—as if Lynn's own plan of playing Dani was working. "You played me."

Dani's jaw set. "You left me to die."

Touché. Lynn swallowed. "But if they knew, why would they send you into a situation that will get you killed? It doesn't make sense."

Dani stopped abruptly and turned to her. The mask fell away some to reveal smoldering, seething anger.

Lynn took a subconscious step back.

"You keep saying that, but you don't know that!" She shook her head. "You can't see the future. You can't tell what's going to happen! Maybe something will try to grab him—or me—on the way back. Maybe the odds are higher because of him, but I am a hunter, Lynn! I'm not some…kid. I'm not you at age twelve without parents! I might not be used to walking long distances or sleeping outdoors, but I know how to handle myself."

Lynn opened her mouth to speak.

"Besides, I'd be in danger if I went with you too! You know damn well that you can die out here like this—" She snapped her fingers in Lynn's face. "So all this bullshit about how you want to save me from certain death is—" She frowned, fumbled for a word. "Bullshit!"

Lynn swallowed. "Based on experience, I think the odds are really high."

Dani searched her features. "Between a two-day journey from Richard's grave to the Homestead and forever in the Wilds with you, which one has the highest odds of me ending up dead?"

Lynn's heart plummeted. Her cheeks grew even hotter. She hadn't considered her proposition like that. Lynn knew she was going to die in the Wilds, even if she kept postponing the inevitable by surviving another day. Yes, the odds of Dani dying with Richard's body acting as lure were high, but the odds of her dying if she went with Lynn were a hundred percent. "I'm still alive."

Dani nodded. "You are. But you could be dead before sundown. Or tomorrow. Or next month."

Lynn had to agree. "Yes."

"And say you got killed before me, then what would happen to me? Do I go back to the Homestead? Do I try to find another group?" She left a pause. "Do I become you and drag someone else from their home?"

The words felt like a slap across the face. Lynn widened her stance and steadied herself enough to speak. "You're making me sound like some sort of predator."

Dani squinted. "You are." She raised the tip of her spear to Lynn's chest. "You're the worst of all predators: you're a predator who thinks they're a victim."

Lynn's ears rang as if the words had been shouted, not hissed. She tried to process them, felt them chafing against everything she'd ever considered herself to be. Instantly, defensive mechanisms arose to counter the accusations; she wasn't a predator, she cared about people, she was a good person. But Dani wasn't done yet.

"You're not a victim." Dani poked the tip of the spear sharply against the leather covering Lynn's chest. "I'm sorry your parents died. I'm sorry you've been alone. My parents are dead too, most likely. I don't have family either, but that hasn't stopped me from making friends. I've built my new family from the ground up. They care about me, and I care about them. There are ways to survive without only taking and never giving anything in return." Dani withdrew the spear and glared at her. With her chin jutting out and her squinted eyes, she looked every bit the proud hunter she was—the hunter Lynn had failed to see in her.

Lynn took a shuddering breath and tried to find a buoy in the onslaught. She opened her mouth in the hopes a defense would form in the chaos that was her brainpan.

"Walk away, Lynn." Dani pointed the way she'd come, then dropped her hand. "That's what you're good at."

Lynn froze.

Dani turned and walked off. She squared her shoulders, tilted her head up, and gripped the spear tightly.

Skeever hurried to catch up, but she ignored him. He looked back at Lynn, his tail stuck between his legs.

Lynn was too crushed to register him or anything other than a hollow pit of darkness inside of her. It spread like burning acid from her stomach all the way to her fingertips, toes, and most of all her head. Dani's words reverberated inside of her skull, etching themselves into her very soul. Panic rushed up. It turned her body from ice-cold to glowing hot in a matter of seconds. She opened her mouth to call Dani back or to explain more, but Dani's dismissal had been absolute.

Skeever trotted back and pressed against her.

For a second, Lynn was unable to formulate a natural response to his attention seeking. Then she dropped to a knee and wrapped him in her arms. *Selfish.* She was hugging him to make him feel better just as much as to make herself feel better.

He bucked against her as he tried to lick her face and then chew her wrist, but she restrained him and inhaled his scent. His love and familiarity strengthened her enough to watch Dani as she navigated around the upturned cars and heat cracks in the road. Watching her walk away hurt in a way that had nothing to do with her blasted ego or her guilt.

This was not how it should have gone. Lynn had planned her escape. She'd had it all thought out. Changing her mind and coming back for Dani had been noble—she'd been trying to save her! But Dani didn't need saving—or maybe she did and she just didn't know it? She groaned in frustration and dropped her head to Skeever's back. Her head hurt. Her soul hurt. Her heart hurt. She felt as if she'd just wrestled a tiger and lost.

Lynn questioned every single one of her actions and thoughts. Who was right about her? Lynn herself or Dani and the Homesteaders? They didn't know her better than she did, did they? But they'd seen right through her plan—and Dani had played her perfectly; she'd tried to keep Lynn with her, but when it became obvious Lynn would leave, she'd made her tell Dani everything she needed to know.

Then a thought hit her: Dani could have gone back to the Homestead to gather the group after Lynn left. She would have been much safer then. Why hadn't she? Lynn didn't buy the story about Kate not taking her back for a second now. Did she really believe she would be able to get Richard's body alone? That she had enough skills to survive whatever came her way? And if so, was that boastful stupidity or reality?

Dani got farther and farther away.

Was she really that good? She'd utterly failed to convey that level of skill with the wolves. Had she been playing that? Lynn couldn't imagine Dani would have stood by and let Lynn get killed. Even if she'd wanted to, Lynn hadn't yet told her where Richard's body was, so Dani had still needed her.

Lynn closed her eyes for a few seconds. She tried to get her thoughts to slow down. It was impossible to keep up with the unending stream of images and conversations up for review, and they didn't get her answers. *Get a grip!* She couldn't sit here in the middle of the road, clutch a dog, and hope that reality would start to make sense on its own.

It wouldn't.

Which way do I go? Back the way she'd come was the most logical route. It was safer—physically and emotionally—but it would also prove Dani right. Lynn swallowed. Dani wasn't right. Yes, she had planned to ditch her, but Dani was most certainly wrong about her personality. Then there was this morning's realization too—that she needed someone.

After Dani, then.

And then what? Force herself upon her? Tell her she wasn't leaving, and risk a spear to the gut? Lynn sighed.

She stood from her crouch and walked after Dani. Maybe she would just keep her distance for a while. She could always catch up with her when Dani made camp.

She looked up to the darkening sky. *Or when the heavens open up.*

Dani, of course, noticed her following almost right away.

She glanced back, then turned and walked backward a few paces before turning back around. After a few more steps, she came to a halt. She turned again and crossed her arms—and the length of the spear—in front of her chest as a barrier—or a warning.

Lynn stifled a sigh and crossed the distance with her head held high.

This time, Skeever stayed with her instead of trying his luck with Dani.

"What are you doing?" Dani arched a brow.

Lynn stared intently at her shoes. "I don't exactly have a plan right now."

"You're following me, in the middle of nowhere, and you don't know why?"

Lynn looked up to discover that Dani's other eyebrow had joined her first, high on her forehead. "Pretty much."

"You're nuts." There wasn't as much loathing in Dani's tone as Lynn had expected.

"Probably." She took a breath. "You're wrong about me—or at least I think you're wrong. And I want to prove it."

"Why?"

Lynn groaned and deflated a little. "Could you stop asking me all these questions I don't have answers to?"

"No." A tiny glimmer of amusement tugged at the corner of Dani's mouth. "I think I'm entitled to some answers or at least to asking the questions that you should be able to answer."

Lynn sighed and patted her thigh with her tomahawk. "I guess..." She thought about the why of it all. "Because of what I said before." She shrugged. "I liked it better when we traveled together, which, I guess, means I like you. And I don't want you to think of me like...that."

"Like what?"

"You're going to make me repeat it?"

"Damn right."

Lynn groaned and threw up her arms. "Fine! Like...a selfish person. Like a predator."

Dani's shoulders sagged a little, which made her posture go from downright hostile to highly reserved. "Go on."

Lynn frowned. *What did I miss? Those were the big ones, right?* She went through the whole conversation again. "I'm not a victim? And I should never have planned to get you stranded in the Wilds."

Dani nodded slowly. "Are you just saying that because you think that's what I want to hear, or do you mean it?"

Lynn hesitated. "I...don't see myself the way you see me." She diverted her gaze to find relief from Dani's intense stare. "But if that's the way you see me, that's what I want to change. Maybe that means changing myself, or maybe it means proving myself to you. I don't know. Either way, I need you present to do it."

Dani inspected her again and waited to speak until Lynn met her eyes. "This is selfish again, you know? I have to stick around so you can feel better about yourself? Selfish."

Lynn groaned. "Come on! Give me a break! That's not fair! First you rip into me and then, when I try to make amends for all the stuff I did, you tell me it's selfish? Don't you want me to make it up to you even a little?"

Dani's eyes, which had softened for a moment, closed off again. "I don't see what the use is, Lynn. You messed up, but you don't owe me anything. You never did. You owed something to human decency, maybe, but it's not like I didn't see your bullshit coming from a mile away. Yeah, I'm angry, and I'm also a little hurt, but mostly I'm just really done with you."

Lynn flinched. The metaphorical knife Dani had previously thrust in her gut twisted to inflict more pain. She swallowed it down. "Fair enough."

Dani sighed and checked around her before she took in Lynn again. "One night."

"What?" Lynn frowned, but her heartbeat quickened.

"You have one night to prove to me you're more than a predator. That storm is going to hit any moment now. If we both set up our own camp, we'd waste resources as well as the possibility of sleep, and that would be stupid. We'll reevaluate in the morning."

"Okay." Lynn nodded quickly. "Okay, sounds good."

"Ask me why you're getting this shot." Dani's stoic face didn't betray any of her emotions.

"Uhhh...why am I getting this shot?"

Dani licked her lips and glanced at her boots. "Because you sat with me in the car when I slept. I remembered grabbing your arm in the morning. I thought it was part of my dream, but then I found my knife on the ground and I kinda pieced together what'd happened. That was a selfless thing you did—pretty much the only selfless thing you've done so far—and if there is more of that person in there, maybe she's worth getting to know."

Dani's soft brown eyes made Lynn feel a little wobbly. The words soothed the sting of her previous reprimands like Ren's healing balm. She blushed. "Okay."

Dani gave her the smallest of smiles. "Okay." She glanced at the sky, then pointed to the left of the road. "There are some houses there. Let's try to find somewhere with a roof."

Lynn followed without comment, but with a head full of thoughts.

Lynn brought her tomahawk down on the goose's spine. It cracked easily. With two more blows, she divided the carcass into four pieces. Its dark meat hung over a small fire Dani tended. The stripped bones were all that remained of the bird. Lynn chopped the ribs from the spine and cracked them once more.

Dani leaned against the wall next to the door and watched the rain come down in buckets.

Skeever, covered in the feathers he'd chased on the pre-storm winds, chewed contentedly on the head and neck of the goose. He'd taken up position on the threshold of the red brick house they'd chosen to occupy for the night.

Two cans of water came to a boil almost at the same time.

Lynn continued to chop the bones into smaller and smaller pieces.

They'd chosen this house because it was three stories high, so even if the roof was shot, the odds were good that they'd find somewhere dry downstairs. There were steps that led up to a plateau in front of the entrance, so they had an overview of the street and the 95 that ran parallel to it, separated from each other by only by a rusty chain-link fence and a patch of green they'd crossed an hour earlier.

Many of the buildings on the street offered protection from the rain through multiple levels and a vantage point by way of an elevated stoop, but none of the others boasted a heavily ornamented awning and low walls on either side that blocked both the rain and the wind and allowed them to make a fire to cook food. Much of the fire's heat was blown away instantly.

Lynn had stocked up on layers of clothing to combat the severe temperature drop.

Dani had wrapped herself up in a blanket.

Lynn dropped as many of the bones as would fit in the boiling water and tossed the remainders to Skeever.

Dani leaned forward and rotated the meat.

The silence wasn't exactly uncomfortable, but it was prolonged. The rain coming down on the awning and the whipping about of tree branches produced enough noise to let the silence stretch without seeming anti-social, but Lynn's time to prove herself was ticking away. She searched for a topic. "You said 'most likely.'" She glanced to the side.

Dani turned her head toward her and frowned. "Most likely?"

"That your parents were 'most likely' dead."

"Ah." Dani turned her head back.

Sure, remind her of her dead parents! Great strategy to show you're not an asshole. She got ready to apologize.

"My father is dead. We were attacked on the road. He told me to run, and I did. They hung him." Dani plucked at her blanket. "I found him the next day."

Lynn swallowed. "I'm really sorry."

Dani shrugged. "Me too."

"How old were you?"

"Seventeen. We'd just left New Town. Have you heard of it?" She looked up to check.

Lynn nodded. "Yeah. Biggest newly established city anywhere, as far as everyone I've ever met knows."

"It's a shit hole. We escaped when—" She licked her lips. "Never mind. We left."

Lynn didn't probe further. "And your mom?"

"She was alive five years ago, but five years is a long time. I assume she's dead."

"You got separated?"

"I guess you could say that." Dani's jaw set.

Back away slowly. "My mom died when I was three. My dad when I was six." Lynn didn't like to talk about it, but Dani had shared first, so it was only right that she told her story as well. She stirred the broth in both tins. "The building we were sleeping in collapsed around us. It killed almost everyone in the group, including my dad." The memories swirled up.

Dani was watching her again. "And your mom?"

"Died while giving birth to my baby brother." Lynn adjusted her coat to busy her hands—and mind.

"Did he—?"

Lynn shook her head.

"I'm sorry." She sounded genuinely upset.

Lynn sighed. "That's how it goes."

Dani nodded slowly. "Yeah. It is." She rotated the meat again.

Lynn needed a few seconds to steel herself before she could go on, but she was determined to give Dani a chance to get to know her.

The rain that pelted down covered the silence.

"The woman who stepped up to care for me—Anna—took me to a nearby settlement after it happened. Predators got her. After that, the group took care of me as best they could. There was an old woman in the camp Anna took me to. Everyone called her Old Lady Senna. In hindsight she probably wasn't that old—late fifties, maybe—but she had all these scars from a bear attack that had left her crippled. She could make anything out of bamboo and reed." Lynn smiled at the memory. Her fingers remembered too: they worked together to weave the air. She watched them as if they were separate from her.

Dani glanced at them too.

"Old Lady Senna used to make these beautiful pieces of art as if it was nothing. Mostly little animals like swans, bears, and wolves. The group had a few kids, and we used to play with the animals she made. I carried one of her little creations around with me for a long time, until it crumbled. I can't make them like she did, but she taught me a lot. Honestly, it's the only relatively useful thing I can do besides hunt and scavenge. I can make snares, bowls, baskets, bags, fishing pods, anything that involves weaving. If I have the right materials, I can weave them tight enough to hold water." She looked up and smiled at Dani.

"She gave me something to do, and it saved my life more times than I can count. Weaving allowed me to carry water, catch food, or make something to trade in exchange for a night spent in safety. I owe her a lot."

Dani examined her, then smiled.

Lynn wondered what she was thinking and felt oddly vulnerable. She didn't like to share things about herself—especially not things that she held dear. These good memories were sacred. If they became tainted somehow, she'd have nothing to fall back on during the times when the weight of the world felt crushing. "She died when I was twelve, and I've been making my own way through since."

"You're still alive, so you're doing something right." Dani's tone was soft.

Lynn shrugged. "I guess. I don't think there is much of an alternative, you know?"

"Yeah, I know." The way Dani looked at her made Lynn feel as if she was missing a glaringly obvious alternative that escaped her.

"Um, I think the meat's about done."

"Yeah, I think so too. Plate?" Dani looked around for her backpack.

"I'll get mine. We can share." Before Dani could protest, she got up and walked past a noisily chewing Skeever to her pack.

When Lynn returned with the plate, Dani pushed the meat off the sticks.

Lynn glanced out into the rain. "Do you want to go inside?"

"Let's eat here."

"Okay. We'll do that." Lynn reached out to take a piece of goose meat, then realized it was rude to help herself first and pushed the plate toward Dani instead.

Dani snorted. "Overdoing it." She smiled a little, so Lynn was okay with the jab.

"Since I'm on a deadline, I figured I'd go the extra mile." She showed her teeth in a grin.

Dani laughed, a short little bark that ended in a nasal snort.

Lynn's gut fluttered upon hearing it. She looked down to the plate so she could select a piece equal in size to the one Dani had taken. It was dark meat, tough, and a little bitter. The complex layers of flavors made her hum. "Perfect."

Dani smiled in response and chewed with her eyes closed.

The second the first bite hit her stomach, Lynn realized how hungry she'd been. It rumbled for more, and Lynn filled it with her fair share of the meat. Then she fed it a large bowl of broth to boot. Afterward, while Dani prepared their bed for the night out of their combined blankets, she sat and added the brittle remains of a side table to the fire.

When Dani said something over the unrelenting rain, Lynn checked to see if she was addressing her.

Dani sat on the bed and spoke to Skeever, who'd come to join her. She stroked his back and scratched him under his jaw until he rolled over so she could rub his chest and belly.

Lynn smiled.

Dani's hair tumbled when she leaned in to rub her face against his fur.

Skeever kicked with his hind leg in a way Lynn had come to recognize as extreme happiness.

She turned away to let the two bond again after their troubled reunion. She really hoped—for his sake as well as her own—that this night wouldn't be the only one they'd get to spend with Dani. Even with the tension, it felt good to get a chance to prove herself.

CHAPTER 11

THERE WAS ONLY SO MUCH one could do to prove their worth during the night, when both parties had to sleep. While Dani slept, Lynn kept the fire going with more ancient furniture and watched out for danger. For most of her shift, the rain plummeted down, and unsurprisingly not a single animal had come close to their shelter. The rain had ended now, but Lynn hadn't seen more than a couple of bats and a troop of monkeys with large eyes that reflected the light of the fire.

She was tired. Her legs ached, and her back felt uncomfortably stiff. Even with small bouts of jumping jacks and short walks around the crumbling fountain in the front yard, she was feeling the aftereffects of yesterday's hard push. The bite on her arm stung, and she'd spent almost an hour pushing pus and grime out of the punctures and patching up her arm with fresh ointment and bandages.

In a way, a night with a watch period was worse than her usual routine of nodding off and waking up: watch periods took forever; they were boring, and you had to stay awake and alert while you got more and more exhausted. On the flip side, once you got to sleep, you could sleep. Unless something barged into your camp, every sound and disturbance would be investigated by the other party, meaning you could just roll over and go back to sleep.

Provided you trusted the other person enough to have your back.

Lynn wasn't sure if she trusted Dani right now, but as soon as her time to sleep came up, Lynn would sleep. Her exhaustion was all-consuming.

She stretched out her legs and groaned. Definitely time for a walk around the house. Lynn descended the steps to the pavement.

Everything was still quiet. The moon shone brightly, just a touch past its full glow. Away from the fire, the world smelled fresh. The roads had been washed clean. Tomorrow, every tree, shrub, and blade of grass would be green and lush. It would be cooler, which made travel more pleasant. Hopefully, it would be sunny. Lynn smiled. Dani would like it that she was enjoying the world around her.

Lynn passed the third house to the left of their shelter and turned around. She walked back to the house. Dani had set up the bed out of sight of anyone or anything passing by, but Lynn could picture her sleeping soundly under the windowsill, with an arm around Skeever.

The thought made her smile. There was a lot of reassurance in knowing that if you called for help, it would be there in seconds. It was also good to have someone to talk to, to shoulder the burden of surviving the night with. Of course, these were all what Dani would call selfish reasons. Lynn still took issue with Dani's assessment of her. Wasn't it a natural thing to like something because it made life better? Lynn could only assume Dani was sleeping more soundly because of Lynn's presence, and she'd enjoyed the goose for sure. So, was that selfish too, or was it only selfish when Lynn did it?

The topic quickly caused another headache. Lynn decided that this was one of those things she wasn't going to figure out. It was time to claim her sleeping period. Maybe she'd have the mental energy required to find a way to prove herself after a few hours of sleep.

Dawn arrived without the desired clarity, but with a general lethargy of too much sleep on a sleep-deprived mind and the gnawing of an empty belly. Lynn turned over and noticed Skeever was gone. She blinked her eyes open and looked around, trying to remember where she was. The memories of the house returned to her in a trickle, followed by a flood of Dani's accusations. She groaned and threw her arm up to hide her face in the crook of her elbow.

"Morning, sunshine." Dani sounded bemused.

"Morning." Lynn sat up. If she'd thought she'd had muscle aches yesterday, today's pains were much more severe. Everything below her ribcage felt like a lemon, squeezed and sour. She yawned, and scratched her belly through her jacket. It was either cloudy or earlier than Lynn had thought, because it was gloomy inside the house. Lynn sheathed her knife in her boot and got up. She stretched, kicked out her legs, and made her way to the door.

Dani sat on the upper step with one of Lynn's tins in her hands. "I made you some too." She pointed behind her. "Rainwater tea with some lemongrass."

On the edge of the fire stood another tin with a sprig of green protruding from its steaming contents.

"Thanks." Lynn checked the temperature of the tin before she took it and joined Dani on the step. She groaned again as she lowered herself down.

"Sore?" Dani's hazel eyes inspected her.

Lynn nodded. "And as stiff as a board. It'll pass." She wrapped her hands around the tin to ward off the chill in the air. It was definitely an overcast day. There would be more rain. "How was your shift?"

"Uneventful." Dani's gaze tracked Skeever as he rummaged through the strip of green separating the parallel road from the 95.

He sat down to poop.

Dani looked away. "Some rustlings and rumblings, but overall it was peaceful. I think the rain scared everything off."

"I had the same feeling." Lynn sipped gingerly. The warm liquid coursed pleasantly down her throat. She cracked her neck. "Do you need the fire for anything else? I was going to make some bread for breakfast."

"Go ahead." Dani's gaze lingered on Lynn before she returned it to Skeever.

Lynn took another sip, then got up to fetch her pack. She measured out flour, added water, and split the dough into balls that she flattened with practiced skill. As she worked, her gaze was drawn to Dani, to check if she was watching her, but Dani seemed more interested in the world around them. Lynn went back to work with a mixture of relief and anxiety in her gut. She was postponing the inevitability of Dani's decision, but it wouldn't be long until the subject came up. Flattening the balls into thin, plate-sized circles was a chore of seconds. They sizzled as she laid them out over the coals. Instantly, the smell of bread filled the air, and Lynn's stomach contracted.

Skeever returned and ambled up the steps.

Dani caught him before he reached the plateau. "Not for doggies." She captured his head and pressed hers against it as she scratched him behind the ears. "That's people breakfast. Go find your own." She turned him around and sent him down the steps.

Skeever merrily left the yard.

Lynn smiled at him and looked around to make sure no surprises awaited him. When she felt confident the area was void of predators, she rummaged through her pack for the pears she'd picked yesterday. "Here." She held up one for Dani.

Dani glanced at it, then up at Lynn before she took it. "Thanks." She bit into it. Juices trickled down her chin. "Very nice."

Lynn shrugged the bit of gratitude away. She bit into her pear and held it between her teeth as she cut up another. Another scavenge through her backpack landed her a couple of chunks of goat cheese. Her fingertips were well-adjusted to heat, and the coals didn't hurt her as she flipped both flatbreads over. Their undersides had bubbled and browned. She wiped some ash off them, then topped each with bits of pear and cheese.

Dani watched her quietly all the while. She ate her pear with small bites and wiped her chin.

Lynn glanced up and met her gaze. "Everything okay?"

"Yeah. Just thinking."

A warning spiked icily down Lynn's spine. "About your decision?"

Dani's gaze flitted to the fire. "Yeah."

There it is. Lynn resigned herself to the inevitable. "Did you decide?"

Dani continued to watch the goat cheese melt. "No."

Their eyes met again.

"No to traveling together, or…?"

A moment of hesitation. "Here's the problem. I am going to get Richard's body, and I am going to bring it to the Homestead. I'd much prefer traveling together, but you don't want me to go through with this, so I'm not sure if this partnership has a chance to succeed."

Lynn hummed. That was pretty much the same conclusion she'd arrived at. She plucked one of the pancake-flat breads from the coals and offered it to Dani on her plate.

Dani took it but made no move to eat.

Lynn pulled the second flatbread from the fire and balanced the stiff disk on her fingertips until the worst of the heat had drained from the bottom. Then she sat on the top step with Dani and watched Skeever. "I don't want to risk my life for this." She blew on her bread, then glanced at Dani.

"I know. That's what I thought."

"But..." Lynn took a deep breath. "The odds are better no one dies if we do this together." She groaned inwardly. *You did it now, Tanner. You just had to go and be stupid.* But she didn't see an alternative. She didn't want to walk away, and she didn't want to go through with it. Sitting on this step forever also wasn't an option, so she chose the one scenario that had the potential to lead to a positive result.

"That's...true." Dani inspected her openly now. "So, that means that if I say I'm okay with you joining me, you'll join?"

Lynn licked her lips as she made up her mind. "Yeah. You have my word on that." She glanced to the side. "To Richard and to the Homestead, unless we die." She smiled wryly.

Dani searched her features and lingered on her eyes. "Swear it on something that matters to you. At least that way, if you break your promise, you'll know what a shitty person you are."

Lynn thought about it. She could just swear it on something that seemed meaningful but wasn't. That would allow her an out. She glanced at Dani and realized she couldn't do that. She was trying to win her trust, and she could only do that with honesty. "I swear it on...the memories of Old Lady Senna." After what she had told her last night, Dani must know that those meant a lot to her.

"That will do." Dani wiped her hand on her pants and held it out. "We'll do it together."

Lynn took the hand and shook it. It felt clammier than hers. The deal was sealed now. A mixture of relief and dread warred inside her stomach and threatened her appetite. To prevent that, Lynn quickly took a bite and chewed. The mixture of salty and sweet over the mild taste of ash was oddly grounding, and she took another bite.

Dani started to eat too. "This is good." She sounded genuinely appreciative.

The tension between them ebbed slowly.

Lynn settled. "Thanks. They came out nice."

The wind had gone down, it would warm up soon, and Lynn had gotten half a night of good sleep. As soon as they got on the road, all aches and pains would vanish too. She was doing pretty good, and most importantly, she wasn't alone. Those were all good things. Still, she faced a massive hurdle: convincing Dani to abandon her quest.

"How long before it starts to rain again?" Dani leaned out to look up past the awning above their heads.

Lynn hesitated. "Probably halfway through the afternoon. Those aren't rainclouds." She pointed above her, then moved her arm down to indicate clouds in the distance. "Those are, and they'll catch up, but not for a while now that the wind has gone down."

Dani inspected the sheen of dark gray on the horizon. "Time to go, then."

Lynn stuffed the last of her bread into her mouth and wiped her hands on her coat. She stood and swallowed. "Time to go."

"Dani? Can I ask you something?" Lynn cast a sweeping glance over the 95.

"Sure." Dani didn't take her eyes off the rustling leaves.

"I've been…I've been trying to figure out what was real about our interaction so far and what was fake."

Dani checked on her.

Lynn averted her gaze.

"What do you mean?"

Lynn shrugged. "You know…you said yesterday that you'd had a plan all along. I've been trying to piece together what part of everything that happened was a setup and which part was genuine."

"Oh." Dani was quiet for a little while. "Fair enough question."

"I thought so too." Lynn smiled to keep the sting out of her voice. "And an answer would be nice."

Dani seemed to consider her question carefully before answering. "I guess it was part of the plan to make you think Kate wouldn't take me back. And that I was really angry with her. We'd discussed that part of the story, Kate and I, I mean. I always knew that if I couldn't get you to come with me, I would have to get you to tell me how to get to Richard's body. When you got antsy and started checking the overhead signs and memorizing the map, I figured you were getting ready to make your escape, so I forced a negotiation instead: your freedom for the location."

Lynn set her jaw as a mixture of anger and shame coursed through her. Hearing how easily Dani and Kate had seen through her was incredibly embarrassing. The answer didn't surprise her, though. She'd gone over every memory since leaving the Homestead with a fine-toothed comb during her watch and now, looking back, she could see the little things that hadn't added up. Letting Lynn get her hands on a map, for example, when keeping Lynn in the dark about her exact location was one of Dani's greatest boons, or Dani letting Lynn talk her into going out alone.

Dani had probably always known Lynn would leave. At that point, only Richard's location had become important, and having a map helped to get there. The only thing that Lynn couldn't figure out was why Dani was so hell-bent on getting Richard's body alone when she had an obvious support system at the Homestead, most likely willing to join her. "Why didn't you go back?"

Dani licked her lips. "I might have. If you hadn't vowed to come along." She looked up.

Lynn felt the world fall out from under her. She stopped walking. Realization dawned on her. "You were still playing me. Right up until this morning, you were playing me." *I don't believe it!* She crossed her arms in front of her chest. "Seriously?"

Dani slowly came to a stop as well. She shrugged, but it was a nervous little shrug. "I-I really hadn't expected you to come back! The plan was to find the spot you'd told me about, confirm Richard's body was there, and then go back to get everyone. I didn't want to drag them out without making sure there was a point." She reached out to touch Lynn's arm.

Lynn stepped back. She squinted at the appendage until it was withdrawn.

Dani wiped her hand on her pants. "When you came back, I figured if I could get you to come with me anyway, I wouldn't have to endanger anyone. You and I doing this was always the plan. You said we could do it at the Homestead, and I meant what I said yesterday, that there are risks—huge risks—but that I think it can be done."

"Who's selfish now?" Lynn's world had only just restored itself a little, and now…? Who was this woman who lied and manipulated to get her way? *You can't really blame her for being better at playing people than you are, Tanner.* But she did. She most certainly did. This went far beyond wounded pride; this was betrayal.

Dani had the decency to look ashamed. "I know. All I can say in my defense is that I'm helping my family. You're just…" She shrugged. "You found Richard's body, and then you found us. Sorry."

Lynn could barely believe what she was hearing—from Dani! Dani, who just yesterday had made her question everything about herself by making her feel like the scum of the earth! Who was scum now? Who was selfish, deceitful, and dishonest? "Y-You're sorry?"

Dani ran her hand through her hair. "To be fair, this was exactly what you were trying to do to me, so don't get too offended. For what it's worth, I did say one thing yesterday I regret, about you being selfish. I think, overall, you're really nice. And you really are very good at surviving out here. Having you with me does make me feel safer, and I really do think we can do this. We're all trying to survive out here—myself included." She tried to reach out again.

Lynn backed up another pace. "Don't touch me. Just…don't try to touch me." She held up her empty hand in front of her. The other squeezed the shaft of her tomahawk so hard she wondered if she'd leave indentations.

"Okay, I won't. And I get that you're angry." Dani swallowed. "But you promised, on your memories. You promised to come with me and bring Richard's body home."

Lynn's anger rose to a new level—one where most rational thought disappeared and left only a single burning thread in her mind that she could actually hear inside her skull as a high-pitched, unrelenting whine. She took another step back because she didn't trust herself not to swing her tomahawk into Dani's skull. "Walk on. I can't be near you right now. Just walk. I need to…to think."

Forming coherent thoughts was impossible right now. Every single one banged against the inside of her skull like a frantic bird. She couldn't catch them, and she couldn't calm them. Not with Dani here.

"Lynn, I—"

"You'll want to walk away now." Lynn's voice sounded detached and far too calm. Eerily calm.

Dani lingered just a little longer. Lynn could see in her eyes she contemplated saying something else, but she didn't. She turned and walked.

When she passed the spot Skeever had been sniffing, he greeted her with enthusiasm.

Dani stroked his head, then walked on. She looked back after a few seconds.

Lynn turned her head away. After Dani put a few more feet of distance between them, she started to walk as well.

What was she going to do? Everyone who had ever mattered in her life had told her the same thing: a promise made was a promise to be kept. That Dani had suckered her into making that promise didn't matter. She didn't have a choice; Dani had played the game perfectly.

When had Dani started strategizing? That night at the Homestead? Or even earlier—the moment Kate had put her in charge of Lynn, after the group had found out about Richard? Had she ever really forgotten Lynn still had her knife, or had she let Lynn believe she was getting away with something and thus was in charge of the situation?

A hundred little examples of possible betrayals presented themselves to her, little acts of kindness or slowness on the part of Dani's intelligence that had made Lynn believe that if push came to shove, she would be able to manipulate Dani and take her in a fight. But if Dani had been aware of her attempts at manipulation all along, then maybe Dani had also been playing Lynn from the very beginning.

The idea was crushing in its enormity.

Lynn stared at Dani's back. She took in the calm movements of her head as she scanned her surroundings, the meticulous way she placed her feet for every step, and the ease with which Dani carried her spear.

Another thought struck her like lightning: had Dani faked the nightmare in the car that night? Had she been awake when she'd sought—what Lynn had perceived to be—comfort? A last-ditch attempt to get her to stay? A call to a softer, more emotional side of Lynn? The result had been delayed, but it had been achieved: Lynn was here. She'd let Dani get to her.

Lynn was still angry, but a sense of admiration began to well up from the part of her that recognized that the number one goal in life was survival. The level of skill and foresight required to befuddle Lynn so completely were beyond Lynn to such a degree, she doubted she would ever be able to match them. Dani had obviously been around people all her life, and she knew how they behaved when under threat. Or maybe Lynn was just very easy to manipulate.

Lynn took a deep breath. She needed to keep an eye on her surroundings, not just sink into her thoughts. She stopped for some water.

Dani stopped too, although she kept her back to Lynn.

Lynn hadn't caught her glancing back even once, but Dani was keeping an eye on her, that much was certain. Did she worry about a tomahawk being thrown in her back? Did she worry if Lynn was all right? At this point, Lynn had nothing to base predictions about Dani's thoughts or behavior on. She knew absolutely nothing about Dani. Was her father really dead? What about the story about her mom? Had she just said those things to make Lynn think they had something in common?

All these questions were driving Lynn insane! And the worst part was that if she asked Dani, she still couldn't be sure she got a true answer. This wasn't the Dani Lynn had thought she knew, and she didn't think she liked the new version very much.

Lynn stared at Dani's back. They had wordlessly kept a forty-foot gap between them while they traveled. When Dani stopped, Lynn stopped, and when Lynn stopped, Dani stopped.

Skeever divided his time between the two—or usually by running back and forth, never lingering long with either before seeking attention on the other side of the divide.

They'd eaten lunch separately, with whatever they'd had in their respective backpacks.

Lynn had stubbornly avoided looking over to Dani, but she'd felt Dani watching her.

Skeever had seemed confused by the lunch arrangements, but getting scraps from both had made everything right. For him, at least.

Lynn still couldn't get over how easily Dani had fooled her. She gave herself credit for having doubted at least some of the story while it was being told to her, but not enough to realize the extent of the hustle. She didn't pride herself on her people skills, but she'd always trusted her gut. This time, it'd been wrong.

Dani stopped.

The change in routine pulled Lynn from her thoughts. She quickly glanced around her to check but saw nothing out of the ordinary.

Skeever looked up at her. He'd been with her for a few minutes now, worn out from the hours of walking they'd put in.

Dani brought her spear up.

By instinct, Lynn raised her tomahawk as well.

The bushes on the left side of the road, way across the tarmac, rustled counter to the wind. Lynn would have missed it if Dani hadn't been watching the spot. She took a few steps closer, then froze.

Three red-and-white monkeys broke through the underbrush. They darted over the remnants of the road, crossed in front of Dani, and disappeared on the other side.

Another monkey followed. Then a pack of about ten monkeys spilled onto the highway. They darted around the asphalt on the lanes leading into the opposite direction.

Dani readied her spear.

Seconds ticked by. Lynn waited. She observed her surroundings as Dani kept her eyes firmly locked on the underbrush.

Four of the monkeys braved the crossing. None of them stayed in place long enough to line up a shot. Then a small female darted within throwing distance.

Dani's spear sailed through the air with absolute accuracy.

The second the monkey jumped the divider, it was knocked off by the impact of the metal rod. The shaft clanked to the ground out of sight.

The underbrush on both sides came to life with fleeing primates. Alarmed hoots went up.

Dani jumped the divider and disappeared.

Lynn stepped onto the concrete blocks between the lanes for a look.

On the other side, Dani made short work of a limp monkey.

I guess dinner is on you tonight. Lynn snorted. *Great.*

The first drops of rain caught Lynn by surprise. She'd been expecting rain since the morning, but most of the storm front was still behind her. Whatever cloud these few drops were falling out of must be a herald, sending travelers fair warning of impending, watery doom. "Shit." With great reluctance, she lengthened her strides to catch up with Dani. Once she got close, she swerved to put a good five feet between them as she came up parallel to her.

Dani glanced at her.

"Rain's here." Lynn kept her voice meticulously flat.

Dani nodded. "I think we have just enough time to find shelter."

Lynn hummed non-committedly. Dani was probably right, though; the drops came down irregularly and a few seconds apart. "I'll lead."

Dani didn't object.

Lynn led her on in a forced march, toward a little green sign in the distance: *Exit 19*. Wordlessly, she guided them up the exit ramp and looked around the intersection. *Left or right?* Left seemed to lead to the opposing ramp onto the 95, so right it was.

The rain intensified. Not by much, but enough for Lynn to quicken her pace. Just like yesterday, the sky darkened to a dull gray that promised to get much darker soon. Spurred on, Lynn took the first ramp down, into *Rye Harrison*, then guided them toward the nearest building she spotted through the green. It had probably been an office before the war. Lynn greatly preferred to sleep in smaller spaces, but they didn't have a lot of options at the moment. The patter of rain on the leaves above as they made their way through the vegetation had become constant.

She reached the edge of the densest growth. Before her lay a strip of asphalt, which—although cracked and covered with grass, moss, and low shrubs—did provide a clearing. From here, she could look up at the building's windows. She slid her gaze from glass plate to shattered glass plate. Nothing moved inside. Either the place was deserted, or everyone inside was staying very still.

Lynn led the way by skirting along the building to the nearest window. She pulled herself up to look through one of the high windows. A sharp stab ran through her injured arm, but she didn't have time for that. She forced herself to hold herself up so she could take in an empty hallway, no lights, and no movement. Then she allowed herself to drop. Her arm continued to pulse dully. She held it up against her chest to decrease the blood flow.

Dani cast her a questioning glance, one eyebrow cocked.

Lynn ignored her. She dropped her arm and skirted along the brick toward the side of the building. The entrance wasn't on this side. Time to find it. When she reached the corner, a rain-soaked, wide-open lot stretched out in front of her. There could be people or creatures hiding in or behind the car husks, but after waiting a while, Lynn began to doubt it. "Let me go ahead."

Dani nodded and reached down to grip Skeever's collar.

Lynn rushed across the lot. She was truly in the open now, fully exposed, and Lynn's heart once more pumped like mad. She skidded to a halt against the side of one of the car husks and crouched. A few cars lay between her and the steps up to the entrance, but the parking lot looked deserted. If she stayed here any longer, she would soak through. She would just have to risk it. Lynn waved Dani over and waited for her and Skeever to join her behind the car. "I say we go for it. Can't stay here, can't check if it's safe until we're in."

Dani clenched her jaw. She inspected Lynn through eyelashes heavy with droplets. Her hair stuck to her head in tangles. "Okay, do it."

Lynn cast one more look at the building, then ran to the steps in front of the entrance and under the overhang. It wasn't a big overhang, but it was enough to fit two people and half a dog. Lynn pressed herself to one side of the double doors, Dani to the other.

Shivering, Skeever leaned against Dani's legs.

The doors had once been made of glass, but it had been shattered long ago. They stood open now. The wind had swept leaves and dirt into the entranceway, but seeing as everything was equally dirty and equally windswept, Lynn couldn't pick out any tracks. Even up close, it was hard to see inside. Lynn caught sight of a solid-looking block of metal and wood, but that was it.

They nodded at each other.

In a crouch, Lynn stepped inside over the smashed glass. The entranceway floor was stained with something dark. There were no signs of debris or cave-ins, so she risked another few steps. Nothing moved. The rain pelting down covered even the noise of her own crunching footsteps.

There was a hallway to the left and one to the right. One branched off to the left of a metal-and-wood block that had most likely served as a desk. The only hallway with closed doors was the latter.

Dani followed her in.

Lynn could only just hear her boots crunch on the glass.

The wind died down and seemed to suck the air out of the building.

Skeever growled.

The sound distorted because of the rain, but it had Lynn turn to check on him.

He stood in the doorway, head low, teeth bared, and his tail between his legs.

Fear brought her heart rate to a frantic gallop, and she swirled back around even as she began to walk backward, toward the exit. "Back!"

Dani began to move, but it was too late.

From a hole in the ceiling, a heavy metal gate, suspended on thick chains, crashed down in front of their only exit.

Skeever jumped back just in time to avoid getting crushed, but his scramble had left him outside, separated from his masters by metal bars. He yelped, then started to bark fiercely. He threw his bulk against the gate, but it didn't budge.

Lynn had never heard him so frantic, which sledgehammered into her mind that the danger wasn't the gate. The danger was still coming. Her fingers trembled as she threw off her backpack. It crashed to the floor with a dull thud. If anything had broken inside, it was a worry for another time. She had only seconds before something would appear. Skeever sounded sure of that.

A dull thud indicated Dani had thrown her pack off too before moving to Lynn's side.

"Get ready." Lynn widened her stance.

"Ready." Dani's voice had raised an octave or two, but it sounded steady.

Lynn chanced a look.

Dani held on to her spear with both hands and had turned to face the right hallway. What Lynn could see of her expression and posture was reassuring: Dani was not going to die today.

Lynn turned to face the hallway to the left.

Skeever howled.

Answering howls echoed through the entryway, and Lynn knew what was coming. She swallowed down bile. Memories wore her nerves ragged.

Wolves. Again.

CHAPTER 12

Claws scraped over stone. Another howl reverberated down the hallway.

"Keep your back to mine." Lynn didn't look behind her to check if Dani followed her order.

Dani didn't reply, but she moved.

Lynn felt the bud of her spear against her shoulder and took a small step forward so she wouldn't get in the way.

No more than ten or fifteen seconds could have passed since the gate had come down, but they seemed to stretch forever as she waited for the inevitable. There was nowhere to run; they would either kill or be killed.

Lynn vowed to herself that this was not the day she'd die. She renewed the grip on her tomahawk as her palm became sweaty.

Dani gasped.

Lynn didn't have time to check. A wolf barreled down the hallway, slipped on the tiles, but corrected its trajectory by throwing itself against the wall before it launched at her.

Lynn flung herself sideways.

It skidded right past her. Teeth clashed as its powerful jaws snapped shut where her thigh had been just a split second prior. Before it could slow itself, it slammed into the opposite wall. The wolf growled, momentarily dazed.

Lynn hit the ground hard. Pain seared through her hip, but this was not the time to dwell on minor injuries. She rolled over and pushed up to her hands and knees. Her heart thundered in her chest.

Out of nowhere, something crashed into her.

Lynn went down again and scrambled away from the claws and teeth of another wolf. She rolled onto her back and sat, darting her gaze about.

Dani still stood. She'd lost her spear somewhere and now clutched her wicked blade. She held out one hand, palm forward, in the direction of the wolf that had first attacked Lynn.

It growled at her, ready for another strike.

Where's the other? Lynn jumped up and raised her tomahawk.

A whine drew her attention to the wolf that had first attacked Dani. Crashing into Lynn had changed its trajectory. It lay close to the marble desk. Dani's spear stuck from its chest. The animal flailed and got up before its front legs gave out and it dropped back down.

The other wolf growled.

Lynn whipped her head back just as it lunged at Dani.

Dani tried to withstand the charge but had to jump to the side. She slashed at it as it passed by but couldn't twist into the strike. The tomahawk made contact, but Lynn knew it wouldn't be a deep cut.

The wolf yelped, skidded, and locked its gaze on her.

The hunger in its yellow eyes made Lynn's skin crawl. Froth dripped to the ground as it snarled, displaying teeth almost as yellow as its eyes.

Skeever stopped barking only long enough to fill his lungs.

The wolf charged.

Lynn had only a second to swing her tomahawk. It connected behind the jawbone, and she used the momentum of the hastily placed blow to spin the predator around her body and into the gate.

Instantly, Skeever bit down into its flank through the bars.

The wolf yowled. Blood dripped down its slack lower jaw and turned the froth pink.

Lynn straightened. For the first time, she realized how mangled these wolves were. Their fur was matted and bloody in places neither of them had landed blows. They were skin over bone.

Dani came up beside her, knife at the ready. She kept her focused gaze on the other wolf now that they were once more flanked. It still hadn't gotten back up. Whatever Dani's spear had hit, the wolf had lost control of its legs.

Lynn's wolf pulled away from the gate. It trembled. Every step seemed like a struggle, but the intensity of its gaze didn't waver. Lynn got the feeling it was operating on hunger and hate alone. It began to circle her.

Lynn moved with it, always keeping it at her front. She would have to trust Dani to protect her from the other wolf. She weathered the wolf's gaze, then weathered the charge. She feinted to the right before she jumped to the left. Its sharp teeth narrowly missed her arm, but her tomahawk impacted perfectly on target. With a crunching sound, vertebrae gave way under the sharp edge of her weapon.

The wolf's howl of agony was cut short as it crashed heavily onto the stone. It slid along the tile and left a streak of red onto what Lynn now realized was an already blood-stained floor. Its chest rose and fell rapidly. Dazed yellow eyes searched the space for its attackers, but it had obviously lost control of its body.

Lynn lurched and stumbled forward to keep herself from falling again. Too late did she realize she'd ended up way too close to the other wolf with Dani's spear protruding from its chest—within biting distance. Panic exploded in her chest. She threw herself backward before the wolf's jaws could snap shut around her leg. Her frantic heart pumped so quickly she felt dizzy.

The wolf tried to scramble after her for another attempt.

Lynn raised her tomahawk even as she struggled not to slip on the bloody floor.

The wolf's jaws opened, and it rushed forward with whatever control it still had of its body—just enough to bridge the divide.

Lynn saw it happen, and she knew she wouldn't get out of the way fast enough. She gripped her tomahawk to strike instead.

Then something gripped the back of her jacket, and she was yanked backward. She landed hard on her ass, just out of reach of snapping jaws. She kicked, but swung only misses because Dani pulled her back another few feet.

The wolf's head fell. It panted. The fire had gone out of its eyes with the failure of its final stand.

Dani rushed forward.

Lynn tried to grab her, but Dani slipped past her groping fingers and sank her knife into the wolf's neck. She jerked the blade up, severing throat and windpipe in one go. A spray of blood hit Dani square in the chest, but she didn't react. She dropped the blade and yanked her spear out. In a fluid motion, she swirled around and forced the tip of it between the other wolf's ribs with a loud cry.

It yowled and threw its head up.

Dani pushed.

The yowl stopped. The wolf twitched. The yellow eyes rolled back into its skull.

Dani let go of the spear and stumbled back. She was out of breath, and her hands were clenched to fists. Both kills had taken only seconds, and Dani had executed them as gracefully as a dancer. She seemed dazed.

Skeever's unrelenting barking wasn't helping matters any.

Lynn whirled to face him. "Quiet!"

He snarled through the bars, all of his hair standing on end. He shivered with rage that couldn't go anywhere but his vocal cords.

"Quiet!" She snapped her fingers in front of his face, but far enough away to make sure he wouldn't bite at them.

He finally looked up at her. For a few seconds, he didn't seem to recognize her, and he snarled darkly. Then Lynn saw the light come on in his eyes. He barked twice more, then turned in a circle. He bumped his side along the gate.

"Stay." Lynn brought her hand down. "Stay."

After the second time she said it, he lay down under the overhang.

Carefully, she reached through the bars and smoothed his fur back down. "Good boy."

He whimpered and licked globs of saliva from his nuzzle. His eyelids fluttered.

Lynn finally allowed the realization that they'd survived to course through her. Her muscles relaxed a fraction, and she took a deep breath, savoring the knowledge it wouldn't be her last.

"We're not done yet."

Dani's voice pulled Lynn's gaze back to her.

Dani retrieved her knife and yanked the spear out. "Someone locked us in with these." She kicked the nearest wolf. "They starved 'em, tortured 'em, and sent them out to kill."

Lynn stared at the dead animals. This species of predator had most successfully navigated the apocalypse. They made their dens in abandoned buildings and roamed the Wilds, hunting for prey. At least once a day, she would catch a glimpse of shaggy gray fur or catch a low growl. Wolves were scary smart, too, which made them even more deadly. But Dani was right; these two hadn't ended up here by accident. She glanced back at the gate. "We need to get this up." She held no illusion that either of them could lift it. It was solid iron, the bars fist-thick. They would have to find whatever mechanism those chains were attached to.

Dani thrust her weapons into Lynn's hands.

Lynn nearly dropped them, surprised by the sudden weight. She clutched them against her chest to keep them from slipping. When she looked up again, Dani had made her way over to the gate.

She squatted, gripped the bars, and tried to lift the barrier with all her might. It didn't produce even an inch of movement. A vein in her neck thumped angrily.

"Dani, that—"

Dani ignored her. She tried to pull the gate aside instead. Again, her efforts had barely an impact.

Skeever got up and wagged his tail. He licked Dani's fingers as they gripped the bars.

"It's not going to work."

Dani yanked one more time, then stepped back. She glared at Lynn, as if this was somehow her fault. "Fine. Then we'll fight our way out. Are you up for that?" Her expression was unreadable, but Lynn didn't trust herself to read Dani anymore.

Lynn's body hurt, and she felt drained already. One fight like this was enough for a day. She nodded anyway. "Left or right?"

"Straight through the middle." Dani headed to the door that had remained closed. She gripped the handle and pulled, then pushed. "Locked." Before Lynn could offer advice, Dani made her way over to a heavy plant by the window. She kicked it over. Dirt and little brown balls scattered across the blood-, piss-, and shit-soaked tiles, but she paid it no heed and picked up the pot. Stumbling under its weight, she walked to the closed doors and threw it against the glass with another cry.

The noise of glass and pot shattering deafened Lynn a moment. It reverberated down the hallways and deeper into the building. It would announce to anyone that they had survived, but she was beyond caring.

Dani took her weapons back. She sheathed the knife behind her belt and gripped her spear. Her hands and arms were bloody, her jaw set. Lynn had snapped Skeever out of his bloodlust, but Dani seemed to use it as fuel. "Time to go."

Lynn followed her down the hallway and rallied her own energy. Dani was right; they would be fighting their way out of this, and Lynn knew weakness would equal death. She gripped the handle of her tomahawk and focused on the task at hand.

There were windows at the end of the hallway, but the walls were blind.

A tall, broad figure rushed around the corner.

Lynn startled and raised her tomahawk.

Dani stepped out, and the spear left her hand.

With only a few feet between her and the figure, they didn't have time to dodge. The spear struck them straight in the throat. The figure went down instantly.

It was a middle-aged man, Lynn saw as she came closer. He wore a leather chest piece, and he'd tied his long hair into a ponytail. He tried to breathe around the blood that filled his lungs. Lynn knew she would never forget the look of absolute horror on his face or the fear in his eyes as she passed him, but for now he was just one man down.

Dani yanked the spear out while he still shuddered. "Do you want the left or right?"

"L-Left." Lynn didn't want to split up, but she understood the need to. This way, they could ensure that even if their captors hoisted the gate, they would always run into one of them.

Dani turned right without sparing her a second glance. She stalked down the hallway, away from Lynn, like a hunter in search of prey.

Lynn's gut clenched. *Let's hope there aren't too many of them, though. Else we're dead.* She turned the other way and channeled her own hunting skills. There was reason to believe she was going to live through this: if their captors had to rely on wolves for protection, they were either weak, small in numbers, or both. She could still wind up dead if she let herself be caught off guard, though. Lynn focused on any sound that rose above the rain and on any scent not blood or mold. She scanned the hallway for movement but saw nothing. The entire right wall was made of windows, but the world outside was as dark as her heart felt. She reached down and gripped her knife in her left hand and renewed her hold on her tomahawk in her right. With a big breath, she pushed forward.

The offices had been raided long ago and were now deserted. Lynn worked to slow her heart rate and breathing; she needed to be able to think clearly. Just like Dani, she'd kill anyone she came across. Survival today was only possible if she took the lives of others.

She moved slowly, checking every room and every niche. The first of the offices was small. It held just a single desk that no one was hiding under. The rest of the hallway's doors led into one big room with at least a dozen desks, most of which had been upturned and ransacked. She weaved through them.

The rustling of her clothes and the creaking of floorboards was drowned out by the rain that beat against the glass.

Her shoulders hunched like those of the wolves they had just put out of their misery. Logic dictated there had to be someone here. The wolf that had first attacked her had come from the left, and the man from the right. He couldn't have released both wolves from their prisons at once, so the logical conclusion was that there was at least one other person here.

She passed another desk and stepped aside to peer under it. Nothing. Another desk, then another. She kept her back to the wall and studied every shifting shadow. Even pulling out a chair to check for people under the desk revealed nothing.

Once she came to the end of the room, she slipped back into the hallway and chanced a glance in the direction Dani had gone. The hallway was empty. Lynn turned back to the unexplored section of the passage. She had to focus on herself.

With her back against the wall, she peeked around the corner. In the seconds she allowed herself to poke her head out, the only thing she registered was a large metal cage, now empty. She stepped out and took a moment to admire it. Someone had put a lot of effort into making an iron cage that could have housed three wolves easily. Whoever had captured the wolves had padded the cage with a layer of grass and sand. Both were coated with dried and fresh blood.

"Bastards!" Abusing an animal into aggressiveness and then using it to do your dirty work. It was a brilliant setup but also completely without honor.

Only when Lynn walked closer to the cage did she see two doors. One was marked with a skirt-wearing figure, while a figure without a skirt graced the other. Listening at the door would be useless with this rain bearing down. She carefully put her knife away before she pushed the door with the skirtless symbol open. It was dark inside. The little light that fell into the room from behind her revealed a single cubicle and oddly shaped fountains—or something similar—along the wall. She let the door fall shut without entering.

The second room was a nearly identical copy in both décor and emptiness. There were no fountains here, and two cubicles instead of one. She carefully lowered herself to the ground to peer under the dividers.

The door of the cubicle flung outward. A figure lunged from within and rushed her way. Something metallic flashed.

Lynn's breath caught. She dropped her tomahawk so she could grab at the attacker's wrist as the woman lunged. They hit the ground hard, and Lynn gasped for air. Long, brown hair obscured her vision.

Her attacker smelled like wolf, smoke, and sweat. She was breathless already.

Lynn tried to push the woman off with her knees, but her attacker was heavier.

The woman grunted as she tried to push the knife down. She was missing a few teeth. The scent of rot hit Lynn as the woman exhaled. Her eyes held a glint of madness.

Lynn's arms trembled as she tried to fight the force applied by the woman above her. She was going to lose: her attacker could put all of her weight behind the motion, and Lynn had just the muscles in her arms. The realization filled her with renewed vigor to break the stalemate. She groped for another way to get the woman off her. Her arms threatened to buckle, which gave her the barest smidgen of an idea. She didn't have time to think about the stupidity of it; she had to go for it—or die.

Lynn lessened her struggle just a bit. This brought the woman closer as she leaned her entire body over Lynn's to put weight behind the blade. The sharp tip of the knife stopped inches above her chest when Lynn pushed to stop the descent of the blade. Every muscle in her body tensed. Her heart pounded wildly, and cold sweat pricked on her forehead. She needed to time this exactly right or risk impaling herself on the knife and doing the woman's work for her. Just as her arms were about to give out, she pushed up with her abdominal muscles and slammed her forehead against the woman's skull hard enough to make herself see stars.

"Fuck!" The woman sat up over Lynn's abdomen and gripped her head.

The knife fell to the floor.

Elation burned hotly in Lynn's system: this was her chance. She swung her tired arm out and brought it down against the woman's ear with as much force as she could muster.

The stranger yelped and lost her balance.

Lynn tilted her hips, bucked her off, then scrambled to get control of the knife.

The woman's eyes widened. She rushed to grab it as well.

Before her attacker could close her hand around the knife, Lynn gripped her wrist. She threw her body into the other woman's until she was sprawled on top of her, and they writhed together on the floor, trying to scratch and bite any part of the other that came close enough to reach. This was fighting at its most animalistic: bare survival without thought of tactics or a next move.

Lynn's tomahawk had clattered somewhere out of sight, and she had her knife in her boot but if she reached for it, the woman would grab the knife and undoubtedly kill her. That weapon needed to be gone before she could even hope to think of what to do next. Lynn elbowed her attacker in the breast.

The woman cried out and went limp just long enough for Lynn to grab the knife. She scrambled to crawl more firmly on top of the woman, sucked in a few gulps of air, then pushed up so she could straddle her hips. Before Lynn's brain could catch up and intervene, Lynn plunged the knife down.

The woman whimpered and froze. Her eyes widened. The look of absolute terror on her attacker's face would be another thing Lynn would remember forever.

Lynn clenched her jaw to steel her resolve and twisted the blade deep inside of the woman's shoulder, just where it met the neck. Then she yanked the knife out.

Now the woman cried out. She thrashed, scratched, hit. She fought like any animal would when it thought it still had a chance to live.

Lynn knew that chance was gone. Even if the woman managed to fight Lynn off, every movement quickened the pace of the gushes with which the arterial spray painted the wall. She was dead; she just didn't know it yet. Lynn fought the urge to squeeze her eyes shut. Instead, she tossed the knife away as far as she could and fought for control of the woman's wrists. Lynn was panting now, and sweat slid down her back. Somewhere in the fight, she'd detached from her emotions. Cold determination was all that was left in her.

"S-Stop! Please!" The other woman sobbed. Her legs kicked out, but Lynn had found a good position, so her attacker couldn't reach her. "Just... wanted...survive!"

Lynn pressed the woman's wrists down with far more ease than only a few seconds prior.

The force and frequency of the spray lessened.

Something wet trailed down Lynn's face—blood or tears, she didn't know. Her chest contracted painfully. Unable to watch a moment longer, she closed her eyes.

The woman's breathing became irregular. She inhaled with ragged shudders and exhaled almost right away.

How much longer will it take?

The resistance slowly wavered. The inhalations became fragmented, seemed to seize, then started again for two or three breaths. It was endless. Lynn opened her eyes and found the world fuzzy with moisture. She had been crying—was still crying.

The woman was watching her with pale blue eyes. She was older than Lynn by at least ten years, maybe more. An ugly scar ran along her left cheek.

"You," Lynn accentuated the word strongly, "attacked us. Not the other way around."

The woman swallowed. Fresh tears spilled from her eyes. She turned her head away and squeezed her eyes shut. She inhaled one more time, twice, then it stopped. This time, her breathing didn't start up again.

Lynn sagged forward. Her arms trembled. She tried to catch her breath, but the second she inhaled, her stomach turned. Lynn felt it coming and stumbled off to vomit violently in a rush of disgust and relief. Finally, only sour slime remained in her mouth. She spit it out and wiped her hand with an arm she could barely control.

As much as she wanted to curl up into a ball and recover, she wasn't done. With great effort, she pulled her shaky legs under her and got up. With her reclaimed tomahawk in hand, she headed back down the hallway.

Dani met her halfway down.

Despite all her lies and schemes, Lynn relaxed just a little as she laid eyes upon her. At least she wasn't alone in this building full of enemies.

Dani inspected her. Judging by the squint that etched into Dani's features, Lynn was showing her wear and tear. "You okay?"

Lynn nodded. She was nowhere near okay either physically or emotionally, but it was useless to dwell on that right now. "One dead."

Dani continued to inspect her.

Lynn tried to weather it.

Eventually, Dani relented. "Good. There's a staircase at the end of the hall. I didn't find anyone else, but I think I heard something upstairs." She observed Lynn. "Are you ready for more?"

Lynn nodded again, without knowing if it was true. "Let's just get this over with." She pushed past Dani and headed down the hallway. She was tired—so tired. Whoever remained, she just wanted to dole out justice, go to sleep, and forget.

There was only darkness up the steps. She forced her tired muscles to grip her tomahawk more tightly and walk up.

Dani followed her quietly.

From halfway up the stairs, Lynn could look through the glass panels of the railing that squared off the staircase. A narrow hallway led all down the length of the building, mirroring the one downstairs. Doors opened into a space that Lynn couldn't see into from here. Waist-height white walls blocked her view. She went up a few more steps until she could look through long panes of glass atop the walls. As quietly as possible, she took the last step up from the stairs and stopped to slide her gaze over the mayhem beyond the glass.

From here, she could just make out the layout of the large space. The left side was piled full of junk—mostly dividers, desks, and chairs—while the right side had been cleared and made up as a living space. Three makeshift beds lay under the windows.

Dani stepped up with her. "Three beds." She whispered the words. They were almost entirely drowned out by the sound of the rain that was more pronounced here, as they were under the roof.

Lynn nodded. Three beds, three people. One of their attackers still lurked somewhere in the building. She rounded the railing and tried the door farthest to the left. It opened easily, and she slipped inside.

Dani followed her in but stayed a few paces behind her. She lowered herself down to the ground and looked through the pile of office paraphernalia. She lay her spear on the floor and took out her knife.

Their gazes met.

Dani nodded slowly.

There hadn't been any communication about the plan of action, but they both knew basic hunting strategies.

Lynn pushed up and rounded the pile. She let her gaze slide over the mess but still saw nothing.

"Come out and meet your death with honor." Despite her anxiety, Lynn's voice was mercifully steady and calm. The hairs on the back of her neck stood on end, and she felt targeted in the middle of the room. There was a good chance the third attacker was hiding somewhere else, and then she'd left herself exposed. She counted to ten. "I know you are in there. Your two companions are already dead. The wolves are dead. You gambled and lost."

Nothing moved. Nothing made a sound. More seconds passed.

Lynn resisted the urge to look at Dani. "Don't make me co—"

The pile moved. There was a small avalanche as a figure pushed out of a hidey-hole in the back of it.

When a desk came tumbling down and crashed in front of her, Lynn jumped back.

The figure climbed over the debris and stumbled toward the open door.

Lynn caught a glint of metal as Dani's blade caught the light.

The figure crumpled but didn't collapse; Dani guided the body down.

Lynn rushed over to confirm the kill.

The boy—he couldn't be more than eleven—coughed blood. His wide eyes fastened on her in terror.

Lynn swallowed. Cold flooded her body from her crown to her toes. "Shit."

Dani held him. She looked up in bewilderment and regret, but the knife stuck out of his chest all the way to the hilt.

There are no do-overs in life. Who had told her that? The memory refused to materialize, perhaps because she was too preoccupied with the death of a child—a death they'd caused.

Dani stroked the boy's matted hair with a hand stained red by his parents' blood. "I'm sorry." She murmured the words close to his face as she rocked him gently.

Lynn crouched down. She felt numb. Her empty stomach rebelled again, but she had nothing left to throw up.

The boy sucked in another breath, then another.

His struggle was all the more painful to watch with images of the inevitable conclusion of his suffering fresh in her memory. "It'll be over soon." Lynn barely managed to get the words out.

The boy groaned. His eyes fell shut, but unlike his mom, he seemed unwilling to lose sight of the world around him. His chest rose and fell. With every exhale, blood bubbled up between his lips. When he tried to inhale, he choked and coughed, spraying droplets.

Dani jumped when the blood hit her, but only tightened her hold. The red drops stood out on her extremely pale skin. Her arms trembled. She continued to stroke his hair. Was she thinking of Toby, as Lynn was? Because she kept seeing Tobias in the boy cradled in Dani's arms.

Lynn slowly reached out to take the boy's hand.

He squeezed it with as much strength as he could muster, then inhaled and exhaled one more time. His grip lessened and then became non-existent. His body relaxed.

Seconds ticked by.

Dani sniffed. "I want to bury him." Her voice was a hoarse whisper.

"Okay." Lynn had been about to say the same. An eleven-year-old boy hadn't thought up this plan. He was just a victim of it, same as them.

Dani continued to stroke his hair.

"Are you…you know? All right?"

Dani hesitated, then her head bobbed up and down almost imperceptibly. "Yeah."

Had Dani believed her when she'd said the same a few minutes ago? Lynn certainly didn't believe her now. She debated whether she should say anything, but then some of the hurt over Dani's betrayal came back and she returned her gaze to the boy. What a mess this was, killing a child.

Dani lifted her hand from the boy's short brown hair and pulled her arm out from under his neck. Slowly, she sat up and took the hilt of the knife with a slightly trembling hand. She slid the knife out. A small stream of blood trickled down over his woolen shirt, too quickly to be absorbed.

Lynn set her jaw. Bile rose again, but she forced it down. She pushed up and took a step back. The distance helped settle her stomach. "We should wrap him. We'll bury him in the morning."

Dani wiped her blade on the carpet. She took a deep breath. "Could you grab a blanket or something?" She nodded toward the beds.

"Yeah." She turned to get one. When she clenched and unclenched her fist to chase away the feeling of the boy's hand in hers, she realized she'd busted up her knuckles when fighting his mother. Her head throbbed.

They wrapped the boy so he was fully encapsulated and protected.

Dani stroked his head one more time through the thick layer of wool before she stood. "Let's get him downstairs."

Lynn could tell she hadn't meant for her voice to break. Dani also hadn't meant for her hands to tremble as she tried to put her knife away, nor for her knees to buckle as the first sob tore through her body.

CHAPTER 13

LYNN RUSHED FORWARD AND CAUGHT Dani as her legs gave out. It was a purely reflexive response, because she had no idea what to do next. She'd been comforted as a child, so she had some memories of that. As far as Lynn could remember, she'd never been on the giving end of such intimate human-to-human contact. Dani's weight against her body made the next step easy. She lowered them both to the floor.

Dani brought her hands up over her face. Their legs tangled as Lynn tried to find a way to hold herself up with her good arm and wrap Dani up with the other. Dani crumpled further and gripped Lynn's jacket high up her chest while the other arm settled around her waist. She buried her face into the crook of Lynn's neck.

Lynn struggled not to tense. This amount of physical contact set off every warning bell inside of her skull. She could picture a thousand ways Dani could kill her from this position. They presented themselves to her in flashes of half-formed images of blood and violence. Rationally, she knew Dani wasn't going to harm her, but years of always being on guard were hard to ignore. Just to make herself more comfortable, she pushed the leg with the knife in her boot out a bit, away from Dani and within easy reach.

Dani was still sobbing. Her body shook with each one.

Her hair tickled Lynn's skin. *Do something, Tanner! Get yourself out of this!* Anna had always rocked her when she'd cried, so she started to rock Dani as well. She really wanted to put distance between them, but she was still determined to prove to Dani that she was a decent person—even though she knew she didn't have anything to prove anymore.

Slowly, some of the tension drained out of Dani. Her grip on Lynn's jacket lessened. After a few more seconds, her clawing fingers relaxed entirely and settled on the leather.

The positive result sent a wave of relief through Lynn. It was a good start. What else had Anna done to calm her? Lynn cautiously slid her hand up over Dani's back.

It caused a momentary stiffening of Dani's body, but when Lynn's hand reached her hair, Dani relaxed again.

Experimentally, Lynn stroked. When Dani's sobs turned to sniffs, she started to work tangles out of Dani's hair with her fingers. This seemed to soothe Dani even more: she slumped against Lynn in surrender, something Lynn found equal parts terrifying, impressive, and endearing—all because she would never have put this kind of trust in another person. *Unless she's playing you again.* But why would she? She already had Lynn committed.

Now that Dani wasn't crying as hard anymore, a quietness settled heavily between them. The rain still came down, but this silence wasn't about the absence of noise. Lynn experienced it as an extreme awareness of Dani's body against hers—heavy, warm, and intimate. The anxiety she felt about letting anyone get so close lingered.

Dani sniffed. She gave no indication of discomfort beyond her inner turmoil.

Lynn looked around the room to find anything that would either further soothe or potentially distract Dani. Her gaze landed on what was probably the mechanism for the gate. The family—or whoever had lived here prior—had managed to cut a hole through the floor close to the wall. The gate extended down on two chains that ran through screw eye hooks in the ceiling above the hole. The chains were long enough to span the breadth of the room, where they ran through two screw eyes again. From there, they fell down past two hooked pins in the wall, just big enough to fit through the chain loops. With proper timing, lowering the gate was probably as easy as yanking the two chains off the pins at the same time and standing back while gravity took hold. Pulling the gate up was going to be a heavy, but doable chore if they both worked at it.

Lynn's inspection had taken a few minutes. By then, stroking Dani's hair had become a repetitive motion without much thought put into it. To Lynn's great surprise, her anxiety level had come down with her distraction.

Yes, she still was very aware of Dani's body curled against her own, but she no longer thought about the many ways this could potentially be lethal.

Dani's breathing had settled. She inhaled and exhaled deeply against the skin of Lynn's neck. Her hand had fallen from Lynn's chest to her lap, but the other arm was still wrapped loosely around Lynn's waist.

"Are you okay?" Lynn kept her voice soft and friendly. She would be mortified to have collapsed so completely, and she didn't want to give Dani the feeling she was judging her, just in case her collapse had been genuine.

Dani took a deep breath and scooted away until there was no more physical contact between them. She cleared her throat, wiped her eyes, and sniffed once. "Yeah." She checked on Lynn. "Sorry."

Lynn didn't know how she felt about the whole affair, so she opted for neutrality. "No problem." She gave Dani a short smile. "I found out how to open the gate, if you want to give that a go."

Dani was on her feet before Lynn finished talking. She swayed lightly. Her expression was flat, her skin pale under the blush of her breakdown.

Lynn tried to catch her gaze, but Dani refused to meet her eyes.

"Where do I go?"

Lynn pointed at the chains. "Back there." She stood as well.

Dani crossed the space and took in the hoisting mechanism. "You want to, um...bury him now?"

Lynn shook her head. "It's raining buckets. I don't want to be out in that for hours. I want the gate up to let Skeever in, and I figured we could get the wolves out. The boy's parents too. We wouldn't have to be out in that downpour for long, and it'll get the stench down."

Dani seemed to consider it, then nodded. "Okay, let's get the gate up, then."

Skeever rushed up the stairs to greet them before they made it even halfway down.

Lynn sidestepped his assault, which meant Dani took the brunt of it.

He pounced on her and almost toppled her over. His momentum forced Dani to lower herself down to the steps, where she accepted him into her arms and buried her head in his fur. Perhaps she took comfort from his familiar scent, as Lynn did.

He doesn't judge us on our mistakes either. Lynn looked away and made her way down to give Dani some time to herself.

Skeever pounced her, almost tipping her over, then took off down the hallway like a bat out of hell, barking once for good measure.

Lynn grinned and shook her head. "Idiot." It was good to see so much life in the face of such horrendous death. She followed him down the hallway. When she stepped over the male body, some of her renewed sense of relief faded. He'd bled out or had choked on his own blood. She reached the smashed doors before she realized Dani was no longer behind her.

Dani stood over the body, her spear hand clenched to a fist. What little color had returned to her features had drained again. Lynn was struck by how little she seemed to have in common with the enraged hunter who'd struck the man down with a single throw. It was hard to watch the horror and regret about her actions dance across Dani's face.

Fueled by a need to comfort, Lynn took a step back down the hallway. "Dani?" She extended her hand. "Come on."

Dani's gaze lingered on the body for a few more seconds before she managed to tear it away. She frowned at the outstretched hand.

Lynn suddenly felt self-conscious about her actions but endured the discomfort. Dani must be feeling much worse right now. "It's in the past, okay? Time to move on."

Dani hesitated. Her gaze flickered back down, then settled on Lynn's hand again. She kept watching it until she closed her own hand around it and squeezed it tightly. Then she met Lynn's eyes. "Thank you." Her voice was raspy.

Lynn squeezed back and smiled a little. Something fluttered from her belly up to her throat. "We're in this together, right?"

Dani smiled a little and nodded. Her gaze dropped to their still-linked hands. "Right." She slowly withdrew her hand and slid her thumb along the back of her own fingers as if she could still feel Lynn's touch. "Together."

Lynn became aware of her heartbeat hammering inside her chest. Her hand tingled. She took a deep breath to steady herself and took in the battlefield. The two wolf carcasses lay next to each other. Their blood had mixed into a darkening puddle, only partially absorbed by soil and the little balls that had come out of the planter. The sight was sobering. Dani still seemed a little dazed, so Lynn started to unbutton her coat. While she had other pants and shirts to wear, she would have to go without a coat tomorrow if it got soaked. "Ready to drag them out?"

Dani finally looked away from her hand. She took in the wolves instead. "Let's get it over with." She followed Lynn's example and took off her jacket.

Lynn decided to leave her boots behind as well.

After a moment's hesitation, Dani did so too.

The wolves were pathetically light. Lynn dragged wolf number one down the stairs by herself and left a blood smear all the way to the center of the parking lot, where she dropped it. Her nose itched, but she swore not to scratch until she was clean; handling the wolf had left her hands stained with blood and who knew what kinds of dirt. The rain pelting down washed some of the grime off right away, but she still felt dirty.

Dani waited for Lynn to walk back before handing over her spear and dragging wolf number two out while Lynn stood watch.

Lynn wasn't proficient with a spear, but she knew the pointy end went into anything that tried to attack.

Skeever ran back and forth, obviously excited by the commotion, but he stayed away from the wolves. Lynn couldn't blame him; their scent still hung heavily in the entryway.

Dani returned. Her hair had matted to her skull even from the few seconds of exposure, and her woolen shirt had soaked up the water like a sponge, making it seem twice as voluminous. "The uh...parents next, right?" Dani's eyes betrayed her reluctance.

Lynn handed the spear back. She was relieved that, just like yesterday, the heavy rain seemed to have driven all the animals into their lairs and dens, and she hadn't had a reason to use it. "I've got it. Stand guard, okay?"

Dani examined her.

Lynn was sure she would refuse the offer, but then Dani nodded.

"Okay." She swallowed and stepped out into the rain, both hands around the shaft of the spear.

Lynn wondered what she was thinking. Did she appreciate Lynn's offer? Did it make her feel better? *I hope so...* She put the thought out of her head since there was grunt work to do.

The dead could be dragged, even though her arms felt like wet rags. Her back protested heavily against the work, but she persevered. She laid first the man, then the woman next to the wolves. She straightened and caught her breath as the rain soaked through her clothes.

Dani hadn't looked at the bodies as she dragged them past her.

Lynn felt her gaze on her back as she inspected the pile of death at her feet. Soon, predators and scavengers would be drawn to the smell and tear them apart. They deserved it, but looking down at their bodies chilled her more than any amount of rain pelting down on her ever could. She glanced at Dani, who stood stock-still where she'd taken up sentry. It was time to go inside. They would both catch their deaths out here. Lynn ascended the steps and stroked Dani's ice-cold hand. "Come on, let's get dry."

Dani blinked and turned her head to look at her. For a second, she didn't seem to recognize her, then she relaxed. "Yes, please."

Lynn peeled off her clothes with difficulty. Everything stuck to her. Goose bumps coursed over her skin. The little office Lynn had directed Dani to was warmer than the rest of the building—the closed door had trapped the day's heat—but the rain had left her shivering.

At the other end of the room, Dani stripped down too. Lean muscle and marred skin came into view. Dani's body was a lot less skeletal than Lynn's own. She didn't have much fat on her, but her bones were much less pronounced and her muscles strong. Homestead living evidently paid off. Dani wrung her hair out before she used a shirt to rub it dry to the point where it didn't drip anymore. She seemed more relaxed, as if removing the bodies had lifted some of her burden.

Lynn was grateful Dani seemed to have control of herself again. Now that there weren't any more bodies to haul, Lynn had no idea how to deal with emotions as powerful as Dani's; she could barely handle her own. All she did was shut down and not think about what had happened.

"You didn't walk away from all your fights unscathed, did you?"

Lynn startled and looked up.

Dani was inspecting her—or, more accurately, her many burns, scars, and other marks. Her gaze lingered on a rather pronounced scar just below Lynn's rib cage. "What happened to give you that?"

Lynn touched the uneven patch of skin. "An unfortunate encounter with an iron rod."

Dani's expression didn't change. Her gaze remained on the round, white mark. "Ouch."

Lynn shrugged it off, as if being impaled hadn't been the single most painful thing she had ever experienced—physically, anyway. The emotional pain of losing her father in the same collapse had been indescribably worse. "It healed, but I did get coughing sickness almost right after, so it took forever until I was on my feet again."

Dani dried the dark hairs under her armpits. "I had that once. I've never felt so miserable in my life. Every time I'd breathe in, I thought I would drown. It was horrible."

Lynn wrung her hair out. "It was the same for me. There was this gurgle in my lungs every time I breathed. I think that's the closest I've gotten to dying without an attack."

"I'm glad you made it." Dani's gaze had fallen away from Lynn's body.

Lynn blinked. She didn't know how to take that. The comment warmed her far more than a few simple words should. *Focus, Lynn, focus. Don't fall for it.* Dani was just trying to assure she came along... Right? "Um... thanks."

Dani smiled but didn't look back up.

The silence that followed left Lynn feeling unbalanced—something she wasn't familiar with. When she looked up, Dani was just drying the curls covering her sex, which made Lynn's insides—and cheeks—even hotter. She quickly looked away and wrestled her damp body into woolen breeches and her sole cotton shirt. "I'm, um, gonna check out the upstairs. Find some food and such. Okay?"

Dani nodded. She was still entirely—gloriously—naked. "Okay."

Lynn felt her gaze on her all the way down the hall, even though she knew the closed door would have blocked Dani's view of her long ago.

Skeever followed her as she made her way to the family's living room.

The moment she entered, her gaze was drawn to the boy's covered body. It was still exactly where they'd left it. *Of course, he's dead.* And yet a small part of her had hoped that maybe it hadn't happened after all. She forced herself to focus on the family's supplies instead.

They had definitely not been the first to fall victim to the family's trap. A wall-to-wall shelving unit held an astonishing variety of items: pre- and post-war jewelry, clothes in various sizes, weapons, food, pots, pans, blankets, fishing gear, hunting traps, cutlery, plates, bottles, cans—pretty much everything that was in Lynn's pack but in quantities that could have supplied a settlement twice as large as the Homestead.

Lynn walked along the shelves and ran her fingers along the neatly sorted piles and stacks. She wanted to take it all, but traveling with nothing more than what fit into and onto your backpack was essential. Anything more and you got slow and encumbered. Either was lethal in the Wilds. But she could upgrade what she already owned and eat well tonight. Whoever had owned all of this before was undoubtedly never going to use it again.

Lynn started with a new backpack. A sturdy backpack was critical, and hers was fraying on all sides. She slipped the empty cow-hide pack over her arms and checked how it settled against her back and onto her shoulders. The fit was comfortable, so it was time to fill it up.

By the time she was done sorting through the massive amount of inventory, she'd found replacements for two woolen sweaters and had added a second cotton shirt, two pairs of pants, and four pairs of socks to her wardrobe. She picked up a long, thin blade more suitable for filleting fish than fighting and added a slingshot and a pouch with pebbles to her arsenal.

A finely crafted bow made her hesitate. She was completely unfamiliar with long-range weapons, so taking it could be a boon if she learned to use it, but bows used up arrows, and she wasn't a fletcher. Learning how to make decent ones and becoming proficient with the weapon could take months. She put the bow back on the shelf. As much as it pained her to leave behind something so precious, hauling something around without a foreseeable payout was against her personal philosophy.

I'll sleep on it.

She did take some of the prettier pieces of jewelry—pre-war pieces specifically. In settlements, there were always people willing to trade for those. One of the family's victims had carried a flat, thin pan to fry things on. She took it without hesitation, even though it was heavy. The family had also amassed quite a collection of containers, many of which in better shape than her cans, so she added them to her quickly filling pack.

Once she came to the food, she hesitated again. There was a small chance the family had poisoned some of it. It was far more likely they would have relied on their heavy gate to keep people out in the first place, but Lynn still discarded anything she found suspect.

She was slowly relaxing. Focusing on a task as mundane as sorting drained the tension from her shoulders and limbs. The heavy gate in front of the door shielded them from danger, and Lynn had found a lot of things that would make their lives easier. There was a lot of food here, and most of it didn't need cooking like the monkey Dani had killed. Since Lynn hadn't found where the family made fire yet—it certainly wasn't indoors—cooking that was out. She supposed there was no time like the present to test the theory that the food was safe to eat.

"Dinner is served." Lynn pushed the door shut behind her, accidently only just allowing Skeever to push in with his tail intact. "Sorry, boy."

He already trotted along the walls of the small office, near incident forgotten.

Dani sat up from the bedding she'd settled on.

Lynn was relieved to note she was dressed again.

"Thanks." Dani took the loaded plate Lynn offered. "Is it safe?" She inspected the various cheeses, carrots, jerky strips, bread, and apple slices Lynn had piled on.

"No guarantees. I tossed out anything I didn't trust." She slid off her new backpack and lowered herself down onto the bedding.

"Okay." Dani licked her lips and settled the plate on her crossed legs so she could break open the chunk of bread and stuff it with cheese and jerky. "Did you find anything good?" She glanced at the bulging brown-and-white-patched pack.

"Yeah, I—" Lynn stopped and held her plate away from an inquisitive snout. "Skeeve, no!" She pushed him away. "Can we give him your monkey?"

"Huh?" Dani stared at her.

Lynn nodded toward Dani's own pack. "The monkey. It'll go bad."

Dani followed her gaze down to the small carcass strapped to her pack. "Sorry. Yeah, sure."

Lynn pushed up again. Her muscles resisted the motion but obeyed under protest. "Hold this." She handed Dani her plate.

Dani took it, already chewing on a big bite of her sandwich.

"Come, Skeeve. Come here." Lynn lured him away from Dani with a snap of her fingers, undid the string holding the monkey tied to the backpack, and took the meat into the hallway.

Skeever followed her with a wagging tail.

Lynn plucked most of the blood-soaked grass from inside the carcass, then tossed it to him. "Enjoy." He started the laborious process of tearing meat from bone with vigor.

Lynn quickly closed the door on him to preserve her appetite. Just enough of the fading daylight remained in the room to notice that Dani watched her as Lynn cleaned her hands on her wet sweater laid out in a corner—she wasn't taking it anyway now that she'd found replacements. When Lynn sat again, Dani silently handed back her plate.

"You were telling me about what you'd found." Dani was already halfway through her bread.

Lynn bit into an apple slice, chewed, and swallowed. "Right. Well, there's lots. You should check it out for yourself. I didn't take anything there wasn't more of. There's also water barrels up there, so we can fill up our bottles before we leave."

"Good. I'll check later." Dani kept looking at her, which brought back that tingly feeling that made Lynn so uncomfortable.

"What?" She halted her assault on her dinner momentarily to meet Dani's inquisitive eyes.

"We should be dead, you know?" Her tone was deceptively light. "Maybe those wolves were just too abused, too weak, but we should be in pieces."

"We're both trained hunters. Two wolves in tight quarters are a challenge, sure, but we made it through."

"We did," Dani said darkly. "But we should still have walked away with injuries. I'm guessing a lot of people weren't so lucky."

Lynn put her plate down and wiped her fingers on her new shirt. She took Dani's hand.

Dani's gaze darted to their linked fingers, but she didn't object.

It felt odd to Lynn too. It also felt nice. Dani's calloused hand was warm, and holding it made Lynn feel warm in turn. "You can't dwell on that. It's in the past. They're dead, we're not. And the people responsible for it are dead as well. That's the law of the Wilds."

"Do you think the wolves got them? The—" Dani hesitated. "The people they killed?"

Lynn shook her head. "No, probably not. Not as food anyway. I really hope they buried them, but I'm afraid that they ended up bait for any wolf that needed replacing." The thought was disturbing enough to quench right away.

"I hate it out here." Dani stared at the plate in her lap.

She sounded so dejected that Lynn looked up at her. "I can't blame you. I don't like the Wilds much either, but it's...home. I guess." She bit into another apple slice as she mulled over how messed up that statement was. It was true, though; she was much better equipped to handle deadly predators than settlement politics.

Dani seemed to think a moment, then captured her gaze. "Maybe you can stay at the Homestead if I talk to the others." She refused to look away, which put even more weight onto the words. "We need someone who can go out and get things done. You could do what Richard did. If we bring him back, they will have to let you stay."

Another warning coursed down her spine. "Is that part of the plan you cooked up with Kate?"

Dani stared at her without comprehension, then the light came on, and she shook her head. "Oh. No. That never came up. We figured the best-case scenario was that you'd help me get him back. They, um, they don't trust you."

The implied rest of the sentence hung heavily in the air.

Lynn decided to voice it. "But you do? Trust me?"

Dani shrugged. "I don't know. So far, you've been pretty honest. Uncomplicated."

"Uncomplicated?" She definitely didn't know if she liked that term.

"I meant...straightforward. Loyal, maybe." She glanced up at Lynn from under her lashes.

Lynn didn't know what to feel about those terms either, but the words heated her chest and cheeks. "Dani..." She sighed and looked down at their joined hands. "You know Kate and the group better than I do, and maybe Kate already talked to you about this, but I-I think Kate wants you to take Richard's place as your group's scout." She watched how the words landed, but the minute twitches and widening of Dani's eyes could mean a host of things. She pushed on.

"If I've learned anything about settlements, it's that the people in them always have to adapt quickly to changing circumstances, and in this case, that means filling a position of vital importance. You were all sure I wasn't going to come back, and you're the most logical person to fulfill the position. You have the basic skills, and Kate trusts you."

Dani opened her mouth to speak, but Lynn had more to say, so she rolled right over what would undoubtedly be Dani's objection. "If Kate already discussed this with you or if you think I'm totally wrong, then I'm sorry for even bringing it up. But what if Kate's banking on you picking up everything you need to know about wilderness survival while you're out with me so you can do the job once you get back?"

"I—" Dani cut herself off. Her hand twitched in Lynn's grip.

Dread settled in Lynn's gut, and she was suddenly sure she was right and that Dani knew it.

Then Dani pulled her hand away, and her certainty faded. Another possibility presented itself to her: maybe Dani thought she was just trying to cause a rift between her and the Homestead people so Dani wouldn't want to go back. *Or maybe she's sad because she thinks you might be right and there wouldn't be room for you.* She shouldn't have brought it up. "Look, maybe I'm wrong. Don't worry about it, okay? We'll just see what happens when we get back."

Dani nodded slowly. She looked down at her lap. "I…I think I need to sleep." She put her plate aside and settled onto the bedding, her back to Lynn.

Lynn pressed her hand against her thigh to chase away the feeling of emptiness. "Okay. Sorry."

As Dani extended her legs, Lynn was forced to scoot away from the wall to make room for them. It felt like a clear dismissal. Lynn knew she'd messed up. Dani must be thinking Lynn was trying to play her again. *Stupid! You were finally getting some solid ground under you!*

"Lynn?"

Lynn whipped her head about so she could look at Dani. "Yeah?"

"Would you, um, stay with me tonight? Like…here. On the bed? I-I think I'll have nightmares." She didn't elaborate on the cause of those nightmares—today's events or her worries about the future.

"Um." She hesitated. A spike of anxiety left a sensation of pinpricks on her skin. "You're not...you know, mad?"

Dani rolled over and frowned up at her. "Mad? No. I'm just... I don't want to think anymore."

Lynn watched her, trying to draw the truth out of her by sheer willpower, but she didn't spot dishonesty in Dani's eyes. Of course that didn't mean anything; she had never been capable of accurately reading her emotions, let alone whether she spoke the truth. "H-How do you...?"

Dani licked her lips. Her shoulder drew up into a little shrug. "Dunno. Whatever you're comfortable with."

I have no idea what I'm comfortable with. "Okay." After a moment's hesitation, she put her plate down and awkwardly lowered herself onto the bedding behind Dani. She made sure their bodies didn't touch anywhere, but she could still feel the warmth radiate off Dani's body. Very lightly, she laid her hand on Dani's hip.

Dani jumped ever so slightly, then relaxed with an audible exhale. She rolled back over until she faced the wall again.

"Is this okay?" Lynn whispered the words. Her breath stirred Dani's half-dried hair.

Dani nodded. She seemed to hesitate, then scooted back until she connected with Lynn's chest. Her ass settled against Lynn's crotch. The back of her legs pressed against Lynn's thighs.

Heat flashed through Lynn. Her eyes widened, and she swallowed down a lump of panic. She hadn't been this physically intimate with someone in years. Her heart rate spiked to a jittery gallop that made her a little light-headed again. She slid her arm more firmly around Dani's waist.

Dani didn't object. "Good night," she whispered.

"Good night." It was all Lynn could get out, completely overloaded by sensations.

CHAPTER 14

SUNLIGHT HIT HER FACE THROUGH the windows. Lynn groaned when wakefulness tugged at her. She blinked her eyes open to scan her surroundings and realized Dani wasn't there. Skeever had taken her place on the bedding. The door was shut.

When Dani had extracted herself from her hold as first light hit the room, Lynn had woken up, and Dani had told her to go back to sleep. In order to avoid any awkwardness, Lynn had.

She sat up, unpleasantly surprised by the amount of pain that flared through her battered limbs. These last few days were taking their toll. The night had been weird too. She hadn't expected to fall asleep, and she didn't remember it happening. She'd slept the sleep of the dead. That was something Lynn had never thought would happen when touching another person—but it had.

Lynn shook her hair out and got up. She didn't want to think about what all of this meant. She had a sneaking suspicion that if she allowed herself to go down that mental road, she'd come to realize that the defining factor in her sleeping so profoundly had been Dani. Thoughts like that would get complicated really fast.

As she pulled the door open, Skeever whimpered but didn't rouse.

Guess someone else is getting a good night's sleep too. Lynn couldn't help smiling. "Dani?" A tiny, nervous flutter coursed through her at the thought of seeing Dani again after last night. Should she bring up holding her? Would it be weird if she did? Would it be weirder if she didn't?

"Over here!" Dani's voice came from upstairs.

Lynn steeled herself. She followed the sound up and looked outside through the windows as she climbed the stairs. The rain had ceased. From what she could see of the sky, it would be a clear, dry day. Perfect for traveling—and for digging a grave. She hadn't forgotten about burying the boy.

Dani sat cross-legged on the floor of the family's living room. She had laid out twenty or so items around her backpack. Some were part of her old gear; some were new additions from the family's stores. Judging by the way Dani's pack stood open and she inspected every item, she was deciding which items were worthy enough to take up valuable space in her inventory.

"Morning." Lynn kept her voice neutral but allowed a small smile.

Dani smiled too. "Morning. I'm almost ready. I already ate too." She pointed at a plate by her leg. "By the time you've finished breakfast, I'll be done."

Lynn inspected her. She seemed more rested too and far more at ease than last night. Something felt off, though, something Lynn couldn't place. Dani seemed a little too chipper. The boy's body lay maybe twenty paces behind her, but that didn't seem to affect her at all. "Sounds like a plan."

She moved past Dani to load up a plate. "So, um…any nightmares?" She chanced a glance over her shoulder.

Dani added some rope to her pack. "No nightmares."

When no further explanation or attempt at communication came, Lynn turned around. "Dani?" She waited for eye contact. "Are things awkward between us now?" Her chest tightened as she awaited a reply.

Dani shook her head. "No. I…I really appreciate that you, you know, held me and everything. And I really didn't have nightmares. I'm just a little overwhelmed, I guess. Yesterday—all of it—was a bit much." She leaned back on her hands. "But it's not, you know, me and you." She smiled, but it didn't reach her eyes.

Lynn nodded. "I can understand that. And I'm glad we're okay. Is there anything I can do?" *Like last night?* With something as simple as holding her, Lynn had managed to chase Dani's fears away—for real this time, not like in the car. Dani had no reason to have an ulterior motive now; Lynn was already committed. She could trust that Dani had made the request simply to feel better, and it had worked. Lynn wanted to do that again.

Dani smiled again and dipped her head down. "I'm not sure a hug's going to solve it this time."

"We could try." The words left her mouth before Lynn had fully vetted them. Now they were out there, and Lynn's heart skipped a beat or two—then another when she realized that maybe she would be okay with a hug. Maybe it would be nice. The thought left her feeling more vulnerable than running into the street naked. "I'm sor—"

"Okay." Dani lifted her head again and nodded. "Let's try."

Lynn closed her mouth. The potentially very embarrassing question of "how?" had threatened to slip out. She put her plate on top of a pile of clothes and walked over. Before she could change her mind, she kneeled and opened her arms. Her cheeks radiated heat, which was horrible but beyond her control.

Dani sat up, wiped her hands on her pants, and scooted forward until their knees met.

Lynn swallowed and held her pose.

Dani had to lean over to wrap her arms around Lynn's torso, just under her armpits.

Lynn met her halfway. She ended up wrapping her arms awkwardly around Dani's neck and leaning in to her to stabilize them. Little sparks raised the hairs on her skin wherever they touched. When Dani settled her head on her shoulder and exhaled against her neck, the sparks spread until all of her skin erupted in goose bumps.

She leaned her head against Dani's as much as she dared. Dani's soft hair tickled her skin. Lynn was very aware of the fact that she had forgotten how to hug, and it didn't come naturally to her. The position also didn't help.

It wasn't the same as yesterday when Dani had broken down; Dani was aware now and nearly as stiff as Lynn knew herself to be. Her breathing was steady, if a little shallow. Her arms and hands didn't move.

Lynn was awash in sensations. Not just the touch, but also the scent of Dani was foreign. It wasn't unpleasant, just new. She let the seconds tick by.

Slowly, Dani relaxed. Two or three fingertips began to travel along Lynn's spine, traversing just a vertebra up, then going back down.

Lynn swallowed as the minute touch flushed her entire system with heat. She tightened her hold a little and shifted her hand so she could rest it against the back of Dani's head, just like yesterday.

Dani's breath hitched.

The puff of air that followed seemed to wrap all the way around Lynn's neck like a caress. She started to stroke too. It had soothed Dani yesterday, and hopefully, it would soothe her now.

After a few seconds, Dani rested a bit more of her weight against Lynn's shoulder. Her hand flattened on Lynn's back.

Lynn closed her eyes. More time passed. She didn't know how much, and she didn't care. She was experiencing things she hadn't experienced in so long. Maybe she had never experienced them at all. She tried to put them into words, to analyze them and file them, to tuck them away to make sense of later, but even as she tried it, she knew she would fail. She couldn't define how Dani affected her; she just did. It was terrifying...and really nice.

"I was wrong."

The words were spoken softer than a whisper, but because Dani's lips were so close to her ear, Lynn caught the words easily. "Wrong about what?"

"This helps. I do feel better."

The almost imperceptible rasp in Dani's voice vibrated down Lynn's entire body and settled hotly in her gut. Her fingers flexed against Dani's skull. "Me too."

Dani sagged a little more. "Good." She exhaled again, and her breath left more goose bumps in its wake. She started to stroke Lynn's spine again, but only for a few moments. Then she slowly pulled back and sat up. Her gaze was slightly dazed when it met Lynn's. She smiled.

Lynn smiled back. It was chilly in the building, but not enough to explain why Lynn suddenly felt cold now Dani had withdrawn. "I should let you pack."

"I think you should." Dani tucked her hair behind her ear and took in the items around her.

When Lynn stood, her legs felt wobbly. They remained unsteady until well into her trip down the stairs. She focused on keeping the food on her plate and on keeping her grin from spreading to the point where her cheeks started to hurt. She wasn't sure what had just transpired between them, but she did know she liked it.

"How about there?" Dani inclined her head to a mossy patch roughly midway between two trees, where Skeever peed to his heart's content.

Lynn dug her fingers deeper into the blanket around the boy's body to keep herself from dropping her side of it. "Sounds good. Let's put him down."

Dani bent down with her. "First watch or first dig?"

"I'll dig." Lynn straightened. Physical labor would get her mind off the memories that had come flooding back the second she'd hoisted the boy's body up.

Dani took off her backpack and pulled her spear out to its full length. She also handed Lynn the shovel she'd found this morning. "Good luck."

When Lynn took the tool, their fingers brushed.

Dani's gaze flitted down, and for a moment, a smile tugged at her lips.

Lynn relaxed a little at the sight. "Thanks." She shrugged off her backpack and jacket. Time to get this over with. She gripped the handle and positioned herself. The first few motions were clumsy, then her muscles remembered the familiar strain and settled into the swing of it. The moss came away easily, and the soil was loose. Almost too loose, Lynn thought, but didn't want to question a gift like that. If the soil conditions held up, they would be out of here well before midday. Then the blade sank into something that crunched under the force of the thrust.

Dani's head turned in her direction, and her eyes opened wider.

Lynn wiggled the handle of the shovel to free the blade. It came away bloody. Realization hit. Her stomach threatened to turn. "Oh no." Her voice reached barely above a whisper.

"Is that…?" Dani sounded as if she was about to throw up. She backed away with her eyes on the shallow hole that now showed just a few patches of blueish skin.

Skeever whined and backed up.

Lynn kicked sand over the trench but gave up when the stench of death rose up violently enough to make her gag. At least now they knew what had happened to the family's victims. She grabbed her pack and hurried to hoist it onto her shoulders. "We'll carry him across the road, bury him there. It's probably littered with bodies here."

Dani vigorously nodded her consent. She had already donned her pack and bent down to pick up Lynn's jacket. She wiped a tear away and wordlessly hoisted the boy's body up as well.

Lynn's skin crawled long after they left the green. As relieved as she was that the family had buried the people they'd killed, the sight—and especially the scent—lingered. She glanced at Dani as they made their way to a patch of green farther away from the building.

Dani had gone pale and her eyes were still moist. She stared down at the blanket.

Was she thinking about Richard? Lynn was. Digging up his body was going to be way worse than this little preview. Lynn shuddered. She didn't want to think about that—not now.

Lynn was the first to break ground again, and this time the soil was a lot less yielding. It made the work harder, but at least Lynn was fairly certain there wouldn't be any more surprises.

Nearly three hours of back-breaking work later, they lowered the boy into the hole.

Sweat ran down Lynn's body in steady streams, and sand had gotten everywhere.

Dani stared at the patches of carefully restored grass. She looked the way Lynn felt: dirty and tired.

Lynn straightened to stretch out her back. "Do you wanna say a few words or…?"

Dani glanced at her. "I'm not sure what to say."

"Try. I think it might, you know, help." Nothing would help them feel better about any of this, but any semblance of closure was good.

After a moment, Dani took a deep breath and released it. "I'm sorry you had to die, boy. May good things grow from all you return to the earth."

Lynn bent her head as Dani spoke. That was pretty much all there was to say about a boy they hadn't known but who shouldn't have been killed. She cleared her throat. "Right. Let's get going. We've lost enough daylight."

Dani fell in line with her upon reaching the 95, and Lynn didn't automatically tense. Something had definitely changed between them: only yesterday, they'd traveled with a good twenty feet of distance between them.

Over the last couple of days, Lynn had gone from an intense desire to get away from Dani, to an intense desire to stay with her. There was logic in that transition. For one, Dani was an asset. She was untrained in prolonged exposure to the Wilds, but on the off chance her terror the first night out hadn't been an act to manipulate Lynn into feeling sorry for her, Dani had been coming to grips quickly with some of the Wild's most pressing terrors. Dani was adaptive, smart, and physically capable. Given time, her feet would heal, and she'd learn to cope with walking long distances every day and sleeping lightly at night.

There was more to it than that, though: Lynn liked her. Dani made her feel something no one else had ever made her feel. She'd lost the desire to touch other people many years ago, but she'd slept soundly through the night while holding Dani, and this morning's hug was fresh in her mind. Every time she thought of it, her skin tingled.

Dani swerved away from her as a car blocked their path.

Skeever took the left with Lynn.

Dani's gaze swept along the tree line in a meticulous pattern that spoke volumes about the progress she'd made on learning how to handle herself out in the Wilds.

Lynn stifled a sigh. Dani had the makings of a Wilder, but no desire to become one. That forced Lynn to examine the flip side of the coin: did Lynn have the makings of a Settler? She had trouble picturing herself functioning as one of the Homestead people. Dani's suggestion she take Richard's place on the team was problematic for a lot of reasons. For one, she doubted Kate had any intention of letting her. It was a job with a lot of responsibility, and it required a lot of trust. Lynn didn't have that trust with the Homesteaders. The only one who perhaps trusted her enough to let her take up Richard's mantle was Dani, and that wasn't enough. Then there was another uncomfortable truth: she didn't want to lay down her life for the well-being of the group.

If push came to shove, maybe Lynn would be willing to risk her own well-being for Dani's, but she only had to think about Dean or Kate to know that if she was ever asked to risk her life for the other Homesteaders, she'd turn the other way. Lynn didn't like the Homesteaders, and the Homesteaders didn't like her.

Besides, Lynn wasn't used to life in a settlement. It was always possible she would unlearn some of the reflexes that had allowed her to survive so far, but she couldn't blame Kate for not wanting someone in her group who turned combative whenever someone spooked her and whose primary concern was her own well-being. The Homesteaders needed someone with Lynn's talents, but not someone with her emotional baggage. They needed a well-trained Dani.

Lynn was convinced her instincts were correct: that Kate had agreed to send Dani out with her so Dani would learn the skills she'd need to replace Richard. It was the only logical conclusion. That would make Lynn entirely redundant. If Dani chose to go back to the Homestead, Lynn didn't see a way for them to stay together. The thought made her swallow heavily. She observed Dani under the pretense of taking in the tree line.

Time was running out. They would reach Richard's body before nightfall. If Dani kept up this pace despite her blistered feet and Lynn remembered the way clearly, they would arrive even earlier. The encroaching deadline made her antsy. Perhaps it was time to just be honest and accept the inevitable if she had to.

Lynn formulated her opening gambit carefully before she spoke. "Dani?"

"Hm?" Dani dragged her gaze away from the tree line only momentarily.

"I have a problem."

This drew Dani's attention a little longer. "Problem?"

Lynn nodded. "Yeah. I have been trying to figure something out, and I'm not getting anywhere. So—" She licked her lips nervously. "I guess I'll just ask. Dani, is there any way I can get you to come with me? Before we bring back Richard's body or after, I don't care anymore at this point. I just… I can't stay at the Homestead, but I don't want to leave there without you either. Not if I, you know, can help it. Somehow." *Naked again.* Lynn hated the feeling, but this was too important to stay in her comfort zone.

Dani stopped to look at her. "Why do you want to stay with me?" Her voice had gone soft again.

Lynn slowed, then stopped too. She looked away under the guise of scouting for danger. "Because it's better out here with you—because I am better out here with you. And I don't just mean things anyone could do like stand guard or find food." The feeling of Dani's body against hers ghosted across her skin, leaving goose bumps in its wake.

"I've met people before who could have traveled with me and been good companions. I've never wanted them to stay. It's different with you, and before you ask me 'why' again, I don't know. I really don't. It's just—" *Trust.* If she hadn't trusted Dani, she wouldn't have gone after her. Still, it was better not to use the word. That would leave her too exposed right now. She was already so far out on the ledge that she was sure she would fall. "... that I know you will have my back when things go wrong."

Dani watched her, then took a deep breath. "I still think we could convince Kate you would be the better choice to replace Richard."

Lynn checked on Skeever for signs of danger, but he had rolled onto his side in a patch of sunlight. She shook her hair out and took her time formulating her reply. "I'm not suited for life in a settlement, Dani. I haven't been able to since I was a little girl. I'd feel trapped when I'd be at the Homestead and chained to it whenever I go out. I...I don't mind sharing what I have with you, but to be responsible for the well-being of people I don't like? I know it's probably selfish of me, but I don't think I can do it." She hesitated, then added: "Besides, I'd still not be out with you. We'd barely see each other, and that's...that's not enough of a pay-off for putting my life in danger for them."

Dani seemed to work that over in her head. The fact that she didn't outright accuse Lynn of being a horrible person was encouraging. Eventually, she shook her head and sighed. "I don't know how we could make it work."

Lynn's insides churned, and she went a little cold despite the heat of the sun. The fear of losing the person that was causing her to feel all these new, good things urged her to take a step forward.

Dani's eyes widened at the sudden move.

"How about this." She met Dani's gaze. "I already promised you I would go with you and get Richard's body. I'm still against it, but if that's something you need to do, we'll do it. If we don't die trying, we'll go back to the Homestead and you can talk to Kate and the others. I'm not going in because they'd take Skeever away from me. We'll set up a place and time to meet so you can tell me what they said. Maybe you can convince me, or maybe their reaction will convince you to come with me. Whatever the case, we'll meet at least one last time to talk things through." She held out her hand. "Deal?"

Dani inspected the hand, then Lynn's face, then the hand again. She swallowed.

Seconds ticked by, and Lynn became sure Dani would refuse. Disappointment crept through her veins. It had taken a lot out of her to put an honest offer out there, and Lynn felt her walls slipping back in place to shield her from the rejection about to come. She was in the process of lowering her hand when Dani's fingers closed around it.

"Deal." Dani's grip was stronger than her tone. "We'll talk things through."

Lynn stared at the slightly darker hand in hers, amazed to feel calloused and warm skin after she had been sure Dani wouldn't reach out. She squeezed and brought her head back up.

Dani's gaze locked with hers.

Lynn still didn't trust herself enough to read it, but there was clear turmoil in Dani's eyes. They had solidified something between them now, something that left open possibilities for the future. What those possibilities were, Lynn wasn't sure, but the intensity of Dani's gaze caused a flutter of something delicate and wild in her stomach.

Dani squeezed before releasing Lynn's hand. "We, uh...we should keep going." She cleared her throat.

Lynn curled her fingers, enjoying the lingering sensations of Dani's touch. A step, a small step, forged in honesty—for once. Then she shifted her tomahawk back into her hand and focused on the feel of the wood instead. "Lead the way."

With eight lanes heading straight on, Dani didn't need more information than that.

"I think this is the right exit." Lynn turned and glanced back out over the road they had just taken. She recognized it—the train tracks ran parallel to it; the station seemed to be where Lynn remembered it should be, and the road did allow them to go right. She didn't remember the number 20 that it had been marked with, but it all seemed to line up.

"Okay, then we'll have a look." Dani scanned the exit that ran up from the interstate to a road that crossed it and branched off in either direction.

Lynn adjusted the straps of her new backpack. They dug into her skin at a slightly different location than the old one had, which made wearing it uncomfortable. She would get used to it soon enough, but the prospect of getting the backpack off had quickened her step in the last hour or so.

They had nearly reached the top of the ramp when Skeever started to growl. He tilted his head to listen.

Lynn instinctively did the same and reached out for Skeever's collar to keep him close.

Dani stopped too. She frowned and gripped her spear more tightly.

After a few seconds of anxious waiting, a sound of very distant thunder reached Lynn's ears. There wasn't a cloud in the sky, so it wasn't that. What else caused this sound? She relaxed when the answer popped into her head. "Hooves."

They spilled onto the overhead pass a few seconds later, as plentiful as if someone had emptied a gargantuan bucket of them: the black-and-white-striped horses Lynn had spotted along the road heading into New York City. They were in full gallop, rushing from right to left as they wove their way between the cars and other obstacles as gracefully as dancers. If Dani held out her spear, she could touch them; they were that close.

"Zebras!"

Dani called out the word loudly enough to chase the jittery creatures away from them. The whole herd swerved around them like water around a rock in a rushing river.

Skeever pulled against her hold and barked his yipping, whiny bark that usually only came into play when she stopped him from eating scat or playing in mud pools.

Lynn watched in awe as the herd of at least fifty or sixty animals thundered past. They didn't move like horses, more like donkeys, and their whinny was high-pitched and very similar to Skeever's bark when he felt as if she was keeping him from something fun and exciting. Kind of like now. Lynn paid him no heed. She marveled at the majestic, stout animals that seemed so alien against the backdrop of green and gray. Their stripes bewildered the eye and made it even harder to get an accurate count. She couldn't imagine an environment they could blend into, but perhaps the dizzying effect of their stripes was enough protection against predators.

Was this the same herd she'd seen just before entering New York City? Lynn couldn't tell; they all looked identical to her. As the last stragglers departed, one seemed to look at their little group with interest—possibly even recognition. Lynn grinned. Maybe going down the same road twice wasn't always such a bad thing.

CHAPTER 15

THE BUILDING HAD AN ODDLY triangular shape that accentuated the corner façade, which had been decorated, pre-war, with a now faded, blue, oval sign with stars on it. Lynn recognized it instantly as they walked up to it. "Yeah, this is it." She took in the area around her. Across the road from the car dealership was a patch of green, barred off by a chain-link fence. "Richard's body should be in there."

Dani took in the building and the trees, then turned her head back toward the building. Was she thinking about her friend who had died there? "Let's make sure the building is secure before we check on the grave." There was a rasp to Dani's voice again. This couldn't be easy for her, but she made her way to the door, regardless.

Skeever seemed equally hesitant. Something about the place made him whine. Did he remember this was where he'd lost his previous owner? Could he still pick up his scent?

Lynn quickened her pace so she could arrive at the door ahead of Dani. She carefully tried the handle. It gave without resistance, so she pulled the door open entirely. Nothing jumped at her; nothing moved within the shadows.

Dani slipped past her, spear and knife at the ready.

"In, Skeever." Lynn inclined her head toward the interior. If they were about to set off another trap, she wanted him with her and not stuck outside again.

Skeever whined but followed Dani as she explored deeper into the building.

Lynn let the door fall closed behind her and watched Dani's progress. She cast sweeping glances across the showroom, aware that every car and every counter was a potential hiding place for predators.

"Where did you find him?" Dani's soft voice carried easily through the building that seemed to hold its breath along with Lynn.

Lynn exhaled. "To the left, in a small office."

Dani diverted from her path until she could push the door open. Lynn knew there was nothing to see there, just a small room, another desk, a chair, some filing cabinets, and trinkets left behind by whoever had worked here. Dani still seemed to soak it in as she stood in the doorway.

Skeever parted ways with her and sniffed his way around the cars, taking his time to familiarize himself with the space—or reacquaint himself, whichever was the case.

Lynn waited patiently for both to finish as she kept an eye out for danger both inside and outside of the building. Except for some prey animals and birds, the outside world was deserted. Indoors, nothing moved but them. Not much had changed around here—nothing at all, as far as Lynn could tell. It was a good sign. Lynn was still tense. That nothing had changed here did not mean the grave was undisturbed. "Ready to check things out across the street?"

The words seemed to draw Dani from her thoughts, as she was slow to reply. "Yeah. Let's get it over with."

Lynn pushed the door open and waited for Dani and Skeever to join her. She squeezed Dani's arm in passing and gave her a look meant to inquire if Dani was all right.

Dani set her jaw and nodded. She dipped her head, but before she could hide her face from Lynn entirely, Lynn could tell Dani was on the verge of tears.

Lynn let go. "Come on. We're doing this together, right?"

Dani nodded again. The nonverbal reply seemed to be all she could manage. She crossed the street and followed Lynn into the driveway of the white house with the red-tiled roof.

Lynn found the little path that led into the overgrown yard and crept through quietly, keeping an eye out for anything that may have found its home here since her last visit.

The gravesite wasn't hard to find. Quietly, she pointed to a bumpy patch of grass with a calf-high boulder on top of it. She had found it in the yard, where it had appeared to serve no obvious purpose, so she had upgraded it to both protector and marker of the grave. It seemed to have done its job: the site looked undisturbed. "There it is."

Dani pushed through the green to overtake her, snapping twigs. She hesitated as she came closer to the stone, then crouched down and laid her hand on it. "He's safe." Dani couldn't quite keep a wobble out of her voice.

Skeever joined her, sniffing the dirt.

Lynn turned away to give them some privacy and to keep watch over them. If the roles had been reversed, she would want a few moments to herself too.

"How are we going to get him home?"

Lynn almost missed the softly spoken words over the rustle of the wind through the leaves.

"I thought about that last night." She turned back around to find Dani watching her with red-rimmed eyes. "We, um, we should make a stretcher. We're at a car shop, so we can probably find something that will serve as wheels too. It won't be pretty, but if we can rig up a cart that one of us can pull alone, the other has her hands free to hold weapons."

Dani seemed to turn the proposal over in her mind, then nodded. She straightened out and looked back down at the stone. "Let's do that first. As soon as we dig him up, we need to move."

"Yeah, that was going to be my suggestion too." She guided everyone back out onto the street.

Dani bent down to pluck a stray twig from Skeever's fur. "What do we need?"

Lynn inspected her, but she knew better than to ask if Dani was all right; of course she wasn't. It was better to focus on the task at hand and find some distraction. Hugs couldn't fix everything. "Two beams for the sides and handlebars, sturdy branches to act as crossbeams, and something to act as tires. I have rope to tie it all together."

Dani seemed to grasp the basic idea. "Okay, then let's find what we don't have."

Finding the branches they needed didn't take long. Lynn's tomahawk was sharp and her arm strong. She cut them from the trees in the garden. Once they were stripped of side branches, they carried them into the car shop and secured the door. Things went a lot faster when no one had to stand guard.

Dani helped her lay out two long branches far enough apart for either of them to stand between and hold one beam in each hand. Then they cut another branch to size and tied it to the two long beams in an H shape. After knotting three more branches to the long beams—first at the end, then two in between—they created a platform to hold Richard's body. What took a little more doing was finding a way to attach the wheels. Tire housings weren't hard to come by—the garage in the back of the building had a few stored neatly away, protected from the elements for all these years—but they didn't have much height to them, so Lynn opted for bike tires instead. As far as she could tell, the only option to secure them was to nail them to another beam. She had to find a way to secure the beam to the stretcher while allowing the beam to rotate instead of having the wheels rotate on a stationary beam. Lynn was pondering it when Dani cleared her throat.

"Lynn?"

"Hm?" She didn't take her gaze off the beam, afraid her half-formed idea would vanish if she lost sight of the required components.

"I don't know if I can do it." Dani's tone was soft and her voice fragile.

Lynn finally looked up.

Dani sat on the floor, arms locked around her drawn-up leg. She rested her chin on her knee as she stared at the cart's frame.

"Can't do what?" The cart was almost done; surely they would figure this wheel problem out soon.

"Dig him up." Dani glanced at her from under her long lashes. Her eyes were moist again.

"Oh?" Lynn sat back on her heels, all thoughts of construction gone. Had Dani changed her mind? Was she satisfied with his burial site? "You want to leave him here?"

"No, that's not—" Dani took a deep breath and squeezed her eyes shut. A tear slid down her cheek, and she wiped it away hastily. "No." She shook her head. "I need to bring him home, but I don't think I can. I keep thinking of the people we found in the woods, the ones the family buried. I can't get the stench out of my nose and the...the sight out of my mind." She sniffed and straightened. "I need—" She faltered. "I need you to do it."

"Oh." Lynn felt a little disappointed, but of course Dani wasn't going to abandon the quest now. She should have known that.

Dani glanced up at her, seemingly gauging her reaction. "I know I don't have the right to ask. You didn't come along to dig him up, just to show me where he is. I just... He was my friend. I can't see him like that." The tears started falling again.

Lynn nodded slowly. This morning's unexpected find was still fresh in her mind as well. She knew how bad this was going to be. If the plea had come from anyone else, she would have flat out refused to dig up what was undoubtedly going to be a bloated, maggot-infested, partially decomposed corpse. She shuddered visibly. But this was Dani.

Dani still looked at her expectantly. Anxiety read clearly in her eyes, and Lynn felt sure she wasn't faking any of this; she was truly horrified at the prospect. Who wouldn't be?

Lynn held out her hand.

Dani took it without a hint of hesitation.

"I get it." Lynn squeezed the calloused hand in hers. *Deep breath.* "I'll get it done. Just help me with this." She nodded at the stretcher. "And help me find some place I can wash up after, and I'll do the digging."

"S-Sure?"

Lynn nodded. She felt those sparks dance along her skin again. "Yeah. I get it."

Renewed tears shone in Dani's eyes. She hurried to close the divide between them and wrapped Lynn up in another hug. "Thank you."

Dani's compact body pressed into her, and hot breath tickled Lynn's skin again. Her brain refused to cooperate and form words. She liberated an arm that had gotten trapped between their bodies and wrapped it around Dani's back. After a moment of hesitation, she brought the other arm up as well. "D-Don't worry about it." She pushed a ball of nerves and worry down and pressed Dani's body a little more tightly against hers.

"Thank you." Dani's repeated words were softer this time, but her hold was still tight. She wasn't stroking now, just holding on to Lynn's neck and shoulders.

"No problem." *How is it not a problem? You just volunteered to dig up a dead guy you don't know!* Lynn leaned the side of her head against Dani's. She listened to her sniffing instead of her own brain anxiously trying to get her to back out of this commitment. In the grand scheme of things, digging up Richard wasn't such a huge sacrifice, and it would make Dani happy. That made it no longer a problem.

Dani sniffed once more, then pulled back. She wiped her eyes and chuckled humorlessly. "So, um, have you found a solution for the wheels yet?" Her voice was barely more than a rasp.

Lynn let her have her emotional space. "Yeah, I think we can use strips of leather to make a holder on both sides of the handlebars at the height where we want the wheels to be—probably all the way in the back because the angle will be pretty steep even now that we've switched to the bike tires. That way, when we put the branch through, it can rotate freely. We'll nail the wheels to the branch, and they'll be able to turn." The idea came to her as she spoke.

"Then we'll do that." Dani gave a weak little smile and got to work.

Lynn woke up with the day's daunting task clear in mind. She postponed the inevitable digging by lingering in bed and pondering Dani. They hadn't slept in the same bed last night; Lynn hadn't known how to bring it up, and Dani hadn't asked. That led Lynn to wonder if sleeping together the night before last had been a one-time thing, and if it was, how she felt about that. If she was completely truthful with herself, she had to admit she'd missed Dani's presence last night, and she hadn't slept nearly as well as when they had shared a bed. It was a little worrying how easy it was to get used to having Dani around.

Lynn listened for sounds of her presence but heard nothing, neither in the bedroom nor in the adjacent showroom. Her bed was empty, and Skeever was gone. That probably meant Dani was outside already. With a groan, she threw off her blanket and sat up. Yesterday's grave-digging efforts had already left her sore. She could only imagine how her shoulders and arms would feel tomorrow morning—tonight even. Once she'd put on her boots and secured her weapons, she made her way out of the office opposite the one Richard had died in. Neither had felt comfortable bunking down there.

The showroom was deserted, but the large glass windows revealed Dani and Skeever beside a fire in the parking lot. It was an overcast, dreary day.

Her mood probably didn't make the outside world seem any happier. She checked to make sure there wasn't any danger, pulled her tomahawk from her belt, and walked out. "Morning."

Dani looked up and smiled. "Morning. I made breakfast." She pointed to two tins and a plate. "Tea, oatmeal, and some fruit."

Lynn sat and eyed the meal. Her stomach rumbled. Still, she hesitated. "I'm afraid I'll just end up throwing it all up."

Dani tensed. "Yeah. I figured if we sat for a while, it would be okay."

Lynn hummed noncommittally but took the tin of oatmeal after testing its heat. "Thanks for this."

"It's the least I can do."

Skeever made his way over and lay by her feet.

She stroked his flank and belly before patting him and returning to her meal. Dani had added apple to the mixture. Lynn watched the apple pieces appear and submerge as she stirred, then spooned the gooey mixture up gratefully; she shouldn't work on an empty stomach, after all.

The cart had survived the night. It sat against the side of the building, handlebars resting on the ground. Hauling it along was going to be rough; the branches weren't entirely straight, so the wheel axle was slightly out of alignment, but they'd both tried pulling it and had managed. They had also found a little creek nearby. It was shallow, but when Dani had gone down to fill their emptied bottles, the water was clear. Everything was ready—everything but Lynn herself.

"Can I, um... Is there any way I can help?" Dani stirred her own oatmeal.

"It's okay. Just get ready to leave."

"I've been thinking about that." Dani fell silent until Lynn prompted her to go on. "Well, I don't know how long it's going to take, but say you get done by noon. Even if you're not too tired to head out, we can't make good ground. We'll need to stop earlier because we'll need to find places to camp that are solidly fortified and where we can separate ourselves from th—from Richard." She winced. "At best, we'd get a few hours of travel time, and you'd be worse for wear. Maybe it's best if we stayed here one more night and start fresh early tomorrow morning?" She glanced up again.

Lynn considered the proposal. It was a good one. As much as she didn't want to stay here with Richard's body on a stretcher, she'd be staying somewhere else with that same body just a few hours later anyway. It made more sense to start their return journey well rested in the morning. "Okay. Solid plan. We'll spend the night here."

Dani smiled all the way to her eyes. "Good. Thanks. You won't have to worry about anything, okay? Food and things, I've got it handled."

"Thanks." Lynn doubted she'd be interested in food the rest of the day, but there was no use in saying so. There was also very little reason to postpone the inevitable any longer: she was only getting more anxious as she sat. She scraped the tin clean, sucked the last of the oatmeal off her spoon, and popped a slice of pear into her mouth. "I'm going to get started."

The sparkle in Dani's eyes died. She tensed and stood when Lynn did, then fidgeted with the hem of her sweater. "Good luck."

Lynn nodded. *I'll need it.* She stepped forward and wrapped her arms around Dani's neck for a quick hug to remind herself why she was doing this. Before Dani could respond, she'd already let go. "Thanks."

Two weeks was long enough for the chunks of grass Lynn had placed over the gravesite to start knitting together again. They broke apart when she pushed the boulder off. All her life, she had been taught death was the enemy. The dead carried diseases that could kill you. Every inch of skin, except for her eyes, was covered. She'd even wrapped cloth around the area where her pants met her boots so nothing could seep into them. She wore two pants and two shirts over each other; her hair was wrapped up in another shirt, and she'd tied a strip of cloth around her nose and mouth. She even had her winter mittens on, tied around her wrist with string. It would make holding the shovel a little more challenging, but the added protection was worth any discomfort.

Lynn grabbed the shovel and examined it, buying herself a few more seconds of respite. This tool had probably aided in the burial of a lot of people—it had belonged to the thieving family, after all—but had it ever dug up anyone? Disturbing the grave felt sacrilegious, but she reminded herself she was committed to doing it. So she started. She didn't bother preserving the slabs of grass as she had when she'd buried him. He wasn't going back in; no one was. She scooped the grass up along with the soil and tried to get her mind to go numb.

With her extra layers of clothing, she was soon sweating profusely and panting. Re-opening a grave was certainly less work than cutting it fresh out of the soil, but it wasn't easier. Not long after she'd started, the sand became infested with maggots. Her insides coiled at the sight of the writhing white worms, then she steeled herself and pressed on. This was nothing, just a prelude.

Under the canopy, she couldn't tell the sun's path. She didn't know how much time passed, but when the shovel hit straining skin, she realized either hours had gone by or she'd buried him shallower than she remembered. A rush of gas puffed up, and no amount of layering could protect her from the stench of rot and putrefaction. Lynn gagged. She tried to weather the assault on her nose, but it was useless; she had to get out of the grave.

She tossed the shovel aside and pressed her elbow over her mouth and nose. The scent of apple from her breakfast made everything worse.

Every inhale sent a warning through her system. Her body and mind screamed at her to get away from the corpse, but instead, she lowered herself down and cleared the dirt off the body with her mitten-covered hands. Icy streams of sweat slid down her back—a mixture of heat, exertion, and sheer miserableness. She ignored it—ignored everything but the scoops of wiggling earth she gathered and placed onto the grass next to the grave. Gather, lift up, gather, lift up, gather, lift up. Every now and again, a few white little bodies toppled back into the grave from the edge and she had to scoop them up again.

Eventually, she stood and balanced precariously over a bloated leg. For the first time, she allowed herself to take in the now fully exposed corpse. Richard looked worse than she had assumed. Where his skin had torn, his flesh had become infested with worms, ants, maggots, and everything else that fed off scavenged meat. His crawling skin made Lynn's crawl sympathetically.

She knew she couldn't give herself time to think about the next step. If the realization of what she would have to do sank in, she wouldn't be able to do it. Instead, she pulled the edge of her rags more securely over her nose to dampen the smell and clambered out of the hole. She kicked the writhing pile of sand farther to the side to make room for the blanket she'd brought and, once done, shook her boot pathetically to get the sand and maggots off. As she climbed into the hip-high grave again, she tried to avoid stepping into the juices that seeped from the disturbed body.

How am I going to do this? The man outweighed her, and the grave was deep. She would have to get the body into a seated position, and that meant full-body contact was unavoidable. Her hair stood on end. *Don't think about it, just do it. Do it!*

She held her breath, bent down, and hesitated only a moment before she pushed through her revulsion and grabbed the sleeves of his once-white shirt. Pulling the arms up, she walked forward until her boots sank into the wet dirt by his waist. She inhaled once, as shallowly as she could, and grabbed the shirt just below Richard's clavicles. With a heave that pulled the muscles in her arms taut, she yanked up as she stepped back.

He bent with her and then toppled forward, against her legs, once he passed the tipping point.

She stumbled. For a disgustingly terrifying moment, the dead, rotting weight threatened to push her off-balance. The back of her legs hit the wall of the grave before she could fall over. Richard's head lolled against her thigh.

Her first instinct was to shove him away, but then he would fall back and she would have to do it all over again, so she fought the urge and carefully stepped aside.

He slumped forward even more, and with effort, Lynn freed her legs. She hurried out of the grave and did a jerky little dance out of sheer disgust, sending maggots and ants flying. "Oh fuck, fuck, fuck, fuck, fuck!" Flapping her arms around wildly, she beat at her clothes until she couldn't see any more bugs. She still felt them, crawling everywhere.

"Gah!" She clenched her hands to fists and squeezed her eyes shut for a few seconds. She wanted to cry. There was no way she could go back into that grave and touch him again—but she had to. Thankfully, she could postpone the inevitable.

She picked up the shovel again and broke the side of the grave opposite Richard's slumped body down to a ramp. Then she tied a rope around a tree and steeled herself before she went down again. The stench instantly overwhelmed her again, and her nausea flared anew. She pushed the bile down and forced herself to see Richard as a package, not a human being. It made it easier to reach under his armpits and tie a rope around his torso. Once she was sure he was secured and the knots would hold, she gratefully clambered back out, wiped bugs from her arms and torso, and got to hoisting.

She sat and planted both feet against the trunk of the tree she'd looped the rope around, then used it to anchor herself to her spot as she pulled the package up the slope. Hand over hand, she pulled the rope around the tree and the package up with it.

It was heavy work. Her muscles didn't get a reprieve: if she let go of the rope, Richard's body slid partway down the ramp. She'd have to cover that distance again, and she didn't trust her arms to hold out for much longer. Finally, the resistance stopped and Lynn checked behind her to see Richard's body entirely freed from the grave. She let go of the rope and fell back onto the grass, too tired to care that she might be lying on bugs.

After taking a moment to breathe in fresh air and settling her heart rate, she returned her mind to the task at hand. That was what it was: a task. Complete it, clean up, move on. With another deep breath that made her breakfast rise up in her throat, she stood. Her legs felt shaky and weak. *Get it done. Quickly!*

She adjusted the blanket spread out on the ground, then crouched down behind the package and slid her arms under his. The force on the rope had turned his skin to mush. Wetness seeped through her shirts. Lynn squeezed her eyes shut and tasted bile when her stomach protested. She didn't linger. She pulled, trying not to stumble and land under the body. One step, two, three, four. With one last blast of energy, she yanked until he was more or less on the blanket, where she dropped him with a wet thud.

I should not have eaten breakfast. Lynn looked down at Richard's swollen face and protruding blue tongue. She was desperate to get it over with, but her legs were numb and her arms shook. Her back had cramped entirely. She stood with her hands on her hips, panting through the rags, bathed in sweat and itching all over from real or imagined bugs. *Fuck!* Lynn hadn't felt this physically uncomfortable in years. Her mind had shut down what felt like hours ago. She was just going on instinct and adrenaline.

Lynn took a deep breath. The stench still upset her stomach, but it was also becoming familiar enough to endure. She bent down and folded a corner of the blanket down over Richard's face, another over his feet, and covered him with a length of the blanket before she rolled him over a couple of times. Getting a rope tied around the package was a chore that once more had sweat running down her back, but she managed. Hours after she'd started, she finally hoisted Richard's body onto the cart, using the same rope-around-the-tree technique as before.

Lynn stumbled and sank to the ground ten feet or so away from the grave. Everything smelled like death. It seemed to spread inside of her. Exhaustion pulled at her limbs like lead weights. *Done. I'm done.*

Dani looked up from the fire as Lynn pulled the cart with Richard's wrapped body out of the bushes. She rushed over, Skeever on her heels, but stopped a few feet off, gaze honed on the package. "You did it."

"Yeah." Just by acknowledging that she had, indeed, gotten it done, the nausea returned, and she had trouble hiding the shivers of panic and relief that coursed up and down her spine. Slowly, they turned into tremors, and she gripped the handlebars to hide it.

"Thank you." Dani tore her gaze away from Richard's body and inspected Lynn carefully. "Do you want to wash?"

Lynn wanted nothing more, but she had one urge even more pressing. "Could you grab the pile of clothes I laid out on my bed?"

"Of course!" Dani's gaze flickered to the back of the cart one more time before she took off at a sprint.

Lynn pulled the cart to the back of the building and then stumbled farther into the lot. With difficulty, she managed to contain her nausea until Dani was out of sight—and hopefully out of earshot—before she retched until her stomach cramped and she didn't even have gall to spew up. Hidden between car wrecks, she tried to expel the memories of her ordeal along with her breakfast. She failed, but eventually she felt gutted enough to dull them somewhat. She stood and tried to get her cramped abdominal muscles to relax.

The feeling of maggots wiggling over her skin plagued her again, even though she knew they weren't really there. She shivered, and her teeth chattered. With a sigh, she ran her forearm over her face and wiped away tears. After a few moments of slow breathing to help her stomach settle, she kicked dirt over her vomit and cracked her neck to relieve the tension in it. Quietly, she headed back to the fire, where Dani waited for her.

Dani stood and reached out, but Lynn pulled her arm away.

A flicker of rejection ghosted across Dani's face.

"I'm filthy." Lynn swallowed. "Sorry."

Dani relaxed a little and nodded. "Time to get you clean."

CHAPTER 16

As Lynn walked, the tremor in her hands spread to her arms, then to her torso. Well before she reached the stream, she was shaking all over. She wrapped her arms around herself in an effort to stop it, but it didn't help much. Every time she blinked, she saw Richard's face—bulging eyes, bloated tongue, maggots crawling—as if she was looking straight at it. No matter what way she turned her head, his face was always right there. Shaking worsened the feeling of things crawling along her skin, under and between the layers of her clothing, maybe even under her skin.

Dani gave her space at first, but then concern for her well-being seemed to take over. "Lynn? Are you okay?" She looked at her as if Lynn was losing her mind.

She might be. Dani's voice seemed to come from much farther away than a foot or two. It was hard to hear her over the pounding of her heart and the shallow, shuddering breaths she drew. Every beat seemed to pump filth through her veins. Every breath was tainted with decay. It wafted off her clothes, off her body. Her shirt stuck to her chest and arms where she'd been forced to squeeze him against her body so she could drag him. Her mittens were stained brown and red with sand and blood. *Why am I still wearing my mittens?*

The question stood out as the only solid thought in the jumble in her brain. This time when she blinked, she saw her once-white mittens dig deep into bloody, maggot-infested soil. Something inside of her snapped. The panic that had been solely physical before crashed into her mind like a tidal wave, drowning out everything else. "Off." She tugged at the strings holding her mittens tight around her wrist.

"W-What?"

Lynn didn't pay Dani any heed. She tried to get a hold of the tiny, twisted, and knotted string on her left wrist, but because her hand was encased in wet wool, she couldn't get a grip. "Off!" Her voice broke, and it was far less a command than a squealed plea. Lynn didn't care. She plucked, trying and failing to unravel tangled string and undo the knot.

Dani gripped both of her hands to get her attention. "Lynn, stop, please. I've got it. Let me do it."

When Lynn looked up, eyes the color of hazelnut husks met her gaze. The wave of panic subsided just a fraction. She nodded.

With precise movements, Dani untangled the string around her wrist, undid the knot, and pulled off the first mitten. The breeze hit Lynn's dirty fingertips and her red-stained skin.

It felt so good. Lynn gasped in relief.

Dani smiled up at her and then wordlessly freed her other hand before she took them both in hers and squeezed. "There. Done. They're off." Those soft eyes inspected her face. "You're crying." Before Lynn could reply, Dani transferred both of Lynn's hands into one of hers and used the fingers of her other hand to brush over her face.

Her skin was warm, not the icy cold that had radiated off Richard, and Lynn leaned into the touch as Dani pulled her hand away, seeking more of it. The grueling hard work and the layers of clothing still on her should have left her cooking from the inside out, but she felt cold—dead cold.

Seemingly sensing Lynn's need for warmth, Dani cupped her cheek.

The touch burned on her skin like an inferno, and Lynn closed her eyes to bask in the glow.

They stood like that for a while. It was good, soothing. Her heart beat steadily again, and her breathing had deepened; neither function drowned out sound anymore.

"Can you go on?" Dani stroked gently with her thumb.

"Think so." With great relief, she realized she actually did feel ready to go on. The tremble had subsided, and the panic had gone down to a tolerable level.

Dani withdrew her fingers from Lynn's face but took her hand instead. With the other, she picked up the mittens from the ground.

They resumed their short journey.

Lynn let herself be pulled along and stared at the place their bodies met as if her hand were a foreign object that had somehow gotten attached to her body. Lynn knew she should be holding her tomahawk instead, and she should be looking out for danger, but her world had gotten very small, and Dani's hand seemed to be the only thing tethering her to reality. She couldn't let go of that—if she did, she'd be swept away by that wave again.

Dani stopped.

Lynn stopped too, but not before bumping into her. She stepped back dully.

"We're here. Come, down to the stream, okay?" Dani pulled her along again, carefully guiding her over grass and rocks. When Dani stopped again and rolled off Lynn's top shirt, Lynn let her. Dani pulled the second shirt free from her pants. Again, Lynn raised her arms dutifully, and Dani slipped it off.

The wind ghosting over her back, belly, and breasts felt wonderful. Lynn hummed and didn't protest when Dani sank to a knee and undid the strips of cloth around her boots, then slipped her boots off. Lynn dug her toes into the cool grass with immense pleasure. Dani laid the tomahawk by Lynn's feet and set her nimble fingers upon the knot in the rope holding up both of Lynn's pants.

Lynn stepped out of them.

"Go on in." Dani looked up at her. "I'll keep watch."

"In?" Lynn frowned.

Dani tilted her head and furrowed her brow. "Into the water."

The words shook loose the memory of scouting out the shallow stream by a bridge near their camp. That memory in turn brought back the day's events. Lynn jolted and blinked. She quickly whipped her head about, all of a sudden realizing she stood naked in the open and Dani's face was level to her crotch. She stepped back. "Wha—?"

Carefully, Dani stood and raised her hands, palms up to show she was unarmed. The tip of her spear bobbed up over her shoulder. "It's okay. Just get in the water. It's...it's been a long day." She looked at Lynn as if she had become a cornered animal with bared teeth.

Lynn felt as if maybe she had. Then something seemed to tumble from her hair, down her back and off the curve of her ass. She gasped and eyed the water by her feet. The need to get clean overwhelmed all other instincts. She stepped in.

The cool water hit her like a slap in the face and cleared some of the fog. She put her other foot in as well and waded out. The water barely came up to her knees at the center of the stream, but that was enough. She lowered herself down and then submerged herself entirely, staying underwater as long as she dared, hoping everything alive would either float off her or drown.

She came up and inhaled deeply. Finally, her lungs didn't fill with the sickening stench of rotting flesh. She inhaled the pure, moist air again and sank back. Slowly, she opened her eyes to make sure everything was all right around her. Nothing beyond an outright attack would get her out of the water.

Dani had climbed up the embankment and stood on the road that led across the creek, her back to Lynn, but casting sweeping glances at their surroundings. A little downstream, hooked behind a branch, were Lynn's clothes, getting a good soak.

As Lynn lay in the stream, ass on a rock, head tilted toward the sun, she felt the touch of death seep out of her slowly. Secure in the knowledge Dani was watching over her, she moved her arms above her head and then back down. The water pressed against her palms and coursed through her spread fingers. Goosebumps played across her skin, and her hair stuck to her scalp. Slowly, Lynn started connecting to her old self again.

Very carefully, she allowed snippets of today's ordeal back into her active memory: blood seeping from ears and eyes, ripped and maggot-infested skin, the weight of him as she pulled. Lynn didn't usually have nightmares, but she would probably have them tonight.

She lay in the stream until she felt cold and clean to her bones and she'd gone over the grueling hours three times in greater and greater detail. Every time a memory caused her panic to rise, she submerged her head and held her breath until her lungs hurt. Physical pain was much easier to deal with than emotional turmoil.

That was a good thing because she had quite a bit of physical pain to deal with. Of course she felt sore all over, but one part of her was far worse than the rest: her left arm. She lifted it out of the water to examine the bite marks. Even though they were almost a week old by now, they were far from being healed. Most of her lower arm had swollen to an alarming size, either from strain or infection. The fact that she couldn't tell which unsettled her even further. The shallower cuts had been healing well and had held up under the stress of grave digging twice in the same number of days, but the deeper punctures had opened up again. She bit back a hiss of pain as she washed them out with her fingers, making sure to get all the blood and yellowish gunk out.

By the time she'd cleaned her arm, it was throbbing but the skin didn't feel half as taut. She was a little woozy from the pain and took her time cleaning the rest of her body. Her hair deserved special attention because the feeling of things creeping around in there just didn't want to budge.

By the time she sat up, she wasn't over the dig, but she'd gotten to a place where she could start to deal with it when she was ready to—and ignore it when she wasn't. She looked around and found Dani staring off into the distance. Her shoulders were drawn up. The tip of the spear she'd gripped to stand guard now drooped.

"Hey, you okay?" Lynn didn't raise her voice. She didn't have to: beside a few singing birds, it was quiet and the wind was still.

Her words shook Dani out of her reverie. She turned and looked down over the railing. "Sorry, I was just thinking."

"About Richard?" Lynn stood and wrung her hair out.

Dani nodded.

The breeze couldn't have hardened her nipples even if it had tried; they were already painfully hard from the cold water. She cupped her breasts to let them settle under the slowly retuning heat of her palms. When she looked back up, she caught Dani staring at her before averting her gaze. The flutter in her belly had nothing to do with nausea this time. "Wait, we'll talk."

Still not looking at her, Dani nodded again.

Once her nipples returned to a state of "erect but no longer able to cut rock," Lynn released her breasts and exhaled in relief. She waded downstream and fished her clothes out of the creek before she climbed up the bank.

Dani's gaze slid down Lynn's body as she drew closer, then she peered at the ground before examining the tree line—looking anywhere but at Lynn.

"How are you holding up?" She examined Dani as she let the water run down her body in streams. The pile of fresh clothes Dani had brought lay on the ground by Dani's feet. Lynn's tomahawk had been placed on top of it.

With a shrug, Dani brought Lynn's attention back to her. "I'm actually doing better knowing he's dug up than I was when he was still in the ground." She tried to put cheerfulness in her voice, but she only partially succeeded. "It's weird. I thought I'd be more anxious, but I'm feeling more in control. We're halfway done now."

Lynn stroked water from her skin and leaned down to fish her pants from the pile. She tugged them on over her clammy skin. "More like three-fourths done. We went the long way 'round on the way here. Depending on how much the cart is going to slow us down, we should be back in two days, probably three."

Dani smiled, but not as broadly as Lynn had assumed she would at the knowledge of returning home victorious in her quest. Instead, Dani found and held her gaze for a few seconds, then leaned down and handed Lynn her shirt. "Here. We should get back. Richard's body is outside."

"I'll hurry." Lynn slipped her shirt on—the newly acquired cotton one—and pulled the wet rope from her previously worn pair of pants to secure the new ones after wringing it out thoroughly. Dani had cleaned the dirt and grime off her boots, which was both surprising and touching. She pulled them on and gathered the wad of wet clothes in one hand as she picked up her tomahawk with the other. Dani's hand had felt better to hold, but Lynn was capable of carrying her own weight again. "Done."

Her clothes left a drippy trail on the cracked concrete as they covered the distance to the camp. This time, Lynn paid attention to her surroundings. Her brain was much clearer, but she was tired, both physically and emotionally. She appreciated Dani's foresight to stay at the camp another night. The thought of getting on the road right now was enough to make Lynn want to cry—and she didn't do crying.

Lynn jolted as she realized something else was out of the norm. She checked around her. "Um, where's Skeever?"

"Oh." Dani blushed. "I locked him in. I figured you wouldn't want an excited dog splashing around, you know?" She checked on Lynn from the corner of her eye.

For a moment, Lynn's feathers were irrationally ruffled—who did Dani think she was to make decisions for her like that?—then she realized Dani was absolutely right. Peacefully soaking in ice-cold water was exactly what she'd needed, not sixty pounds of excited dog jumping all over her and splashing water every which way. "Thanks."

Dani relaxed. "It was literally the least I could do. I owe you. It...it must have been bad. I can't even imagine."

Images flashed before her mind's eye, but Lynn suppressed them as quickly as they came up. "It wasn't fun." There was no point in rehashing the experience. Dani had asked her to do it for a reason; she didn't need the gory details now that it was over.

"Still. Thank you. I really am grateful."

Lynn turned her head to examine Dani openly. "I wouldn't have done it for anyone else."

Dani looked up sharply.

Before she could ask for clarification, Lynn pushed on. "We should get him inside, out of the sun at least. He's... The heat isn't going to do him any good."

Curiosity turned to pained disgust on Dani's features. She bit into her lower lip. "You want to bring him inside? With us?"

Lynn cast a sweeping glance at her surroundings. In the distance, the dealership appeared. "You don't?"

"No! I do! I just... I wasn't sure you'd be okay with it."

"Well, not into the bedroom." She realized instantly that sounded weird and disgusting and hurried to explain. "There's a garage in the back. If we can get the door open, we can get the cart in. The garage is a separate space. It should contain the smell at least a little, and he'd be safe. I don't want to attract the local wildlife any more than you."

"Yes. Thank you. Let's do that." Dani looked at her again. "Thank you."

Lynn chuckled despite her exhaustion and soreness. "You really have to stop saying that. I did it, it's done. It's in the past. Time to move on, okay?"

When Dani responded, it was with hesitation. "Does it...make it easier for you to look at life like that? To just...relegate bad things to the past?"

Does it? "Yeah, I suppose it does. My dad used to tell me to look behind you only to make sure there is nothing there that might kill you. It's smart. You focus on things that you can still influence—and that might kill you."

Dani seemed to ponder that, even as she looked behind her reflexively, as if reminded of potential danger. "It is smart, yeah, but also jaded."

Lynn frowned. "Why jaded?"

"Because there are good things in the past too. And those can keep you going when things get rough."

"Hm." Lynn shrugged. "Maybe." There weren't a lot of good memories in her past, and even those few usually ended in heartache she didn't want to be reminded of. *Like you.* She glanced at Dani and quickly looked away when Dani started to turn her head toward her. *Once we split, all of these memories will be tainted.*

They turned onto the parking lot.

Skeever's frantic bark formed a welcome diversion. "Let's get Richard in before we let Skeever out. If he's smart, he'll stay away, but..." She shrugged sheepishly.

The attempt at levity fizzled. A smile ghosted across Dani's lips, but her gaze was directed at the cart. Reality had hit again.

All worries about the future evaporated in a rush of sympathy. Lynn put her tomahawk away and gently took Dani's arm. "Come on. Let's get him somewhere safe."

For once, everything pre-war cooperated: the garage door could be lifted with a hand crank mounted to the inside wall of the building. It was rusty, and the first few turns were hell on Lynn's sore arms, but she persevered.

Next to her in the dark, Dani waited impatiently. Once the door was up high enough, she slipped under, retrieved the cart, and pulled it inside.

Lynn let go of the crank. The metal door crashed onto the concrete with a grating noise that echoed painfully loudly in her ears. "Dammit." She squinted as the ringing subsided.

Dani stood by the cart, gaze glued to it. She didn't seem rattled by the noise.

This is probably a good time to disappear for a while. "I'll be, uh, around if you need me." Lynn pointed to the door that led back to the showroom even as she walked backward toward it.

"Okay." Dani didn't look up.

Lynn turned and left the heavy atmosphere behind to free Skeever from the bedroom he'd been locked into.

He was excited to see her, of course, but mostly he needed to pee. She let him out and watched him hurry to the nearest patch of green to relieve himself. Before she headed out, she looked back at the door in the far wall, wedged between the two offices that had served a bedroom for them and a morgue for Richard. Dani was behind it, hurting, and Lynn's heart hurt in turn. She was very familiar with the type of pain Dani was feeling. With a sigh, she let the front door fall shut behind her and allowed Dani to say her goodbyes in peace.

She poked up the fire and wrung out her clothes before laying them out in a half circle. She would have loved to burn them instead—just the thought of wearing that outfit again left her with palpitations—but that feeling would pass. They were good clothes, and she didn't have too many of those.

Lynn made use of the quiet time to thoroughly coat her injuries with the ointment Ren had provided and to wrap them up again—just not too tightly, in case the swelling worsened. "Fucking mess." Yeah, it worried her that the injuries weren't healing half as well as she wanted them to, but there was nothing she could do about it. *Resting the damn arm would help.* Sadly, that wasn't an option. Lynn sighed. *Time to make tea.*

Skeever explored around the building but returned often to check in. She scratched him lazily under the jaw or behind his ears whenever he did.

By the time Lynn was halfway through her tea, which settled the last of her lingering nausea, Dani returned. She sat down by Lynn's side wordlessly and took the other tin Lynn had put out. Her hands trembled. She was also paler than Lynn was used to, and her eyes were red-rimmed and bloodshot.

"I take it that was hard."

"Yeah."

Lynn wasn't sure how to make it better. Comforting people was not her strong suit.

Thankfully, Dani either realized that or got tired of waiting, because she scooted closer and leaned her head against Lynn's shoulder.

Lynn saw her coming and wrapped an arm around her.

Dani exhaled audibly and settled.

Now what? She wondered if she should do anything else, but Dani seemed content just being close. Lynn looked out over the lot, now awash in reddening light as the sun slowly went down. Maybe this was something hugs could fix. She'd experienced herself how magical they could be.

"I was staying at another camp before the Homestead, at the coast." Dani's voice was soft, and the story started without preamble. "It wasn't working out. They, um…they wanted me to be…more to the leader. Like—"

"I get it." Lynn pulled her closer. People—men and women—demanding sex as a form of "paying your way" was nothing new to her.

Dani nodded and inhaled shakily. "I refused, things got heated, but where was I going to go? It was pretty horrible, but then Richard showed up. The Homestead and my camp had an agreement to trade once a year—my old camp's dried fish for the Homestead's metalwork tools. When Richard realized what was going on, he took a cut in the fish he was paid for the tools and took me instead. I was terrified and angry. I thought they'd arranged this sort of marriage thing where I was now Richard's wife or something. And Richard kept the idea up too! He told me in private that he was married and had no interest in me that way, that he was just playing the part, but sitting by the campfire with his arm around me made me feel so small. So weak." Dani shifted slightly.

Lynn loosened her hold, but Dani pressed back against her, so Lynn held her close again. "You're not weak."

"I know, and later Richard would tell me that too, but I felt like I was. As soon as we left, Richard became this perfect gentleman. He never tried anything while we traveled or after. I told him I would kick him in the nuts if he did, but he didn't lay off me because of the threats. He genuinely just wanted to take me away from the camp and to a place he knew I would be safe. He had no idea if I would be a good addition. He just saw someone in need and fixed the situation."

Even without seeing her face, Lynn could tell Dani was smiling. "He sounds like a great guy."

"He was. He was reserved, moody, impossible to tie down, and sometimes he was a complete ass too, but he was a really good guy." Dani tilted her head so she could look up at Lynn's face. "Kind of like you."

Lynn laughed to chase away a jumble of emotions that exploded in her stomach at the words. "I'm not a guy."

Dani chuckled and settled her head on Lynn's shoulder again, shifting until she found something softer than bone to rest on. "No, you're not."

Then Lynn felt Dani's hand on her leg. She watched how it settled just above the knee, fingers curling around the inside of her thigh. The ball of emotions flamed down from her stomach—way down. She swallowed and stilled.

"You got quiet."

"S-Sorry. W-What were you saying?"

"That you're an ass."

Lynn frowned, but Dani's hand slipped a few inches up along her leg and her objections evaporated.

"But you're also a good person." Dani's fingers curled.

Lynn could feel the pressure even through the layer of wool between Dani's hand and her own skin—and the warmth. "A-Am I?" She was breathless. Her mind raced with a million thoughts—*Dani's touching me*, *we're outside*, and *what does she want?* primary among them. She glanced around quickly, making sure they were safe.

Dani hummed and tilted her head up a little.

Her breath ghosted along Lynn's jaw, but she didn't dare to turn her head. She shivered under Dani's teasing touch and was completely incapable of coming up with a course of action. Her mind had fogged up for the second time today, but for an entirely different reason. She'd never felt as alive as right now.

"Lynn?" Dani shifted again, and the hand that was not wreaking havoc on Lynn's body and mind cupped Lynn's cheek and angled her head toward hers.

She tried to fight it, tried to catch up with what was happening. "What—?"

Dani angled her head more, and now her breath washed over Lynn's lips.

Lynn shuddered. All thoughts of resisting seized. Dani was going to kiss her, and even though a chorus of warnings urged her to back off, her baser instincts had her lean in. She ended up too conflicted to move.

Dani pushed up and made the decision for her

Their lips brushed.

Goose bumps coursed across Lynn's skin, and her heart skipped a beat or two. Her eyes fluttered shut, and she leaned in, meeting Dani's lips in a full press that ignited her from head to toe. She shivered. How could a brushing of lips affect her so? Light-headed, trembling...hungry.

She wasn't the only one affected: Dani whimpered against her lips and cupped the back of her head to pull her even closer. It was an awkward angle; Lynn was all but holding Dani up, and her neck must be straining painfully, but it didn't seem to matter. Dani initiated another meeting and then parted her lips in invitation before pulling back teasingly.

Lynn gave chase, and when they came together again, she was prepared. Her tongue slid between impossibly soft lips and found Dani's.

Nails dug into Lynn's scalp. Dani shuddered against her. The all-but-forgotten hand on Lynn's leg moved up and squeezed.

She likes it. Lynn was acting purely on theory and instinct, but apparently, she was doing it right. As she moved her tongue over and around Dani's, she very carefully ran her hand up her arm.

Skeever barked loudly.

Lynn jumped up as survival instincts tugged her back to reality. Her tomahawk seemed to materialize in her hand. Her heartbeat galloped, but she wasn't sure which had sent it skyrocketing more: kissing Dani or impending doom.

When Lynn let go, Dani only just managed to throw her arm behind her to keep herself upright.

Skeever trotted over, tail wagging, tongue lolling, just looking for attention.

"Wow." Dani's voice trembled slightly. Her gaze slid across the landscape, but she seemed to come to the same conclusion as Lynn had: there was no danger, just an attention-seeking dog. She ran her hand through her hair and shook her head.

"What the hell, Skeeve." Lynn glared at the dog and lowered herself back down with a deep breath meant to settle the dizzying rush of adrenaline in her system. She accepted a doggy hug and buried her face in his fur to hide the blush heating her cheeks. After a few moments, she dared to put into words what had just transpired, at the risk of making the experience feel even more real than it obviously already was. "You kissed me."

"No," Dani countered instantly. "*We* kissed."

"There's a difference?" Lynn found the courage to look up and sent Skeever away with a pat on the flank.

He ran off, chasing a bird he spotted.

Dani's gaze didn't lift from her. "There's a big difference." Her pupils had dilated, making her eyes seem darker.

"What's the difference, then?"

The same tongue Lynn had tasted wet Dani's lips and drew Lynn's gaze away from Dani's eyes.

She glanced back up.

"That you wanted it too." It was supposed to be a statement, but the way Dani struggled to hold her gaze made Lynn suspect Dani wasn't too sure about that.

Lynn chose her words carefully. "If I told you I did, then what?"

Dani finally couldn't hold eye contact anymore and dropped her gaze to her hands. "Then it would complicate things."

You're not wrong there. "I know. So…do you want me to say I wanted it too? Or do we end it here and never mention it again?" Lynn watched Skeever swallow the bird in large chunks. The gruesome display did nothing to distract her from the conversation.

"Is that what you want?"

"What I want hasn't changed." Lynn licked her lips and tasted Dani. Need flared. "It just got more…" She trailed off. "More."

"For me to come with you. To travel together." Clearly a statement this time.

With a casual shrug, Lynn tried to make this conversation less of a walk through a wolves' den. "It's why I came after you."

"If I say that you can say that you wanted to kiss me too—" She spoke slowly as if to construct the sentence correctly in her head. "Then does that mean I'm promising to stay?"

"No." *But I'd like it to.*

"Then you can say it."

Lynn swallowed down a lump of nerves and looked back at Dani. "I wanted to kiss you too."

Dani didn't outwardly react to that. She paused for a few seconds, seemingly pondering something. Then she drew her gaze up and locked it with Lynn's. "Do you want to do it again?"

When they shut the bedroom door on Skeever, he whined loudly, but Dani smiled.

Lynn turned toward her. It was awkward now, mostly because they hadn't actually discussed what would happen next but also because preparing the camp for the night had taken enough time for Lynn's mind to provide her with enough scenarios of doom to make a second round of kisses—or maybe even more—a very bad idea.

She had romantically kissed exactly one person in her life—and that person was in this room. She hadn't felt the need to be close to another human being since everyone she'd considered family had died. Lynn didn't touch others, and others didn't touch her; that was how it had been for more than half her life.

Dani stood in the center of the room, didn't move, and just...watched. She didn't give any indication of what she was feeling or thinking.

Clearly, Lynn would have to make the next move, which was terrifying. She wanted to kiss Dani again. Even if Dani went back to the Homestead, even if she lost her some other way, she had enjoyed kissing Dani and the way kissing her had made her feel. There was hesitance now too, though. Despite what Dani had said earlier—that Lynn admitting she had wanted to kiss her wouldn't affect Dani's decision once they made it back to the Homestead—it undoubtedly would, and Lynn felt the pressure to perform.

She'd also had plenty of time to think about why Dani had kissed her. The most logical conclusion was that Dani had been confronted with the reality of death in a very brutal and personal way today, and she was just kissing her because it chased the fear of dying and the memories of Richard's corpse away. Lynn hadn't thought of dying when they were kissing. In fact, she'd never felt more alive. If they both felt better while kissing each other, then there was really only one thing to do, right?

While Skeever scratched at the door to be let in, Lynn closed the distance between her and Dani and kissed her again, squarely on the lips.

It wasn't exactly a skillful or gentle coming together. Dani's eyes widened just a touch before Lynn closed hers, but she took a hold of Lynn's shoulder to keep herself from swaying and just...connected. Then she wrapped her other arm around Lynn's back and pressed herself against her.

They were of roughly equal height, so Dani's breasts pressed against Lynn's and her pelvis connected with her too. Even their legs brushed; Dani was that close. It felt very odd, and Lynn had to fight off insidious thoughts like that Dani could reach for her tomahawk and brain her with it. Once she succeeded, Lynn exhaled and relaxed.

With Dani's hand on her arm, the hand of that arm could only go to Dani's hip or side. She settled on her side. The other one could go anywhere. She chose to trace the braid in Dani's hair after lifting it from the curtain of her hair. It felt smooth and tight, with a small bone bead at the end that she could feel was engraved, but she couldn't visualize the pattern. Dani's tongue slipping over her lips and drawing her attention away might have had something to do with it. She parted her lips, but Dani had broken the kiss already.

Lynn chased those lips blindly and met them again, this time instantly connecting with Dani's tongue. The sudden touch had her whimper—which was a sound she had literally never heard herself utter.

With an appreciative hum, Dani rolled her tongue a little more firmly along the edge of Lynn's.

A shiver coursed down all the way to Lynn's toes. When she gently tugged Dani's braid, Dani tilted her head and their mouths connected fully, parting wider instinctively to allow a very real, very firm, very nice kiss.

Another million thoughts popped up, but far less intrusively this time: *Is my tongue cold too? What's that taste? Should I do something else?* They popped up at the rate of one per heartbeat, but once her heartbeat slowed to a regular pace and she could no longer keep track of the times they'd broken apart and come back together for more, they disappeared. Kissing Dani became familiar and fun faster than Lynn had thought possible.

Dani stroked her arm with her fingertips, so Lynn used her thumb to stroke Dani's side. She discovered little kisses anywhere on Dani's lips made her smile. Teasing the corner of her mouth with her tongue made her moan.

Lynn discovered things about herself too: the back of her elbow was extremely ticklish, for example, something Dani noted with glee. When Dani traced her top front teeth with her tongue, she developed goose bumps, but she instantly hated it when Dani pushed her tongue under hers and against the connective tissue between her tongue and the floor of her mouth. She wasn't quite sure how to tell Dani that, so she just sort of fumbled her tongue under Dani's when Dani's tongue seemed to go for the spot. These minor inconveniences did nothing to dampen her enjoyment of the activity. She was probably doing things Dani didn't like and misinterpreting the signs, but Dani didn't seem to mind either.

Slowly, Lynn broke another kiss.

After pecking Lynn's bottom lip, Dani leaned back and continued to scratch the nape of Lynn's neck, where her hand had ended up. "My feet are killing me."

It took a little time for Lynn to realize they were no longer kissing. She enjoyed the rasp of Dani's nails on her skin very much, she'd discovered. When she opened her eyes, enough time had passed for the world to darken considerably since the last time she'd had her eyes open. "Oh."

Dani very distinctly giggled, which was such a foreign sound to Lynn that she dropped her gaze to Dani's lips to watch it happen. They were puffy and red and curved into a big smile.

"Oh?" Dani shook her head, but her eyes were filled with mirth.

Lynn's sluggish brain picked up speed, but not fast enough to come up with anything useful. "Sorry. Um…food?"

Dani watched her for a five count, then burst into laughter. She hugged her, which was somehow a completely different experience than kissing. "Yeah, Wilder, let's eat."

CHAPTER 17

"Is this something we have to talk about?" The long, intense kissing session in question made Lynn dangerously giddy whenever she thought of it, but if they talked about it, they would have to face the consequences of this sudden shift in their relationship. She didn't feel emotionally steady enough to listen to Dani repeating it didn't change anything between them—because their kissing had changed a lot for Lynn, even though she wasn't entirely able to grasp how and how much, nor did she want to.

Dani stretched out her legs and wiggled her toes. The skin of her feet was still riddled with blisters, but the fire seemed to help dry out the popped ones. "I don't know. Do we?"

Lynn plucked at her meat. Skeever had caught a rabbit this morning, and they'd roasted it without much talking but with a good deal of smiles and little touches. "I don't know. If it's going to be a problem then yes, if not, then I guess we don't have to."

It was dark now. The crescent moon and the fire provided the only illumination, but that was more than enough to watch Dani clean the rabbit's juices off her plate with a piece of flatbread. She kept her head down. "It's been a long day."

"Yeah. True." Lynn's leaden arms and aching back reminded her of that with every move. "Does that mean you don't want to talk about it?"

Dani nodded and finally looked at her. The little smile tugging at the corners of her mouth was soothing. "I know we'll have to eventually, but with everything that's happened today, I'm just..." She didn't finish the sentence.

"Tired. I get it. Me too."

Dani's smile spread. "Thanks." After a pause she added, "It was good, though."

Lynn's heart did a somersault. "Yeah?"

Dani's eyes finally lit up with a spark. She sat a little closer on the pavement. "Yeah. Maybe we can do it again sometime."

Lynn laughed and brushed her arm against Dani's. "Yeah, that might be nice." *Potentially stupid, but very nice.*

"Come on, Skeeve, I want to go to bed!" Lynn held the door open for Skeever, who had decided another bathroom call was in order before bed—well after Lynn and Dani had taken care of that themselves.

Dani stood in the doorway of the makeshift bedroom, arms crossed, waiting with a grin.

"Skeever!"

He finally looked up and ran back from the bushes, then shot past her and headed straight for the bedroom.

Once Lynn had bolted the door and joined them in the bedroom, Dani closed the door behind them all.

Skeever settled on Lynn's bed with a happy sigh.

"Ass." Lynn pushed him gently with her foot as she stripped off her jacket. "Go sleep with Dani."

"And that's not mean?" Dani grinned and got under her covers.

Very little light made its way into the back room, but Lynn could see that Dani's face was turned toward her. "Well, a little." She spread her jacket out by the door. "Come, Skeeve. Come here." She patted the leather.

Skeever took his time walking over, then whimpered pathetically as he lay down.

"Whiner." She scratched his neck and side, kissed his nose, and left him to his own sleeping. She lowered herself down on her bed, kicked off her boots, and rolled onto her back with a groan. Every single part of her body was sore, and relaxing her muscles felt like agony. When she brought her arms up to lay her head on, a sharp stab of pain flashed from her wrist to her elbow. She hissed.

"You okay?"

Lynn brought her arms back down and massaged her pulsing left arm. "Yeah, I just keep forgetting about these damn bite marks. All that digging and hauling messed that whole area up." The pain faded slowly.

"Sorry."

Lynn looked toward Dani's general area. The whites of Dani's eyes caught a little light, and she focused her gaze on that. "Don't worry. Really. I'll be fine. I knew it was going to happen and it did."

"Still. I'm grateful. Also for...after. I haven't been thinking of...of Richard half as much as I thought I would be."

Lynn didn't quite know what to think of that. "Was kissing me only a distraction?"

"No!" Dani sat up. "No. Definitely not. It helped, but—" She paused and ran her hand through her hair. "Now we're talking about it anyway."

Lynn smiled in the dark. "Yeah, sorry, I'm just a little out of my league here. We went from playing each other to, well, this, literally overnight."

"Two nights, and a lot happened in between."

"Like?" Lynn shifted onto her side so she could watch Dani more easily.

"Like..." Dani lay down again and looked at her too. "Like not dying because you were with me, and you being there when I...struggled." She sighed. "And you've been wearing on me with that 'come with me' bullshit."

Lynn considered that. "Why is it bullshit?"

Dani groaned. "I don't know! It just is. It's...stupid."

The blankets suddenly felt constricting. Lynn pushed them down to her waist. "But you're thinking about it anyway."

Dani didn't reply for a long time. Finally, she said, "I need to talk to Kate. If you're right, I don't like what her plans are. And I still think you should come with me."

"I'm no—"

"I know what you said. Skeever, shitty scout, I got it." Dani seemed to wave her hand in the air, but it was hard to tell in the dark. "It would just be easier if you did come with me and if you wanted to take over Richard's job."

Lynn didn't reply. She knew down to her bones that wasn't going to work—for anyone.

Dani seemingly got tired of waiting for input. "If she forces me to go out alone like Richard did, well, I have just as much of a chance of dying as I would have with you."

"You wouldn't be alone if you came with me. You'd be safer."

Now it was Dani's turn to pause again. "Unless you left me, then I'd be in just as much danger—more, because I wouldn't have anywhere to go." Her voice trembled.

"I can't make promises." Lynn watched what she thought was Dani's shape as they talked. "Well, I could, but you'd have to trust me to stick to it, and I wouldn't take your word for something as important as this, so I get that making promises is useless." She took a deep breath and let it out again. "It's your choice. And you have to make it. All I can say is that..." *Damn, why is it so hard to get this out?* "That kissing you only made me want you to come with me more."

Only Skeever's breathing filled the silence.

"This is why I didn't want to talk about it."

Dani sounded sad or confused or scared, maybe. Without visual input, Lynn couldn't tell for sure. "We don't have to. We'll stick to the plan: go back, you talk to Kate, you either show up or you don't."

"And you'd be okay with it if I don't?"

Lynn swallowed down a ball of nerves. "I wouldn't be happy," she eventually said. "But I'd understand, and I'd survive. It wouldn't change my plan."

"What plan?"

"Head south, stay warm during the winter. Figure out a way to stay safe." Lynn rattled the list off with ease. It was a simple survival strategy, but one that encompassed all that she'd always thought mattered most. It terrified her that maybe that wasn't enough anymore now that she'd gotten a glimpse of what else life had to offer.

"Did you ever plan for someone else to join you?"

"No." She admitted it honestly. "Well, once I picked up Skeever, he got added to the mix."

"And you'd just as easily fit me in?"

Lynn was instantly presented with a vision of a little farm, fenced off and secure, with Dani working the field as Lynn walked out into the sunlight beyond the patio. Dani looked up and gave her a smile and a wave before wiping sweat off her brow. It was an entirely unrealistic vision of a future that would not—could not—exist in the world they lived in, but it made her smile regardless. "Yeah. Definitely." Her voice was raspy, courtesy of a lightning bolt of longing that tore through her chest.

Dani sighed and turned. "We should sleep."

Shit. Lynn nodded, then realized Dani couldn't see her. "Yeah. Good night."

There was no verbal reply, just the shifting of blankets and a soft sigh.

Lynn wasn't sure if she'd done anything wrong or if it was just Dani struggling with her own thoughts and emotions, but Dani was definitely struggling. Knowing that left her wide-awake, and she tried to work through a confusing mix of anxiety and hope. Here she was, not even sure they would make it back to the Homestead and already worrying about what would happen if Dani didn't choose to come with her.

And what if she did choose to come? What if they ended up butting heads? Especially now this romantic—or maybe just sexual—element had been introduced, the chance of catastrophic failure of their potential partnership was even higher. *Or it'll make us work harder at it.* This whole thing was doing her head in!

She tried to make out Dani's shape, fighting the urge to get up and join her. It felt wrong to know Dani was having a hard time yet to stay away. Then again, maybe Dani liked being apart right now. Maybe some distance was exactly what she needed.

Lynn squeezed her eyes shut and threw her uninjured arm over her face in frustration. *See? This is exactly why this is all a bad idea! You have no clue how to be with another human being—let alone be involved with them.* She moved her arm just enough to peer past it at what she assumed to be the back of Dani's head. *This is stupid! You stare down wolves every other day. Just ask her the damn question and let her decide.* "Dani? Do you want me to come over? Like...like two nights ago?" The seconds that passed before Dani replied felt glacial.

"Yeah." That one word, said softly, was the only reply, but it was a clear answer.

Lynn got up right away. She gathered her knife and tomahawk as well as her blanket.

Dani scooted toward the wall to make room on the bedding and lifted her blanket to allow Lynn under it.

Heat radiated off Dani's body as Lynn settled against her from behind. She put her weapons above her head, then wrapped her arm around Dani's waist. After Dani got her hair out of the way, Lynn laid her head down and smiled. "Is this okay?"

"Yeah." It seemed Dani had been reduced to one-word replies. She was also much more tense than she'd been two nights ago, but her heartbeat was steady and her breathing slow.

"Sleep well," Lynn whispered. "Don't think about anything right now. That's for later."

Dani nodded, and the tension receded from her muscles. "Yeah."

Lynn couldn't help but chuckle. "Can you say anything else?"

"Yeah." This time, there was a small smile in her voice.

"Good." Lynn kissed her shoulder instinctively. "I look forward to hearing more words tomorrow. Now sleep."

Dani exhaled slowly and slid her arm over Lynn's, then covered her hand with hers. She weaved their fingers together and gave a soft squeeze. "You make me very confused."

Even so close to Dani, Lynn had to struggle to hear her. She swallowed. "Trust me," she said just a hint more loudly than Dani. "I came into New York convinced I'd never let another person close ever again, and here I am, holding you, having kissed you, hoping you'll come with me because I like being with you and...and I think life will be better with you. If anyone's confused, it's me."

Dani squeezed her hand again. "Thank you. That helps."

Lynn frowned. "Why?"

"Because you seem to have this all figured out."

Lynn laughed and pushed up so she could try to get a glimpse of Dani's face. "Are you kidding me? I have absolutely no idea what I'm doing, and I'm terrified!" She couldn't help laughing. How could Dani think she had a handle on all of this? "I have been on my own for years. Before you, I'd never even kissed anyone. Not like that. I've definitely never asked anyone to come with me. I have absolutely nothing figured out. I'm just hoping at one point it'll all come together, and it'll be good."

Dani turned around so she could face her in the near dark. So close, Lynn could see that her eyes were shiny and wet. "You've never kissed anyone before?"

"That's what you got out of that?" Lynn squinted at her.

Dani pushed her face against Lynn's chest. "Sorry. I didn't mean it like that. I just... That's special."

Lynn hesitated before cupping the back of Dani's head and lightly scratching her scalp. She remembered how that soothed Dani. It didn't fail to do so now. "Why is it special?"

Dani shrugged. "Because."

Lynn tapped Dani's head with her index finger. "Bad answer."

"Because...I think...you trust me."

Now it was Lynn's turn to tense. Her suddenly frantic mind raced. Was it true? Could she admit that? What would it mean if she did? "I do." The whispered words clawed their way out of her almost constricted throat. It wasn't a hundred percent trust—Lynn doubted she was even capable of that—but she trusted Dani as much as she could. Deep down, she had known that, and it terrified her.

"Your heartbeat went wild." Dani shifted her head against her chest to listen better. "Are you scared?"

"Yes." She inhaled shakily. "Say something."

"I trust you, too."

The whispered words reverberated through Lynn's chest, setting her on fire from head to toe and likewise chilling her entire body as if ice-cold water pushed through her veins.

"Now your heartbeat really went wild." Dani sounded bemused.

Lynn just held on to the back of her head like a tether. She tried to find words in the sea of frantic thoughts raging through her mind. "I don't trust people." She barely recognized her voice, it was so hoarse. "And no one trusts me. That's always been safer."

Dani wrapped her arm around Lynn's waist and pulled herself closer. "Haven't you been lonely?"

The words hit like a sledgehammer. Combined with the warm hold, Dani's breath on her chest, and her own fears, they caused tears to well up in her eyes. "Yes." She curled herself a bit more securely around Dani's body and rested her chin on the top of Dani's head.

Dani's hold intensified. "Then this is better."

"Not if you leave. Then it's horrible."

Dani's fingers played along her spine. "You could stay with us. We could do Richard's job together. It would fix it all: it would be safer, you wouldn't have to deal with the Homesteaders much and...and we'd be together."

Lynn inhaled Dani's comforting scent. "I don't know." She didn't know anything right now, but some weight did lift from her chest as Dani's words seeped slowly into her fried brain. If things didn't work out, she could leave—or escape, if the Homesteaders took her captive again—and Dani would still be safe. On the other hand, it meant settling down and opening herself to loss again. "I don't know." The repeated words came out broken.

Dani shifted and tilted her head up.

Warm lips connected with hers, then parted. Lynn whimpered and gripped Dani's hair as she instantly searched for her tongue. Kissing Dani had chased away all her fears, all her worries, all her thoughts. She needed that more than ever right now.

Dani shuddered. She met Lynn's tongue with a huff of breath, gripped her shirt with both hands, and pulled it up a few inches.

Lynn moved on instinct. She pushed against Dani's mouth, searching for a revelation that would soothe her racing mind. Her tongue stroked with far less coordination than this afternoon. She wasn't merely experiencing now or trying to prove herself—this was a hunt for either clarity or oblivion.

Dani hooked her leg behind Lynn's knee and connected them more fully—breasts, bellies, sexes. She tilted her head to deepen the kiss.

Lynn hummed as heat pooled low in her gut, goading her on. Still she couldn't stop analyzing what was happening. Every one of Dani's movements was noted and logged, along with every move she made herself. Every sound, every reaction, every emotion. Analyze, analyze, analyze. She groaned and rolled Dani onto her back, settling half on top of her, then hissed as pain seared through her injured arm. *Dammit!* She needed to get her weight off that arm and onto the other—which meant covering Dani's body with her own. So she did.

Dani gripped her hips and pushed into her body, rolling against it with a deep moan. They barely broke apart in their kisses, but whenever they did, Dani pushed back up to connect them again, apparently not content to be a passive participant anymore.

Lynn pressed her thigh between Dani's legs and was rewarded with a sound that was a mixture between a hiss and a moan. It quieted her mind for a few seconds. As soon as the thoughts came rolling back, she rolled her hips again.

Dani's nails dug into her skin. "L-Ly—"

Lynn interrupted her with another kiss. She cupped the side of her neck and lightly scraped her skin.

Dani moaned and stopped trying to talk. Instead, she bucked up against Lynn's thigh and pulled her down onto hers.

Now Lynn understood the hiss and moan combination; the sound tore from her own throat the second pleasure buzzed through her. She chased the feeling with another kiss, another buck of her hips, another roll of her body with muscles that fought every movement. She didn't care how tired or sore she was; her mind was going quiet, and Dani was urging her on.

The covers had fallen off. Cool air hit her overheating skin as Dani let go of her hips to pull her shirt up as far as it would go without Lynn shifting. Her hands roamed and examined the evidence of burns, cuts, bites, and the remnants of a whole slew of accidents.

Lynn shivered. The constant rolling of their hips created waves of pleasure that increased in power every time Dani's thigh pushed against her throbbing sex. But something else was building too: a counterwave Lynn couldn't name but that swelled until it drowned out everything else. She whimpered against Dani's lips.

Dani's hands slid up to her shoulder blades and guided her down into a hug.

Lynn buried her face against the crook of Dani's neck.

"Shhhh." Dani stroked the back of her head. "I-It's okay." She was breathless, her voice deep, but her tone was soothing.

It was only then Lynn realized she was crying. *Oh shit! How long have I—* She hurriedly pushed up, but Dani trapped her by the back of her neck.

"Don't. S-Stay." She ran her nails gently over the skin of Lynn's neck, causing the small hairs there to stand on end.

Lynn's body buzzed with need, shook with sobs, and she gave in to the need to be held. She wasn't even sure what she was letting out, but now that the dams had been breached, there was no stopping the flood. She sagged onto Dani's body and let her wrap her arms and a leg around her as she cried herself empty. It took an embarrassingly long time. Whenever she thought she was done, she remembered her dad, felt some sort of pain or ache that reminded her of how fucked up her life was, or Dani did something such as kiss her shoulder or massage the back of her neck, setting her off again. Finally, not even Dani's kindness could coax more tears out of her; she was spent.

"Wow." Dani gathered Lynn's hair and guided it aside so she could trace the shell of her ear. "Better?"

Lynn did feel much lighter, as if she were floating, but she was also embarrassed beyond anything, and she had a skull-splitting headache. *Better* was not an accurate description. She really wanted to pull away, but it would take too much energy, so she buried her face deeper against the crook of Dani's neck.

Dani stroked her hair and rested her cheek against the side of her head. She shifted lightly to get comfortable. "Better?" Dani wanted an answer—deserved an answer.

"Dunno." She sniffed as watery snot threatened to drip from her nose, onto Dani's neck. "S-Sorry."

Dani hummed and kissed the shell of her ear—seemingly the only skin within reach. "You did the same for me, and you were cool about it. It's good you let it out."

Lynn frowned, but gathering enough energy to object was a struggle. "About what h-happened. The crying too, but...us."

Dani was silent for a few seconds. "What exactly are you sorry about?"

The insecurity that snuck into her tone gave Lynn the strength to move. She settled onto her side, still mostly covering Dani, and lifted her head. Her headache dizzied her. She squinted until the pain faded enough to focus again. "Not that it happened," she said softly.

Dani looked at her, then reached out and stroked her cheek with the back of her fingers, either to brush away tears or simply to touch; Lynn couldn't tell. She held her gaze.

"That...that I have no idea what I'm doing. That it stopped. That—"

Dani kissed her again, softly this time. No tongue, just a press of lips.

Lynn relaxed instantly and leaned into the touch just enough to show she was a willing participant.

When Dani pulled away, she met her eyes.

"I know this is hard," Dani said.

"This?" Lynn swallowed. Her arm trembled as she put weight on it to hold herself up.

"Being open." Dani continued to examine her. "You haven't done that for a long time."

Lynn took a shuddering breath and looked away. Her cheeks burned even hotter than before.

Dani gently guided her head back until Lynn was forced to meet her eyes again in the near dark.

Whatever was hidden in the depths of Dani's eyes, Lynn couldn't decipher. She wanted to avert her gaze, but Dani's fingers on her cheek held her in place.

Dani smiled.

Lynn smiled back. Group by group, her muscles relaxed. She exhaled, and her gaze dipped down to Dani's lips. She kissed them softly.

Dani smiled into the touch and ran her fingertips along her jaw. "Better?"

"Yes." Not anywhere near *good*, but better; her fears and confusion still filled her stomach, making her a little nauseous, but she was calm again. And tired.

"Good. Then let's sleep. We'll need our energy tomorrow."

The words were sobering. Tomorrow they would be pulling a cart with a body down a road that was hard to traverse under the best of circumstances, all the while running the risk of getting pounced on by every predator in the area. Lynn wrapped her arm around Dani's waist and pulled her in protectively as she pressed their foreheads together. "This is exactly what I didn't want to have happen."

"What?"

Lynn leaned into Dani's warm hand on her cheek. "To worry about losing you now that we're reaching the part where we'll likely get killed."

Dani shook her head. "We're not going to die."

"Liar." Lynn was only partly joking.

"I'm not. You're an expert in surviving out here, and I am a good hunter. We've already proven we can work together and survive things that should have killed us. I'm not going to let you die, and you're not going to let me die either, so that's settled." Dani sounded so confident.

Lynn wanted to believe her. She really did, but the odds were not in their favor.

"Stop worrying. Come on." Dani shifted until Lynn could spoon her from behind.

Lynn molded herself to Dani's body, staying as close as she could. She also pulled the blankets back up. They had switched places; Dani was on the outside now, Lynn up against the wall.

With great effort, she pushed up one more time to pull her weapons over to this side of the bedding, right above her head, then settled again.

Dani shifted until they were flush. "Sleep well."

Lynn nuzzled against the back of her neck, into Dani's hair. "You too." She had no idea when Dani fell asleep, but Lynn was out like a light within seconds.

Lynn jolted awake. Something pressed against her back, and a weight around her waist held her down. A fleeting pressure and hot breath tickled along her shoulder, moving toward her neck. She gasped and bucked, trying to kick her way to freedom and wakefulness.

The pressure around her waist turned into a firm grip. It kept Lynn from twisting enough to grab a weapon. *Shit, shit, shit!*

"Lynn, it's me! Dani!"

"Wha—?" Lynn blinked but stopped moving. Her mind clawed to wakefulness enough to remember where she was and with whom. She went limp.

Dani relaxed behind her and scooted back a bit.

Lynn took a deep breath to steady her racing heart. *Fucking hell!* This was not her favorite way to wake up. The whole night had been filled with nightmares of grave digging, being buried alive while maggots crawled over and under her skin, and hauling corpses from one location to the other. Being chewed on fitted right in. After a few seconds, she had herself under control enough to turn. She smiled apologetically and wrapped her arm around Dani's waist to show she was okay with physical contact now. "S-Sorry. Habit."

The pale morning light streamed in and revealed the worry in Dani's eyes. "Sorry. I really didn't mean to startle you. Are you sure you're okay?"

Lynn nodded. "That was all on me. I'm used to waking up to things trying to take a bite out of me. I don't usually sleep this deep, so I got all—" She made a gesture to indicate whatever it was she'd turned into upon waking.

"That's okay. I get it." Dani hesitated, then her gaze flickered to Lynn's lips and she crossed the few inches between them to kiss her softly. "I'll remember."

Lynn relaxed and hummed into the soft contact. "Thanks." *Subject change.* "Did you sleep well?"

Dani lay back down and nodded. She ran her fingers along Lynn's arm, all the way from her shoulder to where Lynn had a loose hold of her waist. "Lots of dreams."

Lynn sympathized. "About Richard?"

Dani shrugged. "About a lot of things. Mostly the deadly kind."

Lynn squeezed her side. "Sorry. Do you know what always makes me feel better?"

"What?" Dani met her eyes curiously.

"Breakfast."

Dani slapped her arm. "Impossible." Her shoulders relaxed, though, and her newly acquired smile held.

"Sorry, I'm just that kind of girl." Seeing Dani happier made Lynn feel better in turn. Her brain still felt sluggish, and her body was sore from all the heavy work she'd done yesterday, but once she got moving, she'd be fine.

Dani shook her head but cupped her cheek and kissed her again.

Lynn's eyes fluttered shut. *I could get used to this.* The second the thought hit, reality crashed down again. Getting used to this was dangerous business. She pulled back and cleared her throat. "Could you find us something to eat? I'll check around and get the fire going." She sat up.

"I don't want to get up. Once we get up, everything changes."

Another nervous flutter filled Lynn's belly. She met Dani's gaze. "You can still reconsider. If we don't go back to the Homestead, nothing changes. It'll just be you, me, and Skeever."

Dani groaned and turned her head so she could push her face into the bedding. "I can't."

Lynn ran her hand through her tangled hair and shook it out. "I know, but I had to try."

"I understand." Dani sat up too. "Ready to go?"

Lynn nodded slowly. "Let's do it." With great reluctance, she got up.

Skeever stood from the one blanket Lynn had left behind, wagging his tail.

"Morning, sneaky mutt." Lynn gave him a quick cuddle before she put her boots on and secured her weapons. She opened the door to the showroom and let Skeever search it for danger as she looked back. Dani was putting on her own boots. "I'll see you outside, okay?"

Dani nodded. Lynn caught a glimmer of guilt and worry in her eyes before they faded to blank. "I'll be right out. I'm going to pack our stuff first."

"Sounds good." Fresh air poured past her and washed away the cozy atmosphere in the room. The change had started; the distance between them grew. They were both already preparing for life outside of this building and for the potential threats that came with it. The walls they'd need to survive the Wilds would only become thicker as the day progressed. Lynn had never realized just how heavy those layers of emotional armor were, but she felt its weight settle on her like a yoke, threatening to pull her down. She squared her shoulders and pushed through the showroom and toward the door. She'd always been able to bear it; today wouldn't be any different.

She didn't get attacked the moment she stepped into the pale sunlight. It was always a good morning when she didn't get attacked right out of the gates. Lynn scanned the world around her, then closed the door behind her and Skeever and headed out. She gripped her tomahawk lightly, ready for anything.

Skeever headed for the bushes in a zig-zag pattern as he followed his nose. He made it there safely.

Lynn took her time to adjust to the outdoors again. A few hares hopped across the road, birds flew overhead, but nothing else moved. The sun was just barely up and cast a diffuse glow over the world. The coals showed signs of heat when she poked them with a stick.

A lengthy perimeter check only gave her a single scare as a deer burst from the bushes. Nothing with sharp teeth jumped at her, and the presence of deer was a clear indicator that she was the most dangerous thing around these parts. Well, she and Dani.

"All right, fire." Lynn mumbled the words even as she beelined back to the pit. She blew on the coals, fed them dry leafy material, and coaxed them back into a flame with the patience and nonchalance only someone who did it on a near-daily basis could. Its familiar warmth was soothing and Lynn's focus shifted to the day ahead and what it would entail, offering temporary reprieve from her conflicting emotions.

When Dani came out with both their backpacks, that focus crumbled like a badly stacked woodpile.

Dani had changed into a fresh pair of light leather pants and a dark leather top that left her arms exposed. The well-defined muscles in her arms stood taut under the weight.

Desire sparked hotly in her gut. Lynn swallowed and looked back at the fire. "The, um, tea's almost done."

Dani plopped down next to her and ducked under the strap of her spear before laying it by her feet. "Thanks." She sent her a smile and opened her pack. "Quick meal?"

Lynn nodded.

"Quick meal it is." It was so hard to distance herself from last night. Lynn ate and drank quietly, watching Skeever dart around, chasing his own food, just so she could avoid looking at Dani. The urge to move grew inside of her. The familiarity of walking and the dangers of travel would hopefully put thoughts of Dani out of her mind, at least for a little while. She pushed the last bit of cheese into her mouth, squashed it against her palate, and swallowed. "Ready?"

Dani's head shot up. She looked around dazed, then her focus returned and she nodded. "Ready." She stood right away and pushed the strips of jerky she had left into her mouth. The muscles in her jaw had to work hard to get through the food.

Preparing to leave was worse than leaving. Now that her mind was made up to go, Lynn just wanted to get going, but there was a fire to put out, things to pack, a dog to wrangle, clothes and gear to get on. Every step closer to departing also reminded her that once they arrived at their destination, she might be doing these chores on her own again.

The second she entered the garage, the stench of decay hit her full-force and her tumbling thoughts arrested. She instinctively stepped back and covered her mouth and nose. Breakfast threatened to make a speedy reappearance, but she refused to waste perfectly good food like that. She pushed her nose and mouth into the crook of her elbow and took a shallow breath. She steeled her resolve, pushed inside, and hurried to get the garage door up—both to allow Dani entrance and to get the old air out.

Once the door rolled up, there was another side effect: light. It had been dark in the garage, but now nothing obscured the cart and its cargo.

The package was still right where they'd left it, but the blanket had soaked through and a puddle of fluid had gathered under him. Things she didn't want to inspect writhed inside of it. Lynn gratefully diverted her gaze to Dani as she entered.

Dani pushed in with determination but faltered almost right away. "Oh, that's—" She pinched her nose shut.

Lynn was impressed that Dani managed to keep her breakfast down; she couldn't fault her for being overwhelmed now. "Step aside. I've got it."

Dani backed out with relief obvious on her features.

In order to grip the handlebars, Lynn had to uncover her nose. She took shallow breaths only when she got dizzy. The quickest way to get him out was to push, but that meant stepping into the puddle. Lynn decided to make a half circle instead and pull him out.

Emerging into the light and fresh air was a huge relief. As soon as she was clear of the garage, she inhaled deeply. The cart was a heavy pull, but once she got momentum going, it was easier, so she just kept moving.

Skeever hurried over, as always engaged by anything that moved. As soon as he caught a whiff of the cart's contents, he whined and backed up.

"Didn't you want to tie him down?" Dani hurried after her but stayed about ten paces away from the cart as if repelled by an invisible barrier.

Lynn wished she could do the same. She set her jaw. "Let's just get going. We'll stop if he slips." Her arms felt tired already, and her glutes strained. Stopping would only force her to spend energy she didn't have. She maneuvered toward the main road and focused on avoiding potholes as much as possible.

Of course, Richard's body slipped the second she hit the end of the downslope onto the highway. The weight of the cart and its contents added to her speed, and she hit a crack in the pavement while trying to slow. The wheels jumped; the cart creaked, and Lynn felt the weight shift.

Dani let out a yelp.

Lynn's painful left arm strained to keep the cart from tipping. She dug her heels in. Her calves strained as she pushed against the force. Her heart lunged into her throat. *You're not tipping over, dammit!* She tried to project her thoughts at the cart like a command, and it worked. The wheels found their grip, the load stabilized, and Lynn managed to stop.

She dropped the beams instantly, stepped out, and shook out her arms. "Fucking fuck! This is such a bloody bad idea! Fuck!" She swirled around and glimpsed Dani and Skeever catching up with her at a jog.

"Are you okay?" Dani reached out for her arm.

Lynn pulled away. She was far too antsy to be touched right now. Dying by being overrun by a cart with a corpse on it was very low on the how-I-want-to-die list, just slightly above being eaten alive or starving in a cave-in. "Fuck!" She kicked a hole into the body of a rusted car husk and raised her hands over her head. A stab tore through her arm, adding insult to injury. "And this fucking arm too!" She lowered it again and massaged the sting out of the flesh around the wounds.

Dani watched her, then checked their surroundings. "I'll tie him down."

Lynn clenched her jaw. This was all her fault; she should have just tied him down before they left. *Stubborn and stupid. That'll get you killed, Tanner. That'll get you killed right quick.* She kicked another car but with a lot less passion. "Stupid." She mumbled the word to herself and shook her head. The adrenaline left her system, and her heart rate settled.

"Done." Dani's stepped back from the cart with a slight stumble. Her gaze was glued to its contents. She'd tied Richard's body down with three separate lashes that wrapped around the crossbeams. He wasn't going anywhere now.

"Thank you." She took a deep breath and reeled herself in.

Dani nodded but still looked at the body. Actually touching Richard's cocooned body seemed to have hit her hard.

Lynn set her jaw. Maybe she could help Dani work through it tonight, once they were bunkered down, but not now. Now they needed to get moving again. "Come on." She walked over and patted Dani on the shoulder. "Focus. You're a hunter, you know death. Prioritize." She picked up Dani's spear and handed it back. "You're a hunter." She waited for Dani to meet her eyes and nod before letting go of the metal.

"Got it." Dani twirled the spear and brought it into position by her side. Her shoulders had squared; her chin was up again. There was life in her eyes.

"Yes, you do. Come on." Lynn took up position in front of the cart and gripped the handles.

Time to get this done.

CHAPTER 18

SOMETHING OR SOMEONE HAD DRAGGED the corpses across the parking lot. As Lynn flanked the cart Dani pulled along the front of the office building, she dimly noted the bodies of the wolves and humans were all still there, but spread thirty feet apart.

"Something's come to visit," Dani said.

"Yeah, I saw." Lynn glanced at Dani, who was struggling through her third pulling shift of the day. It was the first bit of conversation they'd had in hours. The hard work and discomfort had chased away the desire to communicate beyond grunted commands and warnings well before noon. "Leave him here. We'll have to make sure the building is safe before we bring him in."

Dani limped along on a swollen knee, which she'd banged on a rock. Lynn felt sore all over from a backward tumble down a rubble pile. The only one in their group who was still fresh was Skeever. He was the first one through the door.

Lynn didn't call him back. The gate was visible in the twilight, and it hadn't moved. Anything could have entered, but Skeever sniffed and went right on in, so Lynn doubted there would be a threat awaiting her. Still, she had her tomahawk in hand before she ducked under the gate and stopped to listen for a sound other than Skeever's as he explored deeper inside the familiar building. She sniffed the air, hoping for a clue, but the smell of blood and feces lingered too strongly in the entryway. Somehow, after a day of frequent whiffs of death, this stench wasn't as off-putting as she remembered it to be.

Dani's boot scraped the tile as she ducked in behind her. "Anything?"

Lynn shook her head. "Skeever's quiet."

"Okay." Dani hobbled ahead of her, using her spear as a crutch to keep some of her weight off her knee.

Lynn quickly caught up and overtook her as lead. As bruised and battered as she felt, unlike Dani, she was still able to keep her weapon raised and ready. If anything attacked, she would keep Dani safe—at least for as long as she could.

Skeever met her upstairs, wagging his tail, seemingly relaxed.

"All clear, huh?"

He leaned into her hand, and she scratched his jaw.

"All clear?" Dani looked up at her from the foot of the staircase.

"I'll have a longer look up here, but yeah, think so. Time to lower the gate and bunk down. I want to check out your knee."

"It's fine." Dani's tone was dismissive, but Lynn knew better.

Lynn leaned over the railing. "Yeah, right. Help me get Richard in, then we'll set up camp."

Dani hesitated a few seconds, then nodded. She tried not to hobble as she walked off, but it was obvious she was in pain.

Shit.

Dani had refused to take shorter pulling shifts or shirk her responsibilities in any other way, but her knee had slowed them down, especially when the cart needed to be pulled out of a ditch or turned to go around something. If her knee didn't improve, they would not be arriving at the Homestead the day after tomorrow.

Lynn guided Skeever downstairs and caught up with Dani halfway down the hall to the entryway. When Dani refused to look at her and trudged on, Lynn let her; the energy required to manage pain left little to socialize with—especially after a long day like this. She would have told Dani to make camp if she didn't need her to get the cart up the steps. "Take the front?" She'd already made her way to the back.

"On three." Dani took up position. "One, two, three."

The second Lynn pushed to set the cart in motion, a fresh lightning bolt of pain coursed up her arm. She set her jaw and marched on, then clenched her teeth as she hoisted the cart up to her shoulders so the wheels would clear the steps. *This is why this quest is a death trap. Not just because we're out here with bait, but also because we'll be too messed up to deal with whatever it draws.* She set the cart down with a groan and watched in relief as Richard's body cleared the gate.

Thankfully, lowering the heavy iron barrier was a one-woman job, so Dani didn't have to go up the stairs. "Set up camp, okay? Maybe get the candle burning. I'm going to see if I can find anything to bring the swelling down."

Dani didn't reply, so Lynn let her drag herself to the office as she made her way upstairs again.

"Coming down!" When no one replied, Lynn pulled the chains off the pegs.

The gate crashed down with a racket that could have woken the dead.

Lynn cringed. Making any kind of noise still rattled her, but at least this cacophony meant they were now safe. She turned toward the shelving the family had put up. The light was all but gone now, but she only needed a bit of illumination to grab what she wanted. The herb bag was still where she remembered it being. It was too large to fit in her backpack and cumbersome to latch on to the outside, so she'd left it. Getting to use its contents to speed up Dani's healing was undoubtedly the second-best thing about only making it as far as this office today. The familiar shelter it provided was the obvious first.

Lynn also took a look at the food that had remained behind. It wasn't much; they'd taken all they'd been able to fit easily, but there was a smoked leg of something big, probably a deer, and she found some more apples, so she took both downstairs.

Dani looked up from the unlit candle as Lynn entered. It was the one Dani had taken from the Homestead and that they'd used in the car. Even though it was halfway burned down now, it would last the night.

Skeever had curled up behind her.

"No light?" Lynn closed the door to the office behind her to keep the heat in.

"I'm having some...issues." Dani sounded annoyed.

Lynn wrapped the food up in a blanket to keep it out of Skeever's reach, then slid of her backpack. "What's the problem?"

"I can't get the wick to catch. Didn't the family have a fireplace? This would be much easier with a fire." Dani sat with her injured leg extended and the other curled under her so she could reach the pot.

"If they liked hot meals, they did. Just not inside, I guess." She shrugged. "Do you want me to have a go?"

Dani sent the candle a withering look. "Yeah, go ahead. I'll get some food ready." She groaned as she got up.

"I brought some more meat and apples." She opened her pack and rummaged in it for her fire-making tools. "Did you get some tinder?"

"It's by the candle."

"Got it." Lynn scooped everything up. "There'll be smoke so I'll take it to the hallway. I'll be back." It took her longer than she would have liked, but eventually she got the candle lit by lighting a big pile of the dried grass on the bottom of the wolf cages, holding a stick in the flames until that caught, and then lighting the wick with that. She stomped on the pile until that went out and returned to the office with her candle. "I've go—" She cut herself off as she caught sight of Dani and Skeever lying together on the bedding.

Dani groaned at the sound of her voice, and her eyelids fluttered. Then she pressed her face deeper into Skeever's fur and exhaled audibly. Within a few seconds, she was very obviously asleep again.

A surprising rush of affection warmed Lynn's chest as she watched. Not just that Dani had fallen asleep got to her—and that she'd sought Skeever's company while she'd done so—but that the noise of Lynn's entrance hadn't been a source of alarm for her. She turned to the desk. Dani didn't have to be awake while Lynn made a poultice for her knee.

Dani had placed her plate of food on the table. Lynn ate while sorting through the bag of herbs. By the time her plate was empty, she had selected and crushed a mix of willow bark, juniper, and comfrey root. All had the reputation of helping a swelling go down. She glanced back at the sleeping Dani to make sure she was all right, then began the laborious process of making a poultice.

"Dani?"

"Whatcha want?" Dani's words came out as a plaintive growl.

Lynn stroked her arm. "I need you to pull your pants down."

"What?" Dani frowned and blinked her eyes open.

Shit! She thinks I want to see her naked. Lynn prayed the light of the candle would hide her blush. "I uh, I made a poultice for your knee. Let me at it. Please."

The blank look persisted a few seconds longer, then Dani's gaze darted to the tin and the cotton strips in Lynn's hand. "Ah." She rolled onto her back and wiggled out of her pants. "You made that?"

Lynn forced herself not to look at the full bush of curls Dani exposed along with her lean legs. "Y-Yeah. We need you in walking shape tomorrow, right?" She chuckled lamely, hoping to chase away the jitters she felt.

Dani hissed as she pulled up her knee. "I really hope you're some kind of witch doctor, because it's not good."

It wasn't. Dani's knee was swollen and bruised where she'd hit the rock.

Lynn slid her fingertips over the skin and found it straining.

Dani sucked in a breath.

"That sore?"

"Pretty much." She lay back down and stared up at the ceiling. "Do what you have to do. I know this is going to suck."

Lynn watched her for a few seconds. When Dani didn't look at her again, she allowed her gaze to slide down Dani's body and lingered on her sex for as long as she dared. Her cheeks heated up, along with her groin. It was an entirely unfamiliar feeling; small sparks of heat seemed to traverse along her bones to radiate out to her skin. She shuddered. "Um. Okay. Just...keep your leg like this. I'm going to apply the poultice, then wrap it up."

"Sounds good. And painful." Dani smiled but gripped the bedding at the same time. "Three, two, one, go."

Lynn scooped a mixture of herbs and molten fat from the candle onto cotton strips, waved the heat out of them, then wrapped the bandage around Dani's knee. Now that she'd started, she had a singular focus to fulfill the task. All other thoughts fell away—right until Dani yelped. Lynn jerked her hands away as if Dani's knee were on fire. "S-Sorry!"

"No!" Dani reached out and gripped her forearm, which had Lynn yelp in turn because of the bite wound.

Dani dropped her hand with equal speed. "Sorry!"

Lynn clutched her arm, realized the absurdity of the situation, and burst out in laughter.

After a moment of shocked silence, Dani joined in. She fell back to the bedding and covered her face with her hands. "Lynn." She shook her head. "This is just—"

"A freakin' mess. Yeah, I know." Lynn grinned and sat back. "Great pair we are, huh?"

Dani uncovered her face and revealed a smile. "Well, we're still alive. You're fixing my knee. So far, your arm hasn't slowed you down one bit." She shrugged shyly. "As far as I'm concerned, you're a badass, and we'll get home."

Lynn opened her mouth to respond to that, but nothing came to her. Was that how Dani saw her? Lynn considered herself to be a lot of things—survivor, hunter, even a killer if she had to be—but a badass?

"Don't look so shocked." Dani winked. "I don't let just anyone undress me."

Lynn's heart missed three beats at least. Her eyes widened, and heat flared in her cheeks. "W-what?" Her voice was painfully high to her own ears. She cleared her throat. "I'm just—"

"Applying bandages. I know. I'm teasing." Her eyes sparkled in the light of the flame. "I do think you're a badass, though."

"So are you. You must have been in a lot of pain today."

Dani pressed her good leg against Lynn's knees.

Lynn looked down and couldn't help catching a glimpse of something far more private, only partially hidden between Dani's legs. She licked her lips. When she looked back up, Dani was watching her intently. She really hoped the reddish glow of the candle's light helped hide what must be a tomato red color on her cheeks.

Dani continued to scan her face. Seconds ticked by.

Lynn became more and more aware of the way her heart seemed to have lodged itself in her throat, constricting her ability to breathe and think.

Dani swallowed visibly. "Were you…done with my knee?"

It took a few seconds for the question to register. "Oh! Uh, no. No, almost." She fumbled with the tin still in her hands and pulled out another strip. Dani still looked at her, but Lynn found relief in focusing on Dani's knee. The bare skin of Dani's leg still radiated heat against her knees, and she was almost sure she could smell Dani's scent, luring her attention back to the junction between her legs. Her hands trembled as she applied the last poultice.

"It smells really nice."

Lynn's head shot up. "W-What?" *Can she read my freaking mind?*

Dani frowned. "I just said the bandages smell nice. What's going on with you?"

"Oh." *Of course that's what she meant, you moron! Why would she say that about her own—about herself?* "Nothing. Just tired." She plastered on a smile and continued to wrap Dani's knee. *Please drop the subject, please drop the subject, please drop the subject, please drop the subject.*

Dani did. The muscles in her calf tensed every time Lynn put tension on the cotton. Her jaw set as she bit back pain.

Lynn finally tied off the bandages. "There, done. We'll leave that on for a while and go from there." She sat back and tried to regain her composure. Since Old Lady Senna's death, she had avoided getting close to anyone, either emotionally or physically, and now she felt herself ill-equipped and unprepared to handle her body's reactions.

Dani pushed up on her elbows and carefully unbent her knee. "The heat feels good already." She paused. "Lynn?"

"Hm?" Lynn turned her head to look at her.

"Thank you." Dani sat up fully and took her hand.

Lynn glanced down at the touch.

Dani's grip slipped on the grease that clung to Lynn's hand, but she held on. "I really appreciate that you went through the trouble. You could have been sleeping, but you decided to help me instead. Thank you."

Lynn cursed the blush that flared right back up. The need to deflect the attention was immediate and unstoppable. "Well, I need you to be able to stand on that leg tomorrow, or I'll have to pull that cart alone." She regretted the words the second she saw Dani tense.

"Right. Got it." Dani started to withdraw her hand.

Lynn tried to hold on, but the fat coating her fingers made it impossible, so she put her hand on Dani's thigh instead. Muscles danced underneath her fingers. "I didn't mean it like that."

Dani pressed her legs together, seemingly curling in on herself by instinct. "It's okay. I get it."

"No, you really don't. Dani—" She scooted forward, chasing Dani's body as she held on to her leg. "I suck at this. Being around people is absolutely beyond my skill set. Out there—" She pointed at the window and the world beyond. "I've got it down. If I die, it's because I forget to apply something I know. With you, I-I feel so...so...stupid. I either mess up or think I've messed up, and then I want to make it right, and it all gets worse."

Dani set her jaw and looked down at the hand Lynn now realized was placed really high up Dani's leg.

Lynn jolted, but she didn't dare remove it. She didn't trust her ability to judge which course of action would cause less damage at this point—except, maybe, honesty. "Like now." She took a shuddering breath. "I just realized that hand's somewhere pretty intimate and that if I leave it there while you're angry, you could get even angrier with me. On the other hand, you could also think I'm rejecting you if I pull my hand away, because you noticed that I only just realized where I'd put my hand." She swallowed. "I don't know what will make you less angry with me right now." She carefully drew her gaze up to Dani's face to check the effect of her words.

Dani was watching her intently, but her expression had taken on that unreadable neutrality Lynn was starting to hate. "You're trying to control me."

"I'm not." Lynn frowned. "Am I?"

Dani took Lynn's hand from her thigh, then pulled at it as she lay down until Lynn had no choice but to settle by Dani's side or fall over far less gracefully. "Yeah, you kind of are."

Lynn stared into hazel eyes and held on to Dani's hand. "Explain, please?"

"Well, tell me something: you look at the landscape and immediately know where the shadows are that might hide a threat, don't you?"

Lynn nodded.

"You know where the wind comes from and how strong it is. You know exactly what's on the ground and how much noise you'll make when you take a step." Dani ran her fingers along Lynn's jaw as she held her gaze. "Analyzing everything around you is what you do to stay alive."

Lynn nodded again. Where was the problem with that? Of course she was hyperaware of her surroundings; of course she knew what was going on around her at all times—except when she got so lost in Dani that she put them both at risk. "Why is that a bad thing?"

Dani smiled and shook her head. "It's not, not out there, but in here—" She brought her hand down and pressed the palm against Lynn's chest. "You can't control everything that happens."

Lynn's heart beat faster as if reacting to Dani's skin so close by, as if it could thump hard enough to close the distance between them. Either that or it was sheer panic that made her heart pound. "I don't understand."

Dani exhaled and slid her hand down Lynn's rigid arm until she could lace their fingers. "You need to trust me."

"I-I already told you I trust you." But even as she said it, Lynn knew how much she was holding back from Dani, how much she guarded her emotions against the impact Dani had on her. She truly didn't know if she would ever be able to break down those barriers.

"I know what you said, and I think you have shown me more of yourself than you've shown anyone else in the world."

Lynn nodded because she didn't trust her voice.

"I know you're scared of getting hurt." Dani's breath coursed over her face; they were that close. "So am I. I can't tell you what's going to happen, but I do know you can't control it. There are decisions to make, of course you control that, but what happens here—" She guided their linked hands between their bodies and pushed them first against Lynn's chest, then her own to indicate their hearts. "Is something we can't control. You can shut it down entirely, but I-I don't think you want to."

As terrifying as it was to admit it to herself, let alone to Dani, she was right. "I don't."

"Good. Neither do I. So maybe you could try to think a little less, hm?" Dani guided Lynn's hand up to her lips and kissed her fingers. "Give up a bit of control? It would be really nice to get to know you better."

Lynn chuckled nervously and shook her head. "There's not much more to know; you seem to have me figured out pretty well." *Embarrassingly well.*

"No, I don't." Dani examined her. "I know almost nothing. I know you lost people and that you've been alone since. That's it."

All these questions were making her antsy, but she forced herself to lie still and smile. It was normal for Dani to want to know more about her, but Lynn wasn't sure what to share. "You're wrong. You know more about me than you think."

"Oh? Like what?" Dani settled more comfortably on her side. She mirrored Lynn's smile.

"Well..." Lynn withdrew her hand from Dani's grasp and wiped it clean on her pants before she used it to fish Dani's braid from her hair. "You know that I'm good at digging holes and that I can kill wolves. You know I can make fires, build carts, and lift heavy things." She ran the bead at the end of the braid through her fingers. "I can make bandages for swollen knees..."

Dani hummed as if she were considering that. "You're right. I knew all of that. And do you know what that tells me?"

Lynn shook her head and hooked the braid behind Dani's ear. "Tell me."

"That you're a good person for using all those skills to make me feel better. I think you care about me."

Lynn met her gaze and held it. She thought she could see a hint of uncertainty in the depths of Dani's eyes, and it urged her to cup Dani's cheek and let go of a bit of her control, even though her heart rate soared. "Yeah, I do. It's scary because I know the odds of losing you are..." She swallowed. "High. Very high."

Dani placed her hand on Lynn's and sighed. "Not high. Uncertain. Too many variables."

"I don't like variables."

Dani cupped her neck. "Me either, but I liked it when we kissed."

Lynn chuckled despite her anxiety. "Yeah, me too."

"So, maybe for now, we don't think about what happens next?"

"I—"

Dani pulled Lynn's head forward and brushed her lips against hers.

The touch instantly made Lynn long for more, and she let her objections fade away. She met Dani's lips in a soft press that was rapidly becoming familiar. She knew Dani would part her lips and anticipated it by teasingly rolling her tongue over them.

Dani's breath caught, and as expected, she parted her lips. Her tongue met Lynn's for a slow kiss. After a few moments, she slid her hand down from Lynn's neck and traced her ribs.

Need flared inside of Lynn. She pulled Dani harder against her and lost herself in the feeling of breath ghosting over her skin, of a strong tongue moving against her own, and of fingers softly tracing her ribs and then the swell of her breast. The touch coursed through her like lightning, making her gasp.

Dani pulled back. "S-Sorry. Too soon?" Her breathing was slightly labored.

Lynn took in her hooded eyes, puffy lips, and strong features. Her stomach tightened. "N-No." She swallowed. "Go on."

When Dani hesitated, Lynn guided her into another kiss and another and another until Dani's hand massaged her breast more firmly and she ran her thumb over Lynn's nipple.

"Ohhh." The unfamiliar spikes of pleasure sent ripples through Lynn.

Dani broke the kiss and licked her way to the corner of her mouth. "Good?"

"Y-Yes." Lynn swallowed, overcome, even though she had hardly been touched. She rolled her body against Dani's to urge her on, unable to ask for whatever Dani had to give.

Full lips trailed down to Lynn's jaw, then her neck, nipping lightly.

Lights exploded behind Lynn's eyelids, and she jerked as the butterfly kisses caused goose bumps to break out across her entire body, especially when Dani's lips ghosted over her ear.

"Can I touch you?"

The words washed away her pleasure-induced headiness like a bucket of ice-cold water. She suddenly realized how vulnerable she was and how much more she would have to expose of herself—physically and emotionally—if she said "yes." Her breath hitched. She froze and pulled back to check Dani's features, needing to reassure herself of...something; she didn't know what she needed right now.

Dani's breathing had shallowed. She searched Lynn's eyes as confusion, then worry flitted across her face. "I'm sorry. I don't want to push you into anything." She pulled her hand back.

The rasp to Dani's voice flared the need inside Lynn's overloaded body, and she hurried to take Dani's hand. "I..." She took a deep breath and dropped her gaze down to their joined hands.

"Lynn, are you okay?"

She met Dani's gaze again. "Y-Yes."

"Are you sure?" Dani's eyes studied her. "You don't look okay."

Lynn couldn't help chuckling. She exhaled and tried to push all the tension in her body out with the stream of air. The warmth radiating from Dani's hand felt good; their tangled legs felt good, and it felt good to be worried over. She cupped Dani's cheek. "I want to trust you." It felt good to admit that, despite her earlier words, she wasn't quite there yet.

Dani didn't get angry, as Lynn had feared. She smiled softly and settled her hand on Lynn's hip. "How can I help?"

Nerves fluttered again. "Tell me this means something to you."

That seemed to rattle Dani. She sucked in a breath. "Lynn, it—" Her gaze fell away, but only for a moment. "It means a lot. Wanting you, liking you... I'm so confused."

"But you want to..." Lynn didn't know what word to use to describe what would come next if she allowed Dani to touch her. *Sex* was too distancing; *making love* came too close. "To touch me?"

Dani blushed. "I do. Even if we are temporary, I want this memory." She licked her lips. "And maybe I'm hoping that if we—" She didn't seem to want to commit to a term either. "...spend the night, you won't leave if I choose to stay at the Homestead."

It surprised Lynn how good it felt to have Dani put her thoughts out in the open, and she realized how fearful she still was of being played. "I can't make promises."

"I know." Dani smiled. "I'm not asking you to. I just want to enjoy being together now."

A smile crept up. "We're enjoying ourselves, huh?"

"Well..." Dani shrugged. Her gaze dipped to Lynn's lips, then moved back up. "There have been moments."

"Moments?" Lynn's stomach did a somersault when Dani met her gaze again.

Dani bit her lip and shrugged.

Still smiling, Lynn slid her hand to Dani's neck and leaned in to kiss her. "The answer is yes," she whispered against her lips. "Yes, you can touch me." Nerves buzzed up and down her spine, but they only made her more eager.

"Are you sure?" Dani's breath ghosted across her lips.

Lynn kissed her again. "Yes. You're right. Even if this ends, I want the memory."

"Me too." Dani slid her hand down and pulled Lynn's shirt up, exposing her hot skin to the air.

The sudden coolness on her skin made Lynn shiver. She pressed close and pulled at Dani's hair so she could kiss her again. "T-Then touch me."

"Hmmm..." Dani ran her tongue along Lynn's teeth, and when Lynn eagerly parted her lips, met her tongue.

Lynn allowed Dani to roll her onto her back. "C-Careful with your k-knee." She hesitated, wondering where to put her hands, then remembered she might only have this once and ran her fingers down Dani's back until she reached her ass. If this was going to be the only time, she wanted to experience it all.

Dani chuckled against her skin. "I'm careful." She slid her lips and tongue—oh, that tongue—down to her neck again as she settled more securely on top of Lynn's buzzing body.

Lynn squeezed the firm flesh under her hands.

Dani moaned and bit down lightly on the skin of her neck.

If her tongue stroking Lynn's neck caused flames of desire, her teeth caused an inferno. "Oh!" Lynn gasped, and her body rolled up instinctively even as she tilted her head to give Dani more space to explore. It wasn't the tiny sting that undid her; it was the reminder that Dani could literally kill her if she bit her with intent, combined with the rush of trusting her not to.

Dani's tongue soothed her pulsing skin, but the torch was lit: Lynn wanted more.

With a quick move, she pushed Dani onto her back and rolled on top of her.

Hazel eyes blinked open, then widened as Lynn pressed her thigh between Dani's legs the way she'd done the night before. This time, only one layer of clothing stood between them, and Lynn wished it gone. She wanted to experience this fully, not with all these barriers.

"L-Lynn..." Dani's breathing had shallowed even more, and need simmered in her eyes—a need to touch, but also to be touched in return. Lynn could feel it in the way Dani's body strained not to rock too wildly against Lynn's stilled thigh and the way Dani's fingers trembled on her back.

She reveled in the reactions she caused in Dani. It was good to be wanted—to feel alive. She held herself up on her good arm and watched the swirls of emotions in Dani's eyes. "Can I touch you too?"

For a second, Dani hesitated, then she took a deep breath and sat up.

Lynn moved with her and sat up over her thigh.

Dani took a hold of the hem of her own sweater and pulled it off in one fluid move. Her abdominal muscles visibly relaxed as she settled back down. "Please."

Lynn's breath caught. She'd seen Dani naked before, but this time she didn't have to look away. She could even touch. Her hand trembled as she reached out.

Dani watched her face, not her hand. Her chest rose and fell rapidly.

Lynn felt light-headed as she traced a line down the valley between Dani's small breasts and watched goose bumps appear on the nearly unmarred skin. Her dark nipples tightened. When she flattened her palm over Dani's belly and guided it down, Dani's abdominal muscles rose to tension in a very slow, rolling wave that kept time with Lynn's hand. Lynn trailed only the tips of her fingers down to the edge of Dani's curls.

When Lynn stopped, Dani whimpered. The firelight added shadows to already contoured muscles and made Dani's body appear even more powerful.

Lynn flattened her hand over Dani's mound and took a shuddering breath. "You are so impressive."

Dani's seemed unable to form words. Her lips parted but closed again seconds after. She licked them slowly. Her cheeks had turned even more intensely red than their kissing had already colored them. "I-I feel like I'm burning up from the inside out." She gripped Lynn's thighs and massaged urgently, as if trying to alleviate her need by touch alone.

Lynn knew exactly how she felt. Her blood pulsed through her veins like wildfire and fueled the desire to consume the beauty literally at her fingertips. She was starting to resent the remaining layers between them, and—as always, it seemed—the layers were put there by her. Dani was naked but Lynn was still fully clothed. She tugged her sweater up.

By the time she lowered her arms and tossed the sweater aside, Dani's gaze had dropped to her breasts and then down to her belly.

Lynn felt self-conscious under her gaze. She'd seen herself naked only a few days ago, so she knew about the protruding bones, the marks, and the flatness of her chest. Dani had at least a little fat to fill her out, but Lynn had none. She swallowed. "S-Sorry I'm not—"

"Shhh..." Dani slid her hands up from Lynn's thighs to her sides and then ran her thumbs over Lynn's hardened nipples.

Lynn gasped, and her eyelids fluttered.

"When was the last time your body felt good?"

"N-Never." All her life her body had been a source of pain, a tool she tried to keep in one piece in order to assure her survival. Dani's touch provoked pleasure for what was probably the first time in her life.

Dani pushed up slowly and smiled up at her as her thumbs continued to tease. "Does it feel good now?"

Lynn opened her eyes with difficulty and met Dani's gaze. Her eyes held nothing but acceptance and enjoyment. Lynn nodded. "Yes."

"How about now?" Dani slid one hand over Lynn's ribcage and replaced her fingers with her warm, wet mouth around her straining nipple.

A loud moan tore from Lynn's throat, and her arms jerked uselessly before she wrapped them around Dani's head and pushed her closer. Every swirl of Dani's tongue overwhelmed her senses. Heat pooled low in her belly, where the ache gained strength by the second.

Dani switched breasts, and her hands traversed down Lynn's back.

Lynn gave in to the need to rock her hips against Dani's thigh. She still didn't know what to do with her arms, so she just held on for dear life.

Thankfully, Dani didn't seem to mind the awkward hold. She let go with a pop and swirled her tongue over the sensitive bud instead.

Lynn withstood the blissful torment as long as she could. When Dani's teeth closed around her nipple and scraped it, she cried out, and something gave way inside of her. A rush of need urged her to grope for Dani's face. She cupped her cheeks and tipped her head up so she could kiss her with the desire to devour.

Dani met her tongue with equal hunger and let her hands roam more freely. They pushed into the back of her pants to squeeze her ass and then guided her down against her leg, helping her move.

Lynn lost the ability to think, which felt just as good as Dani's hands and the pressure between her legs. A base instinct to feel overtook her, and she pushed Dani down, moving with her so she wouldn't have to stop kissing her.

As soon as Dani's back hit the bedding, she started tugging at Lynn's pants.

Lynn pulled up to give her room and held herself up on her uninjured arm so she could help with her free hand. It took some doing to kick off the last barrier between them while she stubbornly refused to let go of Dani's lips and tongue, but when Lynn was finally able to press her body down onto Dani's hot skin, it was all worth it. Nothing could have prepared her for the feel of skin on skin, curls against curls, hard nipples against her breasts. "Ohhh!"

Dani ran her hands up and down her spine, over her ass, her hips, her arms.

Yesterday's manic rocking had given her a glimpse of the pleasure hidden in the joining of their bodies, but it was entirely different and much more intense now that they were both naked. Lynn rubbed herself against Dani's rock-hard thigh and relished the sparks that buzzed through her every time she hit a spot that made her gasp. She struggled for a rhythm that allowed her to push against Dani too and let her experience this as well.

An uncoordinated hand slid into her hair to pull her hard against Dani's lips, where she was instantly met with a probing tongue and hot breath that came out in gasps.

Lynn drowned in the kiss that followed as she rocked against her, searching out a rhythm that made Dani moan. *How can bodies feel this good together? Why didn't I know?*

Dani's hands still roamed with urgency. They felt as if they were everywhere at once—scratching her back, squeezing her ass, gripping her hair. Lynn kissed her way down to Dani's neck and ran her tongue along the strong tendon she found under the skin.

"Ngh!" Dani arched into her and dug her nails into Lynn's back. She tilted her head to the side, and her hips rolled up, creating friction.

Lynn nuzzled her skin. Her heartbeat pounded in her ears in time with Dani's racing pulse. It hammered against her lips, distracting her. Lynn licked again and tasted sweat and dirt and ash.

Dani trembled under her with every stroke of her tongue.

Lynn bit down experimentally.

"L-Lynn!" Dani unraveled under her. She bucked up wildly, coating Lynn's thigh with a slick sheen.

Suddenly, just rocking wasn't enough. The wildfire in Lynn's blood threatened to consume everything unless it was quenched by whatever came next. She swirled her tongue up to Dani's ear. "S-Show me h-how."

Dani raked her fingers through Lynn's hair. Her hips stilled. Just as Lynn started to worry that her inexperience had put Dani off, Dani pushed against her shoulder and rolled them over. She lifted herself up on her arms and looked down at her.

Lynn's insides clenched. Dani's pupils had dilated to the point where the brown of her irises was almost gone. Her lips were parted and swollen. Her hair tumbled freely and framed her sharp features. She was beautiful, and Lynn wanted to freeze them in this perfect moment so she would never have to find out if this would be the only time she got to experience this feeling that could be nothing but love. Lynn reached up and ran her fingertips over Dani's lips, watching with fascination as they moved with her touch.

Dani kissed her fingers, and her eyes fell shut.

"You're breathtaking." Lynn couldn't get out more than a whisper. She ran her fingers over Dani's jawline, then her cheekbones. Her chest constricted as the butterflies returned full-force. She reached behind Dani's head and pulled her into a kiss without knowing if she was doing it to chase the flutters of emotion away or to cement them in her chest forever.

Dani inhaled sharply as their lips met, then cupped her cheek and held on. Slowly, she started to rock again.

Lynn moved with her right away. Now that she was at the bottom, she could use even her painful arm to explore subtle curves and hard muscle, and she did so freely. Her hips remembered the rhythm.

"Y-You feel so good." Dani dipped her head again and scraped her teeth along Lynn's throat.

Stars danced in front of Lynn's eyes. She couldn't help bucking up and curling herself around Dani to urge her on. Her lungs burned. She couldn't get enough air into them to fuel her pounding heart. With anyone else, she'd be overwhelmed, scared even, to lose control of herself so completely, but with Dani she wasn't afraid at all, nor was she ashamed of the sounds of pleasure Dani tore from her throat.

Dani's hand traced a path down her side, trailing streaks of goose bumps behind it.

In a mirror of Dani's movements, Lynn slid her hand to Dani's hip and squeezed when those hips rose.

Soft lips and hard teeth wreaked havoc on the side of her neck even as Dani cupped her sex and pressed.

Lynn didn't have time to react to the touch before Dani pushed into her, and Lynn's entire world exploded and imploded all at once, leaving her reeling. Her eyes flew open as she arched into the touch. Nothing in her life had ever felt this perfect. Nothing Dani had allowed her to experience tonight had even come close to this level of bliss.

Dani lifted her hips and pulled her hand back a bit before rocking into her again.

The second thrust didn't feel as overwhelming as the first, but it was still more than her frayed body could handle and function at the same time. Lynn wanted to reciprocate, but wave upon wave of sensation left her unable to do more than hang on as Dani pleasured her. She planted her foot more securely on the bedding so Dani could at least rub against her thigh.

The renewed pressure seemed to undo Dani some. Her rhythm faltered, and she sagged through the arm holding her up.

Lynn accepted her into her arms and hugged her close. She stroked her sweat-slicked back and kissed whatever part of her came within reach of her lips, be it Dani's shoulder, her neck, or her ear.

Dani was out of breath; her body trembled.

Small sounds of pleasure puffed against Lynn's ear, and she soaked in them. Every gasp, every groan, every moan fueled the fire inside of her until she was sure she would burst. Instead, something much more miraculous happened: Her body arched like a bow, and every muscle in her body tensed. Her mind froze, then fractured as pleasure soaked through her entire being. For a few seconds, she felt nothing but ultimate bliss. She lost track of everything around her and floated in a bright nothingness that radiated up and down her body. Helplessly, she clung to Dani's shaking body.

Dani whimpered and pressed closer. She pulled her hand away and started to rock with fevered urgency, planting her newly liberated hand on the bedding for leverage. After a few rocking motions, she pressed her thigh against Lynn's sensitive sex again.

Lynn gasped. She knew instinctively Dani was chasing the same high Lynn was still recovering from and planted her foot closer to her body as soon as she remembered she actually had feet and a body attached. Her thighs strained from pushing against the force Dani exerted on it, but she withstood it, even though she felt boneless and light. She tilted her head and licked, bit, and nuzzled Dani's neck as best she could, hoping to help Dani get to that state of perfect bliss.

"Ohhh!" Dani sucked in a shallow breath, then another, then stopped breathing altogether. She continued to rock, bucking against Lynn's sex with almost bruising intensity. A deep moan fell from Dani's lips against the shell of Lynn's ear.

Lust caused Lynn's sex to clench, and she rocked up instinctually.

Dani still hadn't taken another breath. Her entire body was covered in sweat, and her damp hair stuck to Lynn's face. She tensed, and her motions lost their fluidity. She sucked in a sudden gasp of air, then ground against Lynn's thigh before she jerked and groaned out her pleasure against Lynn's neck.

Lynn held her by the back of her head, trying to keep her rocking against her leg to give her everything she needed. "E-Enjoy it," she whispered softly and pressed her cheek against Dani's sweaty forehead. She savored this moment because she never wanted to forget any of it.

The shaking lasted several more seconds before Dani crashed on top of her and gasped for breath. "L-Lynn… I-I…" She couldn't finish and swallowed hard. Her breath sounded ragged, and she twisted her head away from Lynn's neck just enough to get oxygen into her lungs more easily.

Her raging heartbeat thumped against Lynn's chest as she held her.

Dani brought her hand up and pressed it to the side of Lynn's skull.

The scent that filled the entire room now was far more intense on Dani's fingers, and Lynn inhaled deeply, memorizing this too.

Silence fell.

Lynn slowly became aware of her surroundings again—of something other than the look, feel, scent, taste, and sound of Dani. She slid her fingers over Dani's back, enjoying the slickness of her sweat as it pooled in the hollow created by the muscles around her spine.

Dani started to play with her hair, and she shifted to nuzzle her neck again. She inhaled and exhaled deeply against Lynn's neck, causing a new wave of goose bumps to rise.

"Are you okay?" Lynn tilted her head to the side.

Dani accommodated her and pulled back just enough for their lips to meet in a soft, slow lock. "Perfect." Dani's voice was a barely recognizable rasp, but she smiled oh-so-happily. Her sticky fingers cupped Lynn's cheek, and she kissed her again, with a bit more strength. "You?"

Lynn chuckled. "I...I've never felt anything like that in my life." Warmth settled in her chest, dangerously near her heart. "Thank you. It was... I won't forget it. Ever."

Dani's smile widened, and she kissed her again. "Me neither." She groaned as she slid off Lynn and onto her side.

Even though they were still heavily entangled, Lynn missed the weight of Dani's body as soon as it left. Cold air hit her hot and sweaty skin and made her shiver. She craned her neck to see where the top blanket had ended up at and tugged it out from under Dani until she could cover them both.

Dani didn't lift her head from Lynn's shoulder the entire time. Her eyes were closed. When Lynn settled again, Dani snuggled closer and kissed her collarbone. It took a few seconds for her to find a comfortable position, but then she exhaled contentedly and hummed. "I don't want to fall asleep."

Lynn smiled and kissed her forehead. "Yeah, I know what you mean." Tomorrow would bring another grueling day filled with pain and danger. She stroked Dani's hair and found her braid again to play with. "You told me to think a little less, so maybe you should take your own advice."

Dani chuckled and tilted her head up for a kiss. "Thank you. That helps."

"Good." Lynn brushed her knuckles over Dani's cheek. "Then sleep."

Dani settled again and wrapped her arm around Lynn's waist under the blanket.

Despite her own brave words, Lynn knew she had just opened herself up to heartache. What if something terrible happened to Dani? What if she got killed? She pushed the thoughts away. She would just have to make sure that did not happen, and for tonight, they had each other and everything was as it should be.

CHAPTER 19

LYNN AWOKE TO A WEIGHT on her chest. Her hand shot out to grab her tomahawk beside the bedding, only to find it missing. Her eyes shot open, and she realized the weight came from Dani's head as it rested on her shoulder. Her tomahawk... She tilted her head and spotted it halfway across the room, beside her backpack. Her knife was probably still on the table by the burned-down candle. *I slept without my weapons. Wow.* That was an absolute first. Then again, there had been a lot of firsts last night. Memories flooded back, and heat settled on her cheeks. She grinned.

Dani nuzzled closer. "It's early. Shhhh."

"Sorry." Lynn shifted to get a bit of relief from the bruising pain in her hips and shoulder blades. The few layers of leather and wool did nothing to alleviate the ache of a night without moving. She was so used to tossing and turning that her whole body felt tight and cramped now that she'd stayed stationary. She was sore somewhere else as well, but that minor ache only served as a reminder of Dani's fingers and the pleasure they had brought. She wrapped her arm around Dani's naked back and held her close as she soaked in this moment of absolute peace. Lynn didn't have a memory of anything like it.

It seemed as if Dani had fallen back asleep, but then she kissed Lynn's shoulder. "Did you sleep well?"

Lynn pressed her cheek against Dani's mushed hair and inhaled her scent. "I thought you wanted to sleep more?"

Dani shrugged. Her hand slid from Lynn's side to her belly under the blanket.

Lynn tensed for a moment, then relaxed under the touch. It felt good, so why not enjoy it?

"I think I like being awake more."

That caused Lynn to smile. "Oh really?"

Dani's fingers traced along her hipbone. "Yeah. This was a pretty...a pretty special night." She finally shifted and lifted her head up so she could look up at Lynn.

Lynn reached over and stroked some locks of hair out of Dani's face. "It was. This is too." It was so foreign to her to lie naked against another human being and let them touch her. She had no weapons nearby, no defense, and—more amazingly—only ruins remained of the walls around her innermost self, even though she'd been sure those would never crumble.

Dani searched her eyes. "Are you scared?"

"Not right now." Lynn shook her head. "I will be the second we get up, but no, not right now."

"Good." Dani leaned in to kiss her.

Flutters filled her belly at the touch of Dani's lips. She cupped Dani's cheek and stroked it lightly. "How about you?"

"Scared?" Dani shook her head against Lynn's shoulder. "No, but I don't want to get up and face it all again. This is good, right here. You and me. No risks, no questions, no decisions." She slid her hand to Lynn's chest and covered—either consciously or subconsciously—her heart.

Lynn swallowed. "Yeah, exactly." She scanned Dani's eyes and found questions burning in their depths. Questions such as *what happens next?* and *how do you feel about me?* Those were questions Lynn knew she couldn't answer. "I am so sore, though."

Dani laughed and groaned. The tension broke. "Me too. Everything hurts."

"Speaking of which..." Lynn extracted herself carefully and sat up. "How's your knee?"

Dani frowned. "Oh, uh, dunno. That's probably a good sign, right?" She pushed the blankets away so she could examine her bandaged leg.

Lynn found herself staring at Dani's body again. In the soft morning light, Dani was just as beautiful, just as lean and powerful. Her muscles danced under her skin as she undid the bandages. Lynn's hand itched to reach out and trace them.

"Wow." Dani whistled as if impressed.

Lynn slid her gaze down to her knee and saw why: the whole area at the base of her knee was a shade of midnight purple, mixed with various hues of blue, green, and yellow, but the swelling had all but disappeared.

Dani bent and stretched her leg experimentally and grinned. "That feels pretty good." She pushed up with a groan and took a few careful steps.

There was no need to fight the urge to take in Dani's body, so Lynn didn't even try. She did focus on Dani's knee after a few seconds, in preparation of the walls she would have to rebuild in order to make it out in the Wilds.

With the start sign to the day given in the form of an erect human being, Skeever jumped up from Lynn's jacket and wagged his tail.

Dani bent down to give him his morning hugs and cuddles.

Lynn waited until she straightened out again. "How is it?"

"Much better than I thought it would be. It's sore, and I wonder how it's going to hold up, but it could have been much worse." Dani let Skeever out into the hallway, then returned and plopped down on the bedding again. "All because of you." She took Lynn's hand. "You and your medicine."

Lynn felt her cheeks sting and knew she was blushing again. "The family had the herbs, why not use them, you know?"

"Yeah, yeah, keep being like that. You thought of it, you wanted to help me, you spent time and effort on it, and it worked. That's pretty damn sweet, and I appreciate it, okay?" Dani squeezed her hand and pulled it onto her lap. "Thank you."

"You're welcome." Lynn didn't mind giving in if the reward was a few more moments together like this.

Dani traced patterns on the back of her hand. "How do we go on from here?" She glanced up but retuned her gaze to Lynn's hand right away.

Lynn's insides clenched. "I...guess we just...focus on getting you to the Homestead." She focused on their joined hands. "Maybe this'll factor into our final decisions, but we still have to make it to the Homestead first."

"Yeah, I know." Dani brought Lynn's hand up to her lips to kiss, then put it back on Lynn's thigh. The symbolism was clear: time for some distance again. She sighed. "Breakfast and go?"

Lynn watched her for a few seconds, then nodded. She grabbed her pants from beside the bedding. "Breakfast and go."

With grim determination, Lynn scraped the sides of the cart through a tunnel created by the side of a car husk and a cement block. Her thigh muscles trembled as she dug her feet in, and the pulsing that continually plagued her arm intensified as she put strain on the muscle. The rusted metal gave, and Lynn shot forward like an arrow. She nearly stumbled but caught herself before she fell flat on the uneven slabs of concrete below.

"Lynn!" Dani hobbled up behind her.

"I'm f-fine." She let the beams fall from her grip and doubled over to catch her breath. "Just fucking done with this." She looked up. The sun was dropping like a stone. "Time to call it a day."

Dani finally reached her side and she ran her hand down Lynn's back soothingly.

"I can take another sh—"

"No, I've got it." Lynn shook her head and straightened out. She was sore in ways she didn't remember ever being, but Dani was worse off. Her knee had held up well for most of the morning, but after a few climbs and two pulling shifts, it had given out again. Lynn had forced her to hand over the cart once her arms had recovered. Dani had resisted, of course, but she was struggling, and they both knew it.

After a few moments, Dani pressed her lips together and nodded. "Yeah, okay." She gripped her spear more tightly and lifted it into position. "Let's find an exit."

Lynn squatted to pick up the beams and had to bite back a groan as her whole body protested against the movement. If something pounced them right now, she wouldn't even be able to hold her tomahawk with her stiff fingers, let alone fight for her life.

They struggled onward side by side. Not being able to contribute by pulling, Dani focused on keeping them safe and making sure Lynn ate and drank enough. It was slightly embarrassing to be fussed over, but it did alleviate the strain and monotone of the pull.

Secretly, Lynn kind of liked it.

Skeever trotted ahead. He had fully adapted to the pace and sniffed his way along with his tail high.

Lynn tried to orientate herself. They'd made more progress than yesterday because the road was a little less broken up, but they hadn't yet reached the house they'd camped out at the night Lynn had caught up to Dani. She'd been too absorbed in her misery to be able to gauge exactly how close to the house they were, but it was probably at least half a day away. At this pace, that meant it was still two full days of travel before they would arrive at the Homestead—and that only if nothing went wrong. At least Lynn wouldn't have to remember the route she'd taken while she'd followed the sound of an elephant being hunted; Dani would know the way.

It felt as if months had passed since that trek through the streets of New York City as she'd tried to picture what could possibly make a sound like that, but in reality it was eleven days. She glanced at Dani. *How can it only have been eleven days?* Lynn felt like an entirely different person than the woman who'd snuck up on a group of Settlers in hope of a meal. Right now, she couldn't say she was better off, but she had definitely changed. What that would mean for her going forward was way beyond her ability to grasp, but just the fact she was thinking that far ahead was a testament to Dani's influence on her.

"I can feel you staring." Dani turned her head to look at her. "What's up?"

Lynn's cheeks heated again. "Nothing, I was just thinking that—Damn it." The left wheel of the cart got caught behind a chunk of stone and jerked her to a halt. She went through the laborious and achingly familiar process of walking backward to create space between the wheel and the obstacle in order to have enough room to maneuver around it. Once back on track, she frowned. "What was I saying?"

"You were going to tell me why you were looking at me and why it made you smile." Dani carefully stepped over a crack in the road, but her gaze only flicked away from Lynn a moment.

"Trust me." Lynn grunted as she put the cart into motion again. "I'm not smiling."

"Oh, you were." Dani seemed eager to drive the point home. "That's why I asked."

Lynn tightened her lips to fight another smile. She carefully picked her path toward the right lane. "I was thinking that it's only been eleven days since we met. It feels like a lot longer."

"Eleven? No, can't be."

"Well, I'm going by nights, really. Homestead closet, ruined building, the car in the garage, then two nights without you, and then we met up. We slept in the house with the steps out front first, then the office, then spent two nights at the car dealership, office again, and now we're here. That's ten nights, eleven days."

"Wow." Dani shook her head. "It feels longer."

"I know. They must be freaking out about you at the Homestead." Lynn felt surprisingly guilty about that. She glanced at Dani. *Maybe it's because this horrible journey has led to something good.*

"Freaking out?"

As they went down the exit, Lynn passed through another narrow path between two rows of cars. "I told Kate it would be a week. It's been eleven days, and it'll be two or three more."

"Oh." Dani swallowed and licked her lips. "No, they'll be fine. They, uh, they knew it would be longer. They're expecting us to be gone two weeks at least."

Lynn took that information in. "Why?"

"Because..." Dani hesitated. She glanced up, then back down as she picked her path—and seemingly her words—carefully. Her shoulders sagged. "The detours were planned."

"Detours?"

"Like, that first night, going the wrong way on the road and taking the long way around over the 95? Kate and I planned that. We knew where you must have come from, so I took you west instead. The idea was to keep you with me as long as possible so I had time to convince you to come with me the whole way. If we'd let you get back to familiar ground right away, you would have abandoned me on day one." Dani seemed to have trouble getting the words out; her volume dropped the longer she spoke.

The familiar feeling of betrayal stabbed at her heart, but it fizzled out quickly. She had realized long ago that there was a plan in play to assure Richard came home; it was just the scale and depth of the planning that surprised her—and how well Dani had played her part. "That's...smart." Lynn took a slow breath. "You two really played me well." They neared the end of the slope, and Lynn looked around for a place to spend the night.

"I didn't know you then. I didn't...care about you like I do now. You didn't give a damn about me either, so I figured turnabout was fair play." Dani turned right.

"It was, I guess." Lynn followed her, away from the highway and its shadowy underpass. "You and Kate were right, I would have left you behind in a heartbeat."

"You did," Dani pointed out.

Lynn chuckled. "Well, it took more than a heartbeat, and I came back. Your strategy worked."

Dani slowed and seemed to hesitate before she put her hand on Lynn's that was holding on to the beam. "I'm sorry, I really am."

Lynn shook her head and halted the cart. "You were surviving, and so was I. It's in the past." She smiled at Dani to make sure she knew they were good. "I do have one more question I didn't want to know the answer to, but since we're getting it all out now, let me ask it anyway: that first day, with the wolves, did you attack that one wolf as part of some strategy I don't know about?" She inspected Dani to see how her words landed.

Dani froze. "What? No!" She placed her body in front of Lynn's so she could easily meet her gaze. "No, that was a mistake, and I feel horrible about it! I really thought there was only one, and I could take one wolf."

Something flashed across Dani's face too swiftly for Lynn to name, but it set off warning bells. Lynn listened to those instinctive signals even if they made her insides feel like a heavy block of ice in her gut. "But...?"

Dani dropped her head and stared at her hand on the shaft of the spear. "But...I could have taken out the wolf that attacked you." She found the courage to look up and push on. "I told you I couldn't find my spear, but I knew where it had landed and I had it in my hands in seconds. I made sure there weren't any others, but I held Skeever back a few seconds while you fought off the wolf, and I didn't help."

The words left Lynn reeling. The ice evaporated in a rush of heat. "You did *what*?"

Dani flinched.

Skeever startled and whimpered.

Lynn dropped the wooden beams and balled her hands to fists instinctively. "Why?" *I can't believe it!* "Why would you—what—?" She couldn't get her words in order and pressed her hands on the back of her head instead. She couldn't wrap her mind around the idea of watching anyone—even your worst enemy—get chewed on by wolves. That wasn't survival; that was cruelty.

Dani licked her lips. She dropped her chin onto her chest. "Judgment call. I really needed you to underestimate me, and as frantic as it was, you had it under control. I took the risk because it served the greater good at the time: getting you to think I'd die the second you left me."

Lynn stared at her, momentarily unable to do anything else. The enormity and compounding of the lies—especially those first few days—was astounding, and it could have cost Lynn her life.

"Say something. Please."

"I, uh…" Lynn shook her head. "I'm shocked. And pissed." She took a deep breath in the hope it would help her get a grip on her raging thoughts and emotions. "Confused, that's probably a good descriptor." She stared. "Dani!"

"I know, I know, and I'm so sorry!" She threw her hands up, causing the spear to bob precariously in her loosened grip. She caught it before it fell. "You would have abandon—"

"Not while you were in immediate danger! I'd *never* have stood by while you were almost killed! Never! I ran right into danger to save your ass, I almost died, and you just *stood there*?" She stepped away from the cart. "How dare you?"

Dani's eyes watered, and her jaw set. "If I could undo it, I would. I panicked and…I-I forgot that it wasn't just about getting you to cooperate."

Anger seeped into every pore and tightened her muscles, priming her for a fight. She took a few blind paces toward the underpass beneath the highway before spinning around again. "How was I going to cooperate with you if I'd died, huh?"

Dani followed her. "I was caught up in it, Lynn. I didn't mean to—"

"Then what did you—" A whiff of heavy animal musk caused Lynn's nostrils to flare. Her stomach dropped. She reached for her tomahawk. *Turn around!*

"Look out!" Dani's eyes widened in fear.

Skeever shot past her with a snarl.

Before Lynn could spin around, something massive hit her back, and she went down. She landed on the concrete with crushing force. A heavy paw pressed into her back and stole her breath. Bottles shattered in her backpack, and tins crushed under the weight. Shards and other sharp object pierced layers of leather as well as her flesh. A heavy musk invaded her senses: a mix of dirt, rot, and shit. Lynn would have gagged if the weight on her back had allowed her muscles to constrict. She clawed at the concrete under her fingertips as panic flooded her.

Skeever barked and growled well beyond her field of vision.

Hot breath hit the nape of her neck. Instinct kicked in, and she froze. *Play dead! Don't be prey!* Lynn fought waves of fear and panic so she could relax her muscles. She whimpered as pain engulfed her body now that the massive weight on her back was held up solely by bones and organs.

Dani's spear flew through the air with a familiar whistling noise.

The animal stomping on her back bellowed.

A rush of pure fear almost undid her threadbare grip on whatever held her all-consuming panic at bay. Only one animal made that kind of sound: bears. Lynn squeezed her eyes shut. *Think!* The reminder cleared some of the fog in her head. *Weapon!* She very slowly inched her hand toward her hip in search of her tomahawk.

"Lynn!" Dani's voice was shrill.

With her one distance weapon gone, Dani would be unable to help her. You didn't go after a bear with a knife unless you wanted to die. *It's okay. I know you would have helped me this time if you could have.*

Teeth sank into her shoulder.

Lynn screamed in agony. There was no holding it back, especially as the bear pulled and shook its massive head, trying to tear muscle from bone. She tried to clear her head enough to focus on her hand. Her world caved in on itself. All that remained was every agonizing inch of progress toward her weapon.

Then her bubble of pain was shattered by a noise so foreign that Lynn couldn't help focusing on it. It was a loud, repetitive banging of metal on metal. "Go! Go, you bastard! Leave us alone!" Dani banged together whatever she had found to bang. "Go!"

The bear let go and grunted.

Lynn sagged onto the pavement as relief washed through her. Whatever Dani had done agitated the bear into lifting its paw long enough for Lynn to suck in air despite the pain.

The bear's nails raked along her arm. The heavy leather of her jacket protected her against much of the onslaught, but fire still spread along the length of her triceps. Lynn clenched her jaw to keep from crying out.

Massive paws moved along her back. Each stomp threatened to crack her spine. Then the bear pushed down and dug its nails in for leverage just below her backpack.

A ragged scream tore from Lynn's throat.

With a bone-rattling growl, the bear pushed off and jerked her body backward like a ragdoll in the process.

She skidded to a stop and breathed in carefully. Sharp pain exploded along her chest and back. She was in too much agony to gauge how broken her body was and in too much shock to find out.

Dani cried out.

The pain in Dani's voice acted like a bucket of ice-cold water. She didn't have time to be hurt. Lynn wiggled her fingers and toes to make sure nothing was irreparably damaged, then pushed up on her hands and knees. The pain was searing and all-consuming, but the impact of it paled in comparison to the view that greeted her when she got herself to lift her head and open her eyes.

Dani's bravery—and absolute stupidity—had spooked the bear, but instead of running away upon hearing the racket, it had charged her. It was a massive animal with matted and muddy fur, half an ear missing and dark wetness coating its flank. She looked upon its broad back as it stood on its hind legs, front paws on the bed of a rusty pickup truck.

As Lynn watched, Dani climbed onto the cabin, knife in hand, and turned to lock gazes with the bear. She crouched and held her abdomen with her knifeless hand.

The only reason Dani wasn't dead yet was Skeever, who hung on to the back of the bear's leg and prevented it from putting its paw on the bed by providing a counterforce.

As Lynn watched, the bear jerked its leg hard enough to shake Skeever off.

Skeever jumped back right away, and his teeth renewed their hold, but the damage was done: the bear was able to push up. The rusty metal creaked, and the bed sank down under the weight.

Dani wobbled and winced as she sank down to her knees. She raised the knife and set her jaw.

"Jump!" Lynn had meant to shout, but the word came out a broken croak instead. She realized the advice was bad anyway—if Dani jumped the six feet to the ground, she wouldn't be able to walk on her knee, let alone run, and the bear would be upon her in seconds.

Dani was trapped.

Lynn's hand shot down to her tomahawk, but it was going to be useless against something as massive as a bear. Instead, she twisted her body to locate Dani's spear. Her heart sped up into an even more frantic gallop as she located it perhaps five feet off. The tip was stained; Dani had already drawn blood. She reached out and closed her hand around the cool metal. As she did, her head throbbed in the same rhythm as her screaming shoulder. She drew the weapon to her and had to pause and squeeze her eyes shut for a second to clear the sparks that exploded behind her eyelids. When she opened her eyes again, the sleeve of her right arm was slowly turning red. Time was running out quickly—the more blood she lost, the more of her meager energy reserves would go with it.

The bear growled and lowered its head, getting ready to pounce.

Dani gripped the knife harder.

Lynn forgot about her pain in the face of certain death for Dani and pushed up. She forced her legs under her, but they almost gave out right away. She used the momentum of her failing muscles to stumble forward and inhaled sharply. "H-Hey!"

The bear ignored her.

"Lynn! Help!" Dani was pale as a sheet. When the bear tried to rake her with its claws, she nearly tumbled off the cabin as she scooted back.

There were maybe twenty feet between Lynn and the pickup, but it could have been a mile for all the progress she was making. Her entire body felt broken and bruised, and she could barely feel her legs. Adrenaline kept her pushing forward, even though her path wavered. "Drop!"

Dani shook her head. There was sheer panic in her eyes.

The bear planted its front paws on the cabin, put its back paw on the side of the truck bed, and pushed up.

Skeever barked and renewed his hold, jerking savagely on the bear's flank.

"Drop! Now!" Lynn reached the back of the truck. Just four or five feet separated her from the bear, but she needed to get closer than that to do damage. She needed to get up. With a pounding heart, she slid the spear onto the bed of the truck, then used whatever power was left in her muscles to push herself up. Her right hand was covered in blood and left a handprint. She ignored it and looked up to check on Dani, who slashed at the bear's paw when it lashed out. "Roll off!"

Dani nodded once and slid off the cabin. She landed with a thud.

The bear pushed up heavily and sniffed the cabin top. Its massive head swung from side to side, searching.

Skeever's nails scratched along the metal as he pushed himself between the bear's flank and the side of the truck bed. His bloody teeth sank into the soft skin where the front leg met the torso.

The bear roared and finally focused all its attention on Skeever. It waggled back, then twisted to snap at Skeever, who scrambled to stay clear but held on.

Lynn finally managed to crawl up the back of the truck and stood on legs almost too weak to take her weight. She sucked in a breath. Her lungs burned; her ribs extended with lightning bolts of pain. She forced herself to pick up and raise the spear. "He-Hey!" She planted her feet more solidly and took a deep breath. "Hey!"

The bear looked up, but its jaws continued to snap. It shook itself to get Skeever off. When he refused to budge, the bear threw itself against the side of the bed.

Skeever yelped as he smashed into the metal and let go.

Before Lynn could react, the bear's jaws snapped shut around Skeever's paw, and it jerked its head up. Muscles rippled under matted fur, and Skeever went flying. He landed out of view beside the truck and whined once, then went silent.

Intense hate flared through Lynn. "You fucker! Yeah, look at me! It's j-just you and me now!" She swayed as she gripped the spear with both hands.

The bear turned in the narrow space and faced her. It shook out its massive body and growled.

Lynn stepped back until she no longer felt the truck bed under her heels. She crouched despite the pain. The spear reflected the blood-red sunlight as she leveled it with the bear's chest. "I'm here, asshole. Yeah, now you see me, don't you?"

Dull brown eyes fastened upon her, and its jaw flapped as it growled. It struck out with a blood-covered paw.

Lynn weathered the threat; the bear was too far away to hit her—and too far away for her to make the kill. *Where's Dani?* She hadn't seen her run away. *And Skeever?* She jabbed with the spear, only barely grazing the bear's forepaw. Worry threatened her focus, but she couldn't afford to let it: she was tempting a bear.

It struck out again, then stepped closer, covering half the width of the bed in a single move.

That's it. Come here! She jabbed again, and now she drew blood.

The bear jerked and shook its entire body before it finally did what Lynn had been both hoping and dreading: it tensed and pounced.

Lynn had exactly one second to panic, then she clutched the shaft of the spear between her side and her arm, tensed all her muscles, and let herself fall backward off the truck.

Too late.

Razor-sharp claws grazed the front of her thighs as the bear landed on the edge of the bed. Its momentum caused it to slide forward.

Lynn landed roughly on the concrete, her fall only slightly broken by her backpack. She managed to hold her head up and kept her grip on the spear.

The bear slid over the edge.

Lynn adjusted the angle of the spear as best she could to hit it square in the chest.

The weight of the animal as it landed on top of her was crushing. The bear howled and trashed. Claws raked across the ground next to her head.

Lynn made herself as small as possible and weathered the assault. The weight on her pain-ridden body made her scream. Warm wetness ran down her arm and chest. She couldn't breathe, couldn't think. Her heart galloped in her chest as hot breath rushed over her, rank and putrid. She shuddered.

The bear whimpered. Its breathing halted, restarted, then stopped. The weight increased.

Seconds ticked by, and Lynn craned her neck, searching for air.

Silence settled over her like a heavy blanket. Her vision swam. She took a tiny breath, as much as her chest would expand. Another. Panic clawed its way up her chest. Dimly, she realized she wouldn't be able to get enough air into her lungs while trapped. Unlike when Dean had tried to choke her, she didn't panic this time. She forced herself to remember all the times she'd held her breath until her lungs nearly burst and forced the panic down. With as much calm as she could muster, she took another shallow breath and tested if she could move anything. Eventually, she found a way to plant her foot against the wheel casing of the truck and use it as leverage to slide out past the shaft of the spear—the only place where something other than Lynn's body held up the dead animal. It took every bit of energy she had, and no amount of worry about Dani or Skeever could get her upright for at least a few minutes.

During those minutes of recovery, Skeever limped over. He sighed and lay down by her side, muzzle on her arm.

Lynn turned her head slowly. A sob tore through her throat. "S-Skeeve." She hissed as she moved her right arm, but it was worth every bit of pain to feel his fur under her fingertips. "Are you okay, boy? You saved our asses, y-you know that, right?"

He licked his muzzle. His eyes pleaded with her to make the pain stop.

"Sorry, Skeeve. I'll have a look soon, okay? I need to find Dani first." The moment she said it, adrenaline drowned out much of the pain. She'd been so consumed with her own suffering that she hadn't realized that she should have heard from or seen Dani by now, and the fact that she hadn't was terrifying.

Getting up was excruciating, but she managed. As she used the truck as leverage to push onto her feet, she also got her first glimpse of the spear tip sticking out from the bears back. It had gone straight through, ripping up everything in its path as the bear's weight forced it on.

Lynn shuddered and swallowed down a rush of bile. *How can I still be alive?*

Skeever got up too. He lifted his left front paw—the one covered in blood—and kept it off the ground as he hobbled alongside her.

Lynn used the truck to make her way to the front of it, both eager to reach it and dreading what she would find when she did.

Dani hadn't moved from where she had fallen. Blood smears covered the windshield and the hood, and a pool of it colored the asphalt underneath Dani's crumpled body red. Her eyes were closed and her skin the color of chalk.

Lynn's legs nearly gave out as she saw her worst fears become a reality.

CHAPTER 20

"No no no no no!" Lynn fell by Dani's side, instantly trying to find where the blood was pouring from. When she pulled up Dani's shredded coat, five gashes of various lengths and depths appeared along Dani's belly. It was hard to judge how extensive the damage was with the sea of red and the diminishing light, but it was bad. Very bad.

Skeever pressed his muzzle against Dani's cheek and lay by her side protectively.

"Dani! Wake up!" Lynn rolled Dani's limp body over and carefully pressed down on Dani's abdomen to see which gashes were deepest.

Dani gasped, and her eyes fluttered open. "Wha—?" She tensed, and blood gushed from the wounds.

Lynn grabbed her hands and held them. "Quiet! Quiet! You're hurt, okay? You're hurt." Her voice broke, and she realized she was crying.

"Lynn..." Dani's voice was barely more than a whisper. She went limp again, but her eyes remained opened to slits. Tears streaked down her dirty cheeks.

"I'm here. You're going to be fine. I'm going to take care of you. Just lie down and try to stay awake for me. Can you do that?" She squeezed her hands.

"T-Think so." Dani sucked in a shallow, shuddering breath.

Lynn forced herself to focus. Her raging heart made her woozy. She was sure her shoulder was mangled, probably still bleeding, and the pain was only getting worse. She had to calm down and prioritize.

"H-How b-bad...?"

Lynn smiled despite the pain. "You're okay." Dani was alive; that was all that mattered. She would keep her alive. "I'm going to bandage you up, though. I like your blood inside your body, if at all possible."

She didn't quite manage to sell the cheer in her voice, but a ghost of a smile flitted across Dani's lips. "M-Me too." She took another shallow breath. "You?"

Me? "Oh, how I am? I'm good. Don't worry. Nothing that can't be patched up. Same as you." She slid her backpack from her shoulders and opened it. Everything was wet, and glass shards had pierced every strip of cloth and leather. She couldn't use any of it to bandage Dani's wounds. "I'm going to find your pack. Lie still, okay? Don't move a muscle."

Dani hummed. Her eyelids fluttered shut.

"Hey!" She tapped Dani's cheek softly. "Stay awake, remember? That's your one job: you have to stay awake, or I'll get really mad at you."

Dani frowned and forced her eyes open. She looked around but seemed unable to focus her gaze on anything.

Lynn's insides churned, but she didn't have time to give in to her worry. Dani was bleeding to death right in front of her eyes, and the only one who could do anything to prevent it was Lynn. "I'll be right back."

"N-Not going…a-anywhere." Dani smiled again. It was so weak that it spurred Lynn on to hurry.

As she retrieved Dani's pack from nearby the cart, her mind kicked into overdrive, spewing out questions she didn't have answers to: Where had the bear come from? Were there more? How was she going to get Dani back to health? When would they be able to travel on? If they missed the two-week deadline the Homesteaders had Dani under, would they come look for her? Would Dani survive long enough to wait for that? She shook her head to clear it. She didn't have time for those questions.

Her gaze landed on the cart. The body could attract all kinds of predators, but she didn't have time to think up a solution to that problem right now. She left it where it was.

Dani was half asleep by the time Lynn fell by her side again. She had started to shiver, and her jaw was set.

"Wake-up call, Dani." She plopped Dani's backpack down and angled it to catch the last of the twilight. She didn't have time to make a fire.

"I-I'm here." Dani turned her head sideways. "V-Very…s-sorry."

"About what?" She finally found a pair of Dani's pants and pulled her knife from her boot to cut it in half through the crotch and then lengthwise down the leg.

"W-Wolf." Dani exhaled shakily and very slowly moved her hand until it touched Lynn's knee.

"Wolf? What?" She looked around but didn't see anything.

Dani's fingers hooked behind her knee and applied just the barest hint of pressure to get her attention. "N-No." She stopped for breath. "Before."

Finally, the dots connected. Lynn shook her head. *Do you really think that matters now?* "Forget about that. I don't care. You're redeemed, if that helps. Just focus on staying awake, and I'll never bring up wolves again, I promise."

Dani managed a nod. "Tha—" She gasped and winced. "Thanks."

"You got it, Settler." She finished the work with two long, broad strips of leather. "Now, this is going to hurt. A lot." Lynn folded one of Dani's woolen sweaters into a rectangular package. "Ready?"

Dani nodded and squeezed her eyes shut. "Go."

Lynn unbuttoned Dani's jacket, pulled her sweater up, and pressed the improvised compress against the wounds.

Dani hissed and tensed, then settled again.

Seeing her in pain was hard, but Lynn had to push on. "Hold it." She put Dani's hand on the wool.

Dani gripped it lightly and pressed with whatever strength she had to give.

Lynn reached under Dani's back and got both cut-open pant legs under her. She tied each down with a hard yank and a strong knot. Applying pressure was all she could do to stop the bleeding without shelter and light.

Dani cried out in agony as Lynn tied the knots. She arched off the ground, then crashed back down. Sweat pearled on her forehead.

"Shhhh... Shhhh." Lynn ran her hand along the unmarred skin of Dani's arm. She'd been carefully holding in her tears, but seeing Dani hurt so much shattered the dam again. "Shhh."

Dani heaved for air. Fresh tears fell.

Lynn sat up and tried to focus. What was the next most pressing issue? She had many: It was getting dark, and she needed shelter. Her own shoulder was messed up and still bleeding, so she had to tend to that. Skeever was hurt, but she didn't have enough light to look him over either. Everything in her pack was drenched and full of glass; Dani's spear was stuck in a bear, and who knew what else was going on that she was forgetting about. There was a lot to think about, but the most important thing they needed was shelter and a fire. Without either, Dani wouldn't survive the night.

Dani groaned. Her shivering was getting worse.

Lynn didn't have time to sit here and think. "I'm going to find somewhere to sleep. Skeever is going to stay with you, and I'll be back before you know it. Do you remember what your job is?"

"S-Stay...a...a-awake."

"Damn right." Lynn got up, but dizziness overtook her instantly, and she had to lean forward and rest her head against the truck's hood before she could straighten fully.

Skeever tried to get to his feet.

Lynn held up her hand. "No, Skeever. No. Stay. Y-You stay with Dani. Do you understand me? Stay with Dani." She took a few steps backward.

Skeever whined and limped to Dani's feet but stopped there. He watched her intently.

"Stay." Lynn turned and walked off, willing herself not to look back.

Lynn didn't believe in a higher power. Some people still worshipped gods—either through the remnants of Old-World religions or by way of newly discovered pantheons and messiahs—but Lynn was sure life just happened the way it happened without outside influence. Even with that extreme certainty, she felt a flicker of doubt as she walked into the first building that emerged from the darkness and found it not only empty but easily defendable. It even had a separate room she could stash Richard's body in.

The building was an old bakery. Its display window was almost too dirty to see through but was intact; the door closed and locked with a deadbolt, and the kitchen had a large back exit and double doors she could shut behind the cart to keep the smell down. It was perfect, but she didn't know where she was going to find the energy to get everyone there.

Lynn knew she was on the verge of physical collapse. She was holding off a complete breakdown on willpower alone, but that wasn't going to sustain her much longer.

When Lynn returned, Skeever lifted his head. He'd pressed up against Dani's side, hopefully keeping her warm.

Lynn smiled at him and dropped down by Dani's side. She gently laid her hand on her chest. "Hey, you. Did you do your job?"

Dani's eyelids fluttered. She licked her dry lips. "Y-Yes." Her voice had lost even more strength. The wind tore the word to shreds long before it reached Lynn's ears, forcing her to lip-read.

"That's good. Very good. I'm going to be making some noise, but Skeever's here, and you'll be safe." She stroked Skeever's head before she undid the bindings that held a blanket to Dani's pack and spread it out over her and Skeever. "If you just do your job and stay awake until I come back, I'm going to get you somewhere safe and near a fire. How does that sound? Good?"

Dani nodded slowly. Her eyelids drooped, but she stubbornly refused to let them close entirely.

Lynn stroked her hair. "Proud of you." She leaned down, ignoring the pain in her protesting back and chest, and kissed her forehead. "I'll be quick."

Dani sighed and seemed to tilt her head toward her a little.

After a moment of hesitation, Lynn kissed her lips as well.

Dani hummed, and a tiny smile tugged at the corners of her mouth.

Lynn kissed her again. "I'll be quick," she repeated. She held her hand up in front of Skeever. "Stay with Dani."

He laid his head down on the pavement and sighed.

Picking up their heavy packs and hauling them to the cart was painful already, but pulling the cart to the back of the bakery was agony on her battered body. Any pressure on the chewed-on muscles in her shoulder caused white spots to dance in front of her eyes, but if she instead used her other arm, her forearm flashed in pain. By the time she closed the outer doors of the bakery's kitchen behind the cart, her vision had deteriorated to a fuzzy blur with white edges.

She didn't give herself time for the fog to clear. Instead, she made her way through the bakery—and walked squarely into the doorpost; she was that dizzy. If she was going to collapse, it would be by Dani's side.

All the car husks, lamp posts, and tree trunks she had viewed as obstacles all day now became her biggest allies because they held her up as she scooted along them toward her destination. She stopped to catch her breath and wipe her forehead but found it dry. That was probably not good since she was working hard enough to build up a sweat. It was another problem she ignored because there was nothing she could do about it right now.

Neither Dani nor Skeever had moved, so she could find them again with nothing but pale moonlight. While Skeever raised his head upon her arrival, Dani didn't react.

"Hey, Dani." She stroked her cheek. "Did you do your job?"

Dani didn't respond. Her eyes were closed.

"Dani?" Lynn's heart beat faster, which worsened the throbbing in her shoulder and forearm to the point of distraction. She checked Dani's pulse with shaking fingers. It was slow, but it was there. The rush of relief made her light-headed.

Skeever licked Dani's cheek.

She worked her hands under Dani's shoulders, then wrapped her undamaged forearm under her breasts, gripped her own wrist, and squatted behind Dani. When her vision stopped swimming, she pushed up and dragged Dani along the ground.

The second Lynn put them into motion, Dani started to scream and resist.

Lynn groaned and sagged to the ground, keeping Dani against her body. "Q-Quiet!" She rasped the word against Dani's ear. "I'm sorry it hurts, but you can't stay out here."

Dani continued to squirm and make small noises of pain and panic.

Holding on to her hurt, but Lynn wasn't going to let go. "D-Do you trust me, Dani? Do you trust me? Then stop struggling and let me get you to safety."

After a few more moments of whimpers and jerks, Dani went limp. Her head fell forward. Either she'd passed out again, or she trusted Lynn enough to drag her.

Lynn didn't have time to wonder which it was. Every second she expended energy on something not absolutely vital, she was damaging their odds of getting through the night alive. She pushed up again. It hurt enough for spots of light to dance in front of her eyes. In fact, her entire vision went hazy, but she was rapidly getting used to that.

Skeever followed her to the bakery, but he avoided putting weight on his leg. He entered ahead of Lynn, found a corner, and curled up. Lynn sank to the floor by one of the small tables that had once seated the people who had eaten the bread and cake depicted on the wall above the counter. Lyn didn't care about the Old-World people, but the tables and chairs were made of wood and could serve as fuel for the fire she was about to make.

When Lynn put her down, Dani whimpered.

"Damn, I forgot your blanket." It would have to wait until she got a fire going. Lynn got up, found her balance, and waddled over to the door to put the deadbolt on. Just that simple act filled her with relief: no matter what else happened, they were safe from further harm. She rested her forehead against the cool glass of the door and inhaled deeply. "Get it done." Tears welled up as the enormity of all the tasks ahead of her settled on her aching shoulders. She sniffed. "Just turn around, find a way to get a fire going, and get it done."

Every whack with her tomahawk caused light-headedness. Every time she bent forward to pick up another chair to put it on a table, her vision swam. She shook her hands to get the tremble out of them before she searched through Dani's pack for anything to start a fire with. It took precious seconds for the bundle of gathered dried leaves to catch flame.

Finally! Lynn was painfully aware of every second that ticked away. Dani moaned every once in a while, so she was still alive, but that was all Lynn knew for sure about her condition, and while she was busy fire building, she couldn't step away to find out more.

When Lynn finally dared to sit up and feed the fire in a way that allowed her to check on her, Dani's eyeballs flitted under her eyelids as if she was suffering through a terrible nightmare. *That's because she is.* This whole damn thing was one big nightmare.

Her vision blurred. She blinked, but it didn't clear. Lynn frowned and looked around. Smoke hung heavily in the room. *Shit.* She had been too rushed to think about the logistics of making a fire indoors, but she would have to figure out a way to ventilate. Lacking the time and energy to time to think about a better solution, she took her tomahawk to the small window above the door. It shattered, and Lynn turned away to avoid the shards. Right away the smoke escaped to the outdoors. *Good, problem solved. Next.*

She dragged Dani closer to the fire.

Dani's groans of complaint were the most beautiful sounds Lynn had ever heard because they meant she was hanging in there, and she was still at least partly responsive to her surroundings. Dani turned her face toward the fire as soon as she felt it and seemed to relax a little.

Lynn sat down by the fire and chewed through a large chunk of dried meat Dani had cut off the deer leg the family had preserved. Had that been just this morning? *Hard to believe.* It was good to get food in her system, though. Maybe it would give her some fuel for what was ahead. Dani had lost a lot of blood, so she needed animal protein as well. Speaking of which...

She clenched the meat between her teeth and shrugged off her wet jacket. The stabs of pain had become part of her ever-increasingly hellish existence, so she hardly noticed them anymore. She draped the jacket over her knees in the hope the back would dry. Getting her shirt off was more painful because the wool had stuck to her open wounds. She suffered through it stoically and twisted her neck to take in as much of the bite marks on the front of her shoulder as she could.

Not as bad as I thought. It certainly wasn't good, but it wasn't as devastating as she'd feared with all the blood. Much like with the wolf, her jacket had limited the damage, but there were two holes just below her clavicle big enough to push the tip of her pinkie into. The muscle below was pierced, but she could still move her hand and arm—although with a lot of pain—so at least the damage wasn't disabling. Since she'd moved with the bear as much as possible, her collarbone was still intact. If the redness that had soaked into her sweater was anything to judge by, she'd lost quite a bit of blood, which was probably why she was so light-headed. She probed the back of her shoulder for damage, but her front had definitely taken the worst of the punishment.

Lynn slid her sweater back on to preserve body heat and chewed up the last of bit of deer jerky. *Think.* They had food left, but not a lot of meat or cheese. *Think.* They needed meat, and there was a dead bear outside. The logical conclusion was that they were having bear for dinner. Exhaustion weighed her down at the thought of having to go outside again, but it had to be done.

Better just get it over with now. She stood with a groan, got her coat back on, and shuddered as the wet wool of her sweater settled more firmly against her back. As miserable as she was, she did feel slightly stronger after soaking up the heat of the fire and getting some food in her system. It would have to be enough.

She didn't want to go out without a fire. Thankfully, she had something that could withstand heat: the bowl that had held the candle. She untied the shovel from the cart and used it to scoop a few charred bits of wood into the bowl, then added small chunks of splintered furniture as fuel for the journey. One of Dani's spare sweaters served as protection for her hand as she balanced the hot bowl in it. With her arm outstretched and the other hand holding her tomahawk as tightly as her shoulder would allow, Lynn slipped out and pulled the door shut behind her. She couldn't bolt it, but she wasn't going to be gone long.

It was maybe three hundred feet to the bear, but they were terrifying. Lynn's heart pounded in her throat as she crept along, searching for the glow of eyes in the light of her wildly dancing flame. Nothing pounced on her, and before long, the splayed out form of the bear came into view. *Maybe I can also pull Dani's spear—*

The carcass moved.

Lynn jumped back and almost dropped the bowl. She fumbled for balance as she peered at the bear's body. She knew it was dead; it *had* to be dead, but then it made noise too, a small growl that sounded nothing like the bellow it had thrown out when attacking them.

Two yellow dots blinked into view in the flickering light.

Lynn's stomach soared up into her throat as fear flashed hotly through her. *I can't fight anymore.* She was too tired; she had nothing left.

Then the eyes and the fuzzy form around them tore away from the larger form and rushed over.

Lynn took another step back, but then she realized what she was looking at: a bear cub. She exhaled in relief.

It was a miniature version of its presumed mother, but Lynn felt no love for it. One day, it would grow into a specimen as big as the one that had all but killed Dani.

She put the bowl down and remained in a crouched position to await the cub. It couldn't be more than half of Skeever's size with big ears, big paws, and a nose it had yet to grow into. She slowly put her tomahawk on the ground and pulled her knife from her boot.

The cub uttered a little growl that sounded more plaintive than aggressive. It stumbled over its own paws on the way to her.

Lynn's fried brain finally put two and two together. "So you're why your mom went after us, huh? Is your den under the overpass?" She gripped the heft of the blade. "This part is going to suck for you, but else you would slowly starve to death, and so would we."

The cub head-butted her knee.

She reached around its muzzle, yanked it over, pressed her knee onto its belly, and pushed its head up to expose its neck. The cub had just enough time to struggle and grunt before Lynn cut its throat.

Lynn clenched her jaw and dropped the knife. She grabbed the front paws to keep herself clear of any scratching nails as the cub gasped for breath, whimpered, and fought. While she watched it struggle, reality caught up with her. *You could have avoided this. If you had paid attention to where you were going, you wouldn't have lured the bear.*

Her prey went limp.

Now you have to make it right. Lynn lifted the cub's lifeless body up by the neck and stood. She had a chance now: ten pounds of bear meat in an easy-to-carry package had been delivered to her. More importantly, the small body held the key to Dani's survival. Blood was literally much easier to swallow than meat, and all energy Dani could preserve was vital. Maybe something was watching over her after all—finally.

Lynn hurried back to the bakery with renewed vigor, pausing only to gather the fire bowl and blanket.

Nothing had changed inside, and Lynn hadn't expected it to. Dani was sleeping or passed out, but her heartbeat was steady upon inspection.

Skeever got up and hobbled over to check her loot, but she sent him off with a pat on the head and the promise of a proper medical exam and food later on. Lynn didn't have time now; she had to skin the cub, drain it, cut it up, roast the meat, and boil the blood. And she couldn't just feed Dani a bowl of blood either. Her body would reject it because it was so heavy and metallic. She'd be throwing up before she got halfway through. No, Lynn would have to make a porridge-type thing that she could feed her over the course of the night and into the following day, a few spoonfuls at a time.

Lynn put her hands on her sides. All she wanted was to lie down, curl herself around Dani, and go to sleep, but she couldn't. She took as deep a breath as her painful ribs allowed. "Time to get to work."

It was well past midnight when Lynn found herself nodding off over three tins with identical contents: a bit of water, flour, whatever goat cheese she'd been able to find, and bear blood. She stirred each in turn as they heated up over the fire. Her porridge had the thickness and consistency of pumpkin soup but with a dark pink hue. An acrid stench that Lynn could taste on her tongue hung heavily in the air. It was like licking her knife but ten times worse, and it drowned out the scent of sizzling bear meat on a stick.

Even Dani reacted to it: her features had scrunched up the moment the blood had heated, and the frown had stuck as the stench lingered.

The mixture in the first of the tins started to bubble beyond the head of foam that had formed.

Lynn forced herself to wakefulness. She took the tin off the fire and tested a spoonful of its contents. The heavy metallic taste tripled, and the mixture of salt and sweet caused her to shudder. She swallowed before she could fully register its flavor nuances. "I'll never learn to appreciate that." She'd eaten a lot of meals featuring blood as a kid. Nothing went to waste, after all, when an animal was killed—especially in a settlement. The other two tins came to a boil as well, and Lynn took them off the coals.

"Dani?" Lynn carried the first tin and her spoon over. She knelt down by Dani's head and stroked her cheek. "Dinnertime."

Dani's features relaxed under the touch, but that was all.

Lynn tapped her cheek. "Dani, wake up."

"Nnnggh." Dani swallowed, and her eyelids fluttered.

Lynn smiled, far more relieved to see such obvious signs of life than she had expected. "That's it. Can you open your eyes?"

Dani struggled visibly with the request, but then her eyelids finally lifted all the way and eyes the color of hazelnuts appeared. After a few seconds, they focused on Lynn's, and Dani whimpered.

"Hey." Lynn swallowed against the lump in her throat. She took Dani's hand and squeezed lightly. "You suck at your job, you know?" The world went blurry as tears welled up.

"L-Ly—" The whispered rasp sounded painful. Dani's eyes closed again.

"Yeah, right here. We're safe. I made you food. It's not going to taste good, but it's good for you. Do you think you can help me by eating it?"

"W-Wha—?"

"Bear's blood, mostly, but with some cheese and flour so you'll be able to stomach it better." Lynn scooted until she could lift Dani's head upon her crossed ankles.

Dani groaned.

"Just relax. Let me move you. Try not to put tension on your stomach, or you'll bleed more." She prepared a small spoonful of the warm mixture and leaned over Dani's head. "Open wide."

Dani licked her lips, then parted them.

Lynn set the spoon on her bottom lip and tipped it so the liquids rolled off.

Dani's face contorted, but she swallowed. She whimpered, then opened her mouth for more.

Lynn prepared another spoonful. "You're going to be okay, you know?"

The second bite went down as well.

"I'll make sure of it."

A single tear slid down the side of Dani's face and disappeared into the hairline by her ear. She opened her mouth again. Her lips and teeth were stained red.

Lynn fed her a third spoonful of the mix, then a fourth.

Dani swallowed them both with grim determination.

"You just have to eat and rest. That's all you have to do. Eat, rest, and we'll be fine."

Dani accepted another bite. Then she struggled to slide up her hand until her fingertips brushed the side of Lynn's knee. She licked her lips and sucked in a breath.

Lynn halted the next spoonful over the tin and leaned forward. "What is it?"

Dani frowned. She seemed to gather energy. "I-I want to…g-go… home."

Who could blame her? She sighed and stroked her cheek. "We'll get there." *I have no idea how or when, but we'll get there.* "As long as you eat."

More tears escaped the corners of Dani's eyes, but she parted her lips. Her fingertips closed around the wool of Lynn's pants, and she held on in a beautiful display of stubborn determination that gave Lynn hope she might actually be able to deliver on the promises she was making.

CHAPTER 21

LYNN WATCHED PEARLS OF SWEAT form on Dani's forehead. Another twitch jerked through her hand. Somewhere around daybreak, Dani had developed a fever. The bear's claws must have carried something that had infected the wounds, and Lynn didn't know what more she could do to make her better.

As night had stretched into morning and rolled into midday, Lynn had settled into a cyclical grind that was about to start its eighth iteration. She took care of the fire, fed Dani, ate and drank herself, completed one chore—take care of Skeever's leg, hang out her clothes, sort food, change Dani's bandages, cut wood—then rested until she jerked awake and did it all over again.

While Dani was losing strength, Lynn was slowly starting to feel better. Her body was still in shambles, but every time she woke up, some strength had returned to her muscles. Her dizziness lessened, then disappeared. Sparks no longer flared up behind her eyelids whenever she stood, and her vision remained steady and clear.

Skeever's paw was broken in at least two places, and he hated the splint Lynn had wrestled around it. He tried to get it off every opportunity he got, but that had become a lot harder to do once Lynn had found enough energy to braid a muzzle out of strips of leather. Now he lay at the opposite side of the fire and sulked.

It was time to face facts: there was a choice to make, and the window to make it was closing rapidly. Within the next two hours, she had to decide if they were staying another night or if she was going to pack everyone and everything up and leave.

She dreaded the thought of pulling the cart for hours on end, and she didn't know if she could physically persevere through the strain, but she had motivation to do so: if she could make it to the house where Dani and she had spent the night when they had first met up again, they would be half a day closer to the Homestead. With Dani's injuries, that was where she had to be. Not only was the Homestead a safe haven—for Dani, at least—but they had food, water, and medical supplies. Ren also seemed to have at least basic knowledge of herbs and other home remedies.

If she didn't leave within the next few hours, she wouldn't make it to the house before nightfall, and she couldn't risk a night in the open in the state they were both in. She could leave tomorrow morning so they could both rest more, but if she delayed getting Dani help even for half a day, the infection might end up killing her.

On the other hand, the same injury that was making Dani sick also made Lynn hesitant to move her. Lynn would have to transport her on the cart, and every bump would open up the wounds again. Dani could bleed to death long before she would be able to get her to the Homestead. Lynn desperately wished she could discuss the situation with Dani, but the greater hold the fever got, the less sense she made, so the burden of deciding was on Lynn.

She reached out and stroked matted hair from Dani's face. So much had changed. Just a few days ago, Lynn wouldn't even have entertained the thought of putting her own physical health at risk for another person, but here she lay by Dani's side, basing her decision almost entirely on whatever would be best for Dani.

Lynn sighed. All of this thinking was giving her a headache. *Time to do something useful.* She pushed up into a seated position and pulled the last of the three tins of blood porridge toward her. It was almost empty, just two more feedings left. That was another reason she would have to make a push soon: they were running out of food, and they were out of water entirely. Lynn had shared the bear meat with Skeever, so only two portions were left.

"Dani? Time for food." She took up station by Dani's head again.

A frown settled on Dani's face. "No." She shook her head. "No more."

Lynn took a deep breath to steady herself and guided Dani's head onto her ankles. Dani had started resisting the monotone meals three feedings ago, about the same time the fever had taken a more solid hold. Getting her to cooperate was becoming harder and harder. "Yes, more. You need it, remember? Your body needs to heal." She kept her voice soft and friendly, but her patience was running a bit low.

"It's not good. Not good." Dani tried to bury her face against Lynn's leg.

Lynn cupped her glowing cheek and guided her head back up. Her heart broke a little over Dani's distress. "How about I make you a deal? You have your meal, and then you get some nice grilled meat to chase it down with? The taste will go away, and you get to chew."

That got Dani's attention. She opened her eyes to slits and tilted her head to look up at her with cloudy eyes. "Promise?"

Lynn smiled. "Cross my heart, hope to die."

Dani dropped her head again. A bead of sweat slid down her forehead. She licked her lips as she seemed to consider the proposal. "Okay. Last time."

Just like the other three times she'd made the promise, Lynn nodded and said, "Definitely the last time."

Lynn pulled the door to the bakery shut behind her and Skeever and sank against the outer wall. It was so good to be out of that smoky, foul-smelling room, even if it was just for a little while. She inhaled deeply and checked her surroundings. The street was deserted, sun-drenched, and in no way reflected the horrors that had taken place on it the evening before.

Skeever hobbled along on three limbs, eager to find the perfect car or pole or tree to relieve himself against.

Dani was sleeping again. She'd chewed and suckled a small cut of meat as if it was the most exquisite dish in the world and had promptly passed out from sheer exhaustion afterward.

Seeing how badly off Dani was—and knowing their supplies were running out—had made up Lynn's mind. Lynn was going to be smart about this journey, though. For one, she was going to be taking all the pulling shifts from now on, and she needed to make that as easy on her body as possible. She was going to craft a harness for herself to wear that she could put the handlebars through. That way, she wouldn't have to use her arms to hold the cart level and pull it forward; she could put that strain on her hips. That would save a lot of energy.

Her second improvement over yesterday's grind was a judgment call: she was going to leave Richard's body behind. She needed the cart for Dani, and she didn't want to have Dani's open wounds near a maggot-ridden corpse. Besides, the stench alone would make Dani even sicker than she already was. Getting rid of Richard lessened the load a lot too, which would make it easier on her painful body and leave room for Skeever and their backpacks in the cart. She just didn't know how the Homesteaders would react if she returned without Richard's body.

Before she left, she would also make a fire pouch—or in this case, a fire tin—so she wouldn't have to go to the trouble of starting a fire from scratch once they arrived at the house. It was something she hadn't done in a while, but she knew how to do it: take semi-dry grass, leaves, and other tinder material, roll it up in flexible bark, tie it as tightly as possible, and sink a hot coal into it so it smoldered but didn't catch flame. Once she stuffed the whole bundle into a tin upside down and poked a few holes into the container to allow the barest bit of air in, the tinder would continue to simmer until it was time to make a fire.

Lynn hoisted herself off the ground. "Better get to it. Come on, Skeeve, we're getting Dani home."

Dani groaned when one of the wheels caught the edge of a pothole Lynn had tried to steer around. She'd packed the cart with layers of cushioning, but every bump and hole in the road was undoubtedly transmitted upward to Dani's body.

"Sorry."

Dani didn't answer, but Lynn hadn't expected her to. She'd passed out when Lynn had hoisted her up onto the cart. Since then, her condition had only gotten worse.

Lynn spared only a quick glance back. With her being strapped in, she'd be in trouble if she tripped while the cart was in motion.

Dani was still securely tied down.

Skeever lay limply by her side, resigned to the ropes holding him too.

She turned her head back just in time to avoid a crack in the asphalt that could have sent her sprawling. *Dammit, focus!* Lynn let the cart roll out and stopped; she needed a breather. Her heart was pounding so fast she felt dizzy from the rush. She could tell how much strength she'd lost by how labored her breathing was only an hour into the trudge. The fact that she'd apparently bruised all of her ribs under the weight of the bear wasn't helping matters any.

She pinched the bridge of her nose until the worst of it had passed, then scanned the tree lines on both sides of the road. Even though everything was quiet, panic surged in her chest. Her attention was scattered among too many tasks: not falling, making sure Dani was settled, watching out for danger, staying on course, minding the weather, and trying not to overexert herself. It was a lot to be mindful of when she was at her peak, but doing it while feeling this tired and in so much pain seemed like an impossible feat.

The spear in her hand felt foreign, which only added to her nervousness. Breaking the fall of a four-hundred-pound bear had warped the shaft enough to jam whatever mechanism was inside to allow it to fold in on itself, but it had a reach advantage over her tomahawk that was crucial with her forced immobility.

Maybe this was a bad idea. Maybe I should have stayed put. Anxiety clawed its way up her spine, but she fought its grip. She didn't have time to panic, and she couldn't look back; she was here now and would just have to make it work.

She took in her surroundings with renewed focus and stretched out to relieve her aching back. The style of the houses only just visible through a strip of green was familiar—very familiar. Realization slowly filtered through the haze of exhaustion. *This can't possibly be...?* She pulled the cart forward until a familiar white house with steps leading up to an awning-covered landing came into view. *No, it is. Is it?* She stared at the house, turned around in the harness to check the road she'd come down on, then turned back to look at the house again. "Well, shit."

Somehow she had gotten her travel distance totally wrong yesterday, probably because she'd spent most of her time looking at her feet. Now here she was, with hours of daylight left, at the only safe stop she could be sure would await them.

Skeever whimpered in the back of the cart.

Lynn checked her surroundings, just in case Skeever was reacting to something she overlooked, but the road was clear. The wind was the only thing upsetting the leaves. She turned in her harness.

Skeever had turned his head up to look at her and struggled against his bindings.

"Pee break?"

He whined again and wiggled.

A vague sense of relief settled inside of her chest. *Maybe we both need a break.* She pulled the cart toward the concrete road dividers and leaned the handlebars on them so the cart would stay level once she undid the knots. The last thing she needed was for Dani to slide off the cart headfirst.

Getting Skeever out took wiggling him downward until his head came free and then restraining him until she could put his muscular body down on the pavement.

He took off right away, entirely unhindered by his useless front paw.

Lynn pulled her sleeve up and checked Dani's temperature with the inside of her wrist. It wasn't an accurate measurement, but it was worrying none the less. "I think your fever went up again." She stroked Dani's overly warm forehead. "Hey, Dani, are you still with me?"

Dani exhaled sharply and smacked her dry lips.

"Yeah, there you are." She smiled, but tears threatened to well up at the weak display of life. Her chest constricted. "I'll find you some water soon, I promise."

With a whimper, Dani turned her head toward the sound of Lynn's voice.

Guilt tugged at her. "I know you're thirsty. I'm sorry." She gathered what little saliva she had in her mouth and leaned over to lick Dani's lips. "It's not much, but maybe it helps a little."

Dani's lips closed, then puckered.

Lynn chuckled even as worry constricted her chest. "I'm trying to wet your lips before they crack too much, not kiss you, you know?" After a second of fighting herself, she kissed Dani anyway and remembered that only a day and a half ago, they had laid entwined, smiling, chatting, and kissing. *What a difference a day makes.* She pulled back and stroked Dani's burning cheek. "You hang in there, okay?" Her voice broke. "I'm not losing you too."

Dani leaned into the touch, and her hot breath coursed over Lynn's wrist.

"I'm taking that as a yes, and I'm holding you to it." She wiped a stray tear away and sniffed. "Okay, let's see how your wounds are doing." She rounded the cart with heavy steps, dreading what she would find once she undid the bandages.

The scent of decay made her nostrils flare and her stomach churn. The bandages were bright red, the claw marks dark and swollen. The deeper gashes were blackening around the edges, and the shallower cuts were filling up with pus.

Lynn set her jaw and used some of the cleaner bandaging to scrape the yellowish fluid out of the wounds.

"Ngggh!" Dani tensed. Fresh trickles of blood coursed along her side.

"Shhh. Shhh." Lynn put her hand on Dani's forehead and stroked. "I've got to get you clean, okay? Shhh."

Dani's frown slowly ceased.

"There you go. Just relax. You only have to do your job, remember. Survive? I'll do everything else." She swallowed against the nausea as she got another whiff of the infected tissue.

Another gasp of air expanded Dani's chest, but her breathing overall was shallow and panicky. It worsened her bleeding, but Lynn didn't know what to do about that. She didn't think there was anything she *could* do except get Dani to someone who might be able to help her. *And do it quickly.*

They were running out of time. She looked up at the house that had served as their camp once and knew that she had to make use of every bit of traveling time she had. Dani was depending on her.

Lynn could barely get her feet off the ground anymore. For every obstacle she managed to step over, she nearly tripped over two. She needed to rest, to eat, to drink—but she didn't have time to sleep or find water, nor could she hunt or gather with a cart strapped to her waist. Her mission was to push on as far as she could get before night fell and to get Dani closer to home. She refused to think about the possibility that the infection had already spread too far to stop it. If she allowed herself to believe anything other than that Dani would be all right once she got to the Homestead, she would collapse and Dani would die for sure.

She'd pushed on for hours and most of that time had been spent trying to piece together every detail about the first time she'd walked this route. How long had it taken her? How had she walked from the bridge to where she'd heard the elephant? What route had the Homesteaders taken from the hunting site to the Homestead? Could she find the way there? Another thought was rapidly becoming more and more obtrusive: *can I find my way to the Homestead by firelight?*

It was an insane thought and one she would never have entertained if she wasn't so worried about Dani, but even a few hours could mean the difference between Dani dying or giving her a shot at life.

Traveling in the dark was the accumulation of everything Lynn considered suicidal. Most predators she feared were nocturnal. Obstacles and the dangers they presented would be harder to spot, and she could easily get lost, which would defeat the entire purpose of pushing through the night. They were back on the 696, though, and Lynn had memorized the map well enough to know that would automatically take her to the 295 and the bridge into New York that she had taken the day she'd met the Homesteaders. If she made a fire now that she still had a bit of daylight left, she could push on until she threatened to lose her way.

She would have to risk it.

The tinder caught flame easily once she pulled it out of the tin and blew. She dropped it into the bowl she'd used to hold the fire yesterday and rushed to add leaves and twigs until the fire became less finicky. The darkness closed in on her as she worked to build a fire that wouldn't blow out at the first gust of wind.

The work kept her mind off the encroaching darkness, but she lost that comfort when she straightened and looked around to find a much smaller world. She had to get moving.

Lynn shrugged her jacket off and pulled her sweater over her head. Her shoulder hated the movement, but she bit back the pain. She quickly slid her jacket back on and buttoned it up before she wrapped her hand and arm up in her sweater. Even through three layers of wool, the bowl radiated heat into her skin, but she could manage the slight sting.

Skeever had twisted onto his belly and huffed plaintively.

"Sorry, boy, we'll be bedding down late tonight. Just hang in there." Lynn rubbed his head and stroked down his back, but her gaze slid to Dani. The sight was heartbreaking, and she had to take a deep breath to steady herself. Maybe the firelight was deepening the shadows on her face; maybe she wasn't so pale in the daylight, but in the flickering light of the fire, Dani looked skeletal. Her chest rose and fell shakily, and she seemed to struggle for each breath.

Lynn remembered Dani telling her about the man who had died of an infected wound just after she'd gotten to the Homestead. Was she bringing Dani home just to die? Fear gripped her heart in its icy claws and squeezed until Lynn's knees threatened to buckle. *Dani's probably going to die.* The thought seared through her brain and tore a sob from her throat.

Maybe she could have shaken off losing Dani if she had chosen staying at the Homestead over going with Lynn, but losing her to death? "No!"

A hint of a frown pulled at Dani's eyebrows.

"No." She pressed her lips down on hot, salty skin and inhaled deeply. "You're not dying." Since last night, she had made Dani a lot of empty promises to soothe her, but this was a promise she vowed to keep. She stroked Dani's hair and lingered as long as she dared to draw strength from the sound of Dani's breathing. "You're going to be okay. I'm getting you home tonight."

Her legs felt strong when she started to pull again. Her arms didn't feel tired. She held up the fire bowl and Dani's spear as she pulled with all her might. *Steady pace, straight ahead.* She might draw every predator in the area to her location, but if they came, she'd kill them all and pull right on. No one was dying tonight, least of all Dani.

CHAPTER 22

The spurt of energy didn't last, but Lynn's determination only grew stronger. Even with cramping leg muscles, she pulled on, and even with trembling arms she kept her grip. The route was simple; finding a path for the cart was more complicated, but Lynn was an expert at cart pulling now. She reached the bridge and crossed it without pause. The ramp down the highway appeared within the circle of light cast by her fire, and she took it, then slowed to orientate herself.

Knowing herself, Lynn had probably gone right. Left would have taken her under the highway, and she always tried to avoid that if at all possible because the shadows could hide any manner of predator. *If only you had remembered that yesterday.*

She set her jaw and maneuvered right. As long as she could find points to orientate herself by, she would push on. If she couldn't, well, she might have to make camp for the night.

Red brick buildings rose above her, illuminated only to their first row of windows by the flickering light cast by her makeshift torch. Lynn hadn't been too afraid on the highway, but this was a whole different experience. Even during the day, an urban area like this, with blown-out windows and gaping holes for doors in every building, would have her on edge. During the night, the darkness beyond those crevices reminded her of gaping mouths and cave entrances, hiding certain death.

Even though she wanted to hurry past them, she forced herself not to since she had to look for landmarks that would help her find the Homestead. Nothing seemed familiar for much longer than she was comfortable with. Then the circle of firelight caught the branches of a tree that grew inside of a house. Lynn exhaled with relief; she remembered that. She turned her gaze right and moved on until she came to the oaks that had housed the yipping monkey. Other animals howled and growled in the distance, well beyond the light of her fire, but if there were monkeys in the oaks, they were silent.

Lynn moved on, following her memories down the maze of streets. It reminded her of a bedtime story Old Lady Senna had told her, about children following breadcrumbs into danger, but Lynn knew she was heading to the witch's gingerbread house and she would be careful to avoid getting burned. The danger didn't matter. She was heading to the Homestead, consequences be damned. She would deal with whatever came her way once Dani had help.

The hike toward the hunting site had been completed mostly by sound, but Lynn—as Dani had pointed out—was always aware of her surroundings. Even with limited light, she remembered the small park she'd cut through and the giant willow tree she'd turned right at. It had been a short dash through the streets last time, but that had been in full daylight and at a jog. Adapting the time for her much slower pace was throwing her off, and before long, she stopped to have a better look around.

Skeever barked.

Lynn nearly had a heart attack. "Skeeve! Quiet!" She hissed the words in his direction and whipped her head about frantically for something to lean the cart's handlebars on so she could untie herself. If they were being attacked, she wanted the freedom to move.

Skeever barked again. She could hear him squirming against his restraints.

Fear pushed through her veins like ice. "Shut up!"

Nothing pushed into the circle of light. No eyes reflected.

She lifted her fire bowl high, hoping to extend the range of the light it cast. Undoing her bindings with the hand that still held Dani's spear seemed to take an eternity as she awaited whatever Skeever had smelled.

Finally, the ropes gave way. She ducked out from under the beams and set the fire bowl down before gripping the spear more tightly. With her left hand, she drew her tomahawk. She'd throw the spear and then switch the tomahawk to her dominant hand.

Slowly, she turned around as she listened for any sound out of the ordinary, but all she heard was the wind through the trees and Skeever finally fighting his way off the cart.

He shot away from her, nose to the ground, stumbling into the dark as he tried to put weight on his leg.

Lynn's stomach dropped. "Skeever!" Now she allowed herself to shout. "Come here! Here!"

After a few terrifying seconds, he did. He almost bowled over her firepot before bumping against her legs.

"What the hell is wrong with you?" Lynn still scanned her surroundings with absolute intensity. She moved to position herself closer to the cart in the hopes she would be able to catch whatever would come charging before it pounced on Dani, but even if she could, it would be a short fight. Her thighs trembled with the strain of hours of heavy pulling, and the pain in her forearm and shoulder was searing.

Skeever trotted to the edge of the circle of light and looked back. He wagged his tail and yipped.

Lynn glanced at him. Nothing attacked either him or her. Then she noticed the twitch running down his tail, which was usually a sign of happiness, not fear. She tried to get that bit of information through her adrenaline- and exhaustion-soaked brain. *Maybe we're not about to be attacked after all. Maybe...* Her eyes widened. "Do you smell them? Do you smell the Homesteaders?"

Skeever walked away from her, then whined. He hobbled forward again, never once putting his injured paw down.

Tears welled up in Lynn's eyes, and she took a deep breath that shuttered as it went down her throat. "Oh thank fuck." She lowered her weapons and doubled over for a few seconds as the adrenaline drop made her dizzy. Lynn beamed. "Okay, wait. Wait." She hurried to gather her things and strap herself in.

Skeever sniffed along the ground and weaved in and out of her view.

"Skeeve! Slow, okay? Slow!" She turned the cart in his direction, then grunted as she put it into motion by sheer leg strength. "Go!"

Of course Skeever took off like a bat out of hell. He stumbled and disappeared.

There was no way she could keep up with his eagerness, even if he had only three functioning legs. She got stuck behind a rock almost right away, then had to maneuver around a bunch of obstacles, all while balancing a hot bowl, trying not to catch her hair on fire, and keeping an eye out for danger. "Skeever! Dammit, get back here!"

He did, and this time he stayed just inside her range of view.

With her hope renewed, Lynn managed to scrape the very last of her energy together and gave the chase her all. Sweat ran down her back and made the spots where her jacket chafed along her skin sting. Her thighs and calves were on fire; her lungs burned, but she pulled.

Skeever took routes that were perfect for dogs but didn't accommodate a cart.

Lynn had to call him back, guide him around, and wait for him to find the scent again, but they managed.

Eventually, Skeever seemed to catch on that if he had to climb over things, Lynn would call him back, and he started choosing his way more carefully.

His pace was just at the top of Lynn's ability, and she didn't want to slow down either. They had to be close and were getting closer with every step. Even when she stumbled and nearly fell, even when she stubbed her toe or jerked to a halt because the cart got caught—making Dani groan—she chased after him. Her vision went fuzzy again; her heart threatened to give out; her lungs felt ragged and sore in her chest, but she followed her dog.

Skeever guided her around a corner and onto a larger street. Then he shot ahead, barking loudly.

Lynn looked up from the pavement and blinked the sweat and blur out of her eyes. It was hard to focus, but her gaze was drawn to the golden glow of a fire atop the only high-rise building in an otherwise leveled area. *The Homestead! Finally!*

A male voice called out, "Kate! They're back!"

Lynn took another step toward the building. The fire bowl slipped from her fingers and shattered with a sharp noise that sounded much farther away than it should have. She pulled the wheels of the cart over the embers.

Figures emerged with fires of their own, but they were shadows against the brightness encroaching on her vision.

Her foot caught behind something, and she went down, entangled in ropes. She managed to catch herself on her hands and knees, bumping them on the hard concrete. The cart's momentum pushed her forward, scraping her knees and palms raw, but the pain barely registered. Everything already hurt, so what were a few more cuts and bruises? She sucked in a breath.

Hands touched her back and arms.

She shook them off. "D-Dani. H-Help…D-Dani!"

Some of the hands disappeared. People talked, but she couldn't grasp the meaning of the words.

Someone undid the ropes around her waist.

Lynn sank down onto the concrete and enjoyed the cold. *Dani's safe.* The cold seeped into her bones and invaded her mind. *I'm done.* She let go of her consciousness, secure in the knowledge that Dani was finally home.

Before anything else, Lynn heard her stomach rumble. When she tried to swallow, she found her mouth dry. Her head throbbed, and thoughts were hard to hold on to. Oblivion still had a hold on her, but she fought against sinking into it again.

She became aware enough to tell she was lying on something soft and covered by blankets, tucked in and comfortable. Lynn tried to focus her sluggish brain and fleeting thoughts. Memories trickled into her awareness in reverse order: collapsing in front of the Homestead, the nighttime chase, lighting the fire, and braving New York City in the dark, and then: Dani's lifeless face.

Fear jolted her system like lightning, and she tried to sit up. Pain flared across her entire body instantly, a mixture of debilitating muscle soreness, stinging injuries, and general fatigue. She barely got her abdominal muscles to rise to tension before she fell back. Dizziness flooded her system, and when she tried to reach up to grip her throbbing head, sharp pain reminded her of her wounds. She couldn't lift her right arm at all, but its root cause lay in a restraining pressure, not her shoulder injuries. Lynn dropped both arms down to the bedding again and tried to open her eyes. The sunlight flooding in seemed to sear her eyeballs. She closed them again and turned her head away from the source.

"Look who's awake."

Lynn froze. The voice was familiar, but she hadn't spent enough time with the Homesteaders to place it instantly. It wasn't Kate, so it had to be— "R-Ren."

"Got it in one."

The tension in her voice knotted up Lynn's stomach. Thoughts of Dani sank to the background as Lynn realized she may have been taken care of, but was far from safe. She tried to open her eyes again but failed. "C-Curtains?"

Ren ignored her request. "How are you feeling?"

Lynn tried to gather her wits. She had a pounding headache that was worsened by her quickening heartbeat. She opened her eyes to slits in the hopes of adjusting them slowly. At the same time, she tested her right arm and found it, indeed, restrained. Pain flared through her shoulder even as she explored the few inches of wiggle room she had. Metal slid over metal. Something had been fastened around her wrist.

"Don't try to get free. You're on mandatory bed rest until we have some clarity."

Lynn tugged at the restraint again. "What? How?" She tried to look down but that damn light was too much.

"I asked you a question, Lynn."

Lynn couldn't give a damn about what Ren had or hadn't asked. Panic tightened her chest. *I'm trapped!* She took a deep breath. *Focus. Think!* She turned her head away from the light—and the sound of Ren's voice. Through her lashes, she could spot a door in the opposite wall and what looked like a hallway beyond. Her eyes were adjusting slowly. *Good, what else? Is anything broken?* She wiggled her toes and fingers. Everything felt sore, but at least she could feel them.

"Fine." Ren sighed. Something creaked. "I'll get Kate."

Lynn's heart stuttered, and she whipped her head about, blinding herself and becoming dizzy all at once. "N-No!" She would much rather deal with Ren than Kate right now. Ren had patched her up before and had probably done so again now. "W-What do you want?" She squeezed her eyes shut as her head swam and spots filled her vision.

Ren sat down again. "How are you feeling?" She accentuated each word as if it were a separate sentence.

"I'll live. My head hurts. Could you close the curtains?" Lynn tried to open her eyes again, but the glare sent daggers through her eyes, into her skull. She gave up and squeezed them shut again.

"Maybe in a while. We'll have a talk first."

A talk. Right. "Okay, let's talk." She shifted to find some comfort—and test her bonds. "How's Dani?"

That gave Ren pause. "That's not what I want to talk to you about."

"I know that's not what you want to talk about—" She tried to twist her hand to escape the clasp around her wrist, but it was too tight. "But it's what you're going to have to tell me before I tell you anything about Richard and what happened on the road."

Ren seemed to consider that. "She's a fighter. That might save her." A small wobble in Ren's voice betrayed her worry.

Fear gripped Lynn's heart, but she clenched her jaw and refused to let it show. *At least she's alive.* "That's not an answer."

"It's an answer, just not one with a lot of information. Tell me something useful, and I'll tell you more about Dani."

Lynn didn't want to give in right away, so she deflected. "Why are you here and not Kate? I figured she'd want to hear the story firsthand."

"She—" Ren hesitated.

Lynn discovered that it wasn't necessary to squeeze her eyes shut anymore, as long as she kept them closed. "Yes?"

"That's none of your business."

Lynn smirked, trying to project a more powerful version of herself than she felt. She needed to be in control of this, not Ren. "Okay, then you have a deal. You answer one of my questions, and I'll answer one of yours."

A few seconds ticked by. "Okay."

Victory! "Okay, is Dani awake?"

"No. What happened to her?"

"Mauled by a bear. Is she going to survive?"

Ren hesitated. "Maybe."

Fear pushed through her veins. "That answer isn't going to get you a lot in return."

"It's the best answer I have."

Lynn chanced opening her eyes to slits. It hurt, but it wasn't the searing pain from before. Ren's blurry shape sat near Lynn's right shin. She blinked to get more focus. "Then explain why you don't know. If you give me a long answer, I'll give you a long answer in return."

"You don't make the rules, you know." Annoyance crept into Ren's voice. "But fine, the cuts on her abdomen are infected, and the flesh has started to rot. The infection is in her blood, and she has a high fever. We're doing what we can, but she's just awake enough to fight us, which makes trying to make her better a lot harder."

Lynn frowned. "Fighting you?"

"It's not your turn."

Frustration mixed with the worry swirling in her gut. *Why the hell are you fighting them, Dani? They're your people!* "Ask your damn question, then."

"Where's Richard?" Ren's voice trembled just a little, betraying how important the answer was—not just to Ren, but most likely also to Lynn's survival.

Lynn took a steadying breath. "I had to leave him behind to get Dani here in time for *you* to save her. If Dani were awake, she would tell you the same thing."

"She's not awake, though." The accusation in the words ruffled Lynn's feathers.

"I got her here! If you're not competent enough to—"

The sudden creaking of the chair prepared Lynn for the slap across her cheek. It still jolted her painful body and sent her heart pounding again. She clenched her jaw and carefully reached up with the arm not tied down to rub the sting from her skin. "Feeling better now?" Through her eyelashes, she watched Ren sink back onto the chair.

Ren sucked in a breath, clearly audible in the otherwise silent room. "I-I've been trying, I—"

"Trying to do what?"

"To get her to eat, to drink. I—" She cut herself off. "I-I'm going to get Kate."

Lynn was angry—and worried—enough not to care. "You do that. Maybe I'll get some real answers then."

The chair creaked again, but Ren got up slowly this time.

Lynn turned her head to track her progress toward the door. She'd won this round of interrogation—she'd learned much more than Ren had—but what the consequences were, she didn't know. At least she'd have a few seconds to herself while Ren got Kate. She really needed to gather her thoughts, take stock of her inventory, and make a plan.

CHAPTER 23

When Kate entered, Lynn met her gaze head-on. Her vision had cleared enough to track her entire progress to the sole chair in the room.

The two intervening weeks had not done Kate a kindness; the bags under her eyes were dark and pronounced, and she'd lost weight. Her machete thumped against the seat of the chair as she lowered herself down onto it. "Where's Richard?"

As much as Lynn hated to give up any information, perhaps a small token of cooperation would help her get out of this shackle quicker. She hadn't found a lock on the entire thing—not on the manacle, not on the chain that ran down from it, and not on the hook that secured the chain to a heavy stone block that she was too weak to tip over, let alone drag. She took as deep a breath as her sore ribs would allow. "At a bakery about a day away. I can tell you where."

Kate didn't outwardly react. "Did you hurt Dani?"

Lynn's insides turned to ice. "What? No, of course I didn't hurt Dani! Why would you even think that?"

"Your threat."

Threat? "What are you talking about?"

"You threatened to lure us into a trap and get us killed if I sent more people than just Dani with you."

A flush of heat crept up to Lynn's cheeks. Now she remembered her heated words during the standoff with Kate. "You didn't send anyone else."

"No," Kate said, "and yet Dani is lying behind that wall, fighting for her life."

Lynn's heart thumped painfully against her bruised ribs. "I-I didn't do that to Dani. Why would I have brought her here if I'd done that? Why risk coming back here without Richard's body?"

Kate didn't respond for what felt like an eternity. "I don't know, Lynn, but I guarantee you I'll find out."

Shit! Lynn swallowed down a surge of panic as she realized she was in a lot more trouble than she'd assumed. They didn't just blame Richard's death on her, but Dani's injuries too. *Don't worry, Dani will tell them they're wrong.* But it wasn't quite so simple: *What if they don't wait for that?* Then all of her fears conglomerated. *What if she dies?* The thought sent her heart racing. Maybe she could fight her way out if the Homesteaders came for her, but what was out there for her if she lost Dani? "Let me prove I didn't hurt her; let me help. I've gotten her to eat and drink before. I can do it again."

Tense seconds passed. Kate leaned forward on the chair. "I don't trust you. I'm not going to let you near Dani again."

Lynn tried to calm herself enough to appear trustworthy. "Kate, I know I can do this. Don't condemn her to a slow, agonizing death."

Kate scanned her eyes.

Lynn forced herself to continue breathing.

"You get one shot." Kate help up a single digit.

Relief coursed through Lynn's system, and she had to stop herself from exhaling in a sigh. She let her air out slowly through her nostrils instead. "That's all I need."

Sweat pearled on her forehead by the time she reached the door to Dani's room. Her leg muscles burned in a way she had never experienced before, and she had to lean against the wall for support to cross the fifteen feet or so between their rooms.

Kate had stared her down impatiently all the way, hand on the doorknob to Dani's room, arching a brow as if to ask why she wasn't moving any faster.

She sent Kate another withering glare. *You try pulling off what I did for your sorry ass and see how well you're walking afterward.* At least the manacles had come with a lock after all, and she wasn't hauling fifty pounds of iron and rock with her.

"Mind yourself in there." Kate placed her hand on the heft of her machete.

Once more, Lynn wished she had a weapon on her, but she wasn't even wearing boots. They'd taken everything off her but her breeches and shirt. She chose to ignore Kate; she needed to brace herself for whatever the other side of the door had in store for her.

The curtains were drawn in the room, but there was enough light to make out the basics. For one, the room was occupied not just by Dani, who lay on the bed. Flint sat in a chair someone had pulled up.

He stood as she entered and put his hand on the pistol in his chest holster. After a few tense seconds of glaring, he stepped back and took up vigil by the window. His hand never left the weapon.

Lynn swallowed and let go of the wall. She wavered a little as she crossed the room but managed to stay upright and on course.

The room contained an assortment of knickknacks—mostly odd objects such as teeth, skulls, shiny stones, and shells, offset by an impressive collection of weapons. It was undoubtedly Dani's room, and it matched her well. Looking around gave her a few seconds of reprieve from the sight she knew would greet her once she finally felt prepared enough to hide her emotions: Dani, on the edge of death.

The moment to confront her fears came when she lowered herself down onto the chair.

Dani looked even sicker than before. Her cheeks had sunken in; her hair stuck to her skull in tangles, and her eyes moved wildly under her eyelids. Even with Dani looking so sick, Lynn couldn't tear her eyes away from Dani's face. Seeing it filled her with a whirling mess of joy and nerves.

"Staring at her isn't going to help." The tremble to Kate's voice took the sting out of the words. "There is a lot of food and fluids there." She pointed at the table by Lynn's side. "If you can get her to eat any of it, that would be good. If you can get her to calm down, Ren can use maggots on her."

"Maggots?" Lynn fought a shudder as memories of Richard's bloated body, crawling with the white buggers, rushed to the forefront of her mind.

"They eat dead flesh. She needs to lie still for the treatment."

But no pressure. Lynn sighed and ran a shaky hand over her hair. "I guess privacy is out of the question?"

Kate snorted. "Damn right it is." She hadn't moved farther than the threshold into the room.

"Understood." She took in the assortment of cups and mugs holding soup, porridge—bloodless, by the looks of it—tea, berries, and even a plate with bread. Turning her head back to Dani took mental strength. It was almost impossible to imagine that the eyes now hidden behind heavy eyelids had stared up at her with desire just a few nights ago.

She reached out to stroke Dani's cheek but stopped herself. If she touched her now, Kate and Flint would see it. It was one thing to be open with Dani while they were alone, but showing that side of her to Kate, who thought she was a murderer, was far beyond what she was comfortable with. She couldn't worry about her own comfort, though. *If you want her to live, you don't have a choice. Just forget about them.*

She closed her eyes and pictured holding Dani in the bakery, feeding her spoonful after spoonful of blood porridge. Without opening her eyes, she leaned forward and stroked Dani's cheek. "Hey, Dani." She swallowed against the rasp in her throat. "We need to have a talk, okay? See, I nearly killed myself trying to get you here, and now you're being a terrible patient. That's not the way this works."

Dani sucked in a shuddering breath. She stirred under the heavy blankets.

The small reactions sent Lynn's heart soaring, and she opened her eyes to search Dani's face. She found her vision blurry and realized she was on the verge of tears. With a sniff, she fought the urge to cry. Two pairs of eyes seemed to be burning holes in her as it was; she didn't want to show that much weakness. "Yeah, you heard me. You have to eat, just like before. That's your job. You promised me you'd fight to stay alive."

Dani groaned. The motions behind her eyelids had stopped. She sucked in air, then her lips parted ever so slightly, just as they had done when Lynn had fed her bits of porridge.

Hope soared inside her chest and constricted her breathing. Maybe it was instinct; Dani could just be holding on to memories from before and copying them now that the first part of the routine had been instigated. Or Dani was more aware of her surroundings than everyone thought, and—her heart fluttered—maybe she recognized Lynn and trusted her to take care of her.

Lynn forgot about her onlookers and hurried to grab the closest food item that looked nutritious enough to qualify for this momentous occasion.

"Here it comes." She scooped something thick onto a spoon and took a bite. *Oatmeal.* That would do. She pushed a small helping between Dani's lips and watched with bated breath how Dani closed her mouth...and swallowed.

Her lips parted again.

Lynn's heart continued to gallop as she fed her another spoonful.

Again, Dani ate. It took her a while to swallow the small scoop, but then her lips parted once more.

Lynn prepared another bite.

"Well then." Flint's voice didn't betray any emotions, but Lynn could feel his interest in her renew.

She blushed but ignored it as she fixed Kate with a glare. "I told you I could get her to eat."

Kate nodded once, then addressed Flint. "Make sure she's secured in her room when she's done here."

"Will do," Flint said behind Lynn's back.

With one last look at Dani, Kate turned on her heel and walked away.

Lynn didn't see her go; her time was better spent watching Dani swallow another bit of oatmeal.

The second the key turned in the lock of her cell, Lynn was wide-awake. Hard-won survival instincts kept her from sleeping more than a few minutes at a time and never deeply, especially now that she was a prisoner again.

Kate closed and locked the door behind her. The key disappeared within the folds of her layered shirts.

Lynn sat up and bit back a groan. A night of interrupted sleep—either because of her own instincts or by getting taken into Dani's room to feed her every couple of hours—hadn't done much to heal her battered body.

Her chain rattled against the side of the bed, reminding her of how vulnerable she was.

"Here." Kate walked over and let a small bag slide from her shoulder onto the bed. "Your food for the day. You'll get dinner tonight, in addition to this."

Lynn was famished. She'd been given dinner yesterday, but she had a lot of days—and miles—to make up for. It took all of her self-control to ignore the bag. Not saying *thank you* was easy, though. "How's Dani?"

Kate pulled up the chair and sat. "I came to ask you where Richard is."

"Okay, great. How's Dani?"

"I would rather not do it this way, but I'll be taking a team out tomorrow to get his body. I wanted to take you along, but it seems Ren will need you to keep Dani fed and switch out the maggots every twenty-four hours."

Lynn chose to stay silent. She didn't want to antagonize Kate further, and she also didn't want to reveal more knowledge about Richard. That—along with her usefulness to keep Dani alive—was all she had to protect herself.

"Tell me, in detail, where Richard's body is. If we find him and confirm your story, well, it might help your case. If you lead us into a trap, and we're not back in two days, Cody will kill you."

Lynn's pushed her eyebrow up even higher. "What about Dani? Ren already said she needs me to help Dani get better. If Cody kills me..."

Kate's jaw set. Something swirled in her eyes that Lynn couldn't place. "A lot can happen in a few days."

"What's that supposed to mean?" Then the emotions in Kate's eyes registered. "You think she's going to die." It wasn't a question.

Kate looked down at her hand. She unclenched her fist. "Where is Richard?"

Lynn barely heard her over the cacophony inside her head. Questions tumbled through her mind: *Why would she think that? Is it really that bad?* One thought quenched all others: *I need to be with her. I need to save her!* And if Dani was really destined to die, she wanted to spend every moment with her, even if Dani was unconscious for all of it. "I'll tell you." Her voice was a rasp. "I'll tell you *exactly* where the body is, but I want to move into Dani's room."

It seemed as if Kate hadn't expected that. Her head came up, and she inspected Lynn with a frown. "Lynn..."

Lynn leaned forward, twisting her chained wrist to get more reach. "You want your husband's body back; I need to be with Dani. It's a fair trade."

Kate hesitated.

Lynn could all but see the questions well up. She didn't want to answer them—didn't even know if she could. Trading the only trump she had left for time with Dani went against everything Lynn had ever been taught, but there wasn't a doubt in her mind that it was worth it.

Seconds ticked by.

"Agreed." Kate's voice broke over the word, but she got it out. Instantly, her shoulders sagged, and she pressed her lips together when they started to tremble.

Relief and fear spiked through Lynn in equal amounts. "There's a map in Dani's backpack. I can point out where he is."

"I'll get it." Kate got up and legged it to the door.

Thinking of Dani's backpack reminded her of their time together, and another stab of pain caused her heart to contract—for an entirely different reason. "Kate?"

She looked back. "Yes?"

Her heart thumped, and she felt just as naked as when she'd asked Dani for a hug. "Can I see Skeever? Please?"

Kate froze.

Lynn held her breath.

After several seconds of silence, Kate retrieved the key, unlocked the door, and pulled it shut behind her.

A short while later, Cody threw the door open wide. "Well, well, well, if it isn't the flower girl up and about!"

Lynn jumped and scrambled off the bed, sending the chain jingling. Her entire being flared with pain, but she could only think about Kate's promise to have Cody kill her. *She doesn't know where Richard is yet! She can't kill me now!* She gripped the chain. *Maybe I can choke him.*

Then Eduardo entered and gave her a nervous little wave.

Lynn hesitated. His amicable behavior muddled her panic.

"Chill. We're moving you to your new digs." Cody smirked as he pushed her aside to make room for him to swing the mattress off the wooden bed frame.

Lynn stumbled and stepped back as much as the chain's slack allowed. *Asshole.* She picked up the food bag that had gone tumbling and hoisted it onto her undamaged shoulder. Slowly, her heartbeat settled. "Where's Kate?" *And Skeever?*

"We'll move the bed first, then we'll come back for you and your leash so Kate can talk to you." Cody turned to Eduardo. "Come on, let's get this done." He pushed the frame away from the wall, bent down, and lifted.

At the other end of the bed, Eduardo hurried to do the same.

Both strained under the weight, but they managed to find a balance.

Lynn watched them struggle to get the bed out of the room and resisted the urge to slump down to the ground as her dropping adrenaline levels left her trembling.

"How far away from your anchor point can you go?" Flint's hand settled on his pistol again.

Lynn gritted her teeth and walked toward him. She stretched out her arms, pulling against the chain. Pain flared in both her shoulder and forearm.

Flint watched her test her range and picked up the chair from beside Dani's bed. He pulled it back to just beyond her reach, ensuring she couldn't harm him, and then sat and watched her. "You can relax again."

Stumbling a little, Lynn stepped back and dropped her arms. She refused to show Flint how much that little exercise had taken out of her, so she strode to her bed as casually as she could and sat down before her legs had a chance to give out.

Cody had left her with a second length of chain. Her new domain centered on her bed and allowed her to come within ten feet of the window on one side and just reach Dani's bed on the other. Of course, the Homesteaders had no intention of leaving her alone with her.

Flint picked up a book from the foot of Dani's bed and opened it. The Old-World relic cracked dangerously but held. He started to read, but Lynn had no doubt he was aware of every little move she made.

Dani lay motionless on the bed, breathing shallowly. Only her fever blush colored her cheeks. They were in the same room now, but she seemed farther away than ever—lost in her own world of misery. Lynn liked to imagine that the real Dani—the person who lived inside the body—was waiting for that body to recover enough to once more be a worthy vessel for a woman as strong as she.

Now was not that time, and Lynn didn't know how to speed up the process. She turned her head away and took in Flint again. "What are you reading?"

"Herman Melville's *Moby-Dick*." He did not look up from the pages.

Never heard of it. "Is it any good?"

Now he did glance at her, just long enough to send her a look that clearly accused her of being an uneducated, uncultured Wilder.

"Whatever." She lay down on the bed. Her stomach growled, but she didn't feel like eating.

Flint flipped the page.

Lynn watched Dani take in shallow, irregular breaths. Her empty stomach slowly filled up with a ball of worry that took all of her hunger away.

The stillness was shattered by a very familiar bark, followed by the scratching of nails against the outside of the door.

Skeever! Lynn pushed up as quickly as she could, heart pounding. *She let him come!*

Kate tried to hold Skeever back as she entered, but with just the one arm, it was impossible to restrain him and open the door at the same time.

He shot out like an arrow from a bow and beelined for her on his three good legs, easily knocking her down.

She didn't care; she laughed as he nuzzled her hair, trying to lick it through the intricate cup she'd woven to cover his muzzle. His tail waggled as if it were possessed. He smelled just right, felt just right, and something inside her reknitted and was made whole. She buried her face in his fur and held on to his wriggling bulk.

Tears pricked in Lynn's eyes, threatening to fall. She held on more tightly and let his presence wash away all her loneliness and the stress of the last few day. After a few moments of intense joy, she pushed at Skeever and met Kate's eyes. "Shhh, quiet." She patted his flank. "Skeeve, quiet."

He stepped back just enough to let Lynn get up.

Her legs trembled with fatigue as she got them under her, but they cooperated long enough for her to sit down on the edge of her bed.

Instinctively, she checked on Dani, who was still out like a light. A sideways glance at the chair showed that Flint had made himself scarce.

Kate heavily lowered herself down onto the seat he'd vacated.

Skeever tried to jump up next to Lynn on the bed but couldn't make it on his three legs. She got him up, then smiled as he settled with his head on her thigh.

"I held up my end, now hold up yours." Exhaustion crept into Kate's voice. She pulled the map from her waistband.

Lynn gathered her thoughts and guts; once she told Kate where to find Richard's body, she would be completely at her mercy. She took a deep breath. "If you go north over the Whitestone Bridge, you'll come to the 695 Interstate." She continued to describe the route she'd taken, adding details such as the exit number and notable landmarks on the way there.

Kate listened, asked clarifying questions, then repeated a summary back to her.

"That should get you there." Lynn stroked Skeever's back. Her stomach growled again.

They both ignored it.

In the silence that followed, Kate studied her. "Am I going to find my husband there, Lynn, or the animal that did that?" She inclined her head to Dani without taking her eyes off Lynn. For the first time, the words didn't sound like an accusation, but a plea.

Lynn felt a small tug at her heartstrings. "The bear's dead, and I have not been lying to you. I didn't lie about how he died, about burying him, nor about where his body is right now. Unless something got in there, he'll be in the bakery, wrapped up and ready to be taken home."

When Kate stood, Lynn gripped Skeever's collar, instinctively fearful he'd be taken away again.

"I'll tell you if you were right in three days." Kate glanced down at Skeever, hesitated, but then turned and walked away.

Lynn fought her relief until the door closed behind Kate, then pulled her painful body up on the bed and wrapped her arms around Skeever. "Let's go see Dani, okay? I'm sure she's missed you too." Hopefully, it would also keep her mind off the possibility that scavengers had found a way into the bakery and Richard's body would no longer be there.

CHAPTER 24

Ren stirred in her chair, and Lynn woke up for what felt like the hundredth time. It wouldn't have been so bad if it had been just one night, but last night had been just as bad, and constantly being observed was grating on her nerves to the point of snapping.

"Could you please just sit still!" She rolled onto her side to face Ren in the lamplight and sent her a glare that, if looks could kill, would have incinerated her.

Ren blinked her eyes open and rubbed them. "Sorry," she mumbled, then seemed to realize who'd yelled at her and scowled. "But you could just ignore it."

"Well, I can't. Seriously, don't you want to go to bed? I am *not* going to hurt Dani. I think that's pretty much a given by now, right?" She pulled her legs under her until she sat cross-legged with her blankets draped over them.

Skeever looked at her accusingly as she roused him from his slumber.

"You probably won't, no." Ren shrugged. "But orders are orders."

Lynn groaned. "Oh, come on!" She rattled her chain. "I am not going anywhere, I am not going to hurt Dani, and your back must be killing you after so many hours on that chair. Kate's not here. Just go to bed. If something changes with Dani, I'll, like, shout or something." They both knew that was a very unlikely scenario anyway.

Ren hesitated. The chair creaked as she shifted, presumably to get comfortable on the hard wood.

"Go to bed." She accentuated each word.

The weight of exhaustion visibly crashed down on Ren and caused her to sag, and after a few seconds, she nodded. "I suppose it won't do harm."

She searched her eyes. "Promise me you won't harm her—and you'll shout for me if she wakes up."

"Will you believe me if I do?"

"No." Ren stood. "But it would make me feel better to hear the words."

"Then I promise." *I'm not going to let anything happen to Dani anyway. I might as well swear it to you.*

Ren exhaled deeply. "Okay. I suppose that'll have to do." She picked up her empty mug. "I'll see you in the morning."

"I'm not going anywhere." She made it a point to wave with her shackled arm, despite the pain in her shoulder as she lifted its weight and the weight of the chain. Its jingle followed Ren down the hallway, since she left the door wide open on her way out.

Lynn glanced at Dani. A sharp longing to be close to her now that she finally had the privacy to do so pierced her heart so suddenly that she gasped out loud. *Not yet.* Maybe Ren would come back, or she'd send Cody to take her place. Lynn didn't want them to see her hold Dani. She needed her armor; she couldn't show that level of affectedness.

When her patience ran out, she tried to keep her chain from jiggling as she slipped off the bed and padded over to Dani's.

Maybe it was the firelight, or maybe she was getting used to seeing her like this, but Dani seemed to be a little less pale. She'd eaten very well yesterday, and Ren had decided to hold off on the third round of maggot therapy. The last time she'd checked, the stitches held, and fluid no longer built up in the wounds. She was still unconscious, and her fever was still sky high.

"Hey." Lynn smiled as she stroked Dani's forehead and hair. "Is there room for me in there?"

Dani smacked her lips, now seemingly always associating Lynn's voice with food.

Lynn's smile widened, and she lifted the blankets. It took some doing with her chain and sore body, but she managed to find a comfortable position on the narrow strip of bedding and carefully laid her hand on Dani's shoulder. She didn't want to risk hurting her by wrapping her arm around her waist, not even high up.

Exhaling contentedly, Dani turned her face toward Lynn.

Lynn didn't mind Dani's morning breath at all. She snuggled a little closer and allowed her leg to brush Dani's, making sure she wasn't rubbing against her bruised knee. Dani's body radiated heat, quickly overheating Lynn as well, but it was so good to be close. She nuzzled closer on Dani's pillow, connecting their foreheads, and slid her hand down over Dani's arm to find her hand.

"This is good." She whispered the words, making Dani smack her lip again. "You really have to come back soon, okay? I need you. These asshole friends of yours don't like me much—which I warned you about." She smiled and squeezed her hand. "You need to wake up and tell them to get off my back."

She leaned in and kissed her cheek, finally allowing herself to inhale Dani's scent much more deeply than before.

A sob tore through her body. Lynn tensed, but there was no stopping the rush of emotions as her walls gave way under the pressure of her hostile environment, her own slow recovery, and most of all her worry about Dani. She buried her face in the crook of Dani's neck and tried to be as quiet as possible as she surrendered to the inevitable.

"I-I didn't bring you back just to watch you die." Sniffling, she let Dani's hand go so she could cup her cheek. She pulled Dani's face more firmly against hers and pressed close. "I didn't open up to you just to lose y—"

Dani coughed.

Lynn froze. Her tears ceased; her heartbeat galloped. "D-Dani?" She barely dared to pull back, but Dani groaned and Lynn hurried to sit up.

Her eyes were open—unfocused, but open.

Lynn's breath caught in her throat. She stroked her cheek with trembling fingers and leaned forward, trying to get Dani's eyes to settle on her. Her heart pounded in her chest, but she forced herself to appear calm. "Dani? Can you hear me?"

Her soft words were enough to draw Dani's attention, but it took a few seconds for her to focus on Lynn's face.

Hope constricted Lynn's throat. She blinked to make sure she didn't imagine it, then released the breath she'd been holding. "Dani?"

Dani's lips parted, but she remained silent. Confusion flickered in her bloodshot eyes.

"You're okay." Lynn smiled and nodded for emphasis. "You have an infection, you're sick, but we're taking care of you at the Homestead. You're home, okay? Home." She checked her forehead, growling in frustration when she got her chain caught behind something and had to pull it free first.

When she looked back, Dani's eyelids fluttered, but her eyes never closed entirely. She struggled to lock their gazes again.

Dizzy with emotion, Lynn gripped Dani's hand. "You're going to be okay." For the first time she dared to believe it herself. Consciousness was a good sign, wasn't it? She should ask Ren, but she didn't want her here, despite what she'd promised. Not yet.

Dani licked her lips, parted them, frowned, and parted them again. This time she managed a broken croak that seemed to frustrate her.

"Don't talk. You don't have to. All that mat—"

Dani squeezed her hand and glared at her.

Okay, shutting up. Lynn leaned in so Dani would be able to whisper.

"D—" She sucked in breath. "D-Did...j-job."

Lynn pulled up and watched her, trying to put the words together in a way that made sense. Then she smiled before giving in to a laugh that seemed to dislodge a lump of darkness in her gut. "Yes, you did do your job." She stroked Dani's cheek and pressed their foreheads together. "You did the best job. Thank you. Thank you so much."

"Sit." Lynn was deftly relegated to her bed while Ren moved in to inspect Dani.

Cody stood by, watching her more than Dani as Ren checked everything from vitals to pupil reactions to Dani's extremities to see if she could feel them all.

Lynn awaited the verdict anxiously.

As if sensing her discomfort, Skeever crawled across the bed until he could lay his head in her lap.

She scratched under his muzzle and made him whimper with relief. Her focus was on Dani's face, however.

Dani searched out her eyes, and something fluttered nervously in Lynn's gut.

Lynn smiled at her, and Dani smiled back.

"Can you stick out your tongue? Dani? Focus, please." Ren tilted Dani's head and broke their eye contact.

Lynn pressed her lips together to keep from telling Ren to fuck off and leave them alone. *She's just worried, like you. Patience.*

Dani struggled to open her mouth and stick out her tongue.

Ren inspected it and even smelled her breath. "Okay, good. You can close it again."

With a lick to her lips, Dani did as told. "H-How?" She struggled to get even that one word out.

Lynn had already realized Dani had trouble controlling her muscles—and she suspected a lot of muscle control went into talking—but hearing the competent hunter reduced to slowly stuttering out her words and ending up breathless from the strain was devastating.

"A bear attack, sweetie. You almost didn't make it." Ren stroked her forehead.

Dani frowned, and her fist clenched. "H-H—"

"I think—" Lynn faltered.

Two people glared at her.

Lynn pushed on. "That she's trying to ask how she's doing." Her heart pounded in her throat, but if she had been in Dani's shoes, that was what she would want to hear first and foremost.

Exhaling, Dani gave a weak little nod.

Ren turned back to her. "Oh. Um. It's…it's good that you're awake." She continued to rattle off the things Lynn already knew—infected wounds, maggot therapy, unconscious for three days—and Lynn tuned her out so she could soak in the fact that Dani's eyes were open and she was listening attentively to Ren's explanations.

Her focus quickly returned when Ren said her name. "…Lynn told us?"

Dani nodded without hesitation. She let her head fall to the side and looked at Lynn, who'd gone hot and cold at the same time.

Oh shit, what did I miss?

Cody and Ren turned to stare at her too.

Lynn scanned their features. *How much trouble am I in?*

Then Cody smirked and shook his head in apparent disbelief. "Bullshit."

Ren took a deep breath, squared her shoulders, and crossed to her bed. "Give me your hand."

Lynn stared up at her, muscles tense. "Why?"

Ren wiggled her fingers. "Dani confirmed your story. I trust her." The implication that she didn't trust Lynn was not lost on her. "I am not going to hold you captive any longer."

After another moment of hesitation, Lynn lifted her arm.

A few seconds later, heavy iron fell to the ground with a rattle and clunk.

She lowered her arm and rubbed her wrist. "Thanks."

"*De nada*." Ren stepped back.

"Aw, so cute." Cody pointed at her. "Don't expect me to join in with the kumbayas just yet. You're a Wilder, and I don't trust Wilders." He glanced at Ren. "Just don't give her anything sharp."

Ren opened her mouth to respond, then closed it and set her jaw. "I'll come back to bed soon, babe."

For a second, anger at the dismissal flashed across Cody's face, then he stretched lazily and scratched his chest. "Yeah, sure. I'll see you." He sent Lynn one more glare before sauntering out.

Instantly, the atmosphere seemed to lighten.

Lynn exhaled audibly and sagged. She glanced at Dani, finding her fast asleep.

Ren checked on her too, but much more in-depth: the usual checkup of her pulse, her eyes, her fever. Then she pulled the blankets down to Dani's hips, exposing small breasts and a blood-soaked bandage below.

After a moment of hesitation, Lynn stood and joined her. The stench that hit her once the covers fell away reminded her far too much of the body she'd left behind in the bakery.

Ren's features scrunched up as well but only for a moment, then she had it under control and carefully undid the bandages.

Dani's hand jerked, and Lynn took it. It was still not a pretty sight. The bear's claws had torn five roughly parallel tears in Dani's skin, three held shut by rows of horse-hair stitches. The skin had flared an angry red, but the cuts seemed to be healing. The other two were the obvious issue: They had once been stitched, judging by rows of small puncture wounds, but the stitches had been pulled out again because of the buildup of fluids and puss that seeped down Dani's side now that the pressure of the bandages had been released. These cuts were caked with dried and fresh blood, and their edges had blackened. Most of the maggots had congregated there.

"It still looks bad." She glanced up at Ren for reassurance but found none.

"They're doing their work." Ren guided some of the wayward maggots back to the cuts. They had at least doubled in size since Lynn had seen them go on. "That she woke up really is a good sign."

Dani whimpered. Maybe she was just dreaming again, but it was more likely the maggots had something to do with it.

Instinctively, Lynn leaned in and kissed Dani's forehead. "It's okay. I'm here."

A deep breath lifted Dani's chest, then her frown lessened.

Lynn groaned as she pushed against the heavy iron door. It gave way just before her strength ran out, and she slipped through the crack and onto the roof.

The strong wind instantly whipped her hair up and pulled at her clothes. The gravel underneath her bare feet was wet and cold. Goose bumps traversed her skin as the unruly weather battered her. The darkness engulfed her only a few paces away from the door.

Lynn pushed her face into the wind, spread her arms as far as she could with her shoulder injury, and inhaled deeply. After all this time cooped up indoors, nothing could have instilled a sense of freedom better than this taste of the Wilds.

When Lynn walked back into the room, Skeever greeted her by standing up on the bed. He prepared to jump off, but then seemed to think better of it as he tried to put weight on his broken paw and jerked it back up.

She crossed the room and helped him down. "Hey, boy, did you miss me?"

He rolled onto his back, and Lynn laboriously lowered herself to the carpet to give him a proper belly rub.

Skeever lifted his damaged leg up so she could reach his chest too and tilted his head back in surrender. His hind leg kicked out in time with her scratching him.

"That's good, right? Yeah, you're good. Saves our lives two times and gets all the belly rubs he'll ever need in return." Lynn pressed her face against his ribcage.

He huffed contentedly.

"You're a very good bo—"

"Mmmm."

Lynn smiled and placed a kiss on Skeever's head. "Sorry, boy. Dani's awake again." She got up and walked over to the bed. "Evening."

Dani's eyes opened, and a sleepy smile spread across her features.

Lynn swallowed down butterflies at the warm welcome. She brushed Dani's hair out of her eyes. "How are you feeling?"

Dani groaned.

"Not good, huh?"

With a sigh, Dani opened her mouth, presumably to talk.

"Shhh." Lynn pulled up the chair and took Dani's hand. "We need to find a way to make answering simple questions easier for you."

Dani tapped her index finger on Lynn's skin. She held her gaze and did it again.

"You agree we need a better system?"

Another tap with the same finger.

"So that means 'yes'?"

Tap. *Yes.*

"How about 'no'?"

Dani thought for a bit, then wove their fingers together. She tapped her middle finger on Lynn's skin.

Lynn laughed. "Okay, fair enough." She resisted the urge to stroke Dani's hot cheek. The laugh died on her lips as she met Dani's gaze. "You really scared me."

A sad little whimper escaped Dani. She tapped out a *yes*. "What… happened?" She huffed, seemingly frustrated by her own lack of energy and her difficulty speaking.

"Long story." Lynn smiled. "Bare bones?"

Yes.

"You took a turn for the worse, so I got Richard off the cart, got you on, and brought you to the Homestead. Everyone was sure I'd lured you into a trap so they kept me locked up—" She showed Dani the chafed skin of her wrist. "Until you woke up and told Ren and Eduardo that I hadn't tried to get you killed. Then they let me go. Kate took everyone else out to get Richard's body. They'll be back some time tomorrow, if nothing went wrong."

It took a while for the words to sink in; Dani stared at her, then blinked. *No.* She tapped her middle finger repeatedly, then dropped her gaze down to Lynn's wrist.

"Don't be surprised. You and everyone else thought I'd killed him when we left, so when I didn't show up with him and you were half dead, there really wasn't much I could do to convince them they'd been wrong."

Dani huffed angrily and glared at the door. She squeezed Lynn's hand.

"Hey." Lynn smiled. "I don't care about them. Just so we're clear, though: do you think I killed Richard?"

No!

The sharp tap and Dani's intense eyes had her smile. "Okay, good. That's all that matters to me."

Something bumped against her leg, and Lynn didn't have to guess who it was.

"Someone wants to say 'hi.'" She helped Skeever up onto the bed and stood so she could better control him. The last thing Dani needed was to be trampled on. "Careful, boy. Careful."

Skeever lay down by Dani's side and laid his head on her chest. His tail wagged energetically.

Dani beamed.

Lynn took Dani's hand and moved it over Skeever's head in a stroking motion. "Without him, you'd be dead."

The smile died on Dani's lips. She sighed and tapped her index finger up against Lynn's hand. Her gaze drew up. "You?"

"I would be dead without you." The horror of the bear attack flashed in front of her mind's eye. "I...I don't know how I would have lived with that if you'd died."

Dani's eyes searched hers. She wiggled her hand, and Lynn took it more firmly.

Lynn could see how badly she wanted to be able to say more, to express whatever was floating inside her brain. Her gaze tugged at something deep inside Lynn, at the source of her worry, her loyalty, and her butterflies.

She held Dani's gaze with difficulty. Heat climbed to her cheeks. *Dammit, how do I say this? How do Settlers ask someone if they like them too?* "Dani?" Her heart thumped in her chest. "Could you tell me if…if what happened between us when we traveled together meant something to you?"

Dani hesitated only a few seconds. She licked her lips and lightly tapped. *Yes.*

Heat spread in Lynn's chest. "It meant something to me too. All of it. It meant a lot."

Dani relaxed and exhaled shakily. She smiled, then rapidly tapped *yes*, urging Lynn on.

A bit of the tension squeezing her heart lifted, and Lynn chuckled. "You know I'm bad at this, right?"

Yes.

"Okay, that's just mean." She shook her head as Dani's eyes sparkled. "Okay, so…I'm not going to try to make it pretty because I'm not good at pretty talk."

Dani smiled and tapped a supportive *yes*.

"But I was lying next to you after the bear attack, watching you get sicker and sicker." She stared at their joined hands where Dani's thumb stroked her skin. "And I realized that I was going to lose you if I didn't do everything I could to stop it." She looked up and tried to swallow down a lump of emotion before she started to cry. "Being with you makes me feel. I haven't felt anything for a long time."

Yes; go on, Dani's finger tapped out.

"I don't know what to do now, Dani. I was going to leave it up to you to choose, but now we're here. You won't be able to travel for a long time, and these people—" She nodded at the hallway and the entirety of the Homestead. "They hate me."

No. Dani frowned.

"Oh yeah, they do. You'll see." She chuckled dryly. "So I don't know what to do now."

Dani tensed in preparation, then she managed to rasp, "What… would…like?" The words left her limp and breathing heavily.

Lynn met her gaze and swallowed. She could see the need in Dani's eyes, along with the fear Lynn felt so strongly herself. She leaned down and met Dani's lips in a soft brush. "I think you know," she said softly.

The tap was expected, and she didn't have to look down to check which finger it was. *Yes.*

CHAPTER 25

Lynn brought the spoon to Dani's lips, and she took the bite of elephant stew, chewed it, and swallowed. Every time a door slammed or someone passed the room, they looked at each other, waited, and when no one entered, Lynn fed her another bite.

Kate's group had arrived back at the Homestead a little while ago. The telltale sounds of their hellos and the shedding of gear left no doubt as to who they were. So far, Kate hadn't made an appearance, but Lynn knew it wouldn't take long.

Dani swallowed her bite and covered Lynn's hand on the cup. She stroked her skin and gave her an encouraging little smile.

"I don't like waiting. I know I locked him up well, but, you know...the Wilds." She shrugged.

If they'd recovered Richard's body, she'd be fully exonerated. If they hadn't, they would forever question Lynn's story, even if Dani confirmed it. What that would mean for Lynn, she didn't know and she didn't want to find out.

Dani squeezed her hand and parted her lips.

With a sigh, Lynn fed her another bite.

As Lynn scraped the last of the stew out of the cup, someone knocked on the door.

Lynn glanced at Dani, received a minute nod, and took a shuddering breath. "Yes?"

Kate pushed the door open. Her ashen complexion was enough for Lynn to know she'd found Richard; she looked as if she had seen a ghost.

To her surprise, Dean followed his mother. They lingered in the doorway.

"Good, you're awake." Kate forced a tired smile onto her features, but her eyes remained dead. "Ren told me you'd woken up."

Lynn took Dani's hand, but Dani didn't use her fingers to communicate. She bit the proverbial bullet. "How did it go?"

Kate's gaze drifted to her slowly. "As you predicted."

Dean sniffed. He wiped his nose on his sleeve.

"Good." Lynn stifled a sigh of relief. "So the cuff stays off?"

"Yes."

Silence settled heavily in the room.

Kate looked at her expectantly.

Maybe I'm not the reason they came by, after all. She checked on Dani to see if she'd come to the same conclusion.

She was looking at Kate and Dean with a frown.

Lynn took the hint. "Um, do you want me to, like, go for a while?"

Relief was instantly evident on Kate's features. "Yes, please. Thank you."

Dani squeezed Lynn's hand before letting go.

"She can't really talk much, so we use taps. Index finger for 'yes,' middle finger for 'no.'" Lynn got up from the chair to make room. After a moment of hesitation, she leaned down and quickly kissed Dani's forehead. "I'll be back soon."

She made it halfway through the room before Dean blocked her path to the door. "Uh, can we talk?" He looked up from his boots.

Lynn jerked to a halt. "Talk?" She took a deep breath and felt Kate's gaze on her back. *Dammit.* "Yeah, sure. Why not. Um…in the hallway?"

Dean shrugged and looked away. He had smudges of dirt on his cheeks, and his boots were mud-caked. "That's fine."

She led him out and looked back at Dani one more time before she closed the door on her and Kate. Then she took Dean in. "What is it?"

He swallowed. "I'm sorry I hit you." It seemed to pain him to say the words, but they didn't feel entirely unauthentic. "I thought you'd killed him."

"I didn't." She kept the sting out of her words.

"I know." He ran a dirty hand through his hair. "Look, my dad was right where you left him, and now we get to bury him at the Homestead. Toby gets to go and visit and stuff. That's important for him."

For you too, I bet. She didn't voice the thought. "And if Dani makes a full recovery, it all works out in the end." She couldn't quite blunt the sharp edge to those words.

He drew his shoulders up like a turtle taking shelter in its shell. "Yeah, exactly. So, um, no hard feelings?"

She stared at him. "There are hard feelings, Dean, but none I can't live with once the dust settles."

He didn't seem to know what to do with that and shifted from one leg to the other. "So it's all good?"

Lynn snorted. "Yeah, just don't go around punching me anymore, and we're good." She held out her hand. "Deal?"

He wiped his hand on his pants and gripped hers. For a moment, he looked very young and very lost. "Yeah, deal." He shook her hand, then let go. "I'll uh, let you do whatever you were going to do. Bye." Before she could respond, he slipped past her.

Lynn turned and watched him walk off. She tried to wrap her head around what had just transpired. *Maybe getting Richard's body back really was what they all needed after all.*

"Do you mind if I join you?"

Lynn looked up from the campfire to find Kate standing over her. "No, I guess not." She scooted to the side to make room for her on the log.

Kate sat and glanced aside. "Dani and I caught up, in as much as that's possible with her current limitations."

Caught up or made amends? Lynn decided it wasn't her place to ask. "That's good." She turned her mug slowly around in her hands and stared down at it.

Kate nodded slowly. "It was." The firelight etched extra-thick grooves into her skin and accentuated just how haggard she looked. "That leaves you and me."

"It does, doesn't it?" She fell silent again and sipped her tea.

Beside her, Kate cleared her throat. "I was hurting. I wanted... vengeance, I suppose. I wish I could say 'justice,' but I wanted someone to blame, and I didn't care who that person was."

When Kate stopped talking and didn't resume, Lynn turned her head toward her. "So validating my story makes it all okay again?"

Kate flinched. "No, but I know I can't blame you for his death anymore. It's this forsaken world." She motioned widely, encompassing the darkness beyond the edges of the roof. "That took him away from me... Not you."

Damn right, it wasn't me. "You put my life in danger." She finally turned her head toward Kate. "You put Dani's life in danger."

Kate shifted and added another log to the fire. "I know." Pain flashed across her features. "It...it was a terrible plan."

Lynn groaned. "Yeah, your plan." She shook her head. "Well, it got you what you wanted."

"Not if Dani takes a turn for the worse. Not if she won't make a full recovery." Kate dug her nails into her own thigh. "Then it didn't work out at all like I wanted."

"True." One thought had been eating away at her. "Kate, I know I didn't give you much choice, but how could you think sending only Dani with me was a good idea? I could have left her—I could have *killed* her."

Kate dug her nails deeper into the leather of her pants. "I should have forced you to take us all, but I convinced myself Dani could handle whatever you or the Wilds had to throw at her, even though she'd never spent that much time away from the Homestead. Dani even assured me she could once you and me struck our deal." She glanced aside. "But you're right, I knew you might try to hurt her, and I still let her go because I—" Emotion cut off her words. She cleared her throat. "I needed him home, and as bad of an idea as it was to let you two go alone, it could have worked—it did work." She looked down at her hand. "But Dani was the victim of my grief."

Lynn could see Kate's pain, and she only had to think of the chance of losing Dani to sympathize with her. After a few seconds of contemplation to test her own limits, she reached out and laid her hand on Kate's.

The older woman stiffened, but then the grip on her thigh relaxed under Lynn's touch.

"Dani will pull through." Lynn stared into the fire. "She'll be out there hunting before you know it."

Kate sighed. "You're hopeful about her recovery."

Lynn shrugged and freed her hand, growing uncomfortable with the prolonged touch. "Yesterday morning she was all but dead to the world. Now she's looking around and answering questions. I'm taking that as a sign that from here on out, things will get better."

"Have you…thought about what you want to do in those weeks? And afterward?"

Kate's gaze made the skin on the side of her head tingle. Lynn swallowed. "No."

"We are short a hunter until Dani is up and about. Once she recovers, we are still short a scout." Kate's voice didn't betray any emotions, but from the corner of her eye, Lynn could see she was plucking twigs and grit off her pants with great intent.

Lynn took a few seconds to absorb the words and to analyze the surge of longing warming her insides. She picked up a piece of bark to occupy her hands with instead of fidgeting. "What makes you think I'd want to stay?"

"Dani. You and her have become…friends. Probably more, from what I've seen and heard."

Lynn felt a blush coming on and tossed the piece of bark into the fire as a lure for Kate's gaze. "Maybe." *Topic change.* If she stayed, she wouldn't just be dealing with Dani, after all. "I get that I'm useful to you and to the rest of the Homesteaders, but it's not easy being around people who like my skills, not me."

"I understand." Kate paused for a few seconds. "But maybe that's just because we don't know you yet." Affability underlay her words.

Lynn checked on her and found her, indeed, smiling. An unfamiliar touch of warmth flitted through her chest. Except for Dani, no one had expressed an interest in getting to know her in a long time, not since she'd been a child. She shrugged, trying to appear unaffected. "Maybe."

Kate didn't appear to be deterred. "You might like us too, if you got to know us as colleagues, even friends, instead of captors."

Would I? And could Kate speak for the whole group? Cody hated her guts, and the others had threatened her life up to a day ago. Was Kate just trying to play her again? Instead of asking, Lynn took the offensive. If Kate snapped at her again, that would tell her all she needed to know about what kind of person she was. She turned to watch Kate in the light cast by the fire. "I really dislike being used, Kate. I thought that was pretty clear by now. If that's why you're offering to keep me around, that's a really shitty foundation for any type of relationship—working or otherwise."

Kate tensed. "Richard and I built this haven with our own bare hands. All that remains of him is here." She cast a sweeping glance about and drew in a deep breath. "I wouldn't open it to people I didn't believe would make it better. Yes, we—I—would take advantage of your unique skillset, but you'd have access to ours as well. Perhaps you could consider it less of a situation in which you are used and more as a way to thrive instead of just surviving."

A surge of hope caused her breath to hitch. She thought about her life on the road, of barely scraping by. Survival had been her sole motivation for decades, but had she ever truly thrived? Her memories of the Wilds blurred together, memories filled with fear, pain, and hunger. In just a few short weeks together, Dani had shown her that life could be so much more than that. How much better could life be for her if she had the Homestead to come back to? And the Homesteaders—if they accepted her and she accepted them. That churned her insides; the Homesteaders hadn't given her much reason to trust them, but maybe now that she was cleared of all charges, that could change. She had grown to trust Dani; maybe she could learn to trust everyone else, even Kate.

The woman in question seemed to take her silence as a call to offer more motivation. "It would also give you and Dani a chance to—" Kate searched for the right word. "Connect."

Lynn pondered the implication of those words as butterflies buzzed distractingly in her gut. She took in the people slowly filtering into the large open space, studied the gardens, the fires, the sheds. The Homestead was still a haven in an ocean of danger and death. More importantly, it was Dani's home. Lynn didn't know if it could ever be her home as well, but the alternative made her feel hollow—and not just because of the thought of losing Dani. She was being offered a chance to elevate her life from just barely surviving to living a good, full life within a well-functioning group.

"You don't have to decide now," Kate said. "How about a trial period? Stay until Dani is back to her old strength, take over her tasks once you are up to it, and see how you like it. If it works out, stay."

Some of the tension in Lynn's gut lessened. A trial period would give her time to get to know the Homesteaders and maybe—hopefully—see what she and Dani could be to one another. She licked her lips and nodded. "Maybe a trial period is not a bad idea." Another smile threatened to settle on her features, and after a moment of hesitation, she allowed it to.

She made it to the bottom of the stairs before she was confronted with another Homesteader: Cody. Lynn steeled herself as he pushed off from the wall he'd been leaning against. *I really wish I had my tomahawk.* "Cody, what a lovely surprise." She allowed every bit of sarcasm she could muster to color her voice.

"Well, you're a hard woman to catch alone." His smirk was full-on present, and he blocked the corridor with his bulk before she could slip past.

Lynn stopped and glanced back. Her legs were already recovering; maybe she could charge up the stairs if he tried anything. "I am remarkably popular today. I guess that's why you're lying in wait in a corridor?"

Cody shrugged with obviously feigned disinterest. "A man's got to do..."

Something in the way he let the words hang unsettled Lynn. She crossed her arms in front of her chest and resisted the urge to take another step back; she didn't want to show that much weakness. "Why don't we cut the crap, hm? You've got something to say, so say it."

His smirk faded. "I've been here long enough to know that Kate either already asked you to stay or she'll do so soon." He took a step forward.

Again, Lynn forced herself not to move back. She jutted her chin up and put her hands on her hips in an attempt to appear bigger than she was—or felt. "What if she did?"

"Then I want you to know I have my eye on you."

Maybe it was the long day she'd had, her body's unrelenting aches, or having to listen to yet another threat, but Lynn finally had enough of his bullshit. "What is your damn problem with me? We got off to a shitty start, but I got your damn leader guy back to you and Dani too! What more do you want from me before you stop acting like a dick?"

For once, she managed to catch him off guard; he deflated a little and his eyes widened. He recovered quickly. "You are my problem! You and all you Wilders!"

"All you Wilders? What does that even mean? It's not like everyone who doesn't live in a settlement is related." She shook her head in dismissal.

"Maybe not, but you all think alike."

"How many of 'us'"—she made air quotes around the word—"have you even met? We don't exactly roam in herds."

"Enough to know that all you care about is yourself."

There was definitely a story there, but she didn't give a damn about Cody's traumas. "Oh, I care, Cody, just not about you." She pushed forward, meeting his bullshit head-on.

He squinted, inspected her. "Then who do you care about, Lynn?"

The use of her name didn't go unnoticed. She realized for the first time that maybe he had a deeper meaning for terrorizing her than just throwing his weight around, but she couldn't put her finger on what it was. She paused long enough for him to push on.

"That's what I mean." He took another step toward her, right into her space. He had to tilt his head down to continue to hold her gaze. "My wife and husband are here." He let that sink in. "If it were up to me, I'd kick you out right now, because if you stay, their lives would depend at least partially on you, and you couldn't care less."

Lynn swallowed heavily and broke the gaze. He was right. She didn't care about Ren or Eduardo the way she cared about Dani. That didn't mean she wanted them to come to harm, though. Maybe before she'd undertaken this journey with Dani, she wouldn't have cared, but now everything had changed. She looked back up. "Nothing is decided yet, but if I stay, I'm staying because I want to be part of the Homestead. That means doing my part to keep it safe—and if anything, you know I can do my part."

Cody set his jaw as he seemed to ponder that. Finally, he straightened and took a deep breath. "If you ever endanger them, I'll kill you."

It sounded to Lynn as if that was as close to acceptance as he was ever going to come.

"I can live with that."

After another pause, he stepped aside and swept his arm out to indicate she could pass.

She did, tensely.

"And Lynn?"

Lynn jolted and turned back. "Hm?"

"The same's true for any of the others: hurt them and you'll have to deal with me." The anger had drained out of his eyes.

She nodded. "Understood." When she turned around this time, she felt much more confident that he wouldn't plant a knife in her back.

Dani was still awake, seemingly waiting for her to return. When Lynn entered, she smiled and settled more comfortably on the bed. Her hazel eyes didn't move away from her. They never did during their talks, and it made Lynn feel special. She had Dani's full attention, and she liked it.

Her own gaze was drawn to a familiar book, lying on the blankets over Dani's legs. *"Moby-Dick?"* She looked at Dani questioningly.

Dani shrugged. She pointed at Lynn.

"What about me?" She sat down on the edge of Dani's bed and picked up the book to leaf through. Some of the pages were original, but many more were hand-written, presumably copied once the originals had started to fall apart. The cover was made out of willow bark.

"For...you." Dani smiled and reached for her hand.

Lynn offered it and squeezed as she laid the book on her lap, holding it protectively. Books were a rarity, and she'd hardly ever seen one, let alone touched any. "The book? But it's Flint's."

Yes. "Borrow." Dani's smile widened. "Read."

Lynn snorted. "He's just trying to educate the Wilder."

"Pffff!" Dani rolled her eyes and tapped: *No!*

"Yes," Lynn countered. She ran her fingers over the cover and found herself smiling despite herself. *Maybe he did do it just to be nice.* With Flint, you never knew. "Anyway!" She turned her attention back to Dani after making a mental note to catch up with Flint later. "I talked to Kate." *And Dean and Cody.* "And so did you. Did it go well?"

Yes. Dani shrugged.

"You'll be having that talk again when you get your words back?"

Dani confirmed that too. Then she tapped her index finger rapidly, urging Lynn on.

Lynn took a deep breath. "She…invited me to stay. At the Homestead."

The tapping stopped. Dani's eyes widened for a moment, then she deliberately tapped her index finger again, just once. The question was clear in her eyes: "Did you say yes?"

"Yeah, I said 'yes,' at least to a trial period." She scanned Dani's features to see how that landed.

A spark appeared in Dani's eyes, bringing them fully to life for the first time since before the bear attack. She tapped her index finger excitedly.

"So, good idea?" Lynn smiled, insides fluttering again at the thought of a trial period not just with Dani but with the Homesteaders as well.

Dani's eyes watered. "Yes." She rasped the word, but it was perfectly clear. She tapped her index finger too. "Stay."

Lynn inspected her face, trying to read every nuance. She was getting very good at it because of the limitations in their communication. "Dani, if…if I stay…" Her heart thumped in her chest. She held Dani's gaze with difficulty. Heat returned to her cheeks. "If I stay, I'd stay to be with you."

Dani tapped her hand.

Before she allowed herself to breathe in relief, Lynn made sure it was her index finger, a "yes."

"You. Me. Together." Dani strained for every word, and the last caused her chest to heave as she ran out of breath.

"Are you sure you want that?"

Yes. Dani's gaze was intense as she all but tried to push her thoughts directly into Lynn's skull.

Lynn took Dani's hand into both of hers and lifted it to her lips for a kiss. The fear was still there, swirling in her gut, reminding her of the scars she carried over people she'd lost, but when Dani smiled at her, it faded. "All right, that's settled, then, I guess. You and I can figure out how to do this…together thing."

Dani rolled her eyes. "Relationship."

The word made Lynn a little dizzy, but in a good way. She held Dani's hand up so Dani could see it and tapped "yes."

EPILOGUE

THE SUN BORE DOWN HEAVILY on Lynn's back as she traversed the broad New York City streets.

Skeever went from rubble pile to rubble pile, sniffing eagerly. He'd found a stick to drag along and did so proudly. The splint was still on his paw, but if Skeever mourned the loss of function in it, it didn't show; he moved as agilely as he had always done.

Lynn kept an eye on him as she followed a now-familiar path through one of New York's many destroyed neighborhoods. "This way, Skeeve." She pointed her tomahawk in the right direction and waited for him to move past her. As she did, she looked around and smiled. It was amazing how quickly she'd become familiar with the city's streets. She was starting to get a grip on its patterns—when the lions hunted, where they rested, where the deer trails were, and where the rabbits had their holes. She knew where to get water and in which of the large ponds alligators lurked under the surface.

The streets of New York City had not lost their dangers, but they were dangers she now knew to expect. Above all, she had a mental map of the many shelters and safe spots strewn about the city blocks. She hadn't been forced to stay out overnight yet, but no matter where she went, she knew she was never more than an hour's walk away from a safe place to sleep and that it would have all the materials she'd need to make a fire in a hurry.

Tonight wouldn't be the first night she'd spend outside; it was midday, and she was closing in on the Homestead. She had two more traps to check, and even if they were empty, she'd go home with enough food to feed every member of her newly found home. Two large hares and a capuchin monkey had been lured into her snares, and today's main target, the fish traps she'd built in an offshoot of the Flushing Bay, had yielded three weakfish and a few menhaden.

She felt good about her haul. Not only was she still proving herself an asset to the Homesteaders, she was also picking up the slack while Dani was recovering and couldn't pull her weight.

Lynn checked the position of the sun and quickened her step. She was running late, and Dani hated it when she was late.

"You're late." Dani smiled and hoisted herself up from the ground by the gate. Her newly repaired spear served as a crutch as she slowly straightened out. Her motions were getting smoother, and it was good to see a healthy glow on her cheeks.

"Sorry, good haul, so a lot of traps to reset." Lynn followed her inside and out of Flint's view as he stood guard on the window washer's rig. She resisted the urge to cup Dani's cheek as she leaned in to kiss her. She'd wiped her hands, but blood and fish guts tended to linger.

Dani hummed and wrapped her arms around her neck. She pressed close and ran her fingers through Lynn's hair in the way that always gave Lynn goose bumps. Dani's tongue running over her lips intensified the feeling, and now Lynn really had to fight to keep her hands off her.

"Mean..." But she claimed another kiss and slipped a little tongue of her own.

This time it was Dani who shuddered. "Mmmm...go clean up, Wilder, we have a date to get to."

Lynn grinned. *A date.* If anyone had told her prior to meeting Dani she'd ever go out into the Wilds for anything other than sheer survival, she would have laughed in their face. Now she ran up five flights of stairs with a wicker basket bouncing on her back and Skeever squirming in her arms just so she would be on time for it.

Ren looked up, startled, as Lynn skidded to a halt in the kitchen.

"I'll take care of these when we get back." She put Skeever down and dropped the basket just inside the door. Her lungs burned much more than she liked from the short run, but she was gaining strength every day. She had time to pace herself now, just not when she was trying to be on time for "date afternoon."

Skeever shook himself out and instantly stuck his nose into the basket.

Lynn hurried to snatch the wicker up and put it on the barrels in the corner instead.

"Good catch?" Ren halted with a brush in one hand and a potato in the other.

"Great catch! Feel free to have a look. Fish for dinner tonight." Lynn made sure to keep her dirty hands away from walls and furniture.

Ren's entire face lit up. Of all the people in the Homestead, she liked fish more than almost everyone else, right after her husband. "I'll tell Cody." Nothing had endeared Lynn to Cody more than the first time she'd brought home a striped bass.

"Tell him to leave some for the rest of us." Lynn had already backed out of the room. "We'll be back. Please watch Skeever."

"Have fun!" Ren shook her head, but the smile that appeared on her features was genuine.

Lynn took the stairs down with equal speed only a few minutes later. This time when Dani appeared in her field of vision, she wrapped her up for a genuine kiss, clean hands traversing her back. She was still careful with Dani's slowly healing wounds, but Ren had taken the stitches out a week ago and Dani had already regained most of the weight she'd lost during her recovery.

Just to have Dani up and about again—although slowly—was a relief Lynn was grateful for every single day she woke up next to her. She didn't have a doubt that before long, Dani would be out with her to trap, hunt, and explore.

The subject of trading and scavenging farther away from the Homestead was often broached but never decided upon. Dani had to be stronger first, and Lynn wasn't at the peak of her abilities yet either. Years of malnutrition and adverse conditions were manifesting now that Lynn had the opportunity to rest, eat regularly, and sometimes even relax and do absolutely nothing. She needed more time to recover, and as long as she provided in her own way, people were patient. Because of their recovery, their trial period was officially still in effect, but so far, Lynn hadn't found a single reason not to extend it indefinitely.

"We're going to miss them," Dani said against her lips. She slid her fingers into Lynn's hair and pulled her closer. Despite Dani's still frail condition, there had been plenty of time to explore and discover, and Dani knew damn well what running her fingers through Lynn's hair did to her.

Lynn shivered and pulled back with great reluctance as a now very familiar need settled low in her gut. She shook her head and took Dani's hand. "It's a block away. We're not going to miss them, unless, of course, you keep teasing me."

Dani shrugged, eyes full of mischief. "I wasn't doing anything of the sort."

Lynn snorted and tugged at Dani's arm so they could start the short walk to their destination. "You are a damn liar, Dani Wilson."

"Am not." Dani laughed and bumped against her as she gripped her hand.

"You are, and I'm okay with it." Lynn glanced aside and took in Dani's sharp features, slowly filling in now that she was eating again and the fever was long gone. Dani's walking speed was still slow, but Lynn didn't feel the need to rush her. They had made the trek at least a dozen times now, and they knew every shadow and obstacle to watch. Lynn wouldn't say she felt safe, but she certainly felt prepared. Her tomahawk lay as comfortably in her hand as Dani's hand did in the other.

They made it up the ladder to the lookout point with only seconds to spare. Dani hurried across the gravel-covered roof as fast as her sore abdomen allowed and eagerly looked out over the street below.

Lynn caught up and wrapped her arms around Dani's waist from behind, laying her chin on her shoulder.

Already the sound of distant thunder filled the air.

She pressed her lips against Dani's shoulder. "I told you we'd make it."

Dani wrapped her arms around Lynn's and stroked the back of her hand with her fingertip. "You were right." She leaned her head back, but her gaze remained glued to the left side of the street.

"I usually am." Lynn took the slap to her arm as well-deserved punishment.

"Here they come." Dani craned her neck.

The herd appeared around the corner like clockwork. They filled the width of the street with ease and bleated warnings about obstacles in their path for the rows of peers behind them. They were heading out of the city for the night after drinking from the park's pond. Lynn had tracked their progress one day, just to see where they were going and where they came from, and once she realized they always came through here, she had taken Dani along as a kind of recovery walk. The black and white stripes still made for a jarring image, and Lynn's eyes failed to settle on any one of the zebras specifically.

Dani's head moved from side to side lightly as she had the same dizzying reaction. "They always make me think of Richard."

"Why?"

"Because they thundered past when we got to the car dealership like a...sign." She swallowed. "I miss him."

Lynn kissed her shoulder softly. "I'm sorry I never met him."

Dani turned her head to brush their lips together. "You two would have gotten along." She returned her gaze to the spectacle in the street. "Very well."

"Do you know what I think of when I see them?" Lynn watched the stragglers trying to catch up with the herd. Once Dani shook her head, she continued. "Of the way my life has changed since I first saw one of them. I think of you and Skeever and the Homestead and that I was so wrong about life."

Dani turned around in her arms and wrapped hers around Lynn's neck. "A lot has changed."

Lynn laughed. She ran her hands up the leather of Dani's vest. "Yeah, you can say that again."

"It was worth everything that happened." Dani leaned in and brushed her lips over hers. "It got me you."

A familiar heat settled on her cheeks. When she slowly broke away and rested her forehead against Dani's, words she'd been dying to say for weeks now bubbled up in her throat. Maybe it was finally time to say them. She lifted her head and captured Dani's gaze. "You know I love you, right?"

For a second, Dani just stared, then a radiant smile spread across her lips, and she nodded. "Yeah, I know. And you know I love you, right?"

Lynn's insides fluttered in a mixture of joy and nervousness. "I do."

Dani exhaled in mock relief. "Good, because if I have to nearly die again to get you to notice me, I—"

Lynn cut her off with a forceful, reaffirming kiss. "Don't you dare, Settler. Trust me, you have claimed my undivided attention."

In the streets below a last straggling zebra bleated as it galloped past, slowing only when it caught up with the waiting herd.

ABOUT MAY DAWNEY

When May was a child, her father read Asimov and Zelazny to her. As a teenager, she gravitated toward science fiction, (future) fantasy, dystopian, and occult stories, even though there was never a character she, as a queer woman, could fully identify with. May's motivation to write comes from the desire to create stories where women turn to women once they stop the apocalypse—be it a global or a personal one. She wants to write the stories she wishes her father could have read to her as a child: riveting tales with a heroine who kicks ass and just so happens to be gay.

CONNECT WITH MAY
Website: www.maydawney.com
Twitter: @MayDawney
E-Mail: contact@maydawney.com

OTHER BOOKS FROM YLVA PUBLISHING

www.ylva-publishing.com

PRIMAL TOUCH

Amber Jacobs

ISBN: 978-3-95533-858-9
Length: 255 pages (99,000 words)

Rumors of a rare, legendary, white tiger lure acclaimed wildlife photographer Ashley Richards deep into the Indian jungle. There, she crosses paths with a ruthless poacher and Leandra, a mysterious, feral woman with a dark past, who seems at one with the fierce felines she protects. In this charged, exotic, lesbian romance, Ashley is caught up in danger, a deadly vendetta, and the clash of two starkly different worlds. It changes everything she knows.

OTHER BOOKS FROM QUEER PACK

www.queer-pack.com

REINTEGRATION

Eden S. French

ISBN: 978-3-95533-926-5
Length: 274 pages (139,000 words)

Streetwise cyborg Lexi Vale brokers deals for gang lords in the anarchic city of Foundation. Her mind-reading implant gives her a crucial edge—but it also makes her brain a hot commodity.

When she's targeted by an augmented hunter, Lexi joins a group of rebels: a murderous vigilante, a daredevil smuggler, a drug-addled surgeon, and a revolutionary whose shared past with Lexi endangers them all.

A queer, dystopian sci-fi about piecing together purpose from the fragments of love and loss, even while the world itself is tearing apart.

Survival Instincts

ISBN: 978-3-95533-934-0

Also available as e-book.

Published by Ylva Publishing, legal entity of Ylva Verlag, e.Kfr.

Ylva Verlag, e.Kfr.
Owner: Astrid Ohletz
Am Kirschgarten 2
65830 Kriftel
Germany

www.ylva-publishing.com

First edition: 2018

Credits
Edited by Sandra Gerth and RJ Samuels
Proofread by A.L. Brooks
Cover Design and Print Layout by Streetlight Graphics

Made in United States
North Haven, CT
01 December 2024